A Romance of Two Worlds

A Romance of Two Worlds

Marie Corelli

MINT EDITIONS

A Romance of Two Worlds was first published in 1886.

This edition published by Mint Editions 2021.

ISBN 9781513277752 | E-ISBN 9781513278162

Published by Mint Editions®

MINT
EDITIONS

minteditionbooks.com

Publishing Director: Jennifer Newens
Design & Production: Rachel Lopez Metzger
Project Manager: Micaela Clark
Typesetting: Westchester Publishing Services

Contents

Prologue

W e live in an age of universal inquiry, ergo of universal scepticism. The prophecies of the poet, the dreams of the philosopher and scientist, are being daily realized—things formerly considered mere fairy-tales have become facts—yet, in spite of the marvels of learning and science that are hourly accomplished among us, the attitude of mankind is one of disbelief. "There is no God!" cries one theorist; "or if there be one, *I* can obtain no proof of His existence!" "There is no Creator!" exclaims another. "The Universe is simply a rushing together of atoms." "There can be no immortality," asserts a third. "We are but dust, and to dust we shall return." "What is called by idealists the SOUL," argues another, "is simply the vital principle composed of heat and air, which escapes from the body at death, and mingles again with its native element. A candle when lit emits flame; blow out the light, the flame vanishes—where? Would it not be madness to assert the flame immortal? Yet the soul, or vital principle of human existence, is no more than the flame of a candle."

If you propound to these theorists the eternal question WHY?—why is the world in existence? why is there a universe? why do we live? why do we think and plan? why do we perish at the last?—their grandiose reply is, "Because of the Law of Universal Necessity." They cannot explain this mysterious Law to themselves, nor can they probe deep enough to find the answer to a still more tremendous WHY—namely, WHY, is there a Law of Universal Necessity?—but they are satisfied with the result of their reasonings, if not wholly, yet in part, and seldom try to search beyond that great vague vast Necessity, lest their finite brains should reel into madness worse than death. Recognizing, therefore, that in this cultivated age a wall of scepticism and cynicism is gradually being built up by intellectual thinkers of every nation against all that treats of the Supernatural and Unseen, I am aware that my narration of the events I have recently experienced will be read with incredulity. At a time when the great empire of the Christian Religion is being assailed, or politely ignored by governments and public speakers and teachers, I realize to the fullest extent how daring is any attempt to prove, even by a plain history of strange occurrences happening to one's self, the actual existence of the Supernatural around us; and the absolute certainty of a future state of being, after the passage through that brief soul-torpor in which the body perishes, known to us as Death.

In the present narration, which I have purposely called a "romance," I do not expect to be believed, as I can only relate what I myself have experienced. I know that men and women of to-day must have proofs, or what they are willing to accept as proofs, before they will credit anything that purports to be of a spiritual tendency;—something startling—some miracle of a stupendous nature, such as according to prophecy they are all unfit to receive. Few will admit the subtle influence and incontestable, though mysterious, authority exercised upon their lives by higher intelligences than their own—intelligences unseen, unknown, but felt. Yes! felt by the most careless, the most cynical; in the uncomfortable prescience of danger, the inner forebodings of guilt—the moral and mental torture endured by those who fight a protracted battle to gain the hardly-won victory in themselves of right over wrong—in the thousand and one sudden appeals made without warning to that compass of a man's life, Conscience—and in those brilliant and startling impulses of generosity, bravery, and self-sacrifice which carry us on, heedless of consequences, to the performance of great and noble deeds, whose fame makes the whole world one resounding echo of glory—deeds that we wonder at ourselves even in the performance of them—acts of heroism in which mere life goes for nothing, and the Soul for a brief space is pre-eminent, obeying blindly the guiding influence of a something akin to itself, yet higher in the realms of Thought.

There are no proofs as to why such things should be; but that they are, is indubitable. The miracles enacted now are silent ones, and are worked in the heart and mind of man alone. Unbelief is nearly supreme in the world to-day. Were an angel to descend from heaven in the middle of a great square, the crowd would think he had got himself up on pulleys and wires, and would try to discover his apparatus. Were he, in wrath, to cast destruction upon them, and with fire blazing from his wings, slay a thousand of them with the mere shaking of a pinion, those who were left alive would either say that a tremendous dynamite explosion had occurred, or that the square was built on an extinct volcano which had suddenly broken out into frightful activity. Anything rather than believe in angels—the nineteenth century protests against the possibility of their existence. It sees no miracle—it pooh-poohs the very enthusiasm that might work them.

"Give a positive sign," it says; "prove clearly that what you say is true, and I, in spite of my Progress and Atom Theory, will believe." The answer to such a request was spoken eighteen hundred years and more

MARIE CORELLI

ago. "A faithless and perverse generation asketh for a sign, and no sign shall be given unto them."

Were I now to assert that a sign had been given to ME—to me, as one out of the thousands who demand it—such daring assurance on my part would meet with the most strenuous opposition from all who peruse the following pages; each person who reads having his own ideas on all subjects, and naturally considering them to be the best if not the only ideas worth anything. Therefore I wish it to be plainly understood that in this book I personally advocate no new theory of either religion or philosophy; nor do I hold myself answerable for the opinions expressed by any of my characters. My aim throughout is to let facts speak for themselves. If they seem strange, unreal, even impossible, I can only say that the things of the invisible world must always appear so to those whose thoughts and desires are centred on this life only.

I

An Artist's Studio

In the winter of 188-, I was afflicted by a series of nervous ailments, brought on by overwork and overworry. Chief among these was a protracted and terrible insomnia, accompanied by the utmost depression of spirits and anxiety of mind. I became filled with the gloomiest anticipations of evil; and my system was strung up by slow degrees to such a high tension of physical and mental excitement, that the quietest and most soothing of friendly voices had no other effect upon me than to jar and irritate. Work was impossible; music, my one passion, intolerable; books became wearisome to my sight; and even a short walk in the open air brought with it such lassitude and exhaustion, that I soon grew to dislike the very thought of moving out of doors. In such a condition of health, medical aid became necessary; and a skilful and amiable physician, Dr. R——, of great repute in nervous ailments, attended me for many weeks, with but slight success. He was not to blame, poor man, for his failure to effect a cure. He had only one way of treatment, and he applied it to all his patients with more or less happy results. Some died, some recovered; it was a lottery on which my medical friend staked his reputation, and won. The patients who died were never heard of more—those who recovered sang the praises of their physician everywhere, and sent him gifts of silver plate and hampers of wine, to testify their gratitude. His popularity was very great; his skill considered marvellous; and his inability to do Me any good arose, I must perforce imagine, out of some defect or hidden obstinacy in my constitution, which was to him a new experience, and for which he was unprepared. Poor Dr. R——! How many bottles of your tastily prepared and expensive medicines have I not swallowed, in blind confidence and blinder ignorance of the offences I thus committed against all the principles of that Nature within me, which, if left to itself, always heroically struggles to recover its own proper balance and effect its own cure; but which, if subjected to the experimental tests of various poisons or drugs, often loses strength in the unnatural contest and sinks exhausted, perhaps never to rise with actual vigour again. Baffled in his attempts to remedy my ailments, Dr. R—— at last resorted to the usual plan adopted by all physicians when their medicines have no power. He recommended change of air and scene, and urged my leaving London, then dark with the fogs of a dreary winter, for the gaiety and sunshine and roses of the Riviera. The idea was not unpleasant to me, and I determined to take the advice proffered. Hearing of my intention, some American friends of mine, Colonel Everard and his charming young wife, decided to accompany me, sharing with me the expenses of the journey and hotel accommodation. We left London all together on a damp foggy evening, when the cold was so intense that it seemed to bite the flesh like the sharp teeth of an animal, and after two days' rapid journey, during which I felt my spirits gradually rising, and my gloomy forebodings vanishing slowly one by one, we arrived at Cannes, and put up at the Hotel de L——. It was a lovely place, and most beautifully situated; the garden was a perfect wilderness of roses in full bloom, and an avenue of orange-trees beginning to flower cast a delicate fragrance on the warm delicious air.

Mrs. Everard was delighted.

"If you do not recover your health here," she said half laughingly to me on the second morning after our arrival, "I am afraid your case is hopeless. What sunshine! What a balmy wind! It is enough to make a cripple cast away his crutches and forget he was ever lame. Don't you think so?"

I smiled in answer, but inwardly I sighed. Beautiful as the scenery, the air, and the general surroundings were, I could not disguise from myself that the temporary exhilaration of my feelings, caused by the novelty and excitement of my journey to Cannes, was slowly but surely passing away. The terrible apathy, against which I had fought for so many months, was again creeping over me with its cruel and resistless force. I did my best to struggle against it; I walked, I rode, I laughed and chatted with Mrs. Everard and her husband, and forced myself into sociability with some of the visitors at the hotel, who were disposed to show us friendly attention. I summoned all my stock of will-power to beat back the insidious physical and mental misery that threatened to sap the very spring of my life; and in some of these efforts I partially succeeded. But it was at night that the terrors of my condition manifested themselves. Then sleep forsook my eyes; a dull throbbing weight of pain encircled my head like a crown of thorns; nervous terrors shook me from head to foot; fragments of my own musical compositions hummed in my ears with wearying persistence—fragments that always left me in a state of distressed conjecture; for I never could remember how they ended, and I puzzled myself vainly over crotchets and quavers that never would consent to arrange themselves in any sort of finale. So the days went on; for Colonel Everard and his wife, those days were full of merriment, sight-seeing, and enjoyment. For me, though outwardly I appeared to share in the universal gaiety, they were laden with increasing despair and wretchedness; for I began to lose hope of ever recovering my once buoyant health and strength, and, what was even worse, I seemed to have utterly parted with all working ability. I was young, and up to within a few months life had stretched brightly before me, with the prospect of a brilliant career. And now what was I? A wretched invalid—a burden to myself and to others—a broken spar flung with other fragments of ship wrecked lives on the great ocean of Time, there to be whirled away and forgotten. But a rescue was approaching; a rescue sudden and marvellous, of which, in my wildest fancies, I had never dreamed.

Staying in the same hotel with us was a young Italian artist, Raffaello Cellini by name. His pictures were beginning to attract a great deal of notice, both in Paris and Rome: not only for their faultless drawing, but for their wonderfully exquisite colouring. So deep and warm and rich were the hues he transferred to his canvases, that others of his art, less fortunate in the management of the palette, declared he must have invented some foreign compound whereby he was enabled to deepen and brighten his colours for the time being; but that the effect was only temporary, and that his pictures, exposed to the air for some eight or ten years, would fade away rapidly, leaving only the traces of an indistinct blur. Others, more generous, congratulated him on having discovered the secrets of the old masters. In short, he was admired, condemned, envied, and flattered, all in a breath; while he himself, being of a singularly serene and unruffled disposition, worked away incessantly, caring little or nothing for the world's praise or blame.

Cellini had a pretty suite of rooms in the Hotel de L——, and my friends Colonel and Mrs. Everard fraternized with him very warmly. He was by no means slow to respond to their overtures of friendship, and so it happened that his studio became a sort of lounge for us, where we would meet to have tea, to chat, to look at the pictures, or to discuss our plans for future enjoyment. These visits to Cellini's studio, strange to say, had a remarkably soothing and calming effect upon my suffering nerves. The lofty and elegant room, furnished with that "admired disorder" and mixed luxuriousness peculiar to artists, with its heavily drooping velvet curtains, its glimpses of white marble busts and broken columns, its flash and fragrance of flowers that bloomed in a tiny conservatory opening out from the studio and leading to the garden, where a fountain bubbled melodiously—all this pleased me and gave me a curious, yet most welcome, sense of absolute rest. Cellini himself had a fascination for me, for exactly the same reason. As an example of this, I remember escaping from Mrs. Everard on one occasion, and hurrying to the most secluded part of the garden, in order to walk up and down alone in an endeavour to calm an attack of nervous agitation which had suddenly seized me. While thus pacing about in feverish restlessness, I saw Cellini approaching, his head bent as if in thought, and his hands clasped behind his back. As he drew near me, he raised his eyes—they were clear and darkly brilliant—he regarded me steadfastly with a kindly smile. Then lifting his hat with the graceful reverence peculiar to an Italian, he passed on, saying no word. But the effect of his momentary presence upon me was remarkable—it was Electric. I was no longer agitated. Calmed, soothed and almost happy, I returned to Mrs. Everard, and entered into her plans for the day with so much alacrity that she was surprised and delighted.

"If you go on like this," she said, "you will be perfectly well in a month."

I was utterly unable to account for the remedial influence Raffaello Cellini's presence had upon me; but such as it was I could not but be grateful for the respite it gave me from nervous suffering, and my now daily visits to the artist's studio were a pleasure and a privilege not to be foregone. Moreover, I was never tired of looking at his pictures. His subjects were all original, and some of them were very weird and fantastic. One large picture particularly attracted me. It was entitled "Lords of our Life and Death." Surrounded by rolling masses of cloud, some silver-crested, some shot through with red flame, was depicted the World, as a globe half in light, half in shade. Poised above it was a great Angel, upon whose calm and noble face rested a mingled expression of deep sorrow, yearning pity, and infinite regret. Tears seemed to glitter on the drooping lashes of this sweet yet stern Spirit; and in his strong right hand he held a drawn sword—the sword of destruction—pointed forever downwards to the fated globe at his feet. Beneath this Angel and the world he dominated was darkness—utter illimitable darkness. But above him the clouds were torn asunder, and through a transparent veil of light golden mist, a face of surpassing beauty was seen—a face on which youth, health, hope, love, and ecstatic joy all shone with ineffable radiance. It was the personification of Life—not life as we know it, brief and full of care—but Life Immortal and Love Triumphant. Often and often I found myself standing before this masterpiece of Cellini's genius, gazing at it, not only with admiration, but with a sense of actual comfort. One afternoon, while resting in my favourite low chair opposite the picture, I roused myself from a reverie, and turning to the artist, who was showing some water-colour sketches to Mrs. Everard, I said abruptly:

"Did you imagine that face of the Angel of Life, Signor Cellini, or had you a model to copy from?"

He looked at me and smiled.

"It is a moderately good portrait of an existing original," he said.

"A woman's face then, I suppose? How very beautiful she must be!"

"Actual beauty is sexless," he replied, and was silent. The expression of his face had become abstracted and dreamy, and he turned over the sketches for Mrs. Everard with an air which showed his thoughts to be far away from his occupation.

"And the Death Angel?" I went on. "Had you a model for that also?"

This time a look of relief, almost of gladness, passed over his features.

"No indeed," he answered with ready frankness; "that is entirely my own creation."

I was about to compliment him on the grandeur and force of his poetical fancy, when he stopped me by a slight gesture of his hand.

"If you really admire the picture," he said, "pray do not say so. If it is in truth a work of art, let it speak to you as art only, and spare the poor workman who has called it into existence the shame of having to confess that it is not above human praise. The only true criticism of high art is silence—silence as grand as heaven itself."

He spoke with energy, and his dark eyes flashed. Amy (Mrs. Everard) looked at him curiously.

"Say now!" she exclaimed, with a ringing laugh, "aren't you a little bit eccentric, signor? You talk like a long-haired prophet! I never met an artist before who couldn't stand praise; it is generally a matter of wonder to me to notice how much of that intoxicating sweet they can swallow without reeling. But you're an exception, I must admit. I congratulate you!"

Cellini bowed gaily in response to the half-friendly, half-mocking curtsey she gave him, and, turning to me again, said:

"I have a favour to ask of you, mademoiselle. Will you sit to me for your portrait?"

"I!" I exclaimed, with astonishment. "Signor Cellini, I cannot imagine why you should wish so to waste your valuable time. There is nothing in my poor physiognomy worthy of your briefest attention."

"You must pardon me, mademoiselle," he replied gravely, "if I presume to differ from you. I am exceedingly anxious to transfer your features to my canvas. I am aware that you are not in strong health, and that your face has not that roundness and colour formerly habitual to it. But I am not an admirer of the milkmaid type of beauty. Everywhere I seek for intelligence, for thought, for inward refinement—in short, mademoiselle, you have the face of one whom the inner soul consumes, and, as such, may I plead again with you to give me a little of your spare time? You Will Not Regret It, I Assure You."

These last words were uttered in a lower tone and with singular impressiveness. I rose from my seat and looked at him steadily; he returned me glance for glance, A strange thrill ran through me, followed by that inexplicable sensation of absolute calm that I had before experienced. I smiled—I could, not help smiling.

"I will come to-morrow," I said.

"A thousand thanks, mademoiselle! Can you be here at noon?"

I looked inquiringly at Amy, who clapped her hands with delighted enthusiasm.

"Of course! Any time you like, signor. We will arrange our excursions so that they shall not interfere with the sittings. It will be most interesting to watch the picture growing day by day. What will you call it, signor? By some fancy title?"

"It will depend on its appearance when completed," he replied, as he threw open the doors of the studio and bowed us out with his usual ceremonious politeness.

"Au revoir, madame! A demain, mademoiselle!" and the violet velvet curtains of the portiere fell softly behind us as we made our exit.

"Is there not something strange about that young man?" said Mrs. Everard, as we walked through the long gallery of the Hotel de L—— back to our own rooms. "Something fiendish or angelic, or a little of both qualities mixed up?"

"I think he is what people term Peculiar, when they fail to understand the poetical vagaries of genius," I replied. "He is certainly very uncommon."

"Well!" continued my friend meditatively, as she contemplated her pretty mignonne face and graceful figure in a long mirror placed attractively in a corner of the hall through which we were passing; "all I can say is that I wouldn't let him paint MY portrait if he were to ask ever so! I should be scared to death. I wonder you, being so nervous, were not afraid of him."

"I thought you liked him," I said.

"So I do. So does my husband. He's awfully handsome and clever, and all that—but his conversation! There now, my dear, you must own he is slightly QUEER. Why, who but a lunatic would say that the only criticism of art is silence? Isn't that utter rubbish?"

"The only TRUE criticism," I corrected her gently.

"Well, it's all the same. How can there be any criticism at all in silence? According to his idea when we admire anything very much we ought to go round with long faces and gags on our mouths. That would be entirely ridiculous! And what was that dreadful thing he said to you?"

"I don't quite understand you," I answered; "I cannot remember his saying anything dreadful."

"Oh, I have it now," continued Amy with rapidity; "it was awful! He said you had the FACE OF ONE WHOM THE SOUL CONSUMES. You know that was most horribly mystical! And when he said it he looked— ghastly! What did he mean by it, I wonder?"

I made no answer; but I thought I knew. I changed the conversation as soon as possible, and my volatile American friend was soon absorbed in a discussion on dress and jewellery. That night was a blessed one for me; I was free from all suffering, and slept as calmly as a child, while in my dreams the face of Cellini's "Angel of life" smiled at me, and seemed to suggest peace.

II

The Mysterious Potion

The next day, punctually at noon, according to my promise, I entered the studio. I was alone, for Amy, after some qualms of conscience respecting chaperonage, propriety, and Mrs. Grundy, had yielded to my entreaties and gone for a drive with some friends. In spite of the fears she began to entertain concerning the Mephistophelian character of Raffaello Cellini, there was one thing of which both she and I felt morally certain: namely, that no truer or more honourable gentleman than he ever walked on the earth. Under his protection the loveliest and loneliest woman that ever lived would have been perfectly safe—as safe as though she were shut up, like the princess in the fairy-tale, in a brazen tower, of which only an undiscoverable serpent possessed the key. When I arrived, the rooms were deserted, save for the presence of a magnificent Newfoundland dog, who, as I entered, rose, and shaking his shaggy body, sat down before me and offered me his huge paw, wagging his tail in the most friendly manner all the while, I at once responded to his cordial greeting, and as I stroked his noble head, I wondered where the animal had come from; for though—we had visited Signor Cellini's studio every day, there had been no sign or mention of this stately, brown-eyed, four-footed companion. I seated myself, and the dog immediately lay down at my feet, every now and then looking up at me with an affectionate glance and a renewed wagging of his tail. Glancing round the well-known room, I noticed that the picture I admired so much was veiled by a curtain of Oriental stuff, in which were embroidered threads of gold mingled with silks of various brilliant hues. On the working easel was a large square canvas, already prepared, as I supposed, for my features to be traced thereon. It was an exceedingly warm morning, and though the windows as well as the glass doors of the conservatory were wide open, I found the air of the studio very oppressive. I perceived on the table a finely-wrought decanter of Venetian glass, in which clear water sparkled temptingly. Rising from my chair, I took an antique silver goblet from the mantelpiece, filled it with the cool fluid, and was about to drink, when the cup was suddenly snatched from my hands, and the voice of Cellini, changed from its usual softness to a tone both imperious and commanding, startled me.

"Do not drink that," he said; "you must not! You dare not! I forbid you!"

I looked up at him in mute astonishment. His face was very pale, and his large dark eyes shone with suppressed excitement. Slowly my self-possession returned to me, and I said calmly:

"You forbid me, signor? Surely you forget yourself. What harm have I done in helping myself to a simple glass of water in your studio? You are not usually so inhospitable."

While I spoke his manner changed, the colour returned to his face, and his eyes softened—he smiled.

"Forgive me, mademoiselle, for my brusquerie. It is true I forgot myself for a moment. But you were in danger, and—"

"In danger!" I exclaimed incredulously.

"Yes, mademoiselle. This," and he held up the Venetian decanter to the light, "is not water simply. If you will observe it now with the sunshine beating full against it, I think you will perceive peculiarities in it that will assure you of my veracity."

I looked as he bade me, and saw, to my surprise, that the fluid was never actually still for a second. A sort of internal bubbling seemed to work in its centre, and curious specks and lines of crimson and gold flashed through it from time to time.

"What is it?" I asked; adding with a half-smile, "Are you the possessor of a specimen of the far-famed Aqua Tofana?"

Cellini placed the decanter carefully on a shelf, and I noticed that he chose a particular spot for it, where the rays of the sun could fall perpendicularly upon the vessel containing it. Then turning to me, he replied:

"Aqua Tofana, mademoiselle, is a deadly poison, known to the ancients and also to many learned chemists of our day. It is a clear and colourless liquid, but it is absolutely still—as still as a stagnant pool. What I have just shown you is not poison, but quite the reverse. I will prove this to you at once." And taking a tiny liqueur glass from a side table, he filled it with the strange fluid and drank it off, carefully replacing the stopper in the decanter.

"But, Signor Cellini," I urged, "if it is so harmless, why did you forbid my tasting it? Why did you say there was danger for me when I was about to drink it?"

"Because, mademoiselle, for You it would be dangerous. Your health is weak, your nerves unstrung. That elixir is a powerful vivifying tonic, acting with great rapidity on the entire system, and rushing through the veins with the swiftness of ELECTRICITY. I am accustomed to it; it is my daily medicine. But I was brought to it by slow, and almost imperceptible degrees. A single teaspoonful of that fluid, mademoiselle, administered to anyone not prepared to receive it, would be instant death, though its actual use is to vivify and strengthen human life. You understand now why I said you were in danger?"

"I understand," I replied, though in sober truth I was mystified and puzzled.

"And you forgive my seeming rudeness?"

"Oh, certainly! But you have aroused my curiosity. I should like to know more about this strange medicine of yours."

"You shall know more if you wish," said Cellini, his usual equable humour and good spirits now quite restored. "You shall know everything; but not to-day. We have too little time. I have not yet commenced your picture. And I forgot—you were thirsty, and I was, as you said, inhospitable. You must permit me to repair my fault."

And with a courteous salute he left the room, to return almost immediately with a tumbler full of some fragrant, golden-coloured liquid, in which lumps of ice glittered refreshingly. A few loose rose-leaves were scattered on the top of this dainty-looking beverage.

"You may enjoy this without fear," said he, smiling; "it will do you good. It is an Eastern wine, unknown to trade, and therefore untampered with. I see you are looking at the rose-leaves on the surface. That is a Persian custom, and I think a pretty one. They float away from your lips in the action of drinking, and therefore they are no obstacle."

I tasted the wine and found it delicious, soft and mellow as summer moonlight. While I sipped it the big Newfoundland, who had stretched himself in a couchant posture on the hearth-rug ever since Cellini had first entered the room, rose and walked majestically to my side and rubbed his head caressingly against the folds of my dress.

"Leo has made friends with you, I see," said Cellini. "You should take that as a great compliment, for he is most particular in his choice of acquaintance, and most steadfast when he has once made up his mind. He has more decision of character than many a statesman."

"How is it we have never seen him before?" I inquired. "You never told us you had such a splendid companion."

"I am not his master," replied the artist. "He only favours me with a visit occasionally. He arrived from Paris last night, and came straight here, sure of his welcome. He does not confide his plans to me, but I suppose he will return to his home when he thinks it advisable. He knows his own business best."

I laughed.

"What a clever dog! Does he journey on foot, or does he take the train?"

"I believe he generally patronizes the railway. All the officials know him, and he gets into the guard's van as a matter of course. Sometimes he will alight at a station en route, and walk the rest of the way. But if he is lazily inclined, he does not stir till the train reaches its destination. At the end of every six months or so, the railway authorities send the bill of Leo's journeyings in to his master, when it is always settled without difficulty."

"And who Is his master?" I ventured to ask.

Cellini's face grew serious and absorbed, and his eyes were full of grave contemplation as he answered:

"His master, mademoiselle, is MY master—one who among men, is supremely intelligent; among teachers, absolutely unselfish; among thinkers, purely impersonal; among friends, inflexibly faithful. To him I owe everything—even life itself. For him no sacrifice, no extreme devotion would be too great, could I hope thereby to show my gratitude. But he is as far above human thanks or human rewards as the sun is above the sea. Not here, not now, dare I say to him, MY FRIEND, BEHOLD HOW MUCH I LOVE THEE! such language would be all too poor and unmeaning; but hereafter—who knows?—" and he broke off abruptly with a half-sigh. Then, as if forcing himself to change the tenor of his thoughts, he continued in a kind tone: "But, mademoiselle, I am wasting your time, and am taking no advantage of the favour you have shown me by your presence to-day. Will you seat yourself here?" and he placed an elaborately carved oaken settee in one corner of the studio, opposite his own easel. "I should be sorry to fatigue you at all," he went on; "do you care for reading?"

I answered eagerly in the affirmative, and he handed me a volume bound in curiously embossed leather, and ornamented with silver clasps. It was entitled "Letters of a Dead Musician."

"You will find clear gems of thought, passion, and feeling in this book," said Cellini; "and being a musician yourself, you will know how to appreciate them. The writer was one of those geniuses whose work the world repays with ridicule and contempt. There is no fate more enviable!"

I looked at the artist with some surprise as I took the volume he recommended, and seated myself in the position he indicated; and while he busied himself in arranging the velvet curtains behind me as a background, I said:

"Do you really consider it enviable, Signor Cellini, to receive the world's ridicule and contempt?"

"I do indeed," he replied, "since it is a certain proof that the world does not understand you. To achieve something that is above human comprehension, THAT is greatness. To have the serene sublimity of the God-man Christ, and consent to be crucified by a gibing world that was fated to be afterwards civilized and dominated by His teachings, what can be more glorious? To have the magnificent versatility of a Shakespeare, who was scarcely recognized in his own day, but whose gifts were so vast and various that the silly multitudes wrangle over his very identity and the authenticity of his plays to this hour—what can be more triumphant? To know that one's own soul can, if strengthened and encouraged by the force of will, rise to a supreme altitude of power— is not that sufficient to compensate for the little whining cries of the common herd of men and women who have forgotten whether they ever had a spiritual spark in them, and who, straining up to see the light of genius that burns too fiercely for their earth-dimmed eyes, exclaim: 'WE see nothing, therefore there CAN be nothing.' Ah, mademoiselle, the knowledge of one's own inner Self-Existence is a knowledge surpassing all the marvels of art and science!"

Cellini spoke with enthusiasm, and his countenance seemed illumined by the eloquence that warmed his speech. I listened with a sort of dreamy satisfaction; the visual sensation of utter rest that I always experienced in this man's presence was upon me, and I watched him with interest as he drew with quick and facile touch the outline of my features on his canvas.

Gradually he became more and more absorbed in his work; he glanced at me from time to time, but did not speak, and his pencil worked rapidly. I turned over the "Letters of a Dead Musician" with some curiosity. Several passages struck me as being remarkable for their originality and depth of thought; but what particularly impressed me as I read on, was the tone of absolute joy and contentment that seemed to light up every page. There were no wailings over disappointed ambition, no regrets for the past, no complaints, no criticism, no word for or against the brothers of his art; everything was treated from a lofty standpoint of splendid equality, save when the writer spoke of himself, and then he became the humblest of the humble, yet never abject, and always happy.

"O Music!" he wrote, "Music, thou Sweetest Spirit of all that serve God, what have I done that thou shouldst so often visit me? It is not well, O thou Lofty and Divine One, that thou shouldst stoop so low as to console him who is the unworthiest of all thy servants. For I am too feeble to tell the world how soft is the sound of thy rustling pinions, how tender is the sighing breath of thy lips, how beyond all things glorious is the vibration of thy lightest whisper! Remain aloft, thou Choicest Essence of the Creator's Voice, remain in that pure and cloudless ether, where alone thou art fitted to dwell. My touch must desecrate thee, my voice affright thee. Suffice it to thy servant, O Beloved, to dream of thee and die!"

Meeting Cellini's glance as I finished reading these lines, I asked:

"Did you know the author of this book, signor?"

"I knew him well," he replied; "he was one of the gentlest souls that ever dwelt in human clay. As ethereal in his music as John Keats in his poetry, he was one of those creatures born of dreams and rapture that rarely visit this planet. Happy fellow! What a death was his!"

"How did he die?" I inquired.

"He was playing the organ in one of the great churches of Rome on the day of the Feast of the Virgin. A choir of finely trained voices sang to his accompaniment his own glorious setting of the "Regina Coeli." The music was wonderful, startling, triumphant—ever rising in power and majesty to a magnificent finale, when suddenly a slight crash was heard; the organ ceased abruptly, the singers broke off. The musician was dead. He had fallen forward on the keys of the instrument, and when they raised him, his face was fairer than the face of any sculptured angel, so serene was its expression, so rapt was its smile. No one could tell exactly the cause of his death—he had always been remarkably strong and healthy. Everyone said it was heart-disease—it is the usual reason assigned by medical savants for these sudden departures out of the world. His loss was regretted by all, save myself and one other who loved him. We rejoiced, and still do rejoice, at his release."

I speculated vaguely on the meaning of these last words, but I felt disinclined to ask any more questions, and Cellini, probably seeing this, worked on at his sketch without further converse. My eyes were growing heavy, and the printed words in the "Dead Musician's Letters" danced before my sight like active little black demons with thin waving arms and legs. A curious yet not unpleasant drowsiness stole over me, in which I heard the humming of the bees at the open window, the singing of the birds, and the voices of people in the hotel gardens, all united in one continuous murmur that seemed a long way off. I saw the sunshine and the shadow—I saw the majestic Leo stretched full length near the easel, and the slight supple form of Raffaello Cellini standing out in bold outline against the light; yet all seemed shifting and mingling strangely into a sort of wide radiance in which there was nothing but varying tints of colour. And could it have been my fancy, or did I actually See the curtain fall gradually away from my favourite picture, just enough for the face of the "Angel of Life" to be seen smiling down upon me? I rubbed my eyes violently, and started to my feet at the sound of the artist's voice.

"I have tried your patience enough for to-day," he said, and his words sounded muffled, as though they were being spoken through, a thick wall. "You can leave me now if you like."

I stood before him mechanically, still holding the book he had lent me clasped in my hand. Irresolutely I raised my eyes towards the "Lords of our Life and Death." It was closely veiled. I had then experienced an optical illusion. I forced myself to speak—to smile—to put back the novel sensations that were overwhelming me.

"I think," I said, and I heard myself speak as though I were somebody else at a great distance off—"I think, Signor Cellini, your Eastern wine has been too potent for me. My head is quite heavy, and I feel dazed."

"It is mere fatigue and the heat of the day," he replied quietly. "I am sure you are not too Dazed, as you call it, to see your favourite picture, are you?"

I trembled. Was not that picture veiled? I looked—there was no curtain at all, and the faces of the two Angels shone out of the canvas with intense brilliancy! Strange to say, I felt no surprise at this circumstance, which, had it occurred a moment previously, would have unquestionably astonished and perhaps alarmed me. The mistiness of my brain suddenly cleared; I saw everything plainly; I heard distinctly; and when I spoke, the tone of my voice sounded as full and ringing as it had previously seemed low and muffled. I gazed steadfastly at the painting, and replied, half smiling:

"I should be indeed 'far gone,' as the saying is, if I could not see that, signor! It is truly your masterpiece. Why have you never exhibited it?"

"Can You ask that?" he said with impressive emphasis, at the same time drawing nearer and fixing upon me the penetrating glance of his dark fathomless eyes. It then seemed to me that some great inner force compelled me to answer this half-inquiry, in words of which I had taken no previous thought, and which, as I uttered them, conveyed no special meaning to my own ears.

"Of course," I said slowly, as if I were repeating a lesson, "you would not so betray the high trust committed to your charge."

"Well said!" replied Cellini; "you are fatigued, mademoiselle. Au revoir! Till to-morrow!" And, throwing open the door of his studio, he stood aside for me to pass out. I looked at him inquiringly.

"Must I come at the same time to-morrow?" I asked.

"If you please."

I passed my hand across my forehead perplexedly, I felt I had something else to say before I left him. He waited patiently, holding back with one hand the curtains of the portiere.

"I think I had a parting word to give you," I said at last, meeting his gaze frankly; "but I seem to have forgotten what it was." Cellini smiled gravely.

"Do not trouble to think about it, mademoiselle. I am unworthy the effort on your part."

A flash of vivid light crossed my eyes for a second, and I exclaimed eagerly:

"I remember now! It was 'Dieu vous garde' signor!"

He bent his head reverentially.

"Merci mille fois, mademoiselle! Dieu vous garde—vous aussi. Au revoir."

And clasping my hand with a light yet friendly pressure, he closed the door of his room behind me. Once alone in the passage, the sense of high elation and contentment that had just possessed me began gradually to decrease. I had not become actually dispirited, but a languid feeling of weariness oppressed me, and my limbs ached as though I had walked incessantly for many miles. I went straight to my own room. I consulted my watch; it was half-past one, the hour at which the hotel luncheon was usually served. Mrs. Everard had evidently not returned from her drive. I did not care to attend the table d'hote alone; besides, I had no inclination to eat. I drew down the window-blinds to shut out the brilliancy of the beautiful Southern sunlight, and throwing myself on my bed I determined to rest quietly till Amy came back. I had brought the "Letters of a Dead Musician" away with me from Cellini's studio, and I began to read, intending to keep myself awake by this means. But I found I could not fix my attention on the page, nor could I think at all connectedly. Little by little my eyelids closed; the book dropped from my nerveless hand; and in a few minutes I was in a deep and tranquil slumber.

III

Three Visions

Roses, roses! An interminable chain of these royal blossoms, red and white, wreathed by the radiant fingers of small rainbow-winged creatures as airy as moonlight mist, as delicate as thistledown! They cluster round me with smiling faces and eager eyes; they place the end of their rose-garland in my hand, and whisper, "Follow!" Gladly I obey, and hasten onward. Guiding myself by the fragrant chain I hold, I pass through a labyrinth of trees, whose luxuriant branches quiver with the flight and song of birds. Then comes a sound of waters; the riotous rushing of a torrent unchecked, that leaps sheer down from rocks a thousand feet high, thundering forth the praise of its own beauty as it tosses in the air triumphant crowns of silver spray. How the living diamonds within it shift, and change, and sparkle! Fain would I linger to watch this magnificence; but the coil of roses still unwinds before me, and the fairy voices still cry, "Follow!" I press on. The trees grow thicker; the songs of the birds cease; the light around me grows pale and subdued. In the far distance I see a golden crescent that seems suspended by some invisible thread in the air. Is it the young moon? No; for as I gaze it breaks apart into a thousand points of vivid light like wandering stars. These meet; they blaze into letters of fire. I strain my dazzled eyes to spell out their meaning. They form one word—Heliobas. I read it. I utter it aloud. The rose-chain breaks at my feet, and disappears. The fairy voices die away on my ear. There is utter silence, utter darkness,— save where that one Name writes itself in burning gold on the blackness of the heavens.

The interior of a vast cathedral is opened before my gaze. The lofty white marble columns support a vaulted roof painted in fresco, from which are suspended a thousand lamps that emit a mild and steady effulgence. The great altar is illuminated; the priests, in glittering raiment, pace slowly to and fro. The large voice of the organ, murmuring to itself awhile, breaks forth in a shout of melody; and a boy's clear, sonorous treble tones pierce the incense-laden air. "Credo!"—and the silver, trumpet-like notes fall from the immense height of the building like a bell ringing in a pure atmosphere—"Credo in unum Deum; Patrem omni-potentum, factorem coeli et terrae, visibilium omnium et invisibilium."

The cathedral echoes with answering voices; and, involuntarily kneeling, I follow the words of the grand chant. I hear the music slacken; the notes of rejoicing change to a sobbing and remorseful wail; the organ shudders like a forest of pines in a tempest, "Crucifixus etiam pro nobis; passus et sepultus est." A darkness grows up around me; my senses swim. The music altogether ceases; but a brilliant radiance streams through a side-door of the church, and twenty maidens, clad in white and crowned with myrtle, pacing two by two, approach me. They gaze at me with joyous eyes. "Art thou also one of us?" they murmur; then they pass onward to the altar, where again the lights are glimmering. I watch them with eager interest; I hear them uplift their fresh young voices in prayer and praise. One of them, whose deep blue eyes are full of lustrous tenderness, leaves her companions, and softly approaches me. She holds a pencil and tablet in her hand.

"Write!" she says, in a thrilling whisper; "and write quickly! for whatsoever thou shalt now inscribe is the clue to thy destiny."

I obey her mechanically, impelled not by my own will, but by some unknown powerful force acting within and around me. I trace upon the tablet one word only; it is a name that startles me even while I myself write it down—HELIOBAS. Scarcely have I written it when a thick white cloud veils the cathedral from my sight; the fair maiden vanishes, and all is again still.

I AM LISTENING TO THE accents of a grave melodious voice, which, from its slow and measured tones, would seem to be in the action of reading or reciting aloud. I see a small room sparely furnished, and at a table covered with books and manuscripts is seated a man of noble features and commanding presence. He is in the full prime of life; his dark hair has no thread of silver to mar its luxuriance; his face is unwrinkled; his forehead unfurrowed by care; his eyes, deeply sunk beneath his shelving brows, are of a singularly clear and penetrating blue, with an absorbed and watchful look in them, like the eyes of one accustomed to gaze far out at sea. His hand rests on the open pages of a massive volume; he is reading, and his expression is intent and earnest— as if he were littering his own thoughts aloud, with the conviction and force of an orator who knows the truth of which he speaks:

"The Universe is upheld solely by the Law of Love. A majestic invisible Protectorate governs the winds, the tides, the incoming and outgoing of the seasons, the birth of the flowers, the growth of forests, the outpourings of the sunlight, the silent glittering of the stars. A wide illimitable Beneficence embraces all creation. A vast Eternal Pity exists for all sorrow, all sin. He who first swung the planets in the air, and bade them revolve till Time shall be no more—He, the Fountain-Head of Absolute Perfection, is no deaf, blind, capricious, or remorseless Being. To Him the death of the smallest singing-bird is as great or as little as the death of a world's emperor. For Him the timeless withering of an innocent flower is as pitiful as the decay of a mighty nation. An infant's first prayer to Him is heard with as tender a patience as the united petitions of thousands of worshippers. For in everything and around everything, from the sun to a grain of sand, He hath a portion, small or great, of His own most Perfect Existence. Should He hate His Creation, He must perforce hate Himself; and that Love should hate Love is an impossibility. Therefore He loves all His work; and as Love, to be perfect, must contain Pity, Forgiveness, and Forbearance, so doth He pity, forgive, and forbear. Shall a mere man deny himself for the sake of his child or friend? and shall the Infinite Love refuse to sacrifice itself— yea, even to as immense a humility as its greatness is immeasurable? Shall we deny those merciful attributes to God which we acknowledge in His creature, Man? O my Soul, rejoice that thou hast pierced the veil of the Beyond; that thou hast seen and known the Truth! that to thee is made clear the Reason of Life, and the Recompense of Death: yet while rejoicing, grieve that thou art not fated to draw more than a few souls to the comfort thou hast thyself attained!"

Fascinated by the speaker's voice and countenance, I listen, straining my ears to catch every word that falls from his lips. He rises; he stands erect; he stretches out his hands as though in solemn entreaty.

"Azul!" he exclaims. "Messenger of my fate; thou who art a guiding spirit of the elements, thou who ridest the storm-cloud and sittest throned on the edge of the lightning! By that electric spark within me, of which thou art the Twin Flame, I ask of thee to send me this one more poor human soul; let me change its unrestfulness into repose, its hesitation to certainty, its weakness to strength, its weary imprisonment to the light of liberty! Azul!"

His voice ceases, his extended hands fall slowly, and gradually, gradually he turns his whole figure towards ME. He faces me—his intense eyes burn through me—his strange yet tender smile absorbs me. Yet I am full of unreasoning terror; I tremble—I strive to turn away from that searching and magnetic gaze. His deep, melodious tones again ring softly on the silence. He addresses me.

"Fearest thou me, my child? Am I not thy friend? Knowest thou not the name of HELIOBAS?"

At this word I start and gasp for breath; I would shriek, but cannot, for a heavy hand seems to close my mouth, and an immense weight presses me down. I struggle violently with this unseen Power—little by little I gain the advantage. One effort more! I win the victory—I wake!

"SAKES ALIVE!" SAYS A FAMILIAR voice; "you HAVE had a spell of sleep! I got home about two, nearly starving, and I found you here curled up 'in a rosy infant slumber,' as the song says. So I hunted up the Colonel and had lunch, for it seemed a sin to disturb you. It's just struck four. Shall we have some tea up here?"

I looked at Mrs. Everard, and smiled assent. So I had been sleeping for two hours and a half, and I had evidently been dreaming all the time; but my dreams had been as vivid as realities. I felt still rather drowsy, but I was thoroughly rested and in a state of delicious tranquillity. My friend rang the bell for the tea, and then turned round and surveyed me with a sort of wonder.

"What have you done to yourself, child?" she said at last, approaching the bed where I lay, and staring fixedly at me.

"What do you mean?"

"Why, you look a different creature. When I left you this morning you were pale and haggard, a sort of die-away delicate invalid; now your eyes are bright; and your cheeks have quite a lovely colour in them; your lips, too, are the right tint. But perhaps," and here she looked alarmed—"perhaps you've got the fever?"

"I don't think so," I said amusedly, and I stretched out my hand for her to feel.

"No, you haven't," she continued, evidently reassured; "your palm is moist and cool, and your pulse is regular. Well, you look spry, anyhow. I shouldn't wonder if you made up your mind to have a dance to-night."

"Dance?" I queried. "What dance, and where?"

"Well, Madame Didier, that jolly little furbelowed Frenchwoman with whom I was driving just now, has got up a regular party to-night—"

"Hans Breitmann gib a barty?" I interposed, with a mock solemn air of inquiry.

Amy laughed.

"Well, yes, it MAY be that kind of thing, for all I know to the contrary. Anyhow, she's hired the band and ordered a right-down elegant supper. Half the folks in the hotel are going, and a lot of outsiders have got invitations. She asked if we couldn't come—myself, the Colonel, and you. I said I could answer for myself and the Colonel, but not for you, as you were an invalid. But if you keep on looking as you do at present, no one will believe that there's anything the matter with you.—Tea, Alphonse!"

This to a polite waiter, who was our special attendant, and who just then knocked at the door to know "madame's" orders.

Utterly disbelieving what my friend said in regard to my improved appearance, I rose from the bed and went to the dressing-table to look in the mirror and judge for myself. I almost recoiled from my own reflection, so great was my surprise. The heavy marks under my eyes, the lines of pain that had been for months deepening in my forehead, the plaintive droop of the mouth that had given me such an air of ill-health and anxiety—all were gone as if by magic. I saw a rose-tinted complexion, a pair of laughing, lustrous eyes, and, altogether, such a happy, mirthful young face smiled back at me, that I half doubted whether it was indeed myself I saw.

"There now!" cried Amy in triumph, watching me as I pushed my clustering hair from my brows, and examined myself more intently. "Did I not tell you so? The change in you is marvellous! I know what it is. You have been getting better unconsciously to yourself in this lovely air and scene, and the long afternoon sleep you've just had has completed the cure."

I smiled at her enthusiasm, but was forced to admit that she was right as far as my actual looks went. No one would believe that I was, or ever had been, ill. In silence I loosened my hair and began to brush it and put it in order before the mirror, and as I did so my thoughts were very busy. I remembered distinctly all that had happened in the studio of Raffaello Cellini, and still more distinctly was I able to recall every detail of the three dreams that had visited me in my slumber. The NAME, too, that had been the key-note of them all I also remembered, but some instinct forbade me to utter it aloud. Once I thought, "Shall I take a pencil and write it down lest I forget it?" and the same instinct said "No." Amy's voluble chatter ran on like the sound of a rippling brook all the time I thus meditated over the occurrences of the day.

"Say, child!" she exclaimed; "will you go to the dance?"

"Certainly I will, with pleasure," I answered, and indeed I felt as if I should thoroughly enjoy it.

"Brava! It will be real fun. There are no end of foreign titles coming, I believe. The Colonel's a bit grumpy about it,—he always is when he has to wear his dress suit. He just hates it. That man hasn't a particle of vanity. He looks handsomer in his evening clothes than in anything else, and yet he doesn't see it. But tell me," and her pretty face became serious with a true feminine anxiety, "whatever will you wear? You've brought no ball fixings, have you?"

I finished twisting up the last coil of my hair, and turned and kissed her affectionately. She was the most sweet-tempered and generous of women, and she would have placed any one of her elaborate costumes at my disposal had I expressed the least desire in that direction. I answered:

"No, dear; I certainly have no regular ball 'fixings,' for I never expected to dance here, or anywhere for that matter. I did not bring the big trunks full of Parisian toilettes that you indulge in, you spoilt bride! Still I have something that may do. In fact it will have to do."

"What is it? Have I seen it? Do show!" and her curiosity was unappeasable.

The discreet Alphonse tapped at the door again just at this moment.

"Entrez!" I answered; and our tea, prepared with the tempting nicety peculiar to the Hotel de L——, appeared. Alphonse set the tray down with his usual artistic nourish, and produced a small note from his vest-pocket.

"For mademoiselle," he said with a bow; and as he handed it to me, his eyes opened wide in surprise. He, too, perceived the change in my appearance. But he was dignity itself, and instantly suppressed his astonishment into the polite impassiveness of a truly accomplished waiter, and gliding from the room on the points of his toes, as was his usual custom, he disappeared. The note was from Cellini, and ran as follows:

"If mademoiselle will be so good as to refrain from choosing any flowers for her toilette this evening, she will confer a favour on her humble friend and servant,

RAFFAELLO CELLINI

I handed it to Amy, who was evidently burning with inquisitiveness to know its contents.

"Didn't I say he was a queer young man?" she exclaimed, as she perused the missive attentively. "This is only his way of saying that he means to send you some flowers himself. But what puzzles me is to think how he could possibly know you were going to make any special 'toilette' this evening. It is really very mysterious when I come to think of it, for Madame Didier said plainly that she would not ask Cellini to the dance till she saw him at the table d'hote to-night."

"Perhaps Alphonse has told him all about it," I suggested.

My friend's countenance brightened.

"Of course! That is it; and Mr. Cellini takes it for granted that a girl of your age would not be likely to refuse a dance. Still there is something odd about it, too. By-the-bye, I forgot to ask you how the picture got on?"

"Oh, very well, I believe," I replied evasively. "Signor Cellini only made a slight outline sketch as a beginning."

"And was it like you?—a really good resemblance?"

"I really did not examine it closely enough to be able to judge."

"What a demure young person you are!" laughed Mrs. Everard. "Now, I should have rushed straight up to the easel and examined every line of what he was doing. You are a model of discretion, really! I shan't be anxious about leaving you alone any more. But about your dress for to-night. Let me see it, there's a good girl."

I opened my trunk and took out a robe of ivory-tinted crepe. It was made with almost severe simplicity, and was unadorned, save by a soft ruffle of old Mechlin lace round the neck and sleeves. Amy examined it critically.

"Now, you would have looked perfectly ghastly in this last night, when you were as pale and hollow-eyed as a sick nun; but to-night," and she raised her eyes to my face, "I believe you will do. Don't you want the bodice cut lower?"

"No, thanks!" I said, smiling. "I will leave that to the portly dowagers—they will expose neck enough for half-a-dozen other women."

My friend laughed.

"Do as you like," she returned; "only I see your gown has short sleeves, and I thought you might like a square neck instead of that little simple Greek round. But perhaps it's better as it is. The stuff is lovely; where did you get it?"

MARIE CORELLI

"At one of the London emporiums of Eastern art," I answered. "My dear, your tea is getting cold."

She laid the dress on the bed, and in doing so, perceived the antique-looking book with the silver clasps which I had left there.

"What's this?" she asked, turning it round to discover its name. "'Letters of a Dead Musician!' What a shivery title! Is it morbid reading?"

"Not at all," I replied, as I leaned comfortably back in an easy-chair and sipped my tea. "It is a very scholarly, poetical, and picturesque work. Signor Cellini lent it to me; the author was a friend of his."

Amy looked at me with a knowing and half-serious expression.

"Say now—take care, take care! Aren't you and Cellini getting to be rather particular friends—something a little beyond the Platonic, eh?"

This notion struck me as so absurd that I laughed heartily. Then, without pausing for one instant to think what I was saying, I answered with amazing readiness and frankness, considering that I really knew nothing about it:

"Why, my dear, Raffaello Cellini is betrothed, and he is a most devoted lover."

A moment after I had uttered this assertion I was surprised at myself. What authority had I for saying that Cellini was betrothed? What did I know about it? Confused, I endeavoured to find some means of retracting this unfounded and rash remark, but no words of explanation would come to my lips that had been so ready and primed to deliver what might be, for all I knew, a falsehood. Amy did not perceive my embarrassment. She was pleased and interested at the idea of Cellini's being in love.

"Really!" she exclaimed, "it makes him a more romantic character than ever! Fancy his telling you that he was betrothed! How delightful! I must ask him all about his chosen fair one. But I'm positively thankful it isn't you, for I'm sure he's just a little bit off his head. Even this book he has lent you looks like a wizard's property;" and she fluttered the leaves of the "Dead Musician's" volume, turning them rapidly over in search of something attractive. Suddenly she paused and cried out: "Why, this is right-down awful! He must have been a regular madman! Just listen!" and she read aloud:

"'How mighty are the Kingdoms of the Air! How vast they are—how densely populated—how glorious are their destinies—how all-powerful and wise are their inhabitants! They possess everlasting health and beauty—their movements are music—their glances are light—they cannot err in their laws or judgments, for their existence is love. Thrones, principalities, and powers are among them, yet all are equal. Each one has a different duty to perform, yet all their labours are lofty. But what a fate is ours on this low earth! For, from the cradle to the grave, we are watched by these spiritual spectators—watched with unflinching interest, unhesitating regard. O Angelic Spirits, what is there in the poor and shabby spectacle of human life to attract your mighty Intelligences? Sorrow, sin, pride, shame, ambition, failure, obstinacy, ignorance, selfishness, forgetfulness—enough to make ye veil your radiant faces in unpierceable clouds to hide forever the sight of so much crime and misery. Yet if there be the faintest, feeblest effort in our souls to answer to the call of your voices, to rise above the earth by force of the same will that pervades your destinies, how the sound of great rejoicing permeates those wide continents ye inhabit, like a wave of thunderous music; and ye are glad, Blessed Spirits!—glad with a gladness beyond that of your own lives, to feel and to know that some vestige, however fragile, is spared from the general wreck of selfish and unbelieving Humanity. Truly we work under the shadow of a "cloud of Witnesses." Disperse, disperse, O dense yet brilliant multitudes! turn away from me your burning, truthful, immutable eyes, filled with that look of divine, perpetual regret and pity! Lo, how unworthy am I to behold your glory! and yet I must see and know and love you all, while the mad blind world rushes on to its own destruction, and none can avert its doom.'"

Here Amy threw down the book with a sort of contempt, and said to me:

"If you are going to muddle your mind with the ravings of a lunatic, you are not what I took you for. Why, it's regular spiritualism! Kingdoms of the air indeed! And his cloud of witnesses! Rubbish!"

"He quotes the CLOUD OF WITNESSES from St. Paul," I remarked.

"More shame for him!" replied my friend, with the usual inconsistent indignation that good Protestants invariably display when their pet corn, the Bible, is accidentally trodden on. "It has been very well said that the devil can quote Scripture, and this musician (a good job he Is dead, I'm sure) is perfectly blasphemous to quote the Testament in support of his ridiculous ideas! St. Paul did not mean by 'a cloud of witnesses,' a lot of 'air multitudes' and 'burning, immutable eyes,' and all that nonsense."

"Well, what DID he mean?" I gently persisted.

"Oh, he meant—why, you know very well what he meant," said Amy, in a tone of reproachful solemnity. "And I wonder at your asking me such a question! Surely you know your Bible, and you must be aware that St. Paul could never have approved of spiritualism."

"'And there are bodies celestial and bodies terrestrial, but one is the glory of the celestial?'" I quoted with, a slight smile.

Mrs. Everard looked shocked and almost angry.

"My dear, I am ashamed of you! You are a believer in spirits, I do declare! Why, I thought Maskelyne and Cook had cured everybody of such notions; and now here's this horrid book going to make you more nervous than ever. I shall have you getting up one night and shrieking about burning, immutable eyes looking at you."

I laughed merrily as I rose to pick up the discarded volume from the floor.

"Don't be afraid," I said; "I'll give back the book to Signor Cellini to-morrow, and I will tell him that you do not like the idea of my reading it, and that I am going to study the Bible instead. Come now, dear, don't look cross!" and I embraced her warmly, for I liked her far too well to wish to offend her. "Let us concentrate our attention on our finery for to-night, when a 'dense and brilliant multitude,' not of air, but of the 'earth earthy,' will pass us under critical survey. I assure you I mean to make the best of my improved looks, as I don't believe they will last. I dare say I shall be the 'sick nun' that you termed me again to-morrow."

"I hope not, dearest," said my friend kindly, returning my caress and forgetting her momentary ill-humour. "A jolly dance will do you good if you are careful to avoid over-exertion. But you are quite right, we must really fix our things ready for the evening, else we shall be all in a flurry at the last moment, and nothing riles the Colonel so much as to see women in a fuss. I shall wear my lace dress; but it wants seeing to. Will you help me?"

Readily assenting, we were soon deep in the arrangement of the numberless little mysteries that make up a woman's toilette; and nothing but the most frivolous conversation ensued. But as I assisted in the sorting of laces, jewels, and other dainty appendages of evening costume, I was deep in earnest meditation. Reviewing in my own mind the various sensations I had experienced since I had tasted that Eastern wine in Cellini's studio, I came to the conclusion that he must have tried an experiment on me with some foreign drug, of which he alone knew the properties. Why he should do this I could not determine; but that he had done it I was certain. Besides this, I felt sure that he personally exerted some influence upon me—a soothing and calming influence

I was forced to admit—still, it could hardly be allowed to continue. To be under the control, however slight, of one who was almost a stranger to me, was, at the least, unnatural and unpleasant. I was bound to ask him a few plain questions. And, supposing Mrs. Everard were to speak to him about his being betrothed, and he were to deny it, and afterwards were to turn round upon me and ask what authority I had for making such a statement, what should I say? Convict myself of falsehood? However, it was no use to puzzle over the solution of this difficulty till it positively presented itself. At any rate, I determined I would ask him frankly, face to face, for some explanation of the strange emotions I had felt ever since meeting him; and thus resolved, I waited patiently for the evening.

IV

A Dance and a Promise

Our little French friend, Madame Didier, was not a woman to do things by halves. She was one of those rare exceptions among Parisian ladies—she was a perfectly happy wife; nay, more, she was in love with her own husband, a fact which, considering the present state of society both in France and England, rendered her almost contemptible in the eyes of all advanced thinkers. She was plump and jolly in appearance; round-eyed and brisk as a lively robin. Her husband, a large, mild-faced placid man—"mon petit mari," as she called him—permitted her to have her own way in everything, and considered all she did as perfectly well done. Therefore, when she had proposed this informal dance at the Hotel de L——, he made no objection, but entered into her plans with spirit; and, what was far more important, opened his purse readily to her demands for the necessary expenses. So nothing was stinted; the beautiful ballroom attached to the hotel was thrown open, and lavishly decorated with flowers, fountains, and twinkling lights; an awning extended from its windows right down the avenue of dark ilex-trees, which were ornamented with Chinese lanterns; an elegant supper was laid out in the large dining-room, and the whole establishment was en fete. The delicious strains of a Viennese band floated to our ears as Colonel Everard, his wife, and myself descended the staircase on our way to the scene of revelry; and suggestions of fairyland were presented to us in the graceful girlish forms, clad in light, diaphanous attire, that flitted here and there, or occasionally passed us. Colonel Everard marched proudly along with the military bearing that always distinguished him, now and then glancing admiringly at his wife, who, indeed, looked her very best. Her dress was of the finest Brussels lace, looped over a skirt of the palest shell-pink satin; deep crimson velvet roses clustered on her breast, and nestled in her rich hair; a necklace of magnificent rubies clasped her neck, and the same jewels glittered on her round white arms. Her eyes shone with pleasurable excitement, and the prettiest colour imaginable tinted her delicate cheeks.

"When an American woman is lovely, she is very lovely," I said. "You will be the belle of the room to-night, Amy!"

"Nonsense!" she replied, well pleased, though, at my remark. "You must remember I have a rival in yourself."

I shrugged my shoulders incredulously.

"It is not like you to be sarcastic," I said. "You know very well I have the air of a resuscitated corpse."

The Colonel wheeled round suddenly, and brought us all up to a standstill before a great mirror.

"If You are like a resuscitated corpse, I'll throw a hundred dollars into the next mud-pond," he observed. "Look at yourself."

I looked, at first indifferently, and then with searching scrutiny. I saw a small, slender girl, clad in white, with a mass of gold hair twisted loosely up from her neck, and fastened with a single star of diamonds. A superb garniture of natural lilies of the valley was fastened on this girl's shoulder; and, falling loosely across her breast, lost itself in the trailing folds of her gown. She held a palm-leaf fan entirely covered with lilies of the valley, and a girdle of the same flowers encircled her waist. Her face was serious, but contented; her eyes were bright, but with an intense and thoughtful lustre; and her cheeks were softly coloured, as though a west wind had blown freshly against them. There was nothing either attractive or repulsive about her that I could see; and yet—I turned away from the mirror hastily with a faint smile.

"The lilies form the best part of my toilette," I said.

"That they do," asserted Amy, with emphasis. "They are the finest specimens I ever saw. It was real elegant of Mr. Cellini to send them all fixed up ready like that, fan and all. You must be a favourite of his!"

"Come, let us proceed," I answered, with some abruptness. "We are losing time."

In a few seconds more we entered the ballroom, and were met at once by Madame Didier, who, resplendent in black lace and diamonds, gave us hearty greeting. She stared at me with unaffected amazement.

"Mon dieu!" she exclaimed—her conversation with us was always a mixture of French and broken English—"I should not 'ave know zis young lady again! She 'ave si bonne mine. You veel dance, sans doute?"

We readily assented, and the usual assortment of dancing-men of all ages and sizes was brought forward for our inspection; while the Colonel, being introduced to a beaming English girl of some seventeen summers, whirled her at once into the merry maze of dancers, who were spinning easily round to the lively melody of one of Strauss's most fascinating waltzes. Presently I also found myself circling the room with an amiable young German, who ambled round with a certain amount of cleverness, considering that he was evidently ignorant of the actual waltz step; and I caught a glimpse now and then of Amy's rubies as they flashed past me in the dance—she was footing it merrily with a handsome Austrian Hussar. The room was pleasantly full—not too crowded for the movements of the dancers; and the whole scene was exceedingly pretty and animated. I had no lack of partners, and I was surprised to find myself so keenly alive to enjoyment, and so completely free from my usual preoccupied condition of nervous misery I looked everywhere for Raffaello Cellini, but he was not to be seen. The lilies that I wore, which he had sent me, seemed quite unaffected by the heat and glare of the gaslight—not a leaf drooped, not a petal withered; and their remarkable whiteness and fragrance elicited many admiring remarks from those with whom I conversed. It was growing very late; there were only two more waltzes before the final cotillon. I was standing near the large open window of the ballroom, conversing with one of my recent partners, when a sudden inexplicable thrill shot through me from head to foot. Instinctively I turned, and saw Cellini approaching. He looked remarkably handsome, though his face was pale and somewhat wearied in expression. He was laughing and conversing gaily with two ladies, one of whom was Mrs. Everard; and as he came towards me he bowed courteously, saying:

"I am too much honoured by the kindness mademoiselle has shown in not discarding my poor flowers."

"They are lovely," I replied simply; "and I am very much obliged to you, signor, for sending them to me."

"And how fresh they keep!" said Amy, burying her little nose in the fragrance of my fan; "yet they have been in the heat of the room all the evening."

"They cannot perish while mademoiselle wears them," said Cellini gallantly. "Her breath is their life."

"Bravo!" cried Amy, clapping her hands. "That is very prettily said, isn't it?"

I was silent. I never could endure compliments. They are seldom sincere, and it gives me no pleasure to be told lies, however prettily they may be worded. Signor Cellini appeared to divine my thoughts, for he said in a lower tone:

"Pardon me, mademoiselle; I see my observation displeased you; but there is more truth in it than you perhaps know."

"Oh, say!" interrupted Mrs. Everard at this juncture; "I am So interested, signor, to hear you are engaged! I suppose she is a dream of beauty?"

The hot colour rushed to my cheeks, and I bit my lips in confusion and inquietude. What WOULD he answer? My anxiety was not of long duration. Cellini smiled, and seemed in no way surprised. He said quietly:

"Who told you, madame, that I am engaged?"

"Why, she did, of course!" went on my friend, nodding towards me, regardless of an imploring look I cast at her. "And said you were perfectly devoted!"

"She is quite right," replied Cellini, with another of those rare sweet smiles of his; "and you also are right, madame, in your supposition: my betrothed is a Dream of Beauty."

I was infinitely relieved. I had not, then, been guilty of a falsehood. But the mystery remained: how had I discovered the truth of the matter at all? While I puzzled my mind over this question, the other lady who had accompanied Mrs. Everard spoke. She was an Austrian of brilliant position and attainments.

"You quite interest me, signor!" she said. "Is your fair fiancee here to-night?"

"No, madame," replied Cellini; "she is not in this country."

"What a pity!" exclaimed Amy. "I want to see her real bad. Don't you?" she asked, turning to me.

I raised my eyes and met the dark clear ones of the artist fixed full upon me.

"Yes," I said hesitatingly; "I should like to meet her. Perhaps the chance will occur at some future time."

"There is not the slightest doubt about that," said Cellini. "And now, mademoiselle, will you give me the pleasure of this waltz with you? or are you promised to another partner?"

I was not engaged, and I at once accepted his proffered arm. Two gentlemen came hurriedly up to claim Amy and her Austrian friend; and for one brief moment Signor Cellini and I stood alone in a comparatively quiet corner of the ballroom, waiting for the music to begin. I opened my lips to ask him a question, when he stopped me by a slight gesture of his hand.

"Patience!" he said in a low and earnest tone. "In a few moments you shall have the opportunity you seek."

The band burst forth just then in the voluptuous strains of a waltz by Gung'l, and together we floated away to its exquisite gliding measure. I use the word FLOATED, advisedly, for no other term could express the delightful sensation I enjoyed. Cellini was a superb dancer. It seemed to me that our feet scarcely touched the floor, so swiftly, so easily and lightly we sped along. A few rapid turns, and I noticed we were nearing the open French windows, and, before I well realized it, we had stopped dancing and were pacing quietly side by side down the ilex avenue, where the little lanterns twinkled like red fireflies and green glow-worms among the dark and leafy branches.

We walked along in silence till we reached the end of the path. There, before us, lay the open garden, with its broad green lawn, bathed in the lovely light of the full moon, sailing aloft in a cloudless sky. The night was very warm, but, regardless of this fact, Cellini wrapped carefully round me a large fleecy white burnous that he had taken from a chair where it was lying, on his way through the avenue.

"I am not cold," I said, smiling.

"No; but you will be, perhaps. It is not wise to run any useless risks."

I was again silent. A low breeze rustled in the tree-tops near us; the music of the ballroom reached us only in faint and far echoes; the scent of roses and myrtle was wafted delicately on the balmy air; the radiance of the moon softened the outlines of the landscape into a dreamy suggestiveness of its reality. Suddenly a sound broke on our ears—a delicious, long, plaintive trill; then a wonderful shower of sparkling roulades; and finally, a clear, imploring, passionate note repeated many times. It was a nightingale, singing as only the nightingales of the South can sing. I listened entranced.

> *"'Thou wast not born for death, immortal Bird!*
> *No hungry generations tread thee down;*
> *The voice I hear this passing night was heard*
> *In ancient days by emperor and clown,'"*

quoted Cellini in earnest tones.

"You admire Keats?" I asked eagerly.

"More than any other poet that has lived," he replied. "His was the most ethereal and delicate muse that ever consented to be tied down to earth. But, mademoiselle, you do not wish to examine me as to my taste in poetry. You have some other questions to put to me, have you not?"

For one instant I hesitated. Then I spoke out frankly, and answered:

"Yes, signor. What was there in that wine you gave me this morning?"

He met my searching gaze unflinchingly.

"A medicine," he said. "An excellent and perfectly simple remedy made of the juice of plants, and absolutely harmless."

"But why," I demanded, "why did you give me this medicine? Was it not wrong to take so much responsibility upon yourself?"

He smiled.

"I think not. If you are injured or offended, then I was wrong; but if, on the contrary, your health and spirits are ever so little improved, as I see they are, I deserve your thanks, mademoiselle."

And he waited with an air of satisfaction and expectancy. I was puzzled and half-angry, yet I could not help acknowledging to myself that I felt better and more cheerful than I had done for many months. I looked up at the artist's dark, intelligent face, and said almost humbly:

"I Do thank you, signor. But surely you will tell me your reasons for constituting yourself my physician without even asking my leave."

He laughed, and his eyes looked very friendly.

"Mademoiselle, I am one of those strangely constituted beings who cannot bear to see any innocent thing suffer. It matters not whether it be a worm in the dust, a butterfly in the air, a bird, a flower, or a human creature. The first time I saw you I knew that your state of health precluded you from the enjoyment of life natural to your sex and age. I also perceived that the physicians had been at work upon you trying to probe into the causes of your ailment, and that they had signally failed. Physicians, mademoiselle, are very clever and estimable men, and there are a few things which come within the limit of their treatment; but there are also other things which baffle their utmost profundity of knowledge. One of these is that wondrous piece of human machinery, the nervous system; that intricate and delicate network of fine threads— electric wires on which run the messages of thought, impulse, affection, emotion. If these threads or wires become, from any subtle cause, entangled, the skill of the mere medical practitioner is of no avail to undo the injurious knot, or to unravel the confused skein. The drugs generally used in such cases are, for the most part, repellent to the human blood and natural instinct, therefore they are always dangerous, and often deadly. I knew, by studying your face, mademoiselle, that you were suffering as acutely as I, too, suffered some five years ago, and I ventured to try upon you a simple vegetable essence, merely to see if you were capable of benefiting by it. The experiment has been so far successful; but—"

He paused, and his face became graver and more abstracted.

"But what?" I queried eagerly.

"I was about to say," he continued, "that the effect is only transitory. Within forty-eight hours you must naturally relapse into your former prostrate condition, and I, unfortunately, am powerless to prevent it."

I sighed wearily, and a feeling of disappointment oppressed me. Was it possible that I must again be the victim of miserable dejection, pain, and stupor?

"You can give me another dose of your remedy," I said.

"That I cannot, mademoiselle," he answered regretfully; "I dare not, without further advice and guidance."

"Advice and guidance from whom?" I inquired.

"From the friend who cured me of my long and almost hopeless illness," said Cellini. "He alone can tell me whether I am right in my theories respecting your nature and constitution."

"And what are those theories?" I asked, becoming deeply interested in the conversation.

Cellini was silent for a minute or so; he seemed absorbed in a sort of inward communion with himself. Then he spoke with impressiveness and gravity:

"In this world, mademoiselle, there are no two natures alike, yet all are born with a small portion of Divinity within them, which we call the Soul. It is a mere spark smouldering in the centre of the weight of clay with which we are encumbered, yet it is there. Now this particular germ or seed can be cultivated if we will—that is, if we desire and insist on its growth. As a child's taste for art or learning can be educated into high capabilities for the future, so can the human Soul be educated into so high, so supreme an attainment, that no merely mortal standard of measurement can reach its magnificence. With much more than half the inhabitants of the globe, this germ of immortality remains always a germ, never sprouting, overlaid and weighted down by the lymphatic laziness and materialistic propensities of its shell or husk—the body. But I must put aside the forlorn prospect of the multitudes in whom the Divine Essence attains to no larger quantity than that proportioned out to a dog or bird—I have only to speak of the rare few with whom the soul is everything—those who, perceiving and admitting its existence within them, devote all their powers to fanning up their spark of light till it becomes a radiant, burning, inextinguishable flame. The mistake made by these examples of beatified Humanity is that they too often sacrifice the body to the demands of the spirit. It is difficult to find the medium path, but it can be found; and the claims of both body and soul can be satisfied without sacrificing the one to the other. I beg your earnest attention, mademoiselle, for what I say concerning THE RARE FEW WITH WHOM THE SOUL IS EVERYTHING. YOU are one of those few, unless I am greatly in error. And you have sacrificed your body so utterly to your spirit that the flesh rebels and suffers. This will not do. You have work before you in the world, and you cannot perform it unless you have bodily health as well as spiritual desire. And why? Because you are a prisoner here on earth, and you must obey the laws of the prison, however unpleasant they may be to you. Were you free as you have been in ages past and as you will be in ages to come, things would be different; but at present you must comply with the orders of your gaolers—the Lords of Life and Death."

I heard him, half awed, half fascinated. His words were full of mysterious suggestions.

"How do you know I am of the temperament you describe?" I asked in a low voice.

"I do not know, mademoiselle; I can only guess. There is but one person who can perhaps judge of you correctly,—a man older than myself by many years—whose life is the very acme of spiritual perfection—whose learning is vast and unprejudiced. I must see and speak to him before I try any more of my, or rather his, remedies. But we have lingered long enough out here, and unless you have something more to say to me, we will return to the ballroom. You will otherwise miss the cotillon;" and he turned to retrace the way through the illuminated grove.

But a sudden thought had struck me, and I resolved to utter it aloud. Laying my hand on his arm and looking him full in the face, I said slowly and distinctly:

"This friend of yours that you speak of—is not his name HELIOBAS?"

Cellini started violently; the blood rushed up to his brows and as quickly receded, leaving him paler than before. His dark eyes glowed with suppressed excitement—his hand trembled. Recovering himself slowly, he met my gaze fixedly; his glance softened, and he bent his head with an air of respect and reverence.

MARIE CORELLI

"Mademoiselle, I see that you must know all. It is your fate. You are greatly to be envied. Come to me to-morrow, and I will tell you everything that is to be told. Afterwards your destiny rests in your own hands. Ask nothing more of me just now."

He escorted me without further words back to the ballroom, where the merriment of the cotillon was then at its height. Whispering to Mrs. Everard as I passed her that I was tired and was going to bed, I reached the outside passage, and there, turning to Cellini, I said gently:

"Good-night, signor. To-morrow at noon I will come."

He replied:

"Good-night, mademoiselle! To-morrow at noon you will find me ready."

With that he saluted me courteously and turned away. I hurried up to my own room, and on arriving there I could not help observing the remarkable freshness of the lilies I wore. They looked as if they had just been gathered. I unfastened them all from my dress, and placed them carefully in water; then quickly disrobing, I was soon in bed. I meditated for a few minutes on the various odd occurrences of the day; but my thoughts soon grew misty and confused, and I travelled quickly off into the Land of Nod, and thence into the region of sleep, where I remained undisturbed by so much as the shadow of a dream.

V

CELLINI'S STORY

The following morning at the appointed hour, I went to Cellini's studio, and was received by him with a sort of gentle courtesy and kindliness that became him very well. I was already beginning to experience an increasing languor and weariness, the sure forerunner of what the artist had prophesied—namely, a return of all my old sufferings. Amy, tired out by the dancing of the previous night, was still in bed, as were many of those who had enjoyed Madame Didier's fete; and the hotel was unusually quiet, almost seeming as though half the visitors had departed during the night. It was a lovely morning, sunny and calm; and Cellini, observing that I looked listless and fatigued, placed a comfortable easy-chair for me near the window, from whence I could see one of the prettiest parterres of the garden, gay with flowers of every colour and perfume. He himself remained standing, one hand resting lightly on his writing-table, which was strewn with a confusion of letters and newspapers.

"Where is Leo?" I asked, as I glanced round the room in search of that noble animal.

"Leo left for Paris last night," replied Cellini; "he carried an important despatch for me, which I feared to trust to the post-office."

"Is it safer in Leo's charge?" I inquired, smiling, for the sagacity of the dog amused as well as interested me.

"Much safer! Leo carries on his collar a small tin case, just large enough to contain several folded sheets of paper. When he knows he has that box to guard during his journeys, he is simply unapproachable. He would fight any one who attempted to touch it with the ferocity of a hungry tiger, and there is no edible dainty yet invented that could tempt his appetite or coax him into any momentary oblivion of his duty. There is no more trustworthy or faithful messenger."

"I suppose you have sent him to your friend—his master," I said.

"Yes. He has gone straight home to—Heliobas."

This name now awakened in me no surprise or even curiosity. It simply sounded homelike and familiar. I gazed abstractedly out of the window at the brilliant blossoms in the garden, that nodded their

MARIE CORELLI

heads at me like so many little elves with coloured caps on, but I said nothing. I felt that Cellini watched me keenly and closely. Presently he continued:

"Shall I tell you everything now, mademoiselle?"

I turned towards him eagerly.

"If you please," I answered.

"May I ask you one question?"

"Certainly."

"How and where did you hear the name of Heliobas?"

I looked up hesitatingly.

"In a dream, signor, strange to say; or rather in three dreams. I will relate them to you."

And I described the visions I had seen, being careful to omit no detail, for, indeed, I remembered everything with curious distinctness.

The artist listened with grave and fixed attention. When I had concluded he said:

"The elixir I gave you acted more potently than even I imagined it would. You are more sensitive than I thought. Do not fatigue yourself any more, mademoiselle, by talking. With your permission I will sit down here opposite to you and tell you my story. Afterwards you must decide for yourself whether you will adopt the method of treatment to which I owe my life, and something more than my life—my reason."

He turned his own library-chair towards me, and seated himself. A few moments passed in silence; his expression was very earnest and absorbed, and he regarded my face with a sympathetic interest which touched me profoundly. Though I felt myself becoming more and more enervated and apathetic as the time went on, and though I knew I was gradually sinking down again into my old Slough of Despond, yet I felt instinctively that I was somehow actively concerned in what was about to be said, therefore I forced myself to attend closely to every word uttered. Cellini began to speak in low and quiet tones as follows:

"You must be aware, mademoiselle, that those who adopt any art as a means of livelihood begin the world heavily handicapped—weighted down, as it were, in the race for fortune. The following of art is a very different thing to the following of trade or mercantile business. In buying or selling, in undertaking the work of import or export, a good head for figures, and an average quantity of shrewd common sense, are all that is necessary in order to win a fair share of success. But in the finer occupations, whose results are found in sculpture, painting, music and poetry, demands are made upon the imagination, the emotions, the entire spiritual susceptibility of man. The most delicate fibres of the brain are taxed; the subtle inner workings of thought are brought into active play; and the temperament becomes daily and hourly more finely strung, more sensitive, more keenly alive to every passing sensation. Of course there are many so-called 'Artists' who are mere shams of the real thing; persons who, having a little surface-education in one or the other branch of the arts, play idly with the paint-brush, or dabble carelessly in the deep waters of literature,—or borrow a few crotchets and quavers from other composers, and putting them together in haste, call it Original Composition. Among these are to be found the self-called 'professors' of painting; the sculptors who allow the work of their 'ghosts' to be admired as their own; the magazine-scribblers; the 'smart' young leader-writers and critics; the half-hearted performers on piano or violin who object to any innovation, and prefer to grind on in the unemotional, coldly correct manner which they are pleased to term the 'classical'—such persons exist, and will exist, so long as good and evil are leading forces of life. They are the aphides on the rose of art. But the men and women I speak of as Artists are those who work day and night to attain even a small degree of perfection, and who are never satisfied with their own best efforts. I was one of these some years ago, and I humbly assert myself still to be of the same disposition; only the difference between myself then and myself now is, that Then I struggled blindly and despairingly, and Now I labour patiently and with calmness, knowing positively that I shall obtain what I seek at the duly appointed hour. I was educated as a painter, mademoiselle, by my father, a good, simple-hearted man, whose little landscapes looked like bits cut out of the actual field and woodland, so fresh and pure were they. But I was not content to follow in the plain path he first taught me to tread. Merely correct drawing, merely correct colouring, were not sufficient for my ambition. I had dazzled my eyes with the loveliness of Correggio's 'Madonna,' and had marvelled at the wondrous blue of her robe—a blue so deep and intense that I used to think one might scrape away the paint till a hole was bored in the canvas and yet not reach the end of that fathomless azure tint; I had studied the warm hues of Titian; I had felt ready to float away in the air with the marvellous 'Angel of the Annunciation'—and with all these thoughts in me, how could I content myself with the ordinary aspiration of modern artists? I grew absorbed in one subject—Colour. I noted how lifeless and pale the colouring

MARIE CORELLI

of to-day appeared beside that of the old masters, and I meditated deeply on the problem thus presented to me. What was the secret of Correggio—of Fra Angelico—of Raphael? I tried various experiments; I bought the most expensive and highly guaranteed pigments. In vain, for they were all adulterated by the dealers! Then I obtained colours in the rough, and ground and mixed them myself; still, though a little better result was obtained, I found trade adulteration still at work with the oils, the varnishes, the mediums—in fact, with everything that painters use to gain effect in their works. I could nowhere escape from vicious dealers, who, to gain a miserable percentage on every article sold, are content to be among the most dishonest men in this dishonest age.

"I assure you, mademoiselle, that not one of the pictures which are now being painted for the salons of Paris and London can possibly last a hundred years. I recently visited that Palace of Art, the South Kensington Museum, in London, and saw there a large fresco by Sir Frederick Leighton. It had just been completed, I was informed. It was already fading! Within a few years it will be a blur of indistinct outlines. I compared its condition with the cartoons of Raphael, and a superb Giorgione in the same building; these were as warm and bright as though recently painted. It is not Leighton's fault that his works are doomed to perish as completely off the canvas as though he had never traced them; it is his dire misfortune, and that of every other nineteenth-century painter, thanks to the magnificent institution of free trade, which has resulted in a vulgar competition of all countries and all classes to see which can most quickly jostle the other out of existence. But I am wearying you, mademoiselle—pardon me! To resume my own story. As I told you, I could think of nothing but the one subject of Colour; it haunted me incessantly. I saw in my dreams visions, of exquisite forms and faces that I longed to transfer to my canvas, but I could never succeed in the attempt. My hand seemed to have lost all skill. About this time my father died, and I, having no other relation in the world, and no ties of home to cling to, lived in utter solitude, and tortured my brain more and more with the one question that baffled and perplexed me. I became moody and irritable; I avoided intercourse with everyone, and at last sleep forsook my eyes. Then came a terrible season of feverish trouble, nervous dejection and despair. At times I would sit silently brooding; at others I started up and walked rapidly for hours, in the hope to calm the wild unrest that took possession of my brain. I was then living in Rome, in the studio that had been my father's.

One evening—how well I remember it!—I was attacked by one of those fierce impulses that forbade me to rest or think or sleep, and, as usual, I hurried out for one of those long aimless excursions I had latterly grown accustomed to. At the open street-door stood the proprietress of the house, a stout, good-natured contadina, with her youngest child Pippa holding to her skirt. As she saw me approaching, she started back with an exclamation of alarm, and catching the little girl up in her arms, she made the sign of the cross rapidly. Astonished at this, I paused in my hasty walk, and said with as much calmness as I could muster:

"'What do you mean by that? Have I the evil-eye, think you?'

"Curly-haired Pippa stretched out her arms to me—I had often caressed the little one, and given her sweetmeats and toys—but her mother held her back with a sort of smothered scream, and muttered:

"'Holy Virgin! Pippa must not touch him; he is mad.'

"Mad? I looked at the woman and child in scornful amazement. Then without further words I turned, and went swiftly away down the street out of their sight. Mad! Was I indeed losing my reason? Was this the terrific meaning of my sleepless nights, my troubled thoughts, my strange inquietude? Fiercely I strode along, heedless whither I was going, till I found myself suddenly on the borders of the desolate Campagna. A young moon gleamed aloft, looking like a slender sickle thrust into the heavens to reap an over-abundant harvest of stars. I paused irresolutely. There was a deep silence everywhere. I felt faint and giddy: curious flashes of light danced past my eyes, and my limbs shook like those of a palsied old man. I sank upon a stone to rest, to try and arrange my scattered ideas into some sort of connection and order. Mad! I clasped my aching head between my hands, and brooded on the fearful prospect looming before me, and in the words of poor King Lear, I prayed in my heart:

"'*O let me not be mad, not mad, sweet heavens!*'

"PRAYER! There was another thought. How could *I* pray? For I was a sceptic. My father had educated me with broadly materialistic views; he himself was a follower of Voltaire, and with his finite rod he took the measure of Divinity, greatly to his own satisfaction. He was a good man, too, and he died with exemplary calmness in the absolute certainty of there being nothing in his composition but dust, to which he was as bound to return. He had not a shred of belief in anything but what he called the Universal Law of Necessity; perhaps this was why all his pictures lacked inspiration. I accepted his theories without thinking much about them, and I had managed to live respectably without any religious belief. But Now—now with the horrible phantom of madness rising before me—my firm nerves quailed. I tried, I longed to PRAY. Yet to whom? To what? To the Universal Law of Necessity? In that there could be no hearing or answering of human petitions. I meditated on this with a kind of sombre ferocity. Who portioned out this Law of Necessity? What brutal Code compels us to be born, to live, to suffer, and to die without recompense or reason? Why should this Universe be an ever-circling Wheel of Torture? Then a fresh impetus came to me. I rose from my recumbent posture and stood erect; I trembled no more. A curious sensation of defiant amusement possessed me so violently that I laughed aloud. Such a laugh, too! I recoiled from the sound, as from a blow, with a shudder. It was the laugh of—a madman! I thought no more; I was resolved. I would fulfil the grim Law of Necessity to its letter. If Necessity caused my birth, it also demanded my death. Necessity could not force me to live against my will. Better eternal nothingness than madness. Slowly and deliberately I took from my vest a Milanese dagger of thin sharp steel—one that I always carried with me as a means of self-defence—I drew it from its sheath, and looked at the fine edge glittering coldly in the pallid moon-rays. I kissed it joyously; it was my final remedy! I poised it aloft with firm fingers— another instant and it would have been buried deep in my heart, when I felt a powerful grasp on my wrist, and a strong arm struggling with mine forced the dagger from my hand. Savagely angry at being thus foiled in my desperate intent, I staggered back a few paces and sullenly stared at my rescuer. He was a tall man, clad in a dark overcoat bordered with fur; he looked like a wealthy Englishman or American travelling for pleasure. His features were fine and commanding; his eyes gleamed with a gentle disdain as he coolly met my resentful gaze. When he spoke his voice was rich and mellifluous, though his accents had a touch in them of grave scorn.

"'So you are tired of your life, young man! All the more reason have you to live. Anyone can die. A murderer has moral force enough to jeer at his hangman. It is very easy to draw the last breath. It can be accomplished successfully by a child or a warrior. One pang of far less anguish than the toothache, and all is over. There is nothing heroic about it, I assure you! It is as common as going to bed; it is almost prosy.

Life is heroism, if you like; but death is a mere cessation of business. And to make a rapid and rude exit off the stage before the prompter gives the sign is always, to say the least of it, ungraceful. Act the part out, no matter how bad the play. What say you?'

"And, balancing the dagger lightly on one finger, as though it were a paper-knife, he smiled at me with so much frank kindliness that it was impossible to resist him. I advanced and held out my hand.

"'Whoever you are,' I said, 'you speak like a true man. But you are ignorant of the causes which compelled me to—' and a hard sob choked my utterance. My new acquaintance pressed my proffered hand cordially, but the gravity of his tone did not vary as he replied:

"'There is no cause, my friend, which compels us to take violent leave of existence, unless it be madness or cowardice.'

"'Aye, and what if it were madness?' I asked him eagerly. He scanned me attentively, and laying his fingers lightly on my wrist, felt my pulse.

"'Pooh, my dear sir!' he said; 'you are no more mad than I am. You are a little overwrought and excited—that I admit. You have some mental worry that consumes you. You shall tell me all about it. I have no doubt I can cure you in a few days.'

"Cure me? I looked at him in wonderment and doubt.

"'Are you a physician?' I asked.

"He laughed. 'Not I! I should be sorry to belong to the profession. Yet I administer medicines and give advice in certain cases. I am simply a remedial agent—not a doctor. But why do we stand here in this bleak place, which must be peopled by the ghosts of olden heroes? Come with me, will you? I am going to the Hotel Costanza, and we can talk there. As for this pretty toy, permit me to return it to you. You will not force it again to the unpleasant task of despatching its owner.'

"And he handed the dagger back to me with a slight bow. I sheathed it at once, feeling somewhat like a chidden child, as I met the slightly satirical gleam of the clear blue eyes that watched me.

"'Will you give me your name, signor?' I asked, as we turned from the Campagna towards the city.

"'With pleasure. I am called Heliobas. A strange name? Oh, not at all! It is pure Chaldee. My mother—as lovely an Eastern houri as Murillo's Madonna, and as devout as Santa Teresa—gave me the Christian saint's name of Casimir also, but Heliobas pur et simple suits me best, and by it I am generally known.'

"'You are a Chaldean?' I inquired.

"'Exactly so. I am descended directly from one of those "wise men of the East" (and, by the way, there were more than three, and they were not all kings), who, being wide awake, happened to notice the birth-star of Christ on the horizon before the rest of the world's inhabitants had so much as rubbed their sleepy eyes. The Chaldeans have been always quick of observation from time immemorial. But in return for my name, you will favour me with yours?'

"I gave it readily, and we walked on together. I felt wonderfully calmed and cheered—as soothed, mademoiselle, as I have noticed you yourself have felt when in My company."

Here Cellini paused, and looked at me as though expecting a question; but I preferred to remain silent till I had heard all he had to say. He therefore resumed:

"We reached the Hotel Costanza, where Heliobas was evidently well known. The waiters addressed him as Monsieur le Comte; but he gave me no information as to this title. He had a superb suite of rooms in the hotel, furnished with every modern luxury; and as soon as we entered a light supper was served. He invited me to partake, and within the space of half an hour I had told him all my history—my ambition—my strivings after the perfection of colour—my disappointment, dejection, and despair—and, finally, the fearful dread of coming madness that had driven me to attempt my own life. He listened patiently and with unbroken attention. When I had finished, he laid one hand on my shoulder, and said gently:

"'Young man, pardon me if I say that up to the present your career has been an inactive, useless, selfish "kicking against the pricks," as St. Paul says. You set before yourself a task of noble effort, namely, to discover the secret of colouring as known to the old masters; and because you meet with the petty difficulty of modern trade adulteration in your materials, you think that there is no chance—that all is lost. Fie! Do you think Nature is overcome by a few dishonest traders? She can still give you in abundance the unspoilt colours she gave to Raphael and Titian; but not in haste—not if you vulgarly scramble for her gifts in a mood that is impatient of obstacle and delay. "Ohne hast, ohne rast," is the motto of the stars. Learn it well. You have injured your bodily health by useless fretfulness and peevish discontent, and with that we have first to deal. In a week's time, I will make a sound, sane man of you; and then I will teach you how to get the colours you seek—yes!' he added, smiling, 'even to the compassing of Correggio's blue.'

"I could not speak for joy and gratitude; I grasped my friend and preserver by the hand. We stood thus together for a brief interval, when suddenly Heliobas drew himself up to the full stateliness of his height and bent his calm eyes deliberately upon me. A strange thrill ran through me; I still held his hand.

"'Rest!' he said in slow and emphatic tones, 'Weary and overwrought frame, take thy full and needful measure of repose! Struggling and deeply injured spirit, be free of thy narrow prison! By that Force which I acknowledge within me and thee and in all created things, I command thee, REST!'

"Fascinated, awed, overcome by his manner, I gazed at him and would have spoken, but my tongue refused its office—my senses swam—my eyes closed—my limbs gave way—I fell senseless."

Cellini again paused and looked at me. Intent on his words, I would not interrupt him. He went on:

"When I say senseless, mademoiselle, I allude of course to my body. But I, myself—that is, my soul—was conscious; I lived, I moved, I heard, I saw. Of that experience I am forbidden to speak. When I returned to mortal existence I found myself lying on a couch in the same room where I had supped with Heliobas, and Heliobas himself sat near me reading. It was broad noonday. A delicious sense of tranquillity and youthful buoyancy was upon me, and without speaking I sprang up from my recumbent position and touched him on the arm. He looked up.

"'Well?' he asked, and his eyes smiled.

"I seized his hand, and pressed it reverently to my lips.

"'My best friend!' I exclaimed. 'What wonders have I not seen—what truths have I not learned—what mysteries!'

"'On all these things be silent,' replied Heliobas. 'They must not be lightly spoken of. And of the questions you naturally desire to ask me, you shall have the answers in due time. What has happened to you is not wonderful; you have simply been acted upon by scientific means. But your cure is not yet complete. A few days more passed with me will restore you thoroughly. Will you consent to remain so long in my company?'

"Gladly and gratefully I consented, and we spent the next ten days together, during which Heliobas administered to me certain remedies, external and internal, which had a marvellous effect in renovating and invigorating my system. By the expiration of that time I was strong and well—a sound and sane man, as my rescuer had promised I should be—my brain was fresh and eager for work, and my mind was filled with new and grand ideas of art. And I had gained through Heliobas two inestimable things—a full comprehension of the truth of religion, and the secret of human destiny; and I had won a LOVE so exquisite!"

Here Cellini paused, and his eyes were uplifted in a sort of wondering rapture. He continued after a pause:

"Yes, mademoiselle, I discovered that I was loved, and watched over and guided by ONE so divinely beautiful, so gloriously faithful, that mortal language fails before the description of such perfection!"

He paused again, and again continued:

"When he found me perfectly healthy again in mind and body, Heliobas showed me his art of mixing colours. From that hour all my works were successful. You know that my pictures are eagerly purchased as soon as completed, and that the colour I obtain in them is to the world a mystery almost magical. Yet there is not one among the humblest of artists who could not, if he chose, make use of the same means as I have done to gain the nearly imperishable hues that still glow on the canvases of Raphael. But of this there is no need to speak just now. I have told you my story, mademoiselle, and it now rests with me to apply its meaning to yourself. You are attending?"

"Perfectly," I replied; and, indeed, my interest at this point was so strong that I could almost hear the expectant beating of my heart. Cellini resumed:

"Electricity, mademoiselle, is, as you are aware, the wonder of our age. No end can be foreseen to the marvels it is capable of accomplishing. But one of the most important branches of this great science is ignorantly derided just now by the larger portion of society—I mean the use of human electricity; that force which is in each one of us—in you and in me—and, to a very large extent, in Heliobas. He has cultivated the electricity in his own system to such an extent that his mere touch, his lightest glance, have healing in them, or the reverse, as he chooses to exert his power—I may say it is never the reverse, for he is full of kindness, sympathy, and pity for all humanity. His influence is so great that he can, without speaking, by his mere presence suggest his own thoughts to other people who are perfect strangers, and cause them to design and carry out certain actions in accordance with his plans. You are incredulous? Mademoiselle, this power is in every one of us; only we do not cultivate it, because our education is yet so imperfect. To prove the truth of what I say, *I*, though I have only advanced a little way in the cultivation of my own electric force, even *I* have influenced You. You cannot deny it. By my thought, impelled to you, you saw clearly my picture that was actually veiled. By MY force, you replied correctly to a question I asked you concerning that same picture. By MY desire, you gave me, without being aware of it, a message from one I love when you said, 'Dieu vous garde!' You remember? And the elixir I gave you, which is one of the simplest remedies discovered by Heliobas, had the effect of making you learn what he intended you to learn—his name."

"He!" I exclaimed. "Why, he does not know me—he can have no intentions towards me!"

"Mademoiselle," replied Cellini gravely, "if you will think again of the last of your three dreams, you will not doubt that he HAS intentions towards you. As I told you, he is a PHYSICAL ELECTRICIAN. By that is meant a great deal. He knows by instinct whether he is or will be needed sooner or later. Let me finish what I have to say. You are ill, mademoiselle—ill from over-work. You are an improvisatrice—that is, you have the emotional genius of music, a spiritual thing unfettered by rules, and utterly misunderstood by the world. You cultivate this faculty, regardless of cost; you suffer, and you will suffer more. In proportion as your powers in music grow, so will your health decline. Go to Heliobas; he will do for you what he did for me. Surely you will not hesitate? Between years of weak invalidism and perfect health, in less than a fortnight, there can be no question of choice."

I rose from my seat slowly.

"Where is this Heliobas?" I asked. "In Paris?"

"Yes, in Paris. If you decide to go there, take my advice, and go alone. You can easily make some excuse to your friends. I will give you the address of a ladies' Pension, where you will be made at home and comfortable. May I do this?"

"If you please," I answered.

He wrote rapidly in pencil on a card of his own:

MADAME DENISE,
36, Avenue du Midi,
Paris,

and handed it to me. I stood still where I had risen, thinking deeply. I had been impressed and somewhat startled by Cellini's story; but I was in no way alarmed at the idea of trusting myself to the hands of a physical electrician such as Heliobas professed to be. I knew that there were many cases of serious illnesses being cured by means of electricity—that electric baths and electric appliances of all descriptions were in ordinary use; and I saw no reason to be surprised at the fact of a man being in existence who had cultivated electric force within himself to such an extent that he was able to use it as a healing power. There seemed to me to be really nothing extraordinary in it. The only part of Cellini's narration I did not credit was the soul-transmigration he professed to have experienced; and I put that down to the over-excitement of his imagination at the time of his first interview with Heliobas. But I kept this thought to myself. In any case, I resolved to go to Paris. The great desire of my life was to be in perfect health, and I determined to omit no means of obtaining this inestimable blessing. Cellini watched me as I remained standing before him in silent abstraction.

"Will you go?" he inquired at last.

"Yes; I will go," I replied. "But will you give me a letter to your friend?"

"Leo has taken it and all necessary explanations already," said Cellini, smiling; "I knew you would go. Heliobas expects you the day after to-morrow. His residence is Hotel Mars, Champs Elysees. You are not angry with me, mademoiselle? I could not help knowing that you would go."

I smiled faintly.

"Electricity again, I suppose! No, I am not angry. Why should I be? I thank you very much, signor, and I shall thank you more if Heliobas indeed effects my cure."

"Oh, that is certain, positively certain," answered Cellini; "you can indulge that hope as much as you like, mademoiselle, for it is one that cannot be disappointed. Before you leave me, you will look at your own picture, will you not?" and, advancing to his easel, he uncovered it.

I was greatly surprised. I thought he had but traced the outline of my features, whereas the head was almost completed. I looked at it as I would look at the portrait of a stranger. It was a wistful, sad-eyed, plaintive face, and on the pale gold of the hair rested a coronal of lilies.

"It will soon be finished," said Cellini, covering the easel again; "I shall not need another sitting, which is fortunate, as it is so necessary for you to go away. And now will you look at the 'Life and Death' once more?"

I raised my eyes to the grand picture, unveiled that day in all its beauty.

"The face of the Life-Angel there," went on Cellini quietly, "is a poor and feeble resemblance of the One I love. You knew I was betrothed, mademoiselle?"

I felt confused, and was endeavouring to find an answer to this when he continued:

"Do not trouble to explain, for *I* know how You knew. But no more of this. Will you leave Cannes to-morrow?"

"Yes. In the morning."

"Then good-bye, mademoiselle. Should I never see you again—"

"Never see me again!" I interrupted. "Why, what do you mean?"

"I do not allude to your destinies, but to mine," he said, with a kindly look. "My business may call me away from here before you come back—our paths may lie apart—many circumstances may occur to prevent our meeting—so that, I repeat, should I never see you again, you will, I hope, bear me in your friendly remembrance as one who was sorry to see you suffer, and who was the humble means of guiding you to renewed health and happiness."

I held out my hand, and my eyes filled with tears. There was something so gentle and chivalrous about him, and withal so warm and sympathetic, that I felt indeed as if I were bidding adieu to one of the truest friends I should ever have in my life.

"I hope nothing will cause you to leave Cannes till I return to it," I said with real earnestness. "I should like you to judge of my restoration to health."

"There will be no need for that," he replied; "I shall know when you are quite recovered through Heliobas."

He pressed my hand warmly.

"I brought back the book you lent me," I went on; "but I should like a copy of it for myself. Can I get it anywhere?"

"Heliobas will give you one with pleasure," replied Cellini; "you have only to make the request. The book is not on sale. It was printed for private circulation only. And now, mademoiselle, we part. I congratulate you on the comfort and joy awaiting you in Paris. Do not forget the address—Hotel Mars, Champs Elysees. Farewell!"

And again shaking my hand cordially, he stood at his door watching me as I passed out and began to ascend the stairs leading to my room. On the landing I paused, and, looking round, saw him still there.

I smiled and waved my hand. He did the same in response, once—twice; then turning abruptly, disappeared.

That afternoon I explained to Colonel and Mrs. Everard that I had resolved to consult a celebrated physician in Paris (whose name, however, I did not mention), and should go there alone for a few days. On hearing that I knew of a well-recommended ladies' Pension, they made no objection to my arrangements, and they agreed to remain at the Hotel de L—— till I returned. I gave them no details of my plans, and of course never mentioned Raffaello Cellini in connection with the matter. A nervous and wretchedly agitated night made me more than ever determined to try the means of cure proposed to me. At ten o'clock the following morning I left Cannes by express train for Paris. Just before starting I noticed that the lilies of the valley Cellini had given me for the dance had, in spite of my care, entirely withered, and were already black with decay—so black that they looked as though they had been scorched by a flash of lightning.

VI

THE HOTEL MARS AND ITS OWNER

I t was between three and four o'clock in the afternoon of the day succeeding the night of my arrival in Paris, when I found myself standing at the door of the Hotel Mars, Champs Elysees. I had proved the Pension kept by Madame Denise to be everything that could be desired; and on my presentation of Raffaello Cellini's card of introduction, I had been welcomed by the maitresse de la maison with a cordial effusiveness that amounted almost to enthusiasm.

"Ce cher Cellini!" the cheery and pleasant little woman had exclaimed, as she set before me a deliciously prepared breakfast. "Je l'aime tant! Il a si bon coeur! et ses beaux yeux! Mon Dieu, comme un ange!"

As soon as I had settled the various little details respecting my room and attendance, and had changed my travelling-dress for a quiet visiting toilette, I started for the abode of Heliobas.

The weather was very cold; I had left the summer behind me at Cannes, to find winter reigning supreme in Paris. A bitter east wind blew, and a few flakes of snow fell now and then from the frowning sky. The house to which I betook myself was situated at a commanding corner of a road facing the Champs Elysees. It was a noble-looking building. The broad steps leading to the entrance were guarded on either side by a sculptured Sphinx, each of whom held, in its massive stone paws, a plain shield, inscribed with the old Roman greeting to strangers, "Salve!" Over the portico was designed a scroll which bore the name "Hotel Mars" in clearly cut capitals, and the monogram "C. H."

I ascended the steps with some hesitation, and twice I extended my hand towards the bell, desiring yet fearing to awaken its summons. I noticed it was an electric bell, not needing to be pulled but pressed; and at last, after many doubts and anxious suppositions, I very gently laid my fingers on the little button which formed its handle. Scarcely had I done this than the great door slid open rapidly without the least noise. I looked for the servant in attendance—there was none. I paused an instant; the door remained invitingly open, and through it I caught a glimpse of flowers. Resolving to be bold, and to hesitate no longer, I entered. As I crossed the threshold, the door closed behind me instantly with its previous swiftness and silence.

I found myself in a spacious hall, light and lofty, surrounded with fluted pillars of white marble. In the centre a fountain bubbled melodiously, and tossed up every now and then a high jet of sparkling spray, while round its basin grew the rarest ferns and exotics, which emitted a subtle and delicate perfume. No cold air penetrated here; it was as warm and balmy as a spring day in Southern Italy. Light Indian bamboo chairs provided with luxurious velvet cushions were placed in various corners between the marble columns, and on one of these I seated myself to rest a minute, wondering what I should do next, and whether anyone would come to ask me the cause of my intrusion. My meditations were soon put to flight by the appearance of a young lad, who crossed the hall from the left-hand side and approached me. He was a handsome boy of twelve or thirteen years of age, and he was attired in a simple Greek costume of white linen, relieved with a broad crimson silk sash. A small flat crimson cap rested on his thick black curls; this he lifted with deferential grace, and, saluting me, said respectfully:

"My master is ready to receive you, mademoiselle."

I rose without a word and followed him, scarcely permitting myself to speculate as to how his master knew I was there at all.

The hall was soon traversed, and the lad paused before a magnificent curtain of deep crimson velvet, heavily bordered with gold. Pulling a twisted cord that hung beside it, the heavy, regal folds parted in twain with noiseless regularity, and displayed an octagon room, so exquisitely designed and ornamented that I gazed upon it as upon some rare and beautiful picture. It was unoccupied, and my young escort placed a chair for me near the central window, informing me as he did so that "Monsieur le Comte" would be with me instantly; whereupon he departed.

Left alone, I gazed in bewilderment at the loveliness round me. The walls and ceiling were painted in fresco. I could not make out the subjects, but I could see faces of surpassing beauty smiling from clouds, and peering between stars and crescents. The furniture appeared to be of very ancient Arabian design; each chair was a perfect masterpiece of wood-carving, picked out and inlaid with gold. The sight of a semi-grand piano, which stood open, brought me back to the realization that I was living in modern times, and not in a dream of the Arabian Nights; while the Paris Figaro and the London Times—both of that day's issue—lying on a side-table, demonstrated the nineteenth century to me with every possible clearness. There were flowers everywhere in this apartment—in graceful vases and in gilded osier baskets—and a queer lop-sided Oriental jar stood quite near me, filled almost to overflowing with Neapolitan violets. Yet it was winter in Paris, and flowers were rare and costly.

Looking about me, I perceived an excellent cabinet photograph of Raffaello Cellini, framed in antique silver; and I rose to examine it more closely, as being the face of a friend. While I looked at it, I heard the sound of an organ in the distance playing softly an old familiar church chant. I listened. Suddenly I bethought myself of the three dreams that had visited me, and a kind of nervous dread came upon me. This Heliobas,—was I right after all in coming to consult him? Was he not perhaps a mere charlatan? and might not his experiments upon me prove fruitless, and possibly fatal? An idea seized me that I would escape while there was yet time. Yes! . . . I would not see him to-day, at any rate; I would write and explain. These and other disjointed thoughts crossed my mind; and yielding to the unreasoning impulse of fear that possessed me, I actually turned to leave the room, when I saw the crimson velvet portiere dividing again in its regular and graceful folds, and Heliobas himself entered.

I stood mute and motionless. I knew him well; he was the very man I had seen in my third and last dream; the same noble, calm features; the same commanding presence; the same keen, clear eyes; the same compelling smile. There was nothing extraordinary about his appearance except his stately bearing and handsome countenance; his dress was that of any well-to-do gentleman of the present day, and there was no affectation of mystery in his manner. He advanced and bowed courteously; then, with a friendly look, held out his hand. I gave him mine at once.

"So you are the young musician?" he said, in those warm mellifluous accents that I had heard before and that I so well remembered. "My friend Raffaello Cellini has written to me about you. I hear you have been suffering from physical depression?"

He spoke as any physician might do who inquired after a patient's health. I was surprised and relieved. I had prepared myself for something darkly mystical, almost cabalistic; but there was nothing unusual in the demeanour of this pleasant and good-looking gentleman who, bidding me be seated, took a chair himself opposite to me, and observed me with that sympathetic and kindly interest which any well-bred doctor would esteem it his duty to exhibit. I became quite at ease, and answered all his questions fully and frankly. He felt my pulse in the customary way, and studied my face attentively. I described all my symptoms, and he listened with the utmost patience. When I had concluded, he leaned back in his chair and appeared to ponder deeply for some moments. Then he spoke.

"You know, of course, that I am not a doctor?"

"I know," I said; "Signer Cellini explained to me."

"Ah!" and Heliobas smiled. "Raffaello explained as much as he might; but not everything. I must tell you I have a simple pharmacopoeia of my own—it contains twelve remedies, and only twelve. In fact there me no more that are of any use to the human mechanism. All are made of the juice of plants, and six of them are electric. Raffaello tried you with one of them, did he not?"

As he put this question, I was aware of a keenly inquiring look sent from the eyes of my interrogator into mine.

"Yes," I answered frankly, "and it made me dream, and I dreamt of You."

Heliobas laughed lightly.

"So!—that is well. Now I am going in the first place to give you what I am sure will be satisfactory information. If you agree to trust yourself to my care, you will be in perfect health in a little less than a fortnight—but you must follow my rules exactly."

I started up from my seat.

"Of course!" I exclaimed eagerly, forgetting all my previous fear of him; "I will do all you advise, even if you wish to magnetize me as you magnetized Signor Cellini!"

"I never MAGNETIZED Raffaello," he said gravely; "he was on the verge of madness, and he had no faith whereby to save himself. I simply set him free for a time, knowing that his was a genius which would find out things for itself or perish in the effort. I let him go on a voyage of discovery, and he came back perfectly satisfied. That is all. You do not need his experience."

"How do you know?" I asked.

"You are a woman—your desire is to be well and strong, health being beauty—to love and to be beloved—to wear pretty toilettes and to be admired; and you have a creed which satisfies you, and which you believe in without proofs."

There was the slightest possible tinge of mockery in his voice as he said these words. A tumultuous rush of feelings overcame me. My high dreams of ambition, my innate scorn of the trite and commonplace, my deep love of art, my desires of fame—all these things bore down upon my heart and overcame it, and a pride too deep for tears arose in me and found utterance.

"You think I am so slight and weak a thing!" I exclaimed. "You, who profess to understand the secrets of electricity—you have no better instinctive knowledge of me than that! Do you deem women all alike— all on one common level, fit for nothing but to be the toys or drudges of men? Can you not realize that there are some among them who despise the inanities of everyday life—who care nothing for the routine of society, and whose hearts are filled with cravings that no mere human love or life can satisfy? Yes—even weak women are capable of greatness; and if we do sometimes dream of what we cannot accomplish through lack of the physical force necessary for large achievements, that is not our fault but our misfortune. We did not create ourselves. We did not ask to be born with the over-sensitiveness, the fatal delicacy, the highly-strung nervousness of the feminine nature. Monsieur Heliobas, you are a learned and far-seeing man, I have no doubt; but you do not read me aright if you judge me as a mere woman who is perfectly contented with the petty commonplaces of ordinary living. And as for my creed, what is it to you whether I kneel in the silence of my own room or in the glory of a lighted cathedral to pour out my very soul to ONE whom I know exists, and whom I am satisfied to believe in, as you say, without proofs, save such proofs as I obtain from my own inner consciousness? I tell you, though, in your opinion it is evident my sex is against me, I would rather die than sink into the miserable nonentity of such lives as are lived by the majority of women."

I paused, overcome by my own feelings. Heliobas smiled.

"So! You are stung!" he said quietly; "stung into action. That is as it should be. Resume your seat, mademoiselle, and do not be angry with me. I am studying you for your own good. In the meantime permit me to analyze your words a little. You are young and inexperienced. You speak of the 'over-sensitiveness, the fatal delicacy, the highly-strung nervousness of the feminine nature.' My dear lady, if you had lived as long as I have, you would know that these are mere stock phrases—for the most part meaningless. As a rule, women are less sensitive than men. There are many of your sex who are nothing but lumps of lymph and fatty matter—women with less instinct than the dumb beasts, and with more brutality. There are others who,—adding the low cunning of the monkey to the vanity of the peacock,—seek no other object but the furtherance of their own designs, which are always petty even when not absolutely mean. There are obese women whose existence is a doze between dinner and tea. There are women with thin lips and pointed noses, who only live to squabble over domestic grievances and interfere in their neighbours' business. There are your murderous women with large almond eyes, fair white hands, and voluptuous red lips, who, deprived of the dagger or the poison-bowl, will slay a reputation in a few lazily enunciated words, delivered with a perfectly high-bred accent. There are the miserly woman, who look after cheese-parings and candle-ends, and lock up the soap. There are the spiteful women whose very breath is acidity and venom. There are the frivolous women whose chitter-chatter and senseless giggle are as empty as the rattling of dry peas on a drum. In fact, the delicacy of women is extremely overrated—their coarseness is never done full justice to. I have heard them recite in public selections of a kind that no man would dare to undertake—such as Tennyson's 'Rizpah,' for instance. I know a woman who utters every line of it, with all its questionable allusions, boldly before any and everybody, without so much as an attempt at blushing. I assure you men are far more delicate than women—far more chivalrous—far larger in their views, and more generous in their sentiments. But I will not deny the existence of about four women in every two hundred and fifty, who may be, and possibly are, examples of what the female sex was originally intended to be—pure-hearted, self-denying, gentle and truthful—filled with tenderness and inspiration. Heaven knows my own mother was all this and more! And my sister is—. But let me speak to you of yourself. You love music, I understand—you are a professional artist?"

"I was," I answered, "till my state of health stopped me from working."

Heliobas bent his eyes upon me in friendly sympathy.

"You were, and you will be again, an improvisatrice" he went on. "Do you not find it difficult to make your audiences understand your aims?"

I smiled as the remembrance of some of my experiences in public came to my mind.

"Yes," I said, half laughing. "In England, at least, people do not know what is meant by Improvising. They think it is to take a little theme and compose variations on it—the mere Abc of the art. But to sit down to the piano and plan a whole sonata or symphony in your head, and play it while planning it, is a thing they do not and will not understand. They come to hear, and they wonder and go away, and the critics declare it to be CLAP-TRAP."

"Exactly!" replied Heliobas. "But you are to be congratulated on having attained this verdict. Everything that people cannot quite understand is called CLAP-TRAP in England; as for instance the matchless violin-playing of Sarasate; the tempestuous splendor of Rubinstein; the wailing throb of passion in Hollmann's violoncello— this is, according to the London press, CLAP-TRAP; while the coldly correct performances of Joachim and the 'icily-null' renderings of Charles Halle are voted 'magnificent' and 'full of colour.' But to return to yourself. Will you play to me?"

"I have not touched the instrument for two months," I said; "I am afraid I am out of practice."

"Then you shall not exert yourself to-day," returned Heliobas kindly. "But I believe I can help you with your improvisations. You compose the music as you play, you tell me. Well, have you any idea how the melodies or the harmonies form themselves in your brain?"

"Not the least in the world," I replied.

"Is the act of thinking them out an effort to you?" he asked.

"Not at all. They come as though someone else were planning them for me."

"Well, well! I think I can certainly be of use to you in this matter as in others. I understand your temperament thoroughly. And now let me give you my first prescription."

He went to a corner of the room and lifted from the floor an ebony casket, curiously carved and ornamented with silver. This he unlocked. It contained twelve flasks of cut glass, stoppered with gold and numbered in order. He next pulled out a side drawer in this casket, and in it I saw several little thin empty glass tubes, about the size of a cigarette-holder. Taking two of these he filled them from two of the larger flasks, corked them tightly, and then turning to me, said:

"To-night, on going to bed, have a warm bath, empty the contents of the tube marked No. 1 into it, and then immerse yourself thoroughly for about five minutes. After the bath, put the fluid in this other tube marked 2, into a tumbler of fresh spring water, and drink it off. Then go straight to bed."

"Shall I have any dreams?" I inquired with a little anxiety.

"Certainly not," replied Heliobas, smiling. "I wish you to sleep as soundly as a year-old child. Dreams are not for you to-night. Can you come to me tomorrow afternoon at five o'clock? If you can arrange to stay to dinner, my sister will be pleased to meet you; but perhaps you are otherwise engaged?"

I told him I was not, and explained where I had taken rooms, adding that I had come to Paris expressly to put myself under his treatment.

"You shall have no cause to regret this journey," he said earnestly. "I can cure you thoroughly, and I will. I forget your nationality—you are not English?"

"No, not entirely. I am half Italian."

"Ah, yes! I remember now. But you have been educated in England?"

"Partly."

"I am glad it is only partly," remarked Heliobas. "If it had been entirely, your improvisations would have had no chance. In fact you never would have improvised. You would have played the piano like poor mechanical Arabella Goddard. As it is, there is some hope of originality in you— you need not be one of the rank and file unless you choose."

"I do not choose," I said.

"Well, but you must take the consequences, and they are bitter. A woman who does not go with her time is voted eccentric; a woman who prefers music to tea and scandal is an undesirable acquaintance; and a woman who prefers Byron to Austin Dobson is—in fact, no measure can gauge her general impossibility!" I laughed gaily. "I will take all the consequences as willingly as I will take your medicines," I said, stretching out my hand for the little vases which he gave me wrapped in paper. "And I thank you very much, monsieur. And"—here I hesitated. Ought I not to ask him his fee? Surely the medicines ought to be paid for?

Heliobas appeared to read my thoughts, for he said, as though answering my unuttered question:

"I do not accept fees, mademoiselle. To relieve your mind from any responsibility of gratitude to me, I will tell you at once that I never promise to effect a cure unless I see that the person who comes to be cured has a certain connection with myself. If the connection exists I am bound by fixed laws to serve him or her. Of course I am able also to cure those who are NOT by nature connected with me; but then I have to ESTABLISH a connection, and this takes time, and is sometimes very difficult to accomplish, almost as tremendous a task as the laying down of the Atlantic cable. But in your case I am actually COMPELLED to do my best for you, so you need be under no sense of obligation."

Here was a strange speech—the first really inexplicable one I had heard from his lips.

"I am connected with you?" I asked, surprised. "How? In what way?"

"It would take too long to explain to you just now," said Heliobas gently; "but I can prove to you in a moment that a connection DOES exist between YOUR inner self, and MY inner self, if you wish it."

"I do wish it very much," I answered.

"Then take my hand," continued Heliobas, stretching it out, "and look steadily at me."

I obeyed, half trembling. As I gazed, a veil appeared to fall from my eyes. A sense of security, of comfort, and of absolute confidence came upon me, and I saw what might be termed THE IMAGE OF ANOTHER FACE looking at me THROUGH or BEHIND the actual form and face of Heliobas. And that other face was his, and yet not his; but whatever it appeared to be, it was the face of a friend to ME, one that I was certain I had known long, long ago, and moreover one that I must have loved in some distant time, for my whole soul seemed to yearn towards that indistinct haze where smiled the fully recognised yet unfamiliar countenance. This strange sensation lasted but a few seconds, for Heliobas suddenly dropped my hand. The room swam round me; the walls seemed to rock; then everything steadied and came right again, and all was as usual, only I was amazed and bewildered.

"What does it mean?" I murmured.

"It means the simplest thing in nature," replied Heliobas quietly, "namely, that your soul and mine are for some reason or other placed on the same circle of electricity. Nothing more nor less. Therefore we must serve each other. Whatever I do for you, you have it in your power to repay me amply for hereafter."

I met the steady glance of his keen eyes, and a sense of some indestructible force within me gave me a sudden courage.

"Decide for me as you please," I answered fearlessly. "I trust you completely, though I do not know why I do so."

"You will know before long. You are satisfied of the fact that my touch can influence you?"

"Yes; most thoroughly."

"Very well. All other explanations, if you desire them, shall be given you in due time. In the power I possess over you and some others, there is neither mesmerism nor magnetism—nothing but a purely scientific fact which can be clearly and reasonably proved and demonstrated. But till you are thoroughly restored to health, we will defer all discussion. And now, mademoiselle, permit me to escort you to the door. I shall expect you to-morrow."

Together we left the beautiful room in which this interview had taken place, and crossed the hall. As we approached the entrance, Heliobas turned towards me and said with a smile:

"Did not the manoeuvres of my street-door astonish you?"

"A little," I confessed.

"It is very simple. The button you touch outside is electric; it opens the door and at the same time rings the bell in my study, thus informing me of a visitor. When the visitor steps across the threshold he treads, whether he will or no, on another apparatus, which closes the door behind him and rings another bell in my page's room, who immediately comes to me for orders. You see how easy? And from within it is managed in almost the same manner."

And he touched a handle similar to the one outside, and the door opened instantly. Heliobas held out his hand—that hand which a few minutes previously had exercised such strange authority over me.

"Good-bye, mademoiselle. You are not afraid of me now?"

I laughed. "I do not think I was ever really afraid of you," I said. "If I was, I am not so any longer. You have promised me health, and that promise is sufficient to give me entire courage."

"That is well," said Heliobas. "Courage and hope in themselves are the precursors of physical and mental energy. Remember to-morrow at five, and do not keep late hours to-night. I should advise you to be in bed by ten at the latest."

I agreed to this, and we shook hands and parted. I walked blithely along, back to the Avenue du Midi, where, on my arrival indoors, I found a letter from Mrs. Everard. She wrote "in haste" to give me the names of some friends of hers whom she had discovered, through the "American Register," to be staying at the Grand Hotel. She begged me to call upon them, and enclosed two letters of introduction for the purpose. She concluded her epistle by saying:

"Raffaello Cellini has been invisible ever since your departure, but our inimitable waiter, Alphonse, says he is very busy finishing a picture for the Salon—something that we have never seen. I shall intrude myself into his studio soon on some pretence or other, and will then let you know all about it. In the meantime, believe me,

Your ever devoted friend,

AMY

I answered this letter, and then spent a pleasant evening at the Pension, chatting sociably with Madame Denise and another cheery little Frenchwoman, a day governess, who boarded there, and who had no end of droll experiences to relate, her enviable temperament being to always see the humorous side of life. I thoroughly enjoyed her sparkling chatter and her expressive gesticulations, and we all three made ourselves merry till bedtime. Acting on the advice of Heliobas, I retired early to my room, where a warm bath had been prepared in compliance with my orders. I uncorked the glass tube No. 1, and poured the colourless fluid it contained into the water, which immediately bubbled gently, as though beginning to boil. After watching it for a minute or two, and observing that this seething movement steadily continued, I undressed quickly and stepped in. Never shall I forget the exquisite sensation I experienced! I can only describe it as the poor little Doll's Dressmaker in "Our Mutual Friend" described her angel visitants, her "blessed children," who used to come and "take her up and make her light." If my body had been composed of no grosser matter than fire and air, I could not have felt more weightless, more buoyant, more thoroughly exhilarated than when, at the end of the prescribed five minutes, I got out of that marvellous bath of healing! As I prepared for bed, I noticed that the bubbling of the water had entirely ceased; but this was easy of comprehension, for if it had contained electricity, as I supposed, my body had absorbed it by contact, which would account for the movement being stilled. I now took the second little phial, and prepared it as I had been told. This time the fluid was motionless. I noticed it was very faintly tinged with amber. I drank it off—it was perfectly tasteless. Once in bed, I seemed to have no power to think any more—my eyes closed readily—the slumber of a year-old child, as Heliobas had said, came upon me with resistless and sudden force, and I remembered no more.

VII

Zara and Prince Ivan

The sun poured brilliantly into my room when I awoke the next morning. I was free from all my customary aches and pains, and a delightful sense of vigour and elasticity pervaded my frame. I rose at once, and, looking at my watch, found to my amazement that it was twelve o'clock in the day! Hastily throwing on my dressing-gown, I rang the bell, and the servant appeared.

"Is it actually mid-day?" I asked her. "Why did you not call me?"

The girl smiled apologetically.

"I did knock at mademoiselle's door, but she gave me no answer. Madame Denise came up also, and entered the room; but seeing mademoiselle in so sound a sleep, she said it was a pity to disturb mademoiselle."

Which statement good Madame Denise, toiling upstairs just then with difficulty, she being stout and short of breath, confirmed with many smiling nods of her head.

"Breakfast shall be served at the instant," she said, rubbing her fat hands together; "but to disturb you when you slept—ah, Heaven! the sleep of an infant—I could not do it! I should have been wicked!"

I thanked her for her care of me; I could have kissed her, she looked so motherly, and kind, and altogether lovable. And I felt so merry and well! She and the servant retired to prepare my coffee, and I proceeded to make my toilette. As I brushed out my hair I heard the sound of a violin. Someone was playing next door. I listened, and recognised a famous Beethoven Concerto. The unseen musician played brilliantly and withal tenderly, both touch and tone reminding me of some beautiful verses in a book of poems I had recently read, called "Love-Letters of a Violinist," in which the poet* talks of his "loved Amati," and says: "I prayed my prayer. I wove into my song

---

* Author of the equally beautiful idyl, "Gladys the Singer," included in the new American copyright edition just issued.

Fervour, and joy, and mystery, and the bleak,
The wan despair that words could never speak.
I prayed as if my spirit did belong
To some old master who was wise and strong,
Because he lov'd and suffered, and was weak.

"I trill'd the notes, and curb'd them to a sigh,
And when they falter'd most, I made them leap
Fierce from my bow, as from a summer sleep
A young she-devil. I was fired thereby
To bolder efforts—and a muffled cry
Came from the strings as if a saint did weep.

"I changed the theme. I dallied with the bow
Just time enough to fit it to a mesh
Of merry tones, and drew it back afresh,
To talk of truth, and constancy, and woe,
And life, and love, and madness, and the glow
Of mine own soul which burns into my flesh."

All my love for music welled freshly up in my heart; I, who had felt disinclined to touch the piano for months, now longed to try my strength again upon the familiar and responsive key-board. For a piano has never been a mere piano to me; it is a friend who answers to my thought, and whose notes meet my fingers with caressing readiness and obedience.

Breakfast came, and I took it with great relish. Then, to pass the day, I went out and called on Mrs. Everard's friends, Mr. and Mrs. Challoner and their daughters. I found them very agreeable, with that easy bonhomie and lack of stiffness that distinguishes the best Americans. Finding out through Mrs. Everard's letter that I was an "artiste" they at once concluded I must need support and patronage, and with impulsive large-heartedness were beginning to plan as to the best means of organizing a concert for me. I was taken by surprise at this, for I had generally found the exact reverse of this sympathy among English patrons of art, who were never tired of murmuring the usual platitudes about there being "so many musicians," "music was overdone," "improvising was not understood or cared for," etc., etc.

But these agreeable Americans, as soon as they discovered that I had not come for any professional reason to Paris, but only to consult a physician about my health, were actually disappointed.

"Oh, we shall persuade you to give a recital some time!" persisted the handsome smiling mother of the family. "I know lots of people in Paris. We'll get it up for you!"

I protested, half laughing, that I had no idea of the kind, but they were incorrigibly generous.

"Nonsense!" said Mrs. Challoner, arranging her diamond rings on her pretty white hand with pardonable pride. "Brains don't go for nothing in Our country. As soon as you are fixed up in health, we'll give you a grand soiree in Paris, and we'll work up all our folks in the place. Don't tell me you are not as glad of dollars as any one of us."

"Dollars are very good," I admitted, "but real appreciation is far better."

"Well, you shall have both from us," said Mrs. Challoner. "And now, will you stop to luncheon?"

I accepted this invitation, given as it was with the most friendly affability, and enjoyed myself very much.

"You don't look ill," said the eldest Miss Challoner to me, later on. "I don't see that you want a physician."

"Oh, I am getting much better now," I replied; "and I hope soon to be quite well."

"Who's your doctor?"

I hesitated. Somehow the name of Heliobas would not come to my lips. Fortunately Mrs. Challoner diverted her daughter's attention at this moment by the announcement that a dressmaker was waiting to see her; and in the face of such an important visit, no one remembered to ask me again the name of my medical adviser.

I left the Grand Hotel in good time to prepare for my second visit to Heliobas. As I was going there to dinner I made a slightly dressy toilette, if a black silk robe relieved with a cluster of pale pink roses can be called dressy. This time I drove to the Hotel Mars, dismissing the coachman, however, before ascending the steps. The door opened and closed as usual, and the first person I saw in the hall was Heliobas himself, seated in one of the easy-chairs, reading a volume of Plato. He rose and greeted me cordially. Before I could speak a word, he said:

"You need not tell me that you slept well. I see it in your eyes and face. You feel better?"

My gratitude to him was so great that I found it difficult to express my thanks. Tears rushed to my eyes, yet I tried to smile, though I could not speak. He saw my emotion, and continued kindly:

"I am as thankful as you can be for the cure which I see has begun, and will soon be effected. My sister is waiting to see you. Will you come to her room?"

We ascended a flight of stairs thickly carpeted, and bordered on each side by tropical ferns and flowers, placed in exquisitely painted china pots and vases. I heard the distant singing of many birds mingled with the ripple and plash of waters. We reached a landing where the afterglow of the set sun streamed through a high oriel window of richly stained glass. Turning towards the left, Heliobas drew aside the folds of some azure satin hangings, and calling in a low voice "Zara!" motioned me to enter. I stepped into a spacious and lofty apartment where the light seemed to soften and merge into many shades of opaline radiance and delicacy—a room the beauty of which would at any other time have astonished and delighted me, but which now appeared as nothing beside the surpassing loveliness of the woman who occupied it. Never shall I behold again any face or form so divinely beautiful! She was about the medium height of women, but her small finely-shaped head was set upon so slender and proud a throat that she appeared taller than she actually was. Her figure was most exquisitely rounded and proportioned, and she came across the room to give me greeting with a sort of gliding graceful movement, like that of a stately swan floating on calm sunlit water. Her complexion was transparently clear—most purely white, most delicately rosy, Her eyes—large, luminous and dark as night, fringed with long silky black lashes—looked like

"Fairy lakes, where tender thoughts
Swam softly to and fro."

Her rich black hair was arranged a la Marguerite, and hung down in one long loose thick braid that nearly reached the end of her dress, and she was attired in a robe of deep old gold Indian silk as soft as cashmere, which was gathered in round her waist by an antique belt of curious jewel-work, in which rubies and turquoises seemed to be thickly studded. On her bosom shone a strange gem, the colour and form of which I could not determine. It was never the same for two minutes together. It glowed with many various hues—now bright crimson, now lightning-blue, sometimes deepening into a rich purple or tawny orange. Its lustre was intense, almost dazzling to the eye. Its beautiful wearer gave me welcome with a radiant smile and a few cordial words, and drawing me by the hand to the low couch she had just vacated, made me sit down beside her. Heliobas had disappeared.

"And so," said Zara—how soft and full of music was her voice!—"so you are one of Casimir's patients? I cannot help considering that you are fortunate in this, for I know my brother's power. If he says he will cure you, you may be sure he means it. And you are already better, are you not?"

"Much better," I said, looking earnestly into the lovely star-like eyes that regarded me with such interest and friendliness. "Indeed, to-day I have felt so well, that I cannot realize ever having been ill."

"I am very glad," said Zara, "I know you are a musician, and I think there can be no bitterer fate than for one belonging to your art to be incapacitated from performance of work by some physical obstacle. Poor grand old Beethoven! Can anything be more pitiful to think of than his deafness? Yet how splendidly he bore up against it! And Chopin, too—so delicate in health that he was too often morbid even in his music. Strength is needed to accomplish great things—the double strength of body and soul."

"Are you, too, a musician?" I inquired.

"No. I love music passionately, and I play a little on the organ in our private chapel; but I follow a different art altogether. I am a mere imitator of noble form—I am a sculptress."

"You?" I said in some wonder, looking at the very small, beautifully formed white hand that lay passively on the edge of the couch beside me. "You make statues in marble like Michael Angelo?"

"Like Angelo?" murmured Zara; and she lowered her brilliant eyes with a reverential gravity. "No one in these modern days can approach the immortal splendour of that great master. He must have known heroes and talked with gods to be able to hew out of the rocks such perfection of shape and attitude as his 'David.' Alas! my strength of brain and hand is mere child's play compared to what Has been done in sculpture, and what Will yet be done; still, I love the work for its own sake, and I am always trying to render a resemblance of—"

Here she broke off abruptly, and a deep blush suffused her cheeks. Then, looking up suddenly, she took my hand impulsively, and pressed it.

"Be my friend," she said, with a caressing inflection in her rich voice, "I have no friends of my own sex, and I wish to love you. My brother has always had so much distrust of the companionship of women for me. You know his theories; and he has always asserted that the sphere of thought in which I have lived all my life is so widely apart from those in which other women exist—that nothing but unhappiness for me could come out of associating us together. When he told me yesterday that you were coming to see me to-day, I knew he must have discovered something in your nature that was not antipathetic to mine; otherwise he would not have brought you to me. Do you think you can like me?—perhaps LOVE me after a little while?"

It would have been a cold heart indeed that would not have responded to such a speech as this, uttered with the pleading prettiness of a loving child. Besides, I had warmed to her from the first moment I had touched her hand; and I was overjoyed to think that she was willing to elect me as a friend. I therefore replied to her words by putting my arm affectionately round her waist and kissing her. My beautiful, tender Zara! How innocently happy she seemed to be thus embraced! and how gently her fragrant lips met mine in that sisterly caress! She leaned her dark head for a moment on my shoulder, and the mysterious jewel on her breast flashed into a weird red hue like the light of a stormy sunset.

"And now we have drawn up, signed, and sealed our compact of friendship," she said gaily, "will you come and see my studio? There is nothing in it that deserves to last, I think; still, one has patience with a child when he builds his brick houses, and you must have equal patience with me. Come!"

And she led the way through her lovely room, which I now noticed was full of delicate statuary, fine paintings, and exquisite embroidery, while flowers were everywhere in abundance. Lifting the hangings at the farther end of the apartment, she passed, I following, into a lofty studio, filled with all the appurtenances of the sculptor's art. Here and there were the usual spectral effects which are always suggested to the mind by unfinished plaster models—an arm in one place, a head in another; a torso, or a single hand, protruding ghost-like from a fold of dark drapery. At the very end of the room stood a large erect figure, the outlines of which could but dimly be seen through its linen coverings; and to this work, whatever it was, Zara did not appear desirous of attracting my attention. She led me to one particular corner; and, throwing aside a small crimson velvet curtain, said:

"This is the last thing I have finished in marble. I call it 'Approaching Evening.'"

I stood silently before the statue, lost in admiration. I could not conceive it possible that the fragile little hand of the woman who stood beside me could have executed such a perfect work. She had depicted "Evening" as a beautiful nude female figure in the act of stepping forward on tip-toe; the eyes were half closed, and the sweet mouth slightly parted in a dreamily serious smile. The right forefinger was laid lightly on the lips, as though suggesting silence; and in the left hand was loosely clasped a bunch of poppies. That was all. But the poetry and force of the whole conception as carried out in the statue was marvellous.

"Do you like it?" asked Zara, half timidly.

"Like it!" I exclaimed. "It is lovely—wonderful! It is worthy to rank with the finest Italian masterpieces."

"Oh, no!" remonstrated Zara; "no, indeed! When the great Italian sculptors lived and worked—ah! one may say with the Scriptures, 'There were giants in those days.' Giants—veritable ones; and we modernists are the pigmies. We can only see Art now through the eyes of others who came before us. We cannot create anything new. We look at painting through Raphael; sculpture through Angelo; poetry through Shakespeare; philosophy through Plato. It is all done for us; we are copyists. The world is getting old—how glorious to have lived when it was young! But nowadays the very children are blase."

"And you—are not you blase to talk like that, with your genius and all the world before you?" I asked laughingly, slipping my arm through hers. "Come, confess!"

Zara looked at me gravely.

"I sincerely hope the world is NOT all before me," she said; "I should be very sorry if I thought so. To have the world all before you in the general acceptation of that term means to live long, to barter whatever genius you have for gold, to hear the fulsome and unmeaning flatteries of the ignorant, who are as ready with condemnation as praise—to be envied and maligned by those less lucky than you are. Heaven defend me from such a fate!"

She spoke with earnestness and solemnity; then, dropping the curtain before her statue, turned away. I was admiring the vine-wreathed head of a young Bacchante that stood on a pedestal near me, and was about to ask Zara what subject she had chosen for the large veiled figure at the farthest end of her studio, when we were interrupted by the entrance of the little Greek page whom I had seen on my first visit to the house. He saluted us both, and addressing himself to Zara, said:

"Monsieur le Comte desires me to tell you, madame, that Prince Ivan will be present at dinner."

Zara looked somewhat vexed; but the shade of annoyance flitted away from her fair face like a passing shadow, as she replied quietly:

"Tell Monsieur le Comte, my brother, that I shall be happy to receive Prince Ivan."

The page bowed deferentially and departed. Zara turned round, and I saw the jewel on her breast flashing with a steely glitter like the blade of a sharp sword.

"I do not like Prince Ivan myself," she said; "but he is a singularly brave and resolute man, and Casimir has some reason for admitting him to our companionship. Though I greatly doubt if—" Here a flood of music broke upon our ears like the sound of a distant orchestra. Zara looked at me and smiled. "Dinner is ready!" she announced; "but you must not imagine that we keep a band to play us to our table in triumph. It is simply a musical instrument worked by electricity that imitates the orchestra; both Casimir and I prefer it to a gong!"

And slipping her arm affectionately through mine, she drew me from the studio into the passage, and together we went down the staircase into a large dining-room, rich with oil-paintings and carved oak, where Heliobas awaited us. Close by him stood another gentleman, who was introduced to me as Prince Ivan Petroffsky. He was a fine-looking, handsome-featured young man, of about thirty, tall and broad-shouldered, though beside the commanding stature of Heliobas, his figure did not show to so much advantage as it might have done beside a less imposing contrast. He bowed to me with easy and courteous grace; but his deeply reverential salute to Zara had something in it of that humility which a slave might render to a queen. She bent her head slightly in answer, and still holding me by the hand, moved to her seat at the bottom of the table, while her brother took the head. My seat was at the right hand of Heliobas, Prince Ivan's at the left, so that we directly faced each other.

There were two men-servants in attendance, dressed in dark livery, who waited upon us with noiseless alacrity. The dinner was exceedingly choice; there was nothing coarse or vulgar in the dishes—no great heavy joints swimming in thin gravy a la Anglaise; no tureens of unpalatable sauce; no clumsy decanters filled with burning sherry or drowsy port. The table itself was laid out in the most perfect taste, with the finest Venetian glass and old Dresden ware, in which tempting fruits gleamed amid clusters of glossy dark leaves. Flowers in tall vases bloomed wherever they could be placed effectively; and in the centre of the board a small fountain played, tinkling as it rose and fell like a very faintly echoing fairy chime. The wines that were served to us were most delicious, though their flavour was quite unknown to me—one in especial, of a pale pink colour, that sparkled slightly as it was poured into my glass, seemed to me a kind of nectar of the gods, so soft it was to the palate. The conversation, at first somewhat desultory, grew more concentrated as the time went on, though Zara spoke little and seemed absorbed in her own thoughts more than once. The Prince, warmed with the wine and the general good cheer, became witty and amusing in his conversation; he was a man who had evidently seen a good deal of the world, and who was accustomed to take everything in life a la bagatelle. He told us gay stories of his life in St. Petersburg; of the pranks he had played in the Florentine Carnival; of his journey to the American States, and his narrow escape from the matrimonial clutches of a Boston heiress.

Heliobas listened to him with a sort of indulgent kindness, only smiling now and then at the preposterous puns the young man would insist on making at every opportunity that presented itself.

"You are a lucky fellow, Ivan," he said at last. "You like the good things of life, and you have got them all without any trouble on your own part. You are one of those men who have absolutely nothing to wish for."

Prince Ivan frowned and pulled his dark moustache with no very satisfied air.

"I am not so sure about that," he returned. "No one is contented in this world, I believe. There is always something left to desire, and the last thing longed for always seems the most necessary to happiness."

"The truest philosophy," said Heliobas, "is not to long for anything in particular, but to accept everything as it comes, and find out the reason of its coming."

"What do you mean by 'the reason of its coming'?" questioned Prince Ivan. "Do you know, Casimir, I find you sometimes as puzzling as Socrates."

"Socrates?—Socrates was as clear as a drop of morning dew, my dear fellow," replied Heliobas. "There was nothing puzzling about him. His remarks were all true and trenchant—hitting smartly home to the heart like daggers plunged down to the hilt. That was the worst of him—he was too clear—too honest—too disdainful of opinions. Society does not love such men. What do I mean, you ask, by accepting everything as it comes, and trying to find out the reason of its coming? Why, I mean what I say. Each circumstance that happens to each one of us brings its own special lesson and meaning—forms a link or part of a link in the chain of our existence. It seems nothing to you that you walk down a particular street at a particular hour, and yet that slight action of yours may lead to a result you wot not of. 'Accept the hint of each new experience,' says the American imitator of Plato—Emerson. If this advice is faithfully followed, we all have enough to occupy us busily from the cradle to the grave."

Prince Ivan looked at Zara, who sat quietly thoughtful, only lifting her bright eyes now and then to glance at her brother as he spoke.

"I tell you," he said, with sudden moroseness, "there are some hints that we cannot accept—some circumstances that we must not yield to. Why should a man, for instance, be subjected to an undeserved and bitter disappointment?"

"Because," said Zara, joining in the conversation for the first time, "he has most likely desired what he is not fated to obtain."

The Prince bit his lips, and gave a forced laugh.

"I know, madame, you are against me in all our arguments," he observed, with some bitterness in his tone. "As Casimir suggests, I am a bad philosopher. I do not pretend to more than the ordinary attributes of an ordinary man; it is fortunate, if I may be permitted to say so, that the rest of the word's inhabitants are very like me, for if everyone reached to the sublime heights of science and knowledge that you and your brother have attained—"

"The course of human destiny would run out, and Paradise would be an established fact," laughed Heliobas. "Come, Ivan! You are a true Epicurean. Have some more wine, and a truce to discussions for the present." And, beckoning to one of the servants, he ordered the Prince's glass to be refilled.

Dessert was now served, and luscious fruits in profusion, including peaches, bananas, plantains, green figs, melons, pine-apples, and magnificent grapes, were offered for our choice. As I made a selection for my own plate, I became aware of something soft rubbing itself gently against my dress; and looking down, I saw the noble head and dark intelligent eyes of my old acquaintance Leo, whom I had last met at Cannes. I gave an exclamation of pleasure, and the dog, encouraged, stood up and laid a caressing paw on my arm.

"You know Leo, of course," said Heliobas, turning to me. "He went to see Raffaello while you were at Cannes. He is a wonderful animal—more valuable to me than his weight in gold."

Prince Ivan, whose transient moodiness had passed away like a bad devil exorcised by the power of good wine, joined heartily in the praise bestowed on this four-footed friend of the family.

"It was really through Leo," he said, "that you were induced to follow out your experiments in human electricity, Casimir, was it not?"

"Yes," replied Heliobas, calling the dog, who went to him immediately to be fondled. "I should never have been much encouraged in my researches, had he not been at hand. I feared to experimentalize much on my sister, she being young at the time—and women are always frail of construction—but Leo was willing and ready to be a victim to science, if necessary. Instead of a martyr he is a living triumph—are you not, old boy?" he continued, stroking the silky coat of the animal, who responded with a short low bark of satisfaction.

My curiosity was much excited by these remarks, and I said eagerly:

"Will you tell me in what way Leo has been useful to you? I have a great affection for dogs, and I never tire of hearing stories of their wonderful intelligence."

"I will certainly tell you," replied Heliobas. "To some people the story might appear improbable, but it is perfectly true and at the same time simple of comprehension. When I was a very young man, younger than Prince Ivan, I absorbed myself in the study of electricity—its wonderful powers, and its various capabilities. From the consideration of electricity in the different forms by which it is known to civilized Europe, I began to look back through history, to what are ignorantly called 'the dark ages,' but which might more justly be termed the enlightened youth of the world. I found that the force of electricity was well understood by the ancients—better understood by them, in fact, than it is by the scientists of our day. The 'MENE, MENE, TEKEL, UPHARSIN' that glittered in unearthly characters on the wall at Belshazzar's feast, was written by electricity; and the Chaldean kings and priests understood a great many secrets of another form of electric force which the world to-day scoffs at and almost ignores—I mean human electricity, which we all possess, but which we do not all cultivate within us. When once I realized the existence of the fact of human electric force, I applied the discovery to myself, and spared no pains to foster and educate whatever germ of this power lay within me. I succeeded with more ease and celerity than I had imagined possible. At the time I pursued these studies, Leo here was quite a young dog, full of the clumsy playfulness and untrained ignorance of a Newfoundland puppy. One day I was very busy reading an interesting Sanskrit scroll which treated of ancient medicines and remedies, and Leo was gambolling in his awkward way about the room, playing with an old slipper and worrying it with his teeth. The noise he made irritated and disturbed me, and I rose in my chair and called him by name, somewhat angrily. He paused in his game and looked up—his eyes met mine exactly. His head drooped; he shivered uneasily, whined, and lay down motionless. He never stirred once from the position he had taken, till I gave him permission—and remember, he was untrained. This strange behaviour led me to try other experiments with him, and all succeeded. I gradually led him up to the point I desired—that is, I FORCED HIM TO RECEIVE MY THOUGHT AND ACT UPON IT, as far as his canine capabilities could do, and he has never once failed. It is sufficient for me to strongly WILL him to do a certain thing, and I can convey that command of mine to his brain without uttering a single word, and he will obey me."

I suppose I showed surprise and incredulity in my face, for Heliobas smiled at me and continued:

"I will put him to the proof at any time you like. If you wish him to fetch anything that he is physically able to carry, and will write the name of whatever it is on a slip of paper, just for me to know what you require, I guarantee Leo's obedience."

I looked at Zara, and she laughed.

"It seems like magic to you, does it not?" she said; "but I assure you it is quite true."

"I am bound to admit," said Prince Ivan, "that I once doubted both Leo and his master, but I am quite converted. Here, mademoiselle," he continued, handing me a leaf from his pocket-book and a pencil— "write down something that you want; only don't send the dog to Italy on an errand just now, as we want him back before we adjourn to the drawing-room."

I remembered that I had left an embroidered handkerchief on the couch in Zara's room, and I wrote this down on the paper, which I passed to Heliobas. He glanced at it and tore it up. Leo was indulging himself with a bone under the table, but came instantly to his master's call.

Heliobas took the dog's head between his two hands, and gazed steadily into the grave brown eyes that regarded him with equal steadiness. This interchange of looks lasted but a few seconds. Leo left the room, walking with an unruffled and dignified pace, while we awaited his return—Heliobas and Zara with indifference, Prince Ivan with amusement, and I with interest and expectancy. Two or three minutes elapsed, and the dog returned with the same majestic demeanour, carrying between his teeth my handkerchief. He came straight to me and placed it in my hand; shook himself, wagged his tail, and conveying a perfectly human expression of satisfaction into his face, went under the table again to his bone. I was utterly amazed, but at the same time convinced. I had not seen the dog since my arrival in Paris, and it was impossible for him to have known where to find my handkerchief, or to recognize it as being mine, unless through the means Heliobas had explained.

"Can you command human beings so?" I asked, with a slight tremor of nervousness.

"Not all," returned Heliobas quietly. "In fact, I may say, very few. Those who are on my own circle of power I can, naturally, draw to or repel from me; but those who are not, have to be treated by different means. Sometimes cases occur in which persons, at first NOT on my circle, are irresistibly attracted to it by a force not mine. Sometimes, in order to perform a cure, I establish a communication between myself and a totally alien sphere of thought; and to do this is a long and laborious effort. But it can be done."

"Then, if it can be done," said Prince Ivan, "why do you not accomplish it for me?"

"Because you are being forcibly drawn towards me without any effort on my part," replied Heliobas, with one of his steady, keen looks. "For what motive I cannot at present determine; but I shall know as soon as you touch the extreme edge of my circle. You are a long way off it yet, but you are coming in spite of yourself, Ivan."

The Prince fidgeted restlessly in his chair, and toyed with the fruit on his plate in a nervous manner.

"If I did not know you to be an absolutely truthful and honourable man, Casimir," he said, "I should think you were trying to deceive me. But I have seen what you can do, therefore I must believe you. Still I confess I do not follow you in your circle theory."

"To begin with," returned Heliobas, "the Universe is a circle. Everything is circular, from the motion of planets down to the human eye, or the cup of a flower, or a drop of dew. My 'circle theory,' as you call it, applied to human electric force, is very simple; but I have proved it to be mathematically correct. Every human being is provided INTERNALLY and EXTERNALLY with a certain amount of electricity, which is as necessary to existence as the life-blood to the heart or fresh air to the lungs. Internally it is the germ of a soul or spirit, and is placed there to be either cultivated or neglected as suits the WILL of man. It is indestructible; yet, if neglected, it remains always a germ; and, at the death of the body it inhabits, goes elsewhere to seek another chance of development. If, on the contrary, its growth is fostered by a persevering, resolute WILL, it becomes a spiritual creature, glorious and supremely powerful, for which a new, brilliant, and endless existence commences when its clay chrysalis perishes. So much for the INTERNAL electrical force. The EXTERNAL binds us all by fixed laws, with which our wills have nothing whatever to do. (Each one of us walks the earth encompassed by an invisible electric ring—wide or narrow according to our capabilities. Sometimes our rings meet and form one, as in the case of two absolutely sympathetic souls, who labour and love together with perfect faith in each other. Sometimes they clash, and storm ensues, as when a strong antipathy between persons causes them almost to loathe each other's presence.) All these human electric rings are capable of attraction and repulsion. If a man, during his courtship of a woman, experiences once or twice a sudden instinctive feeling that there is something in her nature not altogether what he expected or desired, let him take warning and break off the attachment; for the electric circles do not combine, and nothing but unhappiness would come from forcing a union. I would say the same thing to a woman. If my advice were followed, how many unhappy marriages would be avoided! But you have tempted me to talk too much, Ivan. I see the ladies wish to adjourn. Shall we go to the smoking-room for a little, and join them in the drawing-room afterwards?"

We all rose.

"Well," said the Prince gaily, as he prepared to follow his host, "I realize one thing which gives me pleasure, Casimir. If in truth I am being attracted towards your electric circle, I hope I shall reach it soon, as I shall then, I suppose, be more en rapport with madame, your sister."

Zara's luminous eyes surveyed him with a sort of queenly pity and forbearance.

"By the time You arrive at that goal, Prince," she said calmly, "it is most probable that I shall have departed."

And with one arm thrown round my waist, she saluted him gravely, and left the room with me beside her.

"Would you like to see the chapel on your way to the drawing-room?" she asked, as we crossed the hall.

I gladly accepted this proposition, and Zara took me down a flight of marble steps, which terminated in a handsomely-carved oaken door. Pushing this softly open, she made the sign of the cross and sank on her knees. I did the same, and then looked with reverential wonder at the loveliness and serenity of the place. It was small, but lofty, and the painted dome-shaped roof was supported by eight light marble columns, wreathed with minutely-carved garlands of vine-leaves. The chapel was fitted up in accordance with the rites of the Catholic religion, and before the High Altar and Tabernacle burned seven roseate lamps, which were suspended from the roof by slender gilt chains. A large crucifix, bearing a most sorrowful and pathetic figure of Christ, was hung on one of the side walls; and from a corner altar, shining with soft blue and silver, an exquisite statue of the Madonna and Child was dimly seen from where we knelt. A few minutes passed, and Zara rose. Looking towards the Tabernacle, her lips moved as though murmuring a prayer, and then, taking me by the hand, she led me gently out. The heavy oaken door swung softly behind us as we ascended the chapel steps and re-entered the great hall.

"You are a Catholic, are you not?" then said Zara to me.

"Yes," I answered; "but—"

"But you have doubts sometimes, you would say! Of course. One always doubts when one sees the dissensions, the hypocrisies, the false pretences and wickedness of many professing Christians. But Christ and His religion are living facts, in spite of the suicide of souls He would gladly save. You must ask Casimir some day about these things; he will clear up all the knotty points for you. Here we are at the drawing-room door."

It was the same room into which I had first been shown. Zara seated herself, and made me occupy a low chair beside her.

"Tell me," she said, "can you not come here and stay with me while you are under Casimir's treatment?"

I thought of Madame Denise and her Pension.

"I wish I could," I said; "but I fear my friends would want to know where I am staying, and explanations would have to be given, which I do not feel disposed to enter upon."

"Why," went on Zara quietly, "you have only to say that you are being attended by a Dr. Casimir who wishes to have you under his own supervision, and that you are therefore staying in his house under the chaperonage of his sister."

I laughed at the idea of Zara playing the chaperon, and told her she was far too young and beautiful to enact that character.

"Do you know how old I am?" she asked, with a slight smile.

I guessed seventeen, or at any rate not more than twenty.

"I am thirty-eight," said Zara.

Thirty-eight! Impossible! I would not believe it. I could not. I laughed scornfully at such an absurdity, looking at her as she sat there a perfect model of youthful grace and loveliness, with her lustrous eyes and rose-tinted complexion.

"You may doubt me if you choose," she said, still smiling; "but I have told you the truth. I am thirty-eight years of age according to the world's counting. What I am, measured by another standard of time, matters not just now. You see I look young, and, what is more, I am young. I enjoy my youth. I hear that women of society at thirty-eight are often faded and blasé—what a pity it is that they do not understand the first laws of self-preservation! But to resume what I was saying, you know now that I am quite old enough in the eyes of the world to chaperon you or anybody. You had better arrange to stay here. Casimir asked me to settle the matter with, you."

As she spoke, Heliobas and Prince Ivan entered. The latter looked flushed and excited—Heliobas was calm and stately as usual. He addressed himself to me at once.

"I have ordered my carriage, mademoiselle, to take you back this evening to the Avenue du Midi. If you will do as Zara tells you, and explain to your friends the necessity there is for your being under the personal supervision of your doctor, you will find everything will arrange itself very naturally. And the sooner you come here the better—in fact, Zara will expect you here to-morrow early in the afternoon. I may rely upon you?"

He spoke with a certain air of command, evidently expecting no resistance on my part. Indeed, why should I resist? Already I loved Zara, and wished to be more in her company; and then, most probably, my complete restoration to health would be more successfully and quickly accomplished if I were actually in the house of the man who had promised to cure me. Therefore I replied:

"I will do as you wish, monsieur. Having placed myself in your hands, I must obey. In this particular case," I added, looking at Zara, "obedience is very agreeable to me."

Heliobas smiled and seemed satisfied. He then took a small goblet from a side-table and left the room. Returning, however, almost immediately with the cup filled to the brim, he said, handing it to me:

"Drink this—it is your dose for to-night; and then you will go home, and straight to bed."

I drank it off at once. It was delicious in flavour—like very fine Chianti.

"Have you no soothing draught for me?" said Prince Ivan, who had been turning over a volume of photographs in a sullenly abstracted sort of way.

"No," replied Heliobas, with a keen glance at him; "the draught fitted for your present condition might soothe you too thoroughly."

The Prince looked at Zara, but she was mute. She had taken a piece of silk embroidery from a workbasket near her, and was busily employed with it. Heliobas advanced and laid his hand on the young man's arm.

"Sing to us, Ivan," he said, in a kind tone. "Sing us one of your wild Russian airs—Zara loves them, and this young lady would like to hear your voice before she goes."

The Prince hesitated, and then, with another glance at Zara's bent head, went to the piano. He had a brilliant touch, and accompanied himself with great taste and delicacy; but his voice was truly magnificent—a baritone of deep and mellow quality, sonorous, and at the same time tender. He sang a French rendering of a Slavonic love-song, which, as nearly as I can translate it into English, ran as follows:

"As the billows fling shells on the shore,
As the sun poureth light on the sea,
As a lark on the wing scatters song to the spring,
So rushes my love to thee.

"As the ivy clings close to the tower,
As the dew lieth deep in a flower,
As the shadow to light, as the day unto night,
So clings my wild soul to thee!

> "As the moon glitters coldly alone,
> Above earth on her cloud-woven throne,
> As the rocky-bound cave repulses a wave,
> So thy anger repulseth me.

> "As the bitter black frost of a night
> Slays the roses with pitiless might,
> As a sharp dagger-thrust hurls a king to the dust,
> So thy cruelty murdereth me.

> "Yet in spite of thy queenly disdain,
> Thou art seared by my passion and pain;
> Thou shalt hear me repeat, till I die for it, sweet!
> 'I love thee! I dare to love THEE!'"

He ended abruptly and with passion, and rose from the piano directly.

I was enthusiastic in my admiration of the song and of the splendid voice which had given it utterance, and the Prince seemed almost grateful for the praise accorded him both by Heliobas and myself.

The page entered to announce that "the carriage was waiting for mademoiselle," and I prepared to leave. Zara kissed me affectionately, and whispering, "Come early to-morrow," made a graceful salute to Prince Ivan, and left the room immediately.

Heliobas then offered me his arm to take me to the carriage. Prince Ivan accompanied us. As the hall door opened in its usual noiseless manner, I perceived an elegant light brougham drawn by a pair of black horses, who were giving the coachman a great deal of trouble by the fretting and spirited manner in which they pawed the stones and pranced. Before descending the steps I shook hands with Heliobas, and thanked him for the pleasant evening I had passed.

"We will try to make all your time with us pass as pleasantly," he returned. "Good-night! What, Ivan," as he perceived the Prince attiring himself in his great-coat and hat, "are you also going?"

"Yes, I am off," he replied, with a kind of forced gaiety; "I am bad company for anyone to-night, and I won't inflict myself upon you, Casimir. Au revoir! I will put mademoiselle into the carriage if she will permit me."

We went down the steps together, Heliobas watching us from the open door. As the Prince assisted me into the brougham, he whispered:

"Are you one of them!"

I looked at him in bewilderment.

"One of them!" I repeated. "What do you mean?"

"Never mind," he muttered impatiently, as he made a pretence of covering me with the fur rugs inside the carriage: "if you are not now, you will be, or Zara would not have kissed you. If you ever have the chance ask her to think of me at my best. Good-night."

I was touched and a little sorry for him. I held out my hand in silence. He pressed it hard, and calling to the coachman, "36, Avenue du Midi," stood on the pavement bareheaded, looking singularly pale and grave in the starlight, as the carriage rolled swiftly away, and the door of the Hotel Mars closed.

VIII

A Symphony in the Air

Within a very short time I became a temporary resident in the house of Heliobas, and felt myself to be perfectly at home there. I had explained to Madame Denise the cause of my leaving her comfortable Pension, and she had fully approved of my being under a physician's personal care in order to ensure rapid recovery; but when she heard the name of that physician, which I gave (in accordance with Zara's instructions) as Dr. Casimir, she held up her fat hands in dismay.

"Oh, mademoiselle," she exclaimed, "have you not dread of that terrible man? Is it not he that is reported to be a cruel mesmerist who sacrifices everybody—yes, even his own sister, to his medical experiments? Ah, mon Dieu! it makes me to shudder!"

And she shuddered directly, as a proof of her veracity. I was amused. I saw in her an example of the common multitude, who are more ready to believe in vulgar spirit-rapping and mesmerism than to accept an established scientific fact.

"Do you know Dr. Casimir and his sister?" I asked her.

"I have seen them, mademoiselle; perhaps once—twice—three times! It is true madame is lovely as an angel; but they say"—here she lowered her voice mysteriously—"that she is wedded to a devil! It is true, mademoiselle—all people say so. And Suzanne Michot—a very respectable young person, mademoiselle, from Auteuil—she was employed at one time as under-housemaid at Dr. Casimir's, and she had things to say—ah, to make the blood like ice!"

"What did she say?" I asked with a half smile.

"Well," and Madame Denise came close to me and looked confidential, "Suzanne—I assure you a most respectable girl—said that one evening she was crossing the passage near Madame Casimir's boudoir, and she saw a light like fire coming through the curtains of the portiere. And she stopped to listen, and she heard a strange music like the sound of harps. She ventured to go nearer—Suzanne is a brave girl, mademoiselle, and most virtuous—and to raise the curtain the smallest portion just to permit the glance of an eye. And—imagine what she saw."

"Well!" I exclaimed impatiently. "WHAT did she see?"

"Ah, mademoiselle, you will not believe me—but Suzanne Michot has respectable parents, and would not tell a lie—well, Suzanne saw her mistress, Madame Casimir, standing up near her couch with both arms extended as to embrace the air. Round her there was—believe it or not, mademoiselle, as you please—a ring of light like a red fire, which seemed to grow larger and redder always. All suddenly, madame grew pale and more pale, and then fell on her couch as one dead, and all the red fire went out. Suzanne had fear, and she tried to call out—but now see what happened to Suzanne! She was PUSHED from the spot, mademoiselle, pushed along as though by some strong personage; yet she saw no one till she reached her own door, and in her room she fainted from alarm. The very next morning Dr. Casimir dismissed her, with her full wages and a handsome present besides; but he LOOKED at her, Suzanne said, in a manner to make her tremble from head to foot. Now, mademoiselle, judge yourself whether it is fit for one who is suffering with nerves to go to so strange a house!"

I laughed. Her story had not the least effect upon me. In fact, I made up my mind that the so respectable and virtuous Suzanne Michot had been drinking some of her master's wine. I said:

"Your words only make me more desirous to go, Madame Denise. Besides, Dr. Casimir has already done me a great deal of good. You must have heard things of him that are not altogether bad, surely?"

The little woman reflected seriously, and then said, as with some reluctance:

"It is certainly true, mademoiselle, that in the quarter of the poor he is much beloved. Jean Duclos—he is a chiffonnier—had his one child dying of typhoid fever, and he was watching it struggling for breath; it was at the point to die. Monsieur le Comte Casimir, or Dr. Casimir—for he is called both—came in all suddenly, and in half an hour had saved the little one's life. I do not deny that he may have some good in him, and that he understands medicine; but there is something wrong—" And Madame Denise shook her head forlornly a great number of times.

None of her statements deterred me from my intention, and I was delighted when I found myself fairly installed at the Hotel Mars. Zara gave me a beautiful room next to her own; she had taken pains to fit it up herself with everything that was in accordance with my particular tastes, such as a choice selection of books; music, including many of the fascinating scores of Schubert and Wagner; writing materials;

and a pretty, full-toned pianette. My window looked out on a small courtyard, which had been covered over with glass and transformed into a conservatory. I could enter it by going down a few steps, and could have the satisfaction of gathering roses and lilies of the valley, while outside the east wind blew and the cold snowflakes fell over Paris. I wrote to Mrs. Everard from my retreat, and I also informed the Challoners where they could find me if they wanted me. These duties done, I gave myself up to enjoyment. Zara and I became inseparables; we worked together, read together, and together every morning gave those finishing-touches to the ordering and arrangement of the household which are essentially feminine, and which not the wisest philosopher in all the world has been, or ever will be, able to accomplish successfully. We grew to love each other dearly, with that ungrudging, sympathizing, confiding friendship that is very rarely found between two women. In the meantime my cure went on rapidly. Every night on retiring to rest Heliobas prepared a medicinal dose for me, of the qualities of which I was absolutely ignorant, but which I took trustingly from his hand. Every morning a different little phial of liquid was placed in the bathroom for me to empty into the water of my daily bath, and every hour I grew better, brighter, and stronger. The natural vivacity of my temperament returned to me; I suffered no pain, no anxiety, no depression, and I slept as soundly as a child, unvisited by a single dream. The mere fact of my being alive became a joy to me; I felt grateful for everything—for my eyesight, my speech, my hearing, my touch— because all my senses seemed to be sharpened and invigorated and braced up to the keenest delight. This happy condition of my system did not come suddenly—sudden cures mean sudden relapses; it was a gradual, steady, ever-increasing, reliable recovery.

I found the society of Heliobas and his sister very fascinating. Their conversation was both thoughtful and brilliant, their manners were evenly gracious and kindly, and the life they led was a model of perfect household peace and harmony. There was never a fuss about anything: the domestic arrangements seemed to work on smoothly oiled wheels; the different repasts were served with quiet elegance and regularity; the servants were few, but admirably trained; and we all lived in an absolutely calm atmosphere, unruffled by so much as a breath of worry. Nothing of a mysterious nature went on, as far as I could see.

Heliobas passed the greater part of the day in his study—a small, plainly furnished room, the facsimile of the one I had beheld him in when I had dreamed those three dreams at Cannes. Whether he received many or few patients there I could not tell; but that some applied to him for advice I knew, as I often met strangers crossing the hall on their way in and out. He always joined us at dinner, and was invariably cheerful, generally entertaining us with lively converse and sparkling narrative, though now and then the thoughtful tendency of his mind predominated, and gave a serious tone to his remarks.

Zara was uniformly bright and even in her temperament. She was my very ideal of the Greek Psyche, radiant yet calm, pensive yet mirthful. She was full of beautiful ideas and poetical fancies, and so thoroughly untouched by the world and its aims, that she seemed to me just to poise on the earth like a delicate butterfly on a flower; and I should have been scarcely surprised had I seen her unfold a pair of shining wings and fly away to some other region. Yet in spite of this spirituelle nature, she was physically stronger and more robust than any other woman I ever saw. She was gay and active; she was never tired, never ailing, and she enjoyed life with a keen zest such as is unknown to the tired multitudes who toil on hopelessly and wearily, wondering, as they work, why they were born. Zara evidently had no doubts or speculations of this kind; she drank in every minute of her existence as if it were a drop of honey-dew prepared specially for her palate. I never could believe that her age was what she had declared it to be. She seemed to look younger every day; sometimes her eyes had that limpid, lustrous innocence that is seen in the eyes of a very little child; and, again, they would change and glow with the earnest and lofty thought of one who had lived through years of study, research, and discovery. For the first few days of my visit she did not work in her studio at all, but appeared to prefer reading or talking with me. One afternoon, however, when we had returned from a short drive in the Bois de Boulogne, she said half hesitatingly:

"I think I will go to work again to-morrow morning, if you will not think me unsociable."

"Why, Zara dearest!" I replied. "Of course I shall not think you unsociable. I would not interfere with any of your pursuits for the world."

She looked at me with a sort of wistful affection, and continued:

"But you must know I like to work quite alone, and though it may look churlish, still not even you must come into the studio. I never can do anything before a witness; Casimir himself knows that, and keeps away from me."

"Well!" I said, "I should be an ungrateful wretch if I could not oblige you in so small a request. I promise not to disturb you, Zara; and do not think for one moment that I shall be dull. I have books, a piano, flowers—what more do I want? And if I like I can go out; then I have letters to write, and all sorts of things to occupy me. I shall be quite happy, and I shall not come near you till you call me."

Zara kissed me.

"You are a dear girl," she said; "I hate to appear inhospitable, but I know you are a real friend—that you will love me as much away from you as near you, and that you have none of that vulgar curiosity which some women give way to, when what they desire to see is hidden from them. You are not inquisitive, are you?"

I laughed.

"The affairs of other people have never appeared so interesting to me that I have cared to bother myself about them," I replied. "Blue-Beard's Chamber would never have been unlocked had I been that worthy man's wife."

"What a fine moral lesson the old fairy-tale teaches!" said Zara. "I always think those wives of Blue-Beard deserved their fate for not being able to obey him in his one request. But in regard to your pursuits, dear, while I am at work in my studio, you can use the grand piano in the drawing-room when you please, as well as the little one in your own room; and you can improvise on the chapel organ as much as you like."

I was delighted at this idea, and thanked her heartily. She smiled thoughtfully.

"What happiness it must be for you to love music so thoroughly!" she said. "It fills you with enthusiasm. I used to dislike to read the biographies of musical people; they all seemed to find so much fault with one another, and grudged each other every little bit of praise wrung from the world's cold, death-doomed lips. It is to me pathetically absurd to see gifted persons all struggling along, and rudely elbowing each other out of the way to win—what? A few stilted commonplace words of approbation or fault-finding in the newspapers of the day, and a little clapping and shouting from a gathering of ordinary minded persons, who only clap and shout because it is possibly the fashion to do so. It is really ludicrous. If the music the musician offers to the public be really great, it will live by itself and defy praise or blame. Because Schubert died of want and sorrow, that does not interfere with the life of his creations. Because Wagner is voted impossible and absurd by many who think themselves good judges of musical art, that does not offer any obstacle to the steady spread of his fame, which is destined to become as universal as that of Shakespeare. Poor Joachim, the violinist, has got a picture in his private house, in which Wagner is painted as suffering the tortures of hell; can anything be more absurd, when we consider how soon the learned fiddler, who has occupied his life in playing other people's compositions, will be a handful of forgotten dust, while multitudes yet to come will shout their admiration of 'Tristran' and 'Parsifal.' Yes, as I said, I never cared for musical people much, till I met a friend of my brother's—a man whose inner life was an exquisite harmony."

"I know!" I interrupted her. "He wrote the 'Letters of a Dead Musician.'"

"Yes," said Zara. "I suppose you saw the book at Raffaello's studio. Good Raffaello Cellini! his is another absolutely ungrudging and unselfish spirit. But this musician that I speak of was like a child in humility and reverence. Casimir told me he had never sounded so perfect a nature. At one time he, too, was a little anxious for recognition and praise, and Casimir saw that he was likely to wreck himself on that fatal rock of poor ambition. So he took him in hand, and taught him the meaning of his work, and why it was especially given him to do; and that man's life became 'one grand sweet song.' But there are tears in your eyes, dear! What have I said to grieve you?"

And she caressed me tenderly. The tears were indeed thick in my eyes, and a minute or two elapsed before I could master them. At last I raised my head and endeavoured to smile.

"They are not sad tears, Zara," I said; "I think they come from a strong desire I have to be what you are, what your brother is, what that dead musician must have been. Why, I have longed, and do long for fame, for wealth, for the world's applause, for all the things which you seem to think so petty and mean. How can I help it? Is not fame power? Is not money a double power, strong to assist one's self and those one loves? Is not the world's favour a necessary means to gain these things?"

Zara's eyes gleamed with a soft and pitying gentleness.

"Do you understand what you mean by power?" she asked. "World's fame? World's wealth? Will these things make you enjoy life? You will perhaps say yes. I tell you no. Laurels of earth's growing fade; gold of earth's getting is good for a time, but it palls quickly. Suppose a man rich enough to purchase all the treasures of the world—what then? He must die and leave them. Suppose a poet or musician so famous that all nations know and love him: he too must die, and go where nations exist no longer. And you actually would grasp ashes and drink wormwood, little friend? Music, the heaven-born spirit of pure sound, does not teach you so!"

I was silent. The gleam of the strange jewel Zara always wore flashed in my eyes like lightning, and anon changed to the similitude of a crimson star. I watched it, dreamily fascinated by its unearthly glitter.

"Still," I said, "you yourself admit that such fame as that of Shakespeare or Wagner becomes a universal monument to their memories. That is something, surely?"

"Not to them," replied Zara; "they have partly forgotten that they ever were imprisoned in such a narrow gaol as this world. Perhaps they do not care to remember it, though memory is part of immortality."

"Ah!" I sighed restlessly; "your thoughts go beyond me, Zara. I cannot follow your theories."

Zara smiled.

"We will not talk about them any more," she said; "you must tell Casimir—he will teach you far better than I can."

"What shall I tell him?" I asked; "and what will he teach me?"

"You will tell him what a high opinion you have of the world and its judgments," said Zara, "and he will teach you that the world is no more than a grain of dust, measured by the standard of your own soul. This is no mere platitude—no repetition of the poetical statement 'THE MIND'S THE STANDARD OF THE MAN;' it is a fact, and can be proved as completely as that two and two make four. Ask Casimir to set you free."

"To set me free?" I asked, surprised.

"Yes!" and Zara looked at me brightly. "He will know if you are strong enough to travel!" And, nodding her head gaily to me, she left the room to prepare for the dinner-hour which was fast approaching.

I pondered over her words a good deal without arriving at any satisfactory conclusion as to the meaning of them. I did not resume the conversation with her, nor did I speak to Heliobas as yet, and the days went on smoothly and pleasantly till I had been nearly a week in residence at the Hotel Mars. I now felt perfectly well and strong, though Heliobas continued to give me his remedies regularly night and morning. I began an energetic routine of musical practice: the beautiful piano in the drawing-room answered readily to my touch, and many a delightful hour slipped by as I tried various new difficulties on the keyboard, or worked out different combinations of harmony. I spent a great deal of my time at the organ in the little chapel, the bellows of which were worked by electricity, in a manner that gave not the least trouble, and was perfectly simple of management.

The organ itself was peculiarly sweet in tone, the "vox humana" stop especially producing an entrancingly rich and tender sound. The silence, warmth, and beauty of the chapel, with the winter sunlight streaming through its stained windows, and the unbroken solitude I enjoyed there, all gave fresh impetus to the fancies of my brain, and a succession of solemn and tender melodies wove themselves under my fingers as a broidered carpet is woven on the loom.

One particular afternoon, I was sitting at the instrument as usual, and my thoughts began to busy themselves with the sublime tragedy of Calvary. I mused, playing softly all the while, on the wonderful, blameless, glorious life that had ended in the shame and cruelty of the Cross, when suddenly, like a cloud swooping darkly across the heaven of my thoughts, came the suggestive question: "Is it all true? Was Christ indeed Divine—or is it all a myth, a fable—an imposture?" Unconsciously I struck a discordant chord on the organ—a faint tremor shook me, and I ceased playing. An uncomfortable sensation came over me, as of some invisible presence being near me and approaching softly, slowly, yet always more closely; and I hurriedly rose from my seat, shut the organ, and prepared to leave the chapel, overcome by a strange incomprehensible terror. I was glad when I found myself safely outside the door, and I rushed into the hall as though I were being pursued; yet the oddest part of my feeling was, that whoever thus pursued me, did so out of love, not enmity, and that I was almost wrong in running away. I leaned for a moment against one of the columns in the hall, trying to calm the excited beating of my heart, when a deep voice startled me:

"So! you are agitated and alarmed! Unbelief is easily scared!"

I looked up and met the calm eyes of Heliobas. He appeared to be taller, statelier, more like a Chaldean prophet or king than I had ever seen him before. There was something in his steady scrutiny of my face that put me to a sort of shame, and when he spoke again it was in a tone of mild reproof.

"You have been led astray, my child, by the conflicting and vain opinions of mankind. You, like many others in the world, delight to question, to speculate, to weigh this, to measure that, with little or no profit to yourself or your fellow-creatures. And you have come freshly from a land where, in the great Senate-house, a poor perishable lump of clay calling itself a man, dares to stand up boldly and deny the existence of God, while his compeers, less bold than he, pretend a holy displeasure, yet secretly support him—all blind worms denying the existence of the sun; a land where so-called Religion is split into hundreds of cold and narrow sects, gatherings assembled for the practice of hypocrisy, lip-service and lies—where Self, not the Creator, is the prime object of worship; a land, mighty once among the mightiest, but which now, like an over-ripe pear, hangs loosely on its tree, awaiting but a touch to make it fall! A land—let me not name it;—where the wealthy, high-fed ministers of the nation slowly argue away the lives of better men than themselves, with vain words of colder and more cruel force than the whirling spears of untaught savages! What have you, an ardent disciple of music, to do in such a land where favouritism and backstair influence win the day over even the merits of a Schubert? Supposing you were a second Beethoven, what could you do in that land without faith or hope? that land which is like a disappointed, churlish, and aged man with tottering feet and purblind eyes, who has long ago exhausted all enjoyment and sees nothing new under the sun. The world is wide—faith is yet extant—and the teachings of Christ are true. 'Believe and live; doubt and die!' That saying is true also."

I had listened to these words in silence; but now I spoke eagerly and impatiently, remembering what Zara had told me.

"Then," I said, "if I have been misguided by modern opinions—if I have unconsciously absorbed the doctrines of modern fashionable atheism—lead me right. Teach me what you know. I am willing to learn. Let me find out the reason of my life. SET ME FREE!"

Heliobas regarded me with earnest solemnity.

"Set you free!" he murmured, in a low tone. "Do you know what you ask?"

"No," I answered, with reckless fervour. "I do not know what I ask; but I feel that you have the power to show me the unseen things of another world. Did you not yourself tell me in our first interview that you had let Raffaello Cellini 'go on a voyage of discovery, and that he came back perfectly satisfied?' Besides, he told me his history. From you he has gained all that gives him peace and comfort. You possess electric secrets undreamt of by the world. Prove your powers upon me; I am not afraid."

Heliobas smiled. "Not afraid! And you ran out of the chapel just now as if you were pursued by a fiend! You must know that the only

WOMAN I ever tried my greatest experiment upon is my sister Zara. She was trained and prepared for it in the most careful manner; and it succeeded. Now"—and Heliobas looked half-sad, half-triumphant— "she has passed beyond my power; she is dominated by one greater than I. But she cannot use her force for others; she can only employ it to defend herself. Therefore, I am willing to try you if you indeed desire it—to see if the same thing will occur to you as to Zara; and I firmly believe it will."

A slight tremor came over me; but I said with an attempt at indifference:

"You mean that I shall be dominated also by some great force or influence?"

"I think so," replied Heliobas musingly. "Your nature is more prone to love than to command. Try and follow me in the explanation I am going to give you. Do you know some lines by Shelley that run—

> "*Nothing in the world is single,*
> *All things by a law divine*
> *In one another's being mingle—*
> *Why not I with thine?*"

"Yes," I said. "I know the lines well. I used to think them very sentimental and pretty."

"They contain," said Heliobas, "the germ of a great truth, as many of the most fanciful verses of the poets do. As the 'image of a voice' mentioned in the Book of Job hinted at the telephone, and as Shakespeare's 'girdle round the earth' foretold the electric telegraph, so the utterances of the inspired starvelings of the world, known as poets, suggest many more wonders of the universe than may be at first apparent. Poets must always be prophets, or their calling is in vain. Put this standard of judgment to the verse-writers of the day, and where would they be? The English Laureate is no seer: he is a mere relater of pretty stories. Algernon Charles Swinburne has more fire in him, and more wealth of expression, but he does not prophesy; he has a clever way of combining Biblical similes with Provengal passion—et voila tout! The prophets are always poor—the sackcloth and ashes of the world are their portion; and their bodies moulder a hundred years or more in the grave before the world finds out what they meant by their ravings. But apropos of these lines of Shelley. He speaks of the duality of existence. 'Nothing in the world is single.' He might have gone further, and said nothing in the universe is single. Cold and heat, storm and sunshine, good and evil, joy and sorrow—all go in pairs. This double life extends to all the spheres and above the spheres. Do you understand?"

"I understand what you say," I said slowly; "but I cannot see your meaning as applied to myself or yourself."

"I will teach you in a few words," went on Heliobas. "You believe in the soul?"

"Yes."

"Very well. Now realize that there is no soul on this earth that is complete, ALONE. Like everything else, it is dual. It is like half a flame that seeks the other half, and is dissatisfied and restless till it attains its object. Lovers, misled by the blinding light of Love, think they have reached completeness when they are united to the person beloved. Now, in very, very rare cases, perhaps one among a thousand, this desirable result is effected; but the majority of people are content with the union of bodies only, and care little or nothing about the sympathy or attachment between souls. There are people, however, who do care, and who never find their Twin-Flame or companion Spirit at all on earth, and never will find it. And why? Because it is not imprisoned in clay; it is elsewhere."

"Well?" I asked eagerly.

"Well, you seem to ask me by your eyes what this all means. I will apply it at once to myself. By my researches into human electrical science, I discovered that MY companion, MY other half of existence, though not on earth, was near me, and could be commanded by me; and, on being commanded, obeyed. With Zara it was different. She could not COMMAND—she OBEYED; she was the weaker of the two. With you, I think it will be the same thing. Men sacrifice everything to ambition; women to love. It is natural. I see there is much of what I have said that appears to have mystified you; it is no good puzzling your brain any more about it. No doubt you think I am talking very wildly about Twin-Flames and Spiritual Affinities that live for us in another sphere. You do not believe, perhaps, in the existence of beings in the very air that surrounds us, invisible to ordinary human eyes, yet actually akin to us, with a closer relationship than any tie of blood known on earth?"

I hesitated. Heliobas saw my hesitation, and his eyes darkened with a sombre wrath.

"Are you one of those also who must see in order to believe?" he said, half angrily. "Where do you suppose your music comes from? Where do you suppose any music comes from that is not mere imitation? The greatest composers of the world have been mere receptacles of sound; and the emptier they were of self-love and vanity, the greater quantity of heaven-born melody they held. The German Wagner—did he not himself say that he walked up and down in the avenues, 'trying to catch the harmonies as they floated in the air'? Come with me—come back to the place you left, and I will see if you, like Wagner, are able to catch a melody flying."

He grasped my unresisting arm, and led me, half-frightened, half-curious, into the little chapel, where he bade me seat myself at the organ.

"Do not play a single note," he said, "till you are compelled."

And standing beside me, Heliobas laid his hands on my head, then pressed them on my ears, and finally touched my hands, that rested passively on the keyboard.

He then raised his eyes, and uttered the name I had often thought of but never mentioned—the name he had called upon in my dream.

"Azul!" he said, in a low, penetrating voice, "open the gateways of the Air that we may hear the sound of Song!"

A soft rushing noise of wind answered his adjuration. This was followed by a burst of music, transcendently lovely, but unlike any music I had ever heard. There were sounds of delicate and entrancing tenderness such as no instrument made by human hands could produce; there was singing of clear and tender tone, and of infinite purity such as no human voices could be capable of. I listened, perplexed, alarmed, yet entranced. Suddenly I distinguished a melody running through the wonderful air-symphonies—a melody like a flower, fresh and perfect. Instinctively I touched the organ and began to play it; I found I could produce it note for note. I forgot all fear in my delight, and I played on and on in a sort of deepening rapture. Gradually I became aware that the strange sounds about me were dying slowly away; fainter and fainter they grew—softer—farther—and finally ceased. But the melody—that one distinct passage of notes I had followed out—remained with me, and I played it again and again with feverish eagerness lest it should escape me. I had forgotten the presence of Heliobas. But a touch on my shoulder roused me. I looked up and met his eyes fixed upon, me with a steady and earnest regard. A shiver ran through, me, and I felt bewildered.

"Have I lost it?" I asked.

"Lost what?" he demanded.

"The tune I heard—the harmonies."

"No," he replied; "at least I think not. But if you have, no matter. You will hear others. Why do you look so distressed?"

"It is lovely," I said wistfully, "all that music; but it is not MINE;" and tears of regret filled my eyes. "Oh, if it were only mine—my very own composition!"

Heliobas smiled kindly.

"It is as much yours as any thing belongs to anyone. Yours? why, what can you really call your own? Every talent you have, every breath you draw, every drop of blood flowing in your veins, is lent to you only; you must pay it all back. And as far as the arts go, it is a bad sign of poet, painter, or musician, who is arrogant enough to call his work his own. It never was his, and never will be. It is planned by a higher intelligence than his, only he happens to be the hired labourer chosen to carry out the conception; a sort of mechanic in whom boastfulness looks absurd; as absurd as if one of the stonemasons working at the cornice of a cathedral were to vaunt himself as the designer of the whole edifice. And when a work, any work, is completed, it passes out of the labourer's hands; it belongs to the age and the people for whom it was accomplished, and, if deserving, goes on belonging to future ages and future peoples. So far, and only so far, music is your own. But are you convinced? or do you think you have been dreaming all that you heard just now?"

I rose from the organ, closed it gently, and, moved by a sudden impulse, held out both my hands to Heliobas. He took them and held them in a friendly clasp, watching me intently as I spoke.

"I believe in YOU," I said firmly; "and I know thoroughly well that I was not dreaming; I certainly heard strange music, and entrancing voices. But in acknowledging your powers over something unseen, I must explain to you the incredulity I at first felt, which I believe annoyed you. I was made sceptical on one occasion, by attending a so-called spiritual seance, where they tried to convince me of the truth of table-turning—"

Heliobas laughed softly, still holding my hands.

"Your reason will at once tell you that disembodied spirits never become so undignified as to upset furniture or rap on tables. Neither do they write letters in pen and ink and put them under doors. Spiritual beings are purely spiritual; they cannot touch anything human, much less deal in such vulgar display as the throwing about of chairs, and the opening of locked sideboards. You were very rightly sceptical in these matters. But in what I have endeavoured to prove to you, you have no doubts, have you?"

"None in the world," I said. "I only ask you to go on teaching me the wonders that seem so familiar to you. Let me know all I may; and soon!" I spoke with trembling eagerness.

"You have been only eight days in the house, my child," said Heliobas, loosening my hands, and signing me to come out of the chapel with him; "and I do not consider you sufficiently strong as yet for the experiment you wish me to try upon you. Even now you are agitated. Wait one week more, and then you shall be—"

"What?" I asked impatiently.

"Lifted up," he replied. "Lifted up above this little speck called earth. But now, no more of this. Go to Zara; keep your mind well employed; study, read, and pray—pray much and often in few and simple words, and with as utterly unselfish a heart as you can prepare. Think that you are going to some high festival, and attire your soul in readiness. I do not say to you 'Have faith;' I would not compel your belief in anything against your own will. You wish to be convinced of a future existence; you seek proofs; you shall have them. In the meantime avoid all conversation with me on the subject. You can confide your desires to Zara if you like; her experience may be of use to you. You had best join her now. Au revoir!" and with a kind parting gesture, he left me.

I watched his stately figure disappear in the shadow of the passage leading to his own study, and then I hastened to Zara's room. The musical episode in the chapel had certainly startled me, and the words of Heliobas were full of mysterious meaning; but, strange to say, I was in no way rendered anxious or alarmed by the prospect I had before me of being "lifted up," as my physician had expressed it. I thought of Raffaello Cellini and his history, and I determined within myself that no cowardly hesitation or fear should prevent me from making the attempt to see what he professed to have seen. I found Zara reading. She looked up as I entered, and greeted me with her usual bright smile.

"You have had a long practice," she began; "I thought you were never coming."

I sat down beside her, and related at once all that had happened to me that afternoon. Zara listened with deep and almost breathless interest.

"You are quite resolved," she said, when I had concluded, "to let Casimir exert his force upon you?"

"I am quite resolved," I answered.

"And you have no fear?"

"None that I am just now conscious of."

Zara's eyes became darker and deeper in the gravity of her intense meditation. At last she said:

"I can help you to keep your courage firmly to the point, by letting you know at once what Casimir will do to you. Beyond that I cannot go. You understand the nature of an electric shock?"

"Yes," I replied.

"Well, there are different kinds of electric shocks—some that are remedial, some that are fatal. There are cures performed by a careful use of the electric battery—again, people are struck dead by lightning, which is the fatal result of electric force. But all this is EXTERNAL electricity; now what Casimir will use on you will be INTERNAL electricity."

I begged her to explain more clearly. She went on:

"You have internally a certain amount of electricity, which has been increased recently by the remedies prescribed for you by Casimir. But, however much you have, Casimir has more, and he will exert his force over your force, the greater over the lesser. You will experience an INTERNAL electric shock, which, like a sword, will separate in twain body and spirit. The spiritual part of you will be lifted up above material forces; the bodily part will remain inert and useless, till the life, which is actually YOU, returns to put its machinery in motion once more."

"But shall I return at all?" I asked half doubtfully.

"You must return, because God has fixed the limits of your life on earth, and no human power can alter His decree. Casimir's will can set you free for a time, but only for a time. You are bound to return, be it never so reluctantly. Eternal liberty is given by Death alone, and Death cannot be forced to come."

"How about suicide?" I asked.

"The suicide," replied Zara, "has no soul. He kills his body, and by the very act proves that whatever germ of an immortal existence he may have had once, has escaped from its unworthy habitation, and gone, like a flying spark, to find a chance of growth elsewhere. Surely your own reason proves this to you? The very animals have more soul than a man who commits suicide. The beasts of prey slay each other for hunger or in self-defence, but they do not slay themselves. That is a brutality left to man alone, with its companion degradation, drunkenness."

I mused awhile in silence.

"In all the wickedness and cruelty of mankind," I said, "it is almost a wonder that there is any spiritual existence left on earth at all. Why should God trouble Himself to care for such few souls as thoroughly believe in and love Him?—they can be but a mere handful."

"Such a mere handful are worth more than the world to him," said Zara gravely. "Oh, my dear, do not say such things as why should God trouble Himself? Why do you trouble yourself for the safety and happiness of anyone you love?"

Her eyes grew soft and tender, and the jewel she wore glimmered like moonlight on the sea. I felt a little abashed, and, to change the subject, I said:

"Tell me, Zara, what is that stone you always wear? Is it a talisman?"

"It belonged to a king," said Zara,—"at least, it was found in a king's coffin. It has been in our family for generations. Casimir says it is an electric stone—there are such still to be found in remote parts of the sea. Do you like it?"

"It is very brilliant and lovely," I said.

"When I die," went on Zara slowly, "I will leave it to you."

"I hope I shall have to wait a long time before I get it, then," I exclaimed, embracing her affectionately. "Indeed, I will pray never to receive it."

"You will pray wrongly," said Zara, smiling. "But tell me, do you quite understand from my explanation what Casimir will do to you?"

"I think I do."

"And you are not afraid?"

"Not at all. Shall I suffer any pain?"

"No actual pang. You will feel giddy for a moment, and your body will become unconscious. That is all."

I meditated for a few moments, and then looking up, saw Zara's eyes watching me with a wistful inquiring tenderness. I answered her look with a smile, and said, half gaily:

"L'audace, l'audace, et toujours l'audace! That must be my motto, Zara. I have a chance now of proving how far a woman's bravery can go, and I assure you I am proud of the opportunity. Your brother uttered some very cutting remarks on the general inaptitude of the female sex when I first made his acquaintance; so, for the honour of the thing,

I must follow the path I have begun to tread. A plunge into the unseen world is surely a bold step for a woman, and I am determined to take it courageously."

"That is well," said Zara. "I do not think it possible for you ever to regret it. It is growing late—shall we prepare for dinner?"

I assented, and we separated to our different rooms. Before commencing to dress I opened the pianette that stood near my window, and tried very softly to play the melody I had heard in the chapel. To my joy it came at once to my fingers, and I was able to remember every note. I did not attempt to write it down—somehow I felt sure it would not escape me now. A sense of profound gratitude filled my heart, and, remembering the counsel given by Heliobas, I knelt reverently down and thanked God for the joy and grace of music. As I did so, a faint breath of sound, like a distant whisper of harps played in unison, floated past my ears,—then appeared to sweep round in ever-widening circles, till it gradually died away. But it was sweet and entrancing enough for me to understand how glorious and full of rapture must have been the star-symphony played on that winter's night long ago, when the angels chanted together, "Glory to God in the highest, and on earth peace and good-will to Man!"

IX

AN ELECTRIC SHOCK

Prince Ivan Petroffsky was a constant visitor at the Hotel Mars, and I began to take a certain interest in him, not unmingled with pity, for it was evident that he was hopelessly in love with my beautiful friend Zara. She received him always with courtesy and kindness; but her behaviour to him was marked by a somewhat cold dignity, which, like a barrier of ice, repelled the warmth of his admiration and attention. Once or twice, remembering what he had said to me, I endeavoured to speak to her concerning him and his devotion; but she so instantly and decisively turned the conversation that I saw I should displease her if I persisted in it. Heliobas appeared to be really attached to the Prince, at which I secretly wondered; the worldly and frivolous young nobleman was of so entirely different a temperament to that of the thoughtful and studious Chaldean philosopher. Yet there was evidently some mysterious attraction between them—the Prince appeared to be profoundly interested in electric theories and experiments, and Heliobas never wearied of expounding them to so attentive a listener. The wonderful capabilities of the dog Leo also were brought into constant requisition for Prince Ivan's benefit, and without doubt they were most remarkable. This animal, commanded—or, I should say, brain-electrified—by Heliobas, would fetch anything that was named to him through his master's force, providing it was light enough for him to carry; and he would go into the conservatory and pluck off with his teeth any rare or common flower within his reach that was described to him by the same means. Spoken to or commanded by others, he was simply a good-natured intelligent Newfoundland; but under the authority of Heliobas, he became more than human in ready wit and quick obedience, and would have brought in a golden harvest to any great circus or menagerie.

He was a never-failing source of wonder and interest to me, and even more so to the Prince, who made him the subject of many an abstruse and difficult discussion with his friend Casimir. I noticed that Zara seemed to regret the frequent companionship of Ivan Petroffsky and her brother, and a shade of sorrow or vexation often crossed her fair face when she saw them together absorbed in conversation or argument.

One evening a strange circumstance occurred which startled and deeply impressed me. Prince Ivan had dined with us; he was in extraordinarily high spirits—his gaiety was almost boisterous, and his face was deeply flushed. Zara glanced at him half indignantly more than once when his laughter became unusually uproarious, and I saw that Heliobas watched him closely and half-inquiringly, as if he thought there was something amiss.

The Prince, however, heedless of his host's observant eye, tossed off glass after glass of wine, and talked incessantly. After dinner, when we all assembled in the drawing-room, he seated himself at the piano without being asked, and sang several songs. Whether he were influenced by drink or strong excitement, his voice at any rate showed no sign of weakness or deterioration. Never had I heard him sing so magnificently. He seemed possessed not by an angel but by a demon of song. It was impossible not to listen to him, and while listening, equally impossible not to admire him. Even Zara, who was generally indifferent to his music, became, on this particular night, fascinated into a sort of dreamy attention. He perceived this, and suddenly addressed himself to her in softened tones which bore no trace of their previous loudness.

"Madame, you honour me to-night by listening to my poor efforts. It is seldom I am thus rewarded!"

Zara flushed deeply, and then grew very pale.

"Indeed, Prince," she answered quietly, "you mistake me. I always listen with pleasure to your singing—to-night, perhaps, my mood is more fitted to music than is usual with me, and thus I may appear to you to be more attentive. But your voice always delights me as it must delight everybody who hears it."

"While you are in a musical mood then," returned Prince Ivan, "let me sing you an English song—one of the loveliest ever penned. I have set it to music myself, as such words are not of the kind to suit ordinary composers or publishers; they are too much in earnest, too passionate, too full of real human love and sorrow. The songs that suit modern drawing-rooms and concert-halls, as a rule, are those that are full of sham sentiment—a real, strong, throbbing HEART pulsing through a song is too terribly exciting for lackadaisical society. Listen!" And, playing a dreamy, murmuring prelude like the sound of a brook flowing through a hollow cavern, he sang Swinburne's "Leave-Taking," surely one of the saddest and most beautiful poems in the English language.

He subdued his voice to suit the melancholy hopelessness of the lines, and rendered it with so much intensity of pathetic expression that it was difficult to keep tears from filling the eyes. When he came to the last verse, the anguish of a wasted life seemed to declare itself in the complete despair of his low vibrating tones:

> *"Let us go hence and rest; she will not love.*
> *She shall not hear us if we sing hereof,*
> *Nor see love's ways, how sore they are and steep.*
> *Come hence, let be, lie still; it is enough.*
> *Love is a barren sea, bitter and deep;*
> *And though she saw all heaven in flower above,*
> *She would not love!"*

The deep melancholy of the music and the quivering pathos of the deep baritone voice were so affecting that it was almost a relief when the song ceased. I had been looking out of the window at the fantastic patterns of the moonlight on the garden walk, but now I turned to see in Zara's face her appreciation of what we had just heard. To my surprise she had left the room. Heliobas reclined in his easy-chair, glancing up and down the columns of the Figaro; and the Prince still sat at the piano, moving his fingers idly up and down the keys without playing. The little page entered with a letter on a silver salver. It was for his master. Heliobas read it quickly, and rose, saying:

"I must leave you to entertain yourselves for ten minutes while I answer this letter. Will you excuse me?" and with the ever-courteous salute to us which was part of his manner, he left the room.

I still remained at the window. Prince Ivan still dumbly played the piano. There were a few minutes of absolute silence. Then the Prince hastily got up, shut the piano, and approached me.

"Do you know where Zara is?" he demanded in a low, fierce tone.

I looked at him in surprise and a little alarm—he spoke with so much suppressed anger, and his eyes glittered so strangely.

"No," I answered frankly. "I never saw her leave the room."

"I did," he said. "She slipped out like a ghost, or a witch, or an angel, while I was singing the last verse of Swinburne's song. Do you know Swinburne, mademoiselle?"

"No," I replied, wondering at his manner more and more. "I only know him, as you do, to be a poet."

"Poet, madman, or lover—all three should be one and the same thing," muttered the Prince, clenching and unclenching that strong right hand of his on which sparkled a diamond like a star. "I have often wondered if poets feel what they write—whether Swinburne, for instance, ever felt the weight of a dead cold thing within him Here," slightly touching the region of his heart, "and realized that he had to drag that corpse of unburied love with him everywhere—even to the grave, and beyond— O God!—beyond the grave!" I touched him gently on the arm. I was full of pity for him—his despair was so bitter and keen.

"Prince Ivan," I said, "you are excited and overwrought. Zara meant no slight to you in leaving the room before your song was finished. I am quite sure of that. She is kindness itself—her nature is all sweetness and gentleness. She would not willingly offend you—"

"Offend me!" he exclaimed; "she could not offend me if she tried. She could tread upon me, stab me, slay me, but never offend me. I see you are sorry for me—and I thank you. I kiss your hand for your gentle pity, mademoiselle."

And he did so, with a knightly grace that became him well. I thought his momentary anger was passing, but I was mistaken. Suddenly he raised his arm with a fierce gesture, and exclaimed:

"By heaven! I will wait no longer. I am a fool to hesitate. I may wait a century before I draw out of Casimir the secret that would enable me to measure swords with my rival. Listen!" and he grasped my shoulder roughly. "Stay here, you! If Casimir returns, tell him I have gone for a walk of half an hour. Play to him—keep him occupied—be my friend in this one thing—I trust you. Let him not seek for Zara, or for me. I shall not be long absent."

"Stay!" I whispered hurriedly, "What are you going to do? Surely you know the power of Heliobas. He is supreme here. He could find out anything he chose. He could—"

Prince Ivan looked at me fixedly.

"Will you swear to me that you actually do not know?"

"Know what?" I asked, perplexed.

He laughed bitterly, sarcastically.

"Did you ever hear that line of poetry which speaks of 'A woman wailing for her demon-lover'? That is what Zara does. Of one thing I am certain—she does not wail or wait long; he comes quickly."

MARIE CORELLI

"What do you mean?" I exclaimed, utterly mystified. "Who comes quickly? I am sure you do not know what you are talking about."

"I Do know," he replied firmly; "and I am going to prove my knowledge. Remember what I have asked you." And without another word or look, he threw open the velvet curtains of the portiere, and disappeared behind them.

Left to myself, I felt very nervous and excited. All sorts of odd fancies came into my head, and would not go away, but danced about like Will-o'-the-wisps on a morass. What did Prince Ivan mean? Was he mad? or had he drunk too much wine? What strange illusion had he in his mind about Zara and a demon? Suddenly a thought flashed upon me that made me tremble from head to foot. I remembered what Heliobas had said about twin flames and dual affinities; and I also reflected that he had declared Zara to be dominated by a more powerful force than his own. But then, I had accepted it as a matter of course that, whatever the force was, it must be for good, not evil, over a being so pure, so lovely and so intelligent as Zara.

I knew and felt that there were good and evil forces. Now, suppose Zara were commanded by some strange evil thing, unguessed at, undreamt of in the wildest night-mare? I shuddered as with icy cold. It could not be. I resolutely refused to admit such a fearful conjecture. Why, I thought to myself, with a faint smile, I was no better in my imaginings than the so virtuous and ever-respectable Suzanne Michot of whom Madame Denise had spoken. Still the hateful thought came back again and again, and refused to go away.

I went to my old place at the window and looked out. The moonlight fell in cold slanting rays; but an army of dark clouds were hurrying up from the horizon, looking in their weird shapes like the mounted Walkyres in Wagner's "Niebelungen Ring," galloping to Walhalla with the bodies of dead warriors slung before them. A low moaning wind had arisen, and was beginning to sob round the house like the Banshee. Hark! what was that? I started violently. Surely that was a faint shriek? I listened intently. Nothing but the wind rustling among some creaking branches.

"A woman wailing for her demon-lover."

How that line haunted me! And with, it there slowly grew up in my mind a black looming horror; an idea, vague and ghastly, that froze my blood and turned me faint and giddy. Suppose, when I had consented to be experimented upon by Heliobas—when my soul in the electric trance was lifted up to the unseen world—suppose an evil force, terrible and all-compelling, were to dominate ME and hold me forever and ever! I gasped for breath! Oh, so much the more need of prayer!

"Pray much and often, with as unselfish a heart as you can prepare."

Thus Heliobas had said; and I thought to myself, if all those who were on the brink of great sin or crime could only be brought to feel beforehand what I felt when facing the spectral dread of unknown evil, then surely sins would be fewer and crimes never committed. And I murmured softly, "Lead us not into temptation, but deliver us from evil."

The mere utterance of these words seemed to calm and encourage me; and as I gazed up at the sky again, with its gathering clouds, one star, like a bright consoling eye, looked at me, glittering cheerfully amid the surrounding darkness.

More than ten minutes had elapsed since Prince Ivan had left the room, and there was no sound of returning footsteps. And where was Zara? I determined to seek her. I was free to go anywhere in the house, only avoiding her studio during her hours of work; and she never worked at night. I would go to her and confide all my strange thoughts and terrors to her friendly sympathy. I hurried through the hall and up the staircase quickly, and should have gone straight into Zara's boudoir had I not heard a sound of voices which caused me to stop precipitately outside the door. Zara was speaking. Her low, musical accents fell like a silver chime on the air.

"I have told you," she said, "again and again that it is impossible. You waste your life in the pursuit of a phantom; for a phantom I must be to you always—a mere dream, not a woman such as your love would satisfy. You are a strong man, in sound health and spirits; you care for the world and the things that are in it. I do not. You would make me happy, you say. No doubt you would do your best—your wealth and influence, your good looks, your hospitable and friendly nature would make most women happy. But what should *I* care for your family diamonds? for your surroundings? for your ambitions? The society of the world fills me with disgust and prejudice. Marriage, as the world considers it, shocks and outrages my self-respect; the idea of a bodily union without that of souls is to me repulsive and loathsome. Why, therefore, waste your time in seeking a love which does not exist, which never will exist for you?"

I heard the deep, passionate tones of Prince Ivan in answer:

"One light kindles another, Zara! The sunlight melts the snow! I cannot believe but that a long and faithful love may—nay, Must—have its reward at last. Even according to your brother's theories, the emotion of love is capable of powerful attraction. Cannot I hope that my passion—so strong, so great, so true, Zara!—will, with patience, draw you, star of my life, closer and closer, till I at last call you mine?"

I heard the faint rustle of Zara's silk robe, as though she were moving farther from him.

"You speak ignorantly, Prince. Your studies with Casimir appear to have brought you little knowledge. Attraction! How can you attract what is not in your sphere? As well ask for the Moons of Jupiter or the Ring of Saturn! The laws of attraction and repulsion, Prince Ivan, are fixed by a higher authority than yours, and you are as powerless to alter or abate them by one iota, as a child is powerless to repel the advancing waves of the sea."

Prince Ivan spoke again, and his voice quivered, with suppressed anger.

"You may talk as you will, beautiful Zara; but you shall never persuade me against my reason. I am no dreamer; no speculator in aerial nothings; no clever charlatan like Casimir, who, because he is able to magnetize a dog, pretends to the same authority over human beings, and dares to risk the health, perhaps the very sanity, of his own sister, and that of the unfortunate young musician whom he has inveigled in here, all for the sake of proving his dangerous, almost diabolical, experiments. Oh, yes; I see you are indignant, but I speak truth. I am a plain man;—and if I am deficient in electric germs, as Casimir would say, I have plenty of common sense. I wish to rescue you, Zara. You are becoming a prey to morbid fancies; your naturally healthy mind is full of extravagant notions concerning angels and demons and what not; and your entire belief in, and enthusiasm for, your brother is a splendid advertisement for him. Let me tear the veil of credulity from your eyes. Let me teach you how good a thing it is to live and love and laugh like other people, and leave electricity to the telegraph-wires and the lamp-posts."

Again I heard the silken rustle of Zara's dress, and, impelled by a strong curiosity and excitement, I raised a corner of the curtain hanging over the door, and was able to see the room distinctly. The Prince stood, or rather lounged, near the window, and opposite to him was Zara; she had evidently retreated from him as far as possible, and held herself proudly erect, her eyes flashing with unusual brilliancy contrasted with the pallor of her face.

"Your insults to my brother, Prince," she said calmly, "I suffer to pass by me, knowing well to what a depth of wilful blind ignorance you are fallen. I pity you—and—I despise you! You are indeed a plain man, as you say— nothing more and nothing less. You can take advantage of the hospitality of this house, and pretend friendship to the host, while you slander him behind his back, and insult his sister in the privacy of her own apartment. Very manlike, truly; and perfectly in accordance with a reasonable being who likes to live and love and laugh according to the rule of society—a puppet whose wires society pulls, and he dances or dies as society pleases. I told you a gulf existed between us—you have widened it, for which I thank you! As I do not impose any of my wishes upon you, and therefore cannot request you to leave the room, you must excuse me if *I* retire elsewhere."

And she approached the entrance of her studio, which was opposite to where I stood; but the Prince reached it before her, and placed his back against it. His face was deathly pale, and his dark eyes blazed with wrath and love intermingled.

"No, Zara!" he exclaimed in a sort of loud whisper. "If you think to escape me so, you are in error. I came to you reckless and resolved! You shall be mine if I die for it!" And he strove to seize her in his arms. But she escaped him and stood at bay, her lips quivering, her bosom heaving, and her hands clenched.

"I warn you!" she exclaimed. "By the intense loathing I have for you; by the force which makes my spirit rise in arms against you, I warn you! Do not dare to touch me! If you care for your own life, leave me while there is time!"

Never had she looked so supremely, terribly beautiful. I gazed at her from my corner of the doorway, awed, yet fascinated. The jewel on her breast glowed with an angry red lustre, and shot forth dazzling opaline rays, as though it were a sort of living, breathing star. Prince Ivan paused—entranced no doubt, as I was, by her unearthly loveliness. His face flushed—he gave a low laugh of admiration. Then he made two swift strides forward and caught her fiercely in his embrace. His triumph was brief. Scarcely had his strong arm clasped her waist, when it fell numb and powerless—scarcely had his eager lips stooped towards hers, when he reeled and sank heavily on the ground, senseless! The spell that had held me a silent spectator of the scene was broken. Terrified, I rushed into the room, crying out:

"Zara, Zara! What have you done?"

Zara turned her eyes gently upon me—they were soft and humid as though recently filled with tears. All the burning scorn and indignation had gone out of her face—she looked pityingly at the prostrate form of her admirer.

"He is not dead," she said quietly. "I will call Casimir."

I knelt beside the Prince and raised his hand. It was cold and heavy. His lips were blue, and his closed eyelids looked as though, in the words of Homer, "Death's purple finger" had shut them fast forever. No breath—no pulsation of the heart. I looked fearfully at Zara. She smiled half sadly.

"He is not dead," she repeated.

"Are you sure?" I murmured. "What was it, Zara, that made him fall? I was at the door—I saw and heard everything."

"I know you did," said Zara gently; "and I am glad of it. I wished you to see and hear all."

"Is it a fit, do you think?" I asked again, looking sorrowfully at the sad face of the unfortunate Ivan, which seemed to me to have already graven upon it the stern sweet smile of those who have passed all passion and pain forever. "Oh, Zara! do you believe he will recover?" And tears choked my voice—tears of compassion and regret.

Zara came and kissed me.

"Yes, he will recover—do not fret, little one. I have rung my private bell for Casimir; he will be here directly. The Prince has had a shock—not a fatal one, as you will see. You look doubtful—are you afraid of me, dear?"

I gazed at her earnestly. Those clear childlike eyes—that frank smile—that gentle and dignified mien—could they accompany evil thoughts? No! I was sure Zara was good as she was lovely.

"I am not afraid of you, Zara," I said gravely; "I love you too well for that. But I am sorry for the poor Prince; and I cannot understand—"

"You cannot understand why those who trespass against fixed laws should suffer?" observed Zara calmly. "Well, you will understand some day. You will know that in one way or another it is the reason of all suffering, both physical and mental, in the world."

I said no more, but waited in silence till the sound of a firm approaching footstep announced Heliobas. He entered the room quickly—glanced at the motionless form of the Prince, then at me, and lastly at his sister.

"Has he been long thus?" he asked in a low tone.

"Not five minutes," replied Zara.

A pitying and affectionate gentleness of expression filled his keen eyes.

"Reckless boy!" he murmured softly, as he stooped and laid one hand lightly on Ivan's breast. "He is the very type of misguided human bravery. You were too hard upon him, Zara!"

Zara sighed.

"He spoke against you," she said. "Of course he did," returned her brother with a smile. "And it was perfectly natural he should do so. Have I not read his thoughts? Do not I know that he considers me a false pretender and CHARLATAN? And have I not humoured him? In this he is no worse than any one of his race. Every great scientific discovery is voted impossible at the first start. Ivan is not to blame because he is like the rest of the world. He will be wiser in time."

"He attempted to force his desires," began Zara again, and her cheeks flushed indignantly.

"I know," answered her brother. "I foresaw how it would be, but was powerless to prevent it. He was wrong—but bold! Such boldness compels a certain admiration. This fellow would scale the stars, if he knew how to do it, by physical force alone."

I grew impatient, and interrupted these remarks.

"Perhaps he is scaling the stars now," I said; "or at any rate he will do so if death can show him the way."

Heliobas gave me a friendly glance.

"You also are growing courageous when you can speak to your physician thus abruptly," he observed quietly. "Death has nothing to do with our friend as yet, I assure you. Zara, you had better leave us. Your face must not be the first for Ivan's eyes to rest upon. You," nodding to me, "can stay."

Zara pressed my hand gently as she passed me, and entered her studio, the door of which closed behind her, and I heard the key turn in the lock. I became absorbed in the proceedings of Heliobas. Stooping towards the recumbent form of Prince Ivan, he took the heavy lifeless hands firmly in his own, and then fixed his eyes fully and steadily on the pale, set features with an expression of the most forcible calm and absolutely undeniable authority. Not one word did he utter, but remained motionless as a statue in the attitude thus assumed—he seemed scarcely to breathe—not a muscle of his countenance moved. Perhaps twenty or

MARIE CORELLI

thirty seconds might have elapsed, when a warm tinge of colour came back to the apparently dead face—the brows twitched—the lips quivered and parted in a heavy sigh. The braised appearance of the eyelids gave place to the natural tint—they opened, disclosing the eyes, which stared directly into those of the compelling Master who thus forced their obedience. A strong shudder shook the young man's frame; his before nerveless hands grasped those of Heliobas with force and fervour, and still meeting that steady look which seemed to pierce the very centre of his system, Prince Ivan, like Lazarus of old, arose and stood erect. As he did so, Heliobas withdrew his eyes, dropped his hands and smiled.

"You are better, Ivan?" he inquired kindly.

The Prince looked about him, bewildered. He passed one hand across his forehead without replying. Then he turned slightly and perceived me in the window-embrasure, whither I had retreated in fear and wonderment at the marvellous power of Heliobas, thus openly and plainly displayed.

"Tell me," he said, addressing me, "have I been dreaming?"

I could not answer him. I was glad to see him recover, yet I was a little afraid. Heliobas pushed a chair gently towards him.

"Sit down, Ivan," he said quietly.

The Prince obeyed, and covered his face with his hand as though in deep and earnest meditation. I looked on in silence and wonderment. Heliobas spoke not another word, and together we watched the pensive figure in the chair, so absorbed in serious thought. Some minutes passed. The gentle tick of the clock in the outer hall grew almost obtrusive, so loud did it seem in the utter stillness that surrounded us. I longed to speak—to ask questions—to proffer sympathy—but dared not move or utter a syllable. Suddenly the Prince rose; his manner was calm and dignified, yet touched with a strange humility. He advanced to Heliobas, holding out his hand.

"Forgive me, Casimir!" he said simply.

Heliobas at once grasped the proffered palm within his own, and looked at the young man with an almost fatherly tenderness.

"Say no more, Ivan," he returned, his rich voice sounding more than usually mellow in its warmth and heartiness. "We must all learn before we can know, and some of our lessons are sharp and difficult. Whatever you have thought of me, remember I have not, and do not, blame you. To be offended with unbelievers is to show that you are not yourself quite sure of the faith to which you would compel them."

"I would ask you one thing," went on the Prince, speaking in a low tone. "Do not let me stay to fall into fresh errors. Teach me—guide me, Casimir; I will be the most docile of your pupils. As for Zara—"

He paused, as if overcome.

"Come with me," said Heliobas, taking his arm; "a glass of good wine will invigorate you. It is better to see Zara no more for a time. Let me take charge of you. You, mademoiselle," turning to me, "will be kind enough to tell Zara that the Prince has recovered, and sends her a friendly good-night. Will that message suffice?" he inquired of Ivan, with a smile.

The Prince looked at me with a sort of wistful gravity as I came forward to bid him farewell.

"You will embrace her," he said slowly, "without fear. Her eyes will rain sunshine upon you; they will not dart lightning. Her lips will meet yours, and their touch will be warm—not cold, as sharp steel. Yes; bid her good-night for me; tell her that an erring man kisses the hem of her robe, and prays her for pardon. Tell her that I understand; tell her I have seen her lover!"

"With these words, uttered distinctly and emphatically, he turned away with. Heliobas, who still held him by the arm in a friendly, half-protecting manner. The tears stood in my eyes. I called softly:

"Good-night, Prince Ivan!"

He looked back with a faint smile.

"Good-night, mademoiselle!"

Heliobas also looked back and gave me an encouraging nod, which meant several things at once, such as "Do not be anxious," "He will be all right soon," and "Always believe the best." I watched their two figures disappear through the doorway, and then, feeling almost cheerful again, I knocked at the door of Zara's studio. She opened it at once, and came out. I delivered the Prince's message, word for word, as he had given it. She listened, and sighed deeply.

"Are you sorry for him, Zara?" I asked.

"Yes," she replied; "I am sorry for him as far as I can be sorry for anything. I am never actually VERY sorry for any circumstances, however grievous they may appear."

I was surprised at this avowal.

"Why, Zara," I said, "I thought you were so keenly sympathetic?"

"So I am sympathetic, but only with suffering ignorance—a dying bird that knows not why it should die—a withering rose that sees not the reason for its withering; but for human beings who wilfully blind themselves to the teachings of their own instincts, and are always doing what they know they ought not to do in spite of warning, I cannot say I am sorry. And for those who Do study the causes and ultimate results of their existence, there is no occasion to be sorry, as they are perfectly happy, knowing everything that happens to them to be for their advancement and justification."

"Tell me," I asked with a little hesitation, "what did Prince Ivan mean by saying he had seen your lover, Zara?"

"He meant what he said, I suppose," replied Zara, with sudden coldness. "Excuse me, I thought you said you were not inquisitive."

I could not bear this change of tone in her, and I clasped my arms tight about her and smiled in her face.

"You shall not get angry with ME, Zara. I am not going to be treated like poor Ivan. I have found out what you are, and how dangerous it is to admire you; but I do admire and love you. And I defy you to knock me down as unceremoniously as you did the Prince—you beautiful living bit of Lightning!"

Zara moved restlessly in my embrace, but I held her fast. At the last epithet I bestowed on her, she grew very pale; but her eyes resembled the jewels on her breast in their sheeny glitter.

"What have you found out?" she murmured. "What do you know?"

"I cannot say I KNOW," I went on boldly, still keeping my arms round her; "but I have made a guess which I think comes near the truth. Your brother has had the care of you ever since you were a little child, and I believe he has, by some method known only to himself, charged you with electricity. Yes, Zara," for she had started and tried to loosen my hold of her; "and it is that which keeps you young and fresh as a girl of sixteen, at an age when other women lose their bloom and grow wrinkles. It is that which gives you the power to impart a repelling shock to people you dislike, as in the case of Prince Ivan. It is that which gives you such an attractive force for those with whom you have a little sympathy—such as myself, for instance; and you cannot, Zara, with all your electric strength, unclasp my arms from your waist, because you have not the sentiment of repulsion towards me which would enable you to do it. Shall I go on guessing?"

Zara made a sign of assent—the expression of her face had softened, and a dimpling smile played round the corners of her mouth.

"Your lover," I went on steadily and slowly, "is a native of some other sphere—perhaps a creation of your own fancy—perhaps (for I will not be sceptical any more) a beautiful and all-powerful angelic spirit. I will not discuss this with you. I believe that when Prince Ivan fell senseless, he saw, or fancied he saw, that nameless being. And now," I added, loosening my clasp of her, "have I guessed well?"

Zara looked meditative.

"I do not know," she said, "why you should imagine—"

"Stop!" I exclaimed; "there is no imagination in the case. I have reasoned it out. Here is a book I found in the library on electric organs as they are discovered to exist in certain fish. Listen: 'They are nervous apparatuses which in the arrangement of their parts may be compared to a Voltaic pile. They develop electricity and give electrical discharges.'"

"Well!" said Zara.

"You say 'Well!' as if you did not know!" I exclaimed half-angrily, half-laughingly. "These fish have helped me to understand a great deal, I assure you. Your brother must have discovered the seed or commencement of electrical organs like those described, in the human body; and he has cultivated them in you and in himself, and has brought them to a high state of perfection. He has cultivated them in Raffaello Cellini, and he is beginning to cultivate them in me, and I hope most sincerely he will succeed. I think his theory is a magnificent one!"

Zara gazed seriously at me, and her large eyes seemed to grow darker with the intensity of her thought.

"Supposing you had reasoned out the matter correctly," she said—"and I will not deny that you have done a great deal towards the comprehension of it—have you no fear? do you not include some drawbacks in even Casimir's learning such a secret, and being able to cultivate and educate such a deadly force as that of electricity in the human being?"

"If it is deadly, it is also life-giving," I answered. "Remedies are also poisons. You laid the Prince senseless at your feet, but your brother raised him up again. Both these things were done by electricity. I can understand it all now; I see no obscurity, no mystery. And oh, what a superb discovery it is!"

Zara smiled.

"You enthusiast!" she said, "it is nothing new. It was well known to the ancient Chaldeans. It was known to Moses and his followers; it was practised in perfection by Christ and His disciples. To modern civilization it may seem a discovery, because the tendency Of all so-called progress is to forget the past. The scent of the human savage is extraordinarily keen—keener than that of any animal—he can follow a track unerringly by some odour he is able to detect in the air. Again, he can lay back his ears to the wind and catch a faint, far-off sound with, certainty and precision, and tell you what it is. Civilized beings have forgotten all this; they can neither smell nor hear with actual keenness. Just in the same way, they have forgotten the use of the electrical organs they all indubitably possess in large or minute degree. As the muscles of the arm are developed by practice, so can the wonderful internal electrical apparatus of man be strengthened and enlarged by use. The world in its youth knew this; the world in its age forgets, as an old man forgets or smiles disdainfully at the past sports of his childhood. But do not let us talk any more to-night. If you think your ideas of me are correct—"

"I am sure they are!" I cried triumphantly.

Zara held out her arms to me.

"And you are sure you love me?" she asked.

I nestled into her embrace and kissed her.

"Sure!" I answered. "Zara, I love and honour you more than any woman I ever met or ever shall meet. And you love me—I know you do!"

"How can I help it?" she said. "Are you not one of us? Good-night, dearest! Sleep well!"

"Good-night!" I answered. "And remember Prince Ivan asked for your pardon."

"I remember!" she replied softly. "I have already pardoned him, and I will pray for him." And a sort of radiant pity and forbearance illumined her lovely features, as we parted for the night. So might an angel look on some repentant sinner pleading for Heaven's forgiveness.

I lay awake for some time that night, endeavouring to follow out the track of thought I had entered upon in my conversation with Zara. With such electricity as Heliobas practised, once admitting that human electric force existed, a fact which no reasoning person could deny, all things were possible. Even a knowledge of superhuman events might be attained, if there were anything in the universe that WAS superhuman; and surely it would be arrogant and ignorant to refuse to contemplate such a probability. At one time people mocked at the wild idea that a message could flash in a moment of time from one side of the Atlantic to the other by means of a cable laid under the sea; now that it is an established fact, the world has grown accustomed to it, and has ceased to regard it as a wonder. Granting human electricity to exist, why should not a communication be established, like a sort of spiritual Atlantic cable, between man and the beings of other spheres and other solar systems? The more I reflected on the subject the more lost I became in daring speculations concerning that other world, to which I was soon to be lifted. Then in a sort of half-doze, I fancied I saw an interminable glittering chain of vivid light composed of circles that were all looped one in another, which seemed to sweep round the realms of space and to tie up the sun, moon, and stars like flowers in a ribbon of fire. After much anxious and humble research, I found myself to be one of the smallest links in this great chain. I do not know whether I was grateful or afraid at this discovery, for sleep put an end to my drowsy fancies, and dropped a dark curtain over my waking dreams.

X

My Strange Departure

The next morning brought me two letters; one from Mrs. Everard, telling me that she and the Colonel had resolved on coming to Paris. "All the nice people are going away from here," she wrote. "Madame Didier and her husband have started for Naples; and, to crown our lonesomeness, Raffaello Cellini packed up all his traps, and left us yesterday morning en route for Rome. The weather continues to be delicious; but as you seem to be getting on so well in Paris, in spite of the cold there, we have made up our minds to join you, the more especially as I want to renovate my wardrobe. We shall go straight to the Grand Hotel; and I am writing to Mrs. Challoner by this post, asking her to get us rooms. We are so glad you are feeling nearly recovered—of course, you must not leave your physician till you are quite ready. At any rate, we shall not arrive till the end of next week."

I began to calculate. During that strange interview in the chapel, Heliobas had said that in eight days more I should be strong enough to undergo the transmigration he had promised to effect upon me. Those eight days were now completed on this very morning. I was glad of this; for I did not care to see Mrs. Everard or anyone till the experiment was over. The other letter I received was from Mrs. Challoner, who asked me to give an "Improvisation" at the Grand Hotel that day fortnight.

When I went down to breakfast, I mentioned both these letters, and said, addressing myself to Heliobas:

"Is it not rather a sudden freak of Raffaello Cellini's to leave Cannes? We all thought he was settled for the winter there. Did you know he was going to Rome?"

"Yes," replied Heliobas, as he stirred his coffee abstractedly. "I knew he was going there some day this month; his presence is required there on business."

"And are you going to give the Improvisation this Mrs. Challoner asks you for?" inquired Zara.

I glanced at Heliobas. He answered for me.

"I should certainly give it if I were you," he said quietly: "there will be nothing to prevent your doing so at the date named."

I was relieved. I had not been altogether able to divest myself of the idea that I might possibly never come out alive from the electric trance to which I had certainly consented; and this assurance on the part of Heliobas was undoubtedly comforting. We were all very silent that morning; we all wore grave and preoccupied expressions. Zara was very pale, and appeared lost in thought. Heliobas, too, looked slightly careworn, as though he had been up all night, engaged in some brain-exhausting labour. No mention was made of Prince Ivan; we avoided his name by a sort of secret mutual understanding. When the breakfast was over, I looked with a fearless smile at the calm face of Heliobas, which appeared nobler and more dignified than ever with that slight touch of sadness upon it, and said softly:

"The eight days are accomplished!"

He met my gaze fully, with a steady and serious observation of my features, and replied:

"My child, I am aware of it. I expect you in my private room at noon. In the meantime speak to no one—not even to Zara; read no books; touch no note of music. The chapel has been prepared for you; go there and pray. When you see a small point of light touch the extreme edge of the cross upon the altar, it will be twelve o'clock, and you will then come to me."

With these words, uttered in a grave and earnest tone, he left me. A sensation of sudden awe stole upon me. I looked at Zara. She laid her finger on her lips and smiled, enjoining silence; then drawing my hand close within her own, she led me to the door of the chapel. There she took a soft veil of some white transparent fabric, and flung it over me, embracing and kissing me tenderly as she did so, but uttering no word. Taking my hand again, she entered the chapel with me, and accompanied me through what seemed a blaze of light and colour to the high altar, before which was placed a prie-dieu of crimson velvet. Motioning me to kneel, she kissed me once more through the filmy veil that covered me from head to foot; then turning noiselessly away she disappeared, and I heard the heavy oaken door close behind her. Left alone, I was able to quietly take note of everything around me. The altar before which I knelt was ablaze with lighted candles, and a wealth of the purest white flowers decorated it, mingling their delicious fragrance with the faintly perceptible odour of incense. On all sides of the chapel, in every little niche, and at every shrine, tapers were burning like fireflies in a summer twilight. At the foot of the large crucifix, which occupied a somewhat shadowy corner, lay a wreath of magnificent crimson roses. It would seem as though some high festival were about to be celebrated, and I gazed around me with a beating heart, half expecting some invisible touch to awaken the notes of the organ and a chorus of spirit-voices to respond with the "Gloria in excelsis Deo!" But there was silence—absolute, beautiful, restful silence. I strove to collect my thoughts, and turning my eyes towards the jewelled cross that surmounted the high altar, I clasped my hands, and began to wonder how and for what I should pray. Suddenly the idea struck me that surely it was selfish to ask Heaven for anything; would it not be better to reflect on all that had already been given to me, and to offer up thanks? Scarcely had this thought entered my mind when a sort of overwhelming sense of unworthiness came over me. Had I ever been unhappy? I wondered. If so, why? I began to count up my blessings and compare them with my misfortunes. Exhausted pleasure-seekers may be surprised to hear that I proved the joys of my life to have far exceeded my sorrows. I found that I had sight, hearing, youth, sound limbs, an appreciation of the beautiful in art and nature, and an intense power of enjoyment. For all these things, impossible of purchase by mere wealth, should I not give thanks? For every golden ray of sunshine, for every flower that blooms, for the harmonies of the wind and sea, for the singing of birds and the shadows of trees, should I not—should we not all give thanks? For is there any human sorrow so great that the blessing of mere daylight on the earth does not far exceed? We mortals are spoilt and petted children—the more gifts we have the more we crave; and when we burn or wound ourselves by our own obstinacy or carelessness, we are ungratefully prone to blame the Supreme Benefactor for our own faults. We don black mourning robes as a sort of sombre protest against Him for having removed some special object of our choice and love, whereas, if we believed in Him and were grateful to Him, we should wear dazzling white in sign of rejoicing that our treasure is safe in the land of perfect joy where we ourselves desire to be. Do we suffer from illness, loss of money, position, or friends, we rail against Fate—another name for God—and complain like babes who have broken their toys; yet the sun shines on, the seasons come and go, the lovely panorama of Nature unrolls itself all for our benefit, while we murmur and fret and turn our eyes away in anger.

Thinking of these things and kneeling before the altar, my heart became filled with gratitude; and no petition suggested itself to me save one, and that was, "Let me believe and love!" I thought of the fair, strong, stately figure of Christ, standing out in the world's history, like a statue of pure white marble against a dark background; I mused on the endurance, patience, forgiveness, and perfect innocence of that most spotless life which was finished on the cross, and again I murmured, "Let me believe and love!" And I became so absorbed in meditation that the time fled fast, till a sudden sparkle of flame flashing across the altar-steps caused me to look up. The jewelled cross had become a cross of fire. The point of light I had been, told to watch for had not only touched the extreme edge, but had crept down among all the precious stones and lit them up like stars. I afterwards learned that this effect was produced by means of a thin, electric wire, which, communicating with a timepiece constructed on the same system, illuminated the cross at sunrise, noon, and sunset. It was time for me to join Heliobas. I rose gently, and left the chapel with a quiet and reverent step, for I have always thought that to manifest hurry and impatience in any place set apart for the worship of the Creator is to prove yourself one of the unworthiest things created. Once outside the door I laid aside my veil, and then, with a perfectly composed and fearless mind, went straight to the Electrician's study. I shall never forget the intense quiet of the house that morning. The very fountain in the hall seemed to tinkle in a sort of subdued whisper. I found Heliobas seated at his table, reading. How my dream came vividly back to me, as I saw him in that attitude! I felt that I knew what he was reading. He looked up as I entered, and greeted me with a kindly yet grave smile. I broke silence abruptly.

"Your book is open," I said, "at a passage commencing thus: 'The universe is upheld solely by the Law of Love. A majestic invisible Protectorate governs the winds, the tides.' Is it not so?"

"It is so," returned Heliobas. "Are you acquainted with the book?"

"Only through the dream I had of you at Cannes," I answered. "I do think Signor Cellini had some power over me."

"Of course he had in your then weak state. But now that you are as strong as he is, he could not influence you at all. Let us be brief in our converse, my child. I have a few serious things to say to you before you leave me, on your celestial journey."

I trembled slightly, but took the chair he pointed out to me—a large easy-chair in which one could recline and sleep.

"Listen," continued Heliobas; "I told you, when you first came here, that whatever I might do to restore you to health, you would have it in your power to repay me amply. You ARE restored to health; will you give me my reward?"

"I would and will do anything to prove my gratitude to you," I said earnestly. "Only tell me how."

"You are aware," he went on, "of my theories respecting the Electric Spirit or Soul in Man. It is progressive, as I have told you—it begins as a germ—it goes on increasing in power and beauty for ever, till it is great and pure enough to enter the last of all worlds—God's World. But there are sometimes hindrances to its progression—obstacles in its path, which cause it to recoil and retire a long way back—so far back occasionally that it has to commence its journey over again. Now, by my earnest researches, I am able to study and watch the progress of my own inner force or soul. So far, all has been well—prayerfully and humbly I may say I believe all has been well. But I foresee an approaching shadow—a difficulty—a danger—which, if it cannot be repelled or passed in some way, threatens to violently push back my advancing spiritual nature, so that, with much grief and pain, I shall have to re-commence the work that I had hoped was done. I cannot, with all my best effort, discover WHAT this darkening obstacle is—but You, yes, You"—for I had started up in surprise—"you, when you are lifted up high enough to behold these things, may, being perfectly unselfish in this research, attain to the knowledge of it and explain it to me, when you return. In trying to probe the secret for myself, it is of course purely for my own interest; and nothing clear, nothing satisfactory can be spiritually obtained, in which selfishness has ever so slight a share. You, if indeed I deserve your gratitude for the aid I have given you—you will be able to search out the matter more certainly, being in the position of one soul working for another. Still, I cannot compel you to do this for me—I only ask, WILL you?"

His entreating and anxious tone touched me keenly; but I was amazed and perplexed, and could not yet realize what strange thing was going to happen to me. But whatever occurred I was resolved to give a ready consent to his request, therefore I said firmly:

"I will do my best, I promise you. Remember that I do not know, I cannot even guess where I am going, or what strange sensations will overcome me; but if I am permitted to have any recollection of earth at all, I will try to find out what you ask."

Heliobas seemed satisfied, and rising from his chair, unlocked a heavily-bound iron safe. From this he took a glass flask of a strange, ever-moving, glittering fluid, the same in appearance as that which Raffaello Cellini had forbidden me to drink. He then paused and looked searchingly at me.

"Tell me," he said in an authoritative tone, "tell me WHY you wish to see what to mortals is unseen? What motive have you? What ulterior plan?"

I hesitated. Then I gathered my strength together and answered decisively:

"I desire to know why this world, this universe exists; and also wish to prove, if possible, the truth and necessity of religion. And I think I would give my life, if it were worth anything, to be certain of the truth of Christianity."

Heliobas gazed in my face with a sort of half-pity, half-censure.

"You have a daring aim," he said slowly, "and you are a bold seeker. But shame, repentance and sorrow await you where you are going, as well as rapture and amazement. 'I WOULD GIVE MY LIFE IF IT WERE WORTH ANYTHING.' That utterance has saved you—otherwise to soar into an unexplored wilderness of spheres, weighted by your own doubts and guided solely by your own wild desires, would be a fruitless journey."

I felt abashed as I met his steady, scrutinizing eyes.

"Surely it is well to wish to know the reason of things?" I asked, with some timidity.

"The desire of knowledge is a great virtue, certainly," he replied; "it is not truly felt by one in a thousand. Most persons are content to live and die, absorbed in their own petty commonplace affairs, without troubling themselves as to the reasons of their existence. Yet it is almost better, like these, to wallow in blind ignorance than wantonly to doubt the Creator because He is unseen, or to put a self-opinionated construction on His mysteries because He chooses to veil them from our eyes."

"I do not doubt!" I exclaimed earnestly. "I only want to make sure, and then perhaps I may persuade others."

"You can never compel faith," said Heliobas calmly. "You are going to see wonderful things that no tongue or pen can adequately describe. Well, when you return to earth again, do you suppose you can make people believe the story of your experiences? Never! Be thankful if you are the possessor of a secret joy yourself, and do not attempt to impart it to others, who will only repel and mock you."

"Not even to one other?" I asked hesitatingly.

A warm, kindly smile seemed to illuminate his face as I put this question.

"Yes, to one other, the other half of yourself—you may tell all things," he said. "But now, no more converse. If you are quite ready, drink this."

He held out to me a small tumbler filled with the sparkling volatile liquid he had poured from the flask. For one moment my courage almost forsook me, and an icy shiver ran through my veins. Then I bethought myself of all my boasted bravery; was it possible that I should fail now at this critical moment? I allowed myself no more time for reflection, but took the glass from his hand and drained its contents to the last drop. It was tasteless, but sparkling and warm on the tongue. Scarcely had I swallowed it, when a curiously light, dizzy sensation overcame me, and the figure of Heliobas standing before me seemed to assume gigantic proportions. I saw his hands extend—his eyes, like lamps of electric flame, burned through and through me—and like a distant echo, I heard the deep vibrating tones of his voice uttering the following words:

"Azul! Azul! Lift up this light and daring spirit unto thyself; be its pioneer upon the path it must pursue; suffer it to float untrammelled through the wide and glorious Continents of Air; give it form and force to alight on any of the vast and beautiful spheres it may desire to behold; and if worthy, permit it to gaze, if only for a brief interval, upon the supreme vision of the First and Last of worlds. By the force thou givest unto me, I free this soul; do thou, Azul, quickly receive it!"

A dense darkness now grew thickly around me—I lost all power over my limbs—I felt myself being lifted up forcibly and rapidly, up, up, into some illimitable, terrible space of blackness and nothingness. I could not think, move, or cry out—I could only feel that I was rising, rising, steadily, swiftly, breathlessly. . . when suddenly a long quivering flash of radiance, like the fragment of a rainbow, struck dazzlingly across my sight. Darkness? What had I to do with darkness? I knew not the word—I was only conscious of light—light exquisitely pure and brilliant—light through which I stepped as easily as a bird flies in air. Perfectly awake to my sensations, I felt somehow that there was nothing remarkable in them—I seemed to be at home in some familiar element. Delicate hands held mine—a face far lovelier than the loveliest face of woman ever dreamed by poet or painter, smiled radiantly at me, and I smiled back again. A voice whispered in strange musical murmurs, such as I well seemed to know and comprehend:

"Gaze behind thee ere the picture fades."

I obeyed, half reluctantly, and saw as a passing shadow in a glass, or a sort of blurred miniature painting, the room where Heliobas stood, watching some strange imperfect shape, which I seemed faintly to recognise. It looked like a small cast in clay, very badly executed, of the shape I at present wore; but it was incomplete, as though the sculptor had given it up as a failure and gone away, leaving it unfinished.

"Did I dwell in that body?" I mused to myself, as I felt the perfection of my then state of being. "How came I shut in such a prison? How poor a form—how destitute of faculties—how full of infirmities—how limited in capabilities—how narrow in all intelligence—how ignorant—how mean!"

And I turned for relief to the shining companion who held me, and obeying an impulse suddenly imparted, I felt myself floating higher and higher till the last limits of the atmosphere surrounding the Earth were passed, and fields of pure and cloudless ether extended before us. Here we met myriads of creatures like ourselves, all hastening in various directions—all lovely and radiant as a dream of the fairies. Some of these beings were quite tiny and delicate—some of lofty stature and glorious appearance: their forms were human, yet so refined, improved, and perfected, that they were unlike, while so like humanity.

"Askest thou nothing?" whispered the voice beside me.

"Tell me," I answered, "what I must know."

"These spirits that we behold," went on the voice, "are the guardians of all the inhabitants of all the planets. Their labours are those of love and penitence. Their work is to draw other souls to God—to attract them by warnings, by pleading, by praying. They have all worn the garb of mortality themselves, and they teach mortals by their own experience. For these radiant creatures are expiating sins of their own in thus striving to save others—the oftener they succeed the nearer they approach to Heaven. This is what is vaguely understood on your earth as purgatory; the sufferings of spirits who love and long for the presence of their Creator, and who yet are not pure enough to approach Him. Only by serving and saving others can they obtain at last their own joy. Every act of ingratitude and forgetfulness and wickedness committed by a mortal, detains one or another of these patient workers longer away from Heaven—imagine then what a weary while many of them have to wait."

I made no answer, and we floated on. Higher and higher—higher and higher—till at last my guide, whom I knew to be that being whom

Heliobas had called Azul, bade me pause. We were floating close together in what seemed a sea of translucent light. From this point I could learn something of the mighty workings of the Universe. I gazed upon countless solar systems, that like wheels within wheels revolved with such rapidity that they seemed all one wheel. I saw planets whirl around and around with breathless swiftness, like glittering balls flung through the air—burning comets flared fiercely past like torches of alarm for God's wars against Evil—a marvellous procession of indescribable wonders sweeping on for ever in circles, grand, huge, and immeasurable. And as I watched the superb pageant, I was not startled or confused—I looked upon it as anyone might look on any quiet landscape scene in what we know of Nature. I scarcely could perceive the Earth from whence I had come—so tiny a speck was it—nothing but a mere pin's point in the burning whirl of immensities. I felt, however, perfectly conscious of a superior force in myself to all these enormous forces around me—I knew without needing any explanation that I was formed of an indestructible essence, and that were all these stars and systems suddenly to end in one fell burst of brilliant horror, I should still exist—I should know and remember and feel—should be able to watch the birth of a new Universe, and take my part in its growth and design.

"Remind me why these wonders exist," I said, turning to my guide, and speaking in those dulcet sounds which were like music and yet like speech; "and why amid them all the Earth is believed by its inhabitants to have merited destruction, and yet to have been found worthy of redemption?"

"Thy last question shall be answered first," replied Azul. "Seest thou yonder planet circled with a ring? It is known to the dwellers on Earth, of whom when in clay thou art one, as Saturn. Descend with me!"

And in a breath of time we floated downwards and alighted on a broad and beautiful plain, where flowers of strange shape and colour grew in profusion. Here we were met by creatures of lofty stature and dazzling beauty, human in shape, yet angelic in countenance. They knelt to us with reverence and joy, and then passed on to their toil or pleasure, whichever invited them, and I looked to Azul for explanation.

"To these children of the Creator," said that radiant guide, "is granted the ability to see and to converse with the spirits of the air. They know them and love them, and implore their protection. In this planet sickness and old age are unknown, and death comes as a quiet sleep. The period of existence is about two hundred years, according to the Earth's standard of time; and the process of decay is no more unlovely than the gentle withering of roses. The influence of the electric belt around their world is a bar to pestilence and disease, and scatters health with light. All sciences, arts, and inventions known on Earth are known here, only to greater perfection. The three important differences between the inhabitants of this planet and those who dwell on Earth are these: first they have no rulers in authority, as each one perfectly governs himself; second, they do not marry, as the law of attraction which draws together any two of opposite sexes, holds them fast in inviolable fidelity; thirdly, there is no creature in all the immensity of this magnificent sphere who has ever doubted, or who ever will doubt, the existence of the Creator."

A thrill of fiery shame seemed to dart through my spiritual being as I heard this, and I made no answer. Some fairy-like little creatures, the children of the Saturnites, as I supposed, here came running towards us and knelt down, reverently clasping their hands in prayer. They then gathered flowers and flung them on that portion of ground where we stood, and gazed at us fearlessly and lovingly, as they might have gazed at some rare bird or butterfly.

Azul signed to me, and we rose while yet in their sight, and soaring through the radiance of the ring, which was like a sun woven into a circle, we soon left Saturn far behind us, and alighted on Venus. Here seas, mountains, forests, lakes, and meadows were one vast garden, in which the bloom and verdure of all worlds seemed to find a home. Here were realized the dreams of sculptors and painters, in the graceful forms and exquisite faces of the women, and the splendid strength and godlike beauty of the men. A brief glance was sufficient to show me that the moving spring of all the civilization of this radiant planet was the love of Nature and Art united. There were no wars—for there were no different nations. All the inhabitants were like one vast family; they worked for one another, and vied with each other in paying homage to those of the loftiest genius among them. They had one supreme Monarch to whom they all rendered glad obedience; and he was a Poet, ready to sacrifice his throne with joy as soon as his people should discover a greater than he. For they all loved not the artist but the Art; and selfishness was a vice unknown. Here, none loved or were wedded save those who had spiritual sympathies, and here, too, no creature existed who did not believe in and worship the Creator. The same state of things existed in Jupiter, the planet we next visited, where everything was performed by electricity. Here persons living hundreds of miles apart could yet converse together with perfect ease through an electric medium; ships ploughed the seas by electricity; printing, an art of which the dwellers on Earth are so proud, was accomplished by electricity—in fact, everything in the way of science, art, and invention known to us was also known in Jupiter, only to greater perfection, because tempered and strengthened by an electric force which never failed. From Jupiter, Azul guided me to many other fair and splendid worlds—yet none of them were Paradise; all had some slight drawback—some physical or spiritual ailment, as it were, which had to be combated with and conquered. All the inhabitants of each star longed for something they had not—something better, greater, and higher—and therefore all had discontent. They could not realize their best desires in the state of existence they then were, therefore they all suffered disappointment. They were all compelled to work in some way or another; they were all doomed to die. Yet, unlike the dwellers on Earth, they did not, because their lives were more or less constrained and painful, complain of or deny the goodness of God— on the contrary, they believed in a future state which should be as perfect as their present one was imperfect; and the chief aim and object of all their labours was to become worthy of attaining that final grand result—Eternal Happiness and Peace.

"Readest thou the lesson in these glowing spheres, teeming with life and learning?" murmured Azul to me, as we soared swiftly on together. "Know that not one smallest world in all the myriad systems circling before thee, holds a single human creature who doubts his Maker. Not one! except thine own doomed star! Behold it yonder—sparkling feebly, like a faint flame amid sunshine—how poor a speck it is—how like a scarcely visible point in all the brilliancy of the ever-revolving wheel of Life! Yet there dwell the dwarfs of clay—the men and women who pretend to love while they secretly hate and despise one another. There, wealth is a god, and the greed of gain a virtue. There, genius starves, and heroism dies unrewarded. There, faith is martyred, and unbelief elected sovereign monarch of the people. There, the sublime, unreachable mysteries of the Universe are haggled over by poor finite minds who cannot call their lives their own. There, nation wars against nation, creed against creed, soul against soul. Alas, fated planet! how soon shalt thou be extinct, and thy place shall know thee no more!"

I gazed earnestly at my radiant guide. "If that is true," I said, "why then should we have a legend that God, in the person of one called Christ, came to die for so miserable and mean a race of beings?"

Azul answered not, but turned her luminous eyes upon me with a sort of wide dazzling wonder. Some strange impelling force bore me onward, and before I could realize it I was alone. Alone, in a vast area of light through which I floated, serene and conscious of power. A sound falling from a great height reached me; it was first like a grand organ-chord, and then like a voice, trumpet-clear and far-echoing.

"Spirit that searchest for the Unseen," it said, "because I will not that no atom of true worth should perish, unto thee shall be given a vision—unto thee shall be taught a lesson thou dreamest not of. THOU shalt create; THOU shalt design and plan; THOU shalt be worshipped, and THOU shalt destroy! Rest therefore in the light and behold the things that are in the light, for the tune cometh when all that seemeth clear and visible now shall be but darkness. And they that love me not shall have no place of abode in that hour!"

The voice ceased. Awed, yet consoled, I listened for it again. There was no more sound. Around me was illimitable light—illimitable silence. But a strange scene unfolded itself swiftly before me—a sort of shifting dream that was a reality, yet so wonderfully unreal—a vision that impressed itself on every portion of my intelligence; a kind of spirit-drama in which I was forced to enact the chief part, and where a mystery that I had deemed impenetrable was made perfectly clear and simple of comprehension.

XI

A Miniature Creation

In my heaven-uplifted dream, I thought I saw a circular spacious garden in which all the lovely landscapes of a superior world appeared to form themselves by swift degrees. The longer I looked at it, the more beautiful it became, and a little star shone above it like a sun. Trees and flowers sprang up under my gaze, and all stretched themselves towards me, as though for protection. Birds flew about and sang; some of them tried to get as near as possible to the little sun they saw; and other living creatures began to move about in the shadows of the groves, and on the fresh green grass. All the wonderful workings of Nature, as known to us in the world, took place over again in this garden, which seemed somehow to belong to me; and I watched everything with a certain satisfaction and delight. Then the idea came to me that the place would be fairer if there were either men or angels to inhabit it; and quick as light a whisper came to me:

"Create!"

And I thought in my dream that by the mere desire of my being, expressed in waves of electric warmth that floated downwards from me to the earth I possessed, my garden was suddenly filled with men, women and children, each of whom had a small portion of myself in them, inasmuch as it was I who made them move and talk and occupy themselves in all manner of amusements. Many of them knelt down to me and prayed, and offered thanksgivings for having been created; but some of them went instead to the little star, which they called a sun, and thanked that, and prayed to that instead. Then others went and cut down the trees in the garden, and dug up stones, and built themselves little cities, where they all dwelt together like flocks of sheep, and ate and drank and made merry with the things I had given them. Then I thought that I increased their intelligence and quickness of perception, and by-and-by they grew so proud that they forgot everything but themselves. They ceased to remember how they were created, and they cared no more to offer praises to their little sun that through me gave them light and heat. But because something of my essence still was in them, they always instinctively sought to worship a superior creature to themselves; and puzzling themselves in their folly, they made hideous images of wood and clay, unlike anything in heaven or earth, and offered sacrifices and prayer to these lifeless puppets instead of to me. Then I turned away my eyes in sorrow and pity, but never in anger; for I could not be wrathful with these children of my own creation. And when I thus turned away my eyes, all manner of evil came upon the once fair scene—pestilence and storm, disease and vice. A dark shadow stole between my little world and me—the shadow of the people's own wickedness. And as every delicate fibre of my spiritual being repelled evil by the necessity of the pure light in which I dwelt serene. I waited patiently for the mists to clear, so that I might again behold the beauty of my garden. Suddenly a soft clamour smote upon my sense of hearing, and a slender stream of light, like a connecting ray, seemed to be flung upwards through the darkness that hid me from the people I had created and loved. I knew the sound—it was the mingled music of the prayers of children. An infinite pity and pleasure touched me, my being thrilled with love and tenderness; and yielding to these little ones who asked me for protection, I turned my eyes again towards the garden I had designed for fairness and pleasure. But alas! how changed it had become! No longer fresh and sweet, the people had turned it into a wilderness; they had divided it into small portions, and in so doing had divided themselves into separate companies called nations, all of whom fought with each other fiercely for their different little parterres or flower-beds. Some haggled and talked incessantly over the mere possession of a stone which they called a rock; others busied themselves in digging a little yellow metal out of the earth, which, when once obtained, seemed to make the owners of it mad, for they straightway forgot everything else. As I looked, the darkness between me and my creation grew denser, and was only pierced at last by those long wide shafts of radiance caused by the innocent prayers of those who still remembered me. And I was full of regret, for I saw my people wandering hither and thither, restless and dissatisfied, perplexed by their own errors, and caring nothing for the love I bore them. Then some of them advanced and began to question why they had been created, forgetting completely how their lives had been originally designed by me for happiness, love and wisdom. Then they accused me of the existence of evil, refusing to see that where there is light there is also darkness, and that darkness is the rival force of the Universe, whence cometh silently the Unnamable Oblivion of Souls. They could not see, my self-willed children, that they had of their own desire sought the darkness and found it; and now, because it gloomed above them like a pall, they refused to believe in the light where still I was loving and striving to attract them still. Yet it was not all darkness, and I knew that even what there was might be repelled and cleared away if only my people would turn towards me once more. So I sent down upon them all possible blessings—some they rejected angrily, some they snatched at and threw away again, as though they were poor and trivial—none of them were they thankful for, and none did they desire to keep. And the darkness above them deepened, while my anxious pity and love for them increased. For how could I turn altogether away from them, as long as but a few remembered me? There were some of these weak children of mine who loved and honoured me so well that they absorbed some of my light into themselves, and became heroes, poets, musicians, teachers of high and noble thought, and unselfish, devoted martyrs for the sake of the reverence they bore me. There were women pure and sweet, who wore their existence as innocently as lilies, and who turned to me to seek protection, not for themselves, but for those they loved. There were little children, whose asking voices were like waves of delicious music to my being, and for whom I had a surpassing tenderness. And yet all these were a mere handful compared to the numbers who denied my existence, and who had wilfully crushed out and repelled every spark of my essence in themselves. And as I contemplated this, the voice I had heard at the commencement of my dream rushed towards me like a mighty wind broken through by thunder:

"Destroy!"

A great pity and love possessed me. In deep awe, yet solemn earnestness, I pleaded with that vast commanding voice.

"Bid me not destroy!" I implored. "Command me not to disperse into nothingness these children of my fancy, some of whom yet love and trust to me for safety. Let me strive once more to bring them out of their darkness into the light—to bring them to the happiness I designed them to enjoy. They have not all forgotten me—let me give them more time for thought and recollection!"

Again the great voice shook the air:

"They love darkness rather than light; they love the perishable earth of which they are in part composed, better than the germ of immortality with which they were in the beginning endowed. This garden of thine is but a caprice of thy intelligence; the creatures that inhabit it are soulless and unworthy, and are an offence to that indestructible radiance of which thou art one ray. Therefore I say unto thee again—DESTROY!"

My yearning love grew stronger, and I pleaded with renewed force.

"Oh, thou Unseen Glory!" I cried; "thou who hast filled me with this emotion of love and pity which permeates and supports my existence, how canst thou bid me take this sudden revenge upon my frail creation! No caprice was it that caused me to design it; nothing but a thought of love and a desire of beauty. Even yet I will fulfil my plan—even yet shall these erring children of mine return to me in time, with patience. While one of them still lifts a hand in prayer to me, or gratitude, I cannot destroy! Bid me rather sink into the darkness of the uttermost deep of shadow; only let me save these feeble little ones from destruction!"

The voice replied not. A flashing opal brilliancy shot across the light in which I rested, and I beheld an Angel, grand, lofty, majestic, with a countenance in which shone the lustre of a myriad summer mornings.

"Spirit that art escaped from the Sorrowful Star," it said in accents clear and sonorous, "wouldst thou indeed be content to suffer the loss of heavenly joy and peace, in order to rescue thy perishing creation?"

"I would!" I answered; "if I understood death, I would die to save one of those frail creatures, who seek to know me and yet cannot find me through the darkness they have brought upon themselves."

"To die," said the Angel, "to understand death, thou wouldst need to become one of them, to take upon thyself their form—to imprison all that brilliancy of which thou art now composed, into a mean and common case of clay; and even if thou couldst accomplish this, would thy children know thee or receive thee?"

"Nay, but if I could suffer shame by them," I cried impetuously, "I could not suffer sin. My being would be incapable of error, and I would show these creatures of mine the bliss of purity, the joy of wisdom, the ecstasy of light, the certainty of immortality, if they followed me. And then I would die to show them death is easy, and that in dying they would come to me and find their happiness for ever!"

The stature of the Angel grew more lofty and magnificent, and its star-like eyes flashed fire.

MARIE CORELLI

"Then, oh thou wanderer from the Earth!" it said, "understandest thou not the Christ?"

A deep awe trembled through me. Meanwhile the garden I had thought a world appeared to roll up like a cloudy scroll, and vanished, and I knew that it had been a vision, and no more.

"Oh doubting and foolish Spirit!" went on the Angel—"thou who art but one point of living light in the Supreme Radiance, even THOU wouldst consent to immure thyself in the darkness of mortality for sake of thy fancied creation! Even THOU wouldst submit to suffer and to die, in order to show the frail children of thy dream a purely sinless and spiritual example! Even THOU hast had the courage to plead with the One All-Sufficing Voice against the destruction of what to thee was but a mirage floating in this ether! Even THOU hast had love, forgiveness, pity! Even THOU wouldst be willing to dwell among the creatures of thy fancy as one of them, knowing in thy inner self that by so doing, thy spiritual presence would have marked thy little world for ever as sanctified and impossible to destroy. Even THOU wouldst sacrifice a glory to answer a child's prayer—even thou wouldst have patience! And yet thou hast dared to deny to God those attributes which thou thyself dost possess—He is so great and vast—thou so small and slight! For the love thou feelest throbbing through thy being, He is the very commencement and perfection of all love; if thou hast pity, He has ten thousand times more pity; if THOU canst forgive, remember that from Him flows all thy power of forgiveness! There is nothing thou canst do, even at the highest height of spiritual perfection, that He cannot surpass by a thousand million fold! Neither shalt thou refuse to believe that He can also suffer. Know that nothing is more godlike than unselfish sorrow—and the grief of the Creator over one erring human soul is as vast as He Himself is vast. Why wouldst thou make of Him a being destitute of the best emotions that He Himself bestows upon thee? THOU wouldst have entered into thy dream-world and lived in it and died in it, if by so doing thou couldst have drawn one of thy creatures back to the love of thee; and wilt thou not receive the Christ?"

I bowed my head, and a flood of joy rushed through me.

"I believe—I believe and I love!" I murmured. "Desert me not, O radiant Angel! I feel and know that all these wonders must soon pass away from my sight; but wilt thou also go?"

The Angel smiled and touched me.

"I am thy guardian," it said. "I have been with thee always. I can never leave thee so long as thy soul seeks spiritual things. Asleep or awake on the Earth, wherever thou art, I also am. There have been times when I have warned thee and thou wouldst not listen, when I have tried to draw thee onward and thou wouldst not come; but now I fear no more thy disobedience, for thy restlessness is past. Come with me; it is permitted thee to see far off the vision of the Last Circle."

The glorious figure raised me gently by the hand, and we floated on and on, higher and higher, past little circles which my guide told me were all solar systems, though they looked nothing but slender garlands of fire, so rapidly did they revolve and so swiftly did we pass them. Higher and higher we went, till even to my untiring spirit the way seemed long. Beautiful creatures in human shape, but as delicate as gossamer, passed us every now and then, some in bands of twos and threes, some alone; and the higher we soared the more dazzlingly lovely these inhabitants of the air seemed to be.

"They are all born of the Great Circle," my guardian Angel explained to me: "and to them is given the power of communicating high thought or inspiration. Among them are the Spirits of Music, of Poesy, of Prophecy, and of all Art ever known in all worlds. The success of their teaching depends on how much purity and unselfishness there is in the soul to which they whisper their divine messages—messages as brief as telegrams which must be listened to with entire attention and acted upon at once, or the lesson is lost and may never come again."

Just then I saw a Shape coming towards me as of a lovely fair-haired child, who seemed to be playing softly on a strange glittering instrument like a broken cloud strung through with sunbeams. Heedless of consequences, I caught at its misty robe in a wild effort to detain it. It obeyed my touch, and turned its deeply luminous eyes first upon me, and then upon the Angel who accompanied my flight.

"What seekest thou?" it asked in a voice like the murmuring of the wind among flowers.

"Music!" I answered. "Sing me thy melodies—fill me with harmonies divine and unreachable—and I will strive to be worthy of thy teachings!"

The young Shape smiled and drew closer towards me.

"Thy wish is granted, Sister Spirit!" it replied. "The pity I shall feel for thy fate when thou art again pent in clay, shall be taught thee in minor music—thou shalt possess the secret of unwritten sound, and I will sing to thee and bring thee comfort. On Earth, call but my name—

Aeon! and thou shalt behold me. For thy longing voice is known to the Children of Music, and hath oft shaken the vibrating light wherein they dwell. Fear not! As long as thou dost love me, I am thine." And parting slowly, still smiling, the lovely vision, with its small radiant hands ever wandering among the starry strings of its cloud-like lyre, floated onward.

Suddenly a clear voice said "Welcome!" and looking up I saw my first friend, Azul. I smiled in glad recognition—I would have spoken—but lo! a wide immensity of blazing glory broke like many-coloured lightning around me—so dazzling, so overpowering, that I instinctively drew back and paused—I felt I could go no further.

"Here," said my guardian gently—"here ends thy journey. Would that it were possible, poor Spirit, for thee to pass this boundary! But that may not be—as yet. In the meanwhile thou mayest gaze for a brief space upon the majestic sphere which mortals dream of as Heaven. Behold and see how fair is the incorruptible perfection of God's World!"

I looked and trembled—I should have sunk yet further backward, had not Azul and my Angel-guide held me with their light yet forcible clasp. My heart fails me now as I try to write of that tremendous, that sublime scene—the Centre of the Universe—the Cause of all Creation. How unlike Heaven such as we in our ignorance have tried to depict! though it is far better we should have a mistaken idea than none at all. What I beheld was a circle, so huge that no mortal measurements could compass it—a wide Ring composed of seven colours, rainbow-like, but flashing with perpetual motion and brilliancy, as though a thousand million suns were for ever being woven into it to feed its transcendent lustre. From every part of this Ring darted long broad shafts of light, some of which stretched out so far that I could not see where they ended; sometimes a bubbling shower of lightning sparks would be flung out on the pure ether, and this would instantly form into circles, small or great, and whirl round and round the enormous girdle of flame from which they had been cast, with the most inconceivable rapidity. But wonderful as the Ring was, it encompassed a Sphere yet more marvellous and dazzling; a great Globe of opal-tinted light, revolving as it were upon its own axis, and ever surrounded by that scintillating, jewel-like wreath of electricity, whose only motion was to shine and burn within itself for ever. I could not bear to look upon the brightness of that magnificent central World—so large that multiplying the size of the sun by a hundred thousand millions, no adequate idea could be formed of its vast proportions. And ever it revolved—and ever the Rainbow Ring around it glittered and cast forth those other rings which I knew now were living solar systems cast forth from that electric band as a volcano casts forth fire and lava. My Angel-guide motioned me to look towards that side of the Ring which was nearest to the position of the Earth. I looked, and perceived that there the shafts of descending light formed themselves as they fell into the shape of a Cross. At this, such sorrow, love, and shame overcame me, that I knew not where to turn. I murmured:

"Send me back again, dear Angel—send me back to that Star of Sorrow and Error! Let me hasten to make amends there for all my folly—let me try to teach others what now I know. I am unworthy to be here beside thee—I am unfit to look on yonder splendid World—let me return to do penance for my sins and shortcomings; for what am I that God should bless me? and though I should consume myself in labour and suffering, how can I ever hope to deserve the smallest place in that heavenly glory I now partly behold?" And could spirits shed tears, I should have wept with remorse and grief.

Azul spoke, softly and tenderly:

"Now thou dost believe—henceforth thou must love! Love alone can pass yon flaming barrier—love alone can gain for thee eternal bliss. In love and for love were all things made—God loveth His creatures, even so let His creatures love Him, and so shall the twain be drawn together."

"Listen!" added my Angel-guide. "Thou hast not travelled so far as yet to remain in ignorance. That burning Ring thou seest is the result of the Creator's ever-working Intelligence; from it all the Universe hath sprung. It is exhaustless and perpetually creative; it is pure and perfect Light. The smallest spark of that fiery essence in a mortal frame is sufficient to form a soul or spirit, such as mine, or that of Azul, or thine, when thou art perfected. The huge world rolling within the Ring is where God dwells. Dare not thou to question His shape, His look, His mien! Know that He is the Supreme Spirit in which all Beauty, all Perfection, all Love, find consummation. His breath is the fire of the Ring; His look, His pleasure, cause the motion of His World and all worlds. There where He dwells, dwell also all pure souls; there all desires have fulfilment without satiety, and there all loveliness, wisdom or pleasure known in any or all of the other spheres are also known. Speak, Azul, and tell this wanderer from Earth what she will gain in winning her place in Heaven."

MARIE CORELLI

Azul looked tenderly upon me and said:

"When thou hast slept the brief sleep of death, when thou art permitted to throw off for ever thy garb of clay, and when by thine own ceaseless love and longing thou hast won the right to pass the Great Circle, thou shalt find thyself in a land where the glories of the natural scenery alone shall overpower thee with joy—scenery that for ever changes into new wonders and greater beauty. Thou shalt hear music such as thou canst not dream of. Thou shalt find friends, beyond all imagination fair and faithful. Thou shalt read and see the history of all the planets, produced for thee in an ever-moving panorama. Thou shalt love and be beloved for ever by thine own Twin Soul; wherever that spirit may be now, it must join thee hereafter. The joys of learning, memory, consciousness, sleep, waking, and exercise shall all be thine. Sin, sorrow, pain, disease and death thou shalt know no more. Thou shalt be able to remember happiness, to possess it, and to look forward to it. Thou shalt have full and pleasant occupation without fatigue—thy food and substance shall be light and air. Flowers, rare and imperishable, shall bloom for thee; birds of exquisite form and tender voice shall sing to thee; angels shall be thy companions. Thou shalt have fresh and glad desires to offer to God with every portion of thy existence, and each one shall be granted as soon as asked, for then thou wilt not be able to ask anything that is displeasing to Him. But because it is a joy to wish, thou shalt wish! and because it is a joy to grant, so also will He grant. No delight, small or great, is wanting in that vast sphere; only sorrow is lacking, and satiety and disappointment have no place. Wilt thou seek for admittance there or wilt thou faint by the way and grow weary?"

I raised my eyes full of ecstasy and reverence.

"My mere efforts must count as nothing," I said; "but if Love can help me, I will love and long for God's World until I die!"

My guardian Angel pointed to those rays of light I had before noticed, that slanted downwards towards Earth in the form of a Cross.

"That is the path by which THOU must travel. Mark it well! All pilgrims from the Sorrowful Star must journey by that road. Woe to them that turn aside to roam mid spheres they know not of, to lose themselves in seas of light wherein they cannot steer! Remember my warning! And now, Spirit who art commended to my watchful care, thy brief liberty is ended. Thou hast been lifted up to the outer edge of the Electric Circle, further we dare not take thee. Hast thou aught else to ask before the veil of mortality again enshrouds thee?"

I answered not, but within myself I formed a wild desire. The Electric Ring flashed fiercely on my uplifted eyes, but I kept them fixed hopefully and lovingly on its intensely deep brilliancy.

"If Love and Faith can avail me," I murmured, "I shall see what I have sought."

I was not disappointed. The fiery waves of light parted on either side of the spot where I with my companions rested; and a Figure,—majestic, unutterably grand and beautiful,—approached me. At the same moment a number of other faces and forms shone hoveringly out of the Ring; one I noticed like an exquisitely lovely woman, with floating hair and clear, earnest, unfathomable eyes. Azul and the Angel sank reverently down and drooped their radiant heads like flowers in hot sunshine. I alone, daringly, yet with inexpressible affection welling up within me, watched with unshrinking gaze the swift advance of that supreme Figure, upon whose broad brows rested the faint semblance of a Crown of Thorns. A voice penetratingly sweet addressed me:

"Mortal from the Star I saved from ruin, because thou hast desired Me, I come! Even as thy former unbelief, shall be now thy faith. Because thou lovest Me, I am with thee. For do I not know thee better than the Angels can? Have I not dwelt in thy clay, suffered thy sorrows, wept thy tears, died thy deaths? One with My Father, and yet one with thee, I demand thy love, and so through Me shalt thou attain immortal life!"

I felt a touch upon me like a scorching flame—a thrill rushed through my being—and then I knew that I was sinking down, down, further and further away. I saw that wondrous Figure standing serene and smiling between the retiring waves of electric radiance. I saw the great inner sphere revolve, and glitter as it rolled, like an enormous diamond encircled with gold and sapphire, and then all suddenly the air grew dim and cloudy, and the sensation of falling became more and more rapid. Azul was beside me still, and I also perceived the outline of my guardian Angel's form, though that was growing indistinct. I now recalled the request of Heliobas, and spoke:

"Azul, tell me what shadow rests upon the life of him to whom I am now returning?"

Azul looked at me earnestly, and replied:

"Thou daring one! Seekest thou to pierce the future fate of others? Is it not enough for thee to have heard the voice that maketh the Angel's singing silent, and wouldst thou yet know more?"

I was full of a strange unhesitating courage, therefore I said fearlessly:

"He is thy Beloved one, Azul—thy Twin Soul; and wilt thou let him fall away from thee when a word or sign might save him?"

"Even as he is my Beloved, so let him not fail to hear my voice," replied Azul, with a tinge of melancholy. "For though he has accomplished much, he is as yet but mortal. Thou canst guide him thus far; tell him, when death lies like a gift in his hand, let him withhold it, and remember me. And now, my friend—farewell!"

I would have spoken again, but could not. An oppressed sensation came over me, and I seemed to plunge coldly into a depth of inextricable blackness. I felt cramped for room, and struggled for existence, for motion, for breath. What had happened to me? I wondered indignantly. Was I a fettered prisoner? had I lost the use of my light aerial limbs that had borne me so swiftly through the realms of space? What crushing weight overpowered me? why such want of air and loss of delightful ease? I sighed restlessly and impatiently at the narrow darkness in which I found myself—a sorrowful, deep, shuddering sigh. . . and WOKE! That is to say, I languidly opened mortal eyes to find myself once more pent up in mortal frame, though I retained a perfect remembrance and consciousness of everything I had experienced during my spirit-wanderings. Heliobas stood in front of me with outstretched hands, and his eyes were fixed on mine with a mingled expression of anxiety and authority, which changed into a look of relief and gladness as I smiled at him and uttered his name aloud.

XII

Secrets of the Sun and Moon

Have I been long away?" I asked, as I raised myself upright in the chair where I had been resting.

"I sent you from hence on Thursday morning at noon," replied Heliobas. "It is now Friday evening, and within a few minutes of midnight. I was growing alarmed. I have never known anyone stay absent for so long; and you resisted my authority so powerfully, that I began to fear you would never come back at all."

"I wish I had not been compelled to do so!" I said regretfully.

He smiled.

"No doubt you do. It is the general complaint. Will you stand up now and see how you feel?"

I obeyed. There was still a slight sensation about me as of being cramped for space; but this was passing, and otherwise I felt singularly strong, bright and vigorous. I stretched out my hands in unspeakable gratitude to him through whose scientific power I had gained my recent experience.

"I can never thank you enough!" I said earnestly. "I dare say you know something of what I have seen on my journey?"

"Something, but not all," he replied. "Of course I know what worlds and systems you saw, but what was said to you, or what special lessons were given you for your comfort, I cannot tell." "Then I will describe everything while it is fresh upon me," I returned. "I feel that I must do so in order that you may understand how glad I am,—how grateful I am to you."

I then related the different scenes through which I had passed, omitting no detail. Heliobas listened with profound interest and attention. When I had finished, he said:

"Yours has been a most wonderful, I may say almost exceptional, experience. It proves to me more than ever the omnipotence of WILL. Most of those who have been placed by my means in the Uplifted or Electric state of being, have consented to it simply to gratify a sense of curiosity—few therefore have gone beyond the pure ether, where, as in a sea, the planets swim. Cellini, for instance, never went farther than Venus, because in the atmosphere of that planet he met the Spirit that rules and divides his destiny. Zara—she was daring, and reached the outer rim of the Great Circle; but even she never caught a glimpse of the great Central Sphere. You, differing from these, started with a daring aim which you never lost sight of till you had fulfilled it. How true are those words: 'Ask, and it shall be given you; seek, and ye shall find; knock, and it shall be opened unto you'! It is not possible," and here he sighed, "that amid such wonders you could have remembered me—it were foolish on my part to expect it."

"I confess I thought nothing of you," I said frankly, "till I was approaching Earth again; but then my memory prompted me in time, and I did not forget your request."

"And what did you learn?" he asked anxiously.

"Simply this. Azul said that I might deliver you this message: When death lies like a gift in your hand, withhold it, and remember her."

"As if I did not always guide myself by her promptings!" exclaimed Heliobas, with a tender smile.

"You might forget to do so for once," I said.

"Never!" he replied fervently. "It could not be. But I thank you, my child, for having thought of me—the message you bring shall be impressed strongly on my mind. Now, before you leave me to-night, I must say a few necessary words."

He paused, and appeared to consider profoundly for some minutes. At last he spoke.

"I have selected certain writings for your perusal," he said. "In them you will find full and clear instructions how to cultivate and educate the electric force within you, and thus continue the work I have begun. With these you will also perceive that I have written out the receipt for the volatile fluid which, if taken in a small quantity every day, will keep you in health, strength, and intellectual vigour, while it will preserve your youth and enjoyment of life to a very much longer extent than that usually experienced by the majority. Understand me well—this liquid of itself cannot put you into an uplifted state of existence; you need HUMAN electric force applied strongly to your system to compass this; and as it is dangerous to try the experiment too often—dangerous to the body, I mean—it will be as well, as you have work to do yet in this life, not to attempt it again. But if you drink the fluid every morning of your life, and at the same time obey my written manual as to the cultivation of your own inner force, which is already existent in a large degree, you will attain to certain advantages over the rest of the people you meet, which will give you not only physical, but mental power."

He paused a minute or two, and again went on:

"When you have educated your Will to a certain height of electric command, you can at your pleasure see at any time, and see plainly, the spirits who inhabit the air; and also those who, descending to long distances below the Great Circle, come within the range of human electricity, or the attractive matter contained in the Earth's atmosphere. You can converse with them, and they with you. You will also be able, at your desire, to see the parted spirits of dead persons, so long as they linger within Earth's radius, which they seldom do, being always anxious to escape from it as soon as possible. Love may sometimes detain them, or remorse; but even these have to yield to the superior longings which possess them the instant they are set free. You will, in your intercourse with your fellow-mortals, be able to discern their motives quickly and unerringly—you will at once discover where you are loved and where you are disliked; and not all the learning and logic of so-called philosophers shall be able to cloud your instinct. You will have a keener appreciation of good and beautiful things—a delightful sense of humour, and invariable cheerfulness; and whatever you do, unless you make some mistake by your own folly, will carry with it its success. And, what is perhaps a greater privilege, you will find that all who are brought into very close contact with you will be beneficially influenced, or the reverse, exactly as you choose to exert your power. I do not think, after what you have seen, you will ever desire to exert a malign influence, knowing that the Creator of your being is all love and forgiveness. At any rate, the greatest force in the universe, electricity, is yours—that is, it has begun to form itself in you—and you have nothing to do but to encourage its growth, just as you would encourage a taste for music or the fine arts. Now let me give you the writings."

He unlocked a desk, and took from it two small rolls of parchment, one tied with a gold ribbon, the other secured in a kind of case with a clasp. This last he held up before my eyes, and said:

"This contains my private instructions to you. Never make a single one of them public. The world is not ready for wisdom, and the secrets of science can only be explained to the few. Therefore keep this parchment safely under lock and key, and never let any eye but your own look upon its contents."

I promised, and he handed it to me. Then taking the other roll, which was tied with ribbon, he said,

"Here is written out what I call the Electric Principle of Christianity. This is for your own study and consideration; still, if you ever desire to explain my theory to others, I do not forbid you. But as I told you before, you can never compel belief—the goldfish in a glass bowl will never understand the existence of the ocean. Be satisfied if you can guide yourself by the compass you have found, but do not grieve if you are unable to guide others. You may try, but it will not be surprising if you fail. Nor will it be your fault. The only sorrow that might happen to you in these efforts would be in case you should love someone very dearly, and yet be unable to instil the truth of what yon know into that particular soul. You would then have to make a discovery, which is always more or less painful—namely, that your love was misplaced, inasmuch as the nature you had selected as worthy of love had no part with yours; and that separation utter and eternal must therefore occur, if not in this life, then in the future. So I would say beware of loving, lest you should not love rightly—though I believe you will soon be able to discern clearly the spirit that is by fate destined to complete and perfect your own. And now, though I know you are scarcely fatigued enough to sleep, I will say good-night."

I took the second roll of parchment from his hand, and opening it a little way, I saw that it was covered with very fine small writing. Then I said:

"Does Zara know how long I have been absent?"

"Yes," replied Heliobas; "and she, like myself, was surprised and anxious. I think she went to bed long ago; but you may look into her room and see if she is awake, before you yourself retire to rest."

As he spoke of Zara his eyes grew melancholy and his brow clouded. An instinctive sense of fear came upon me.

"Is she not well?" I asked.

"She is perfectly well," he answered. "Why should you imagine her to be otherwise?"

"Pardon me," I said; "I fancied that you looked unhappy when I mentioned her."

Heliobas made no answer. He stepped to the window, and throwing back the curtain, called me to his side.

"Look out yonder." he said in low and earnest tones; "look at the dark blue veil strewn with stars, through which so lately your daring soul pierced its flight! See how the small Moon hangs like a lamp in Heaven, apparently outshining the myriad worlds around her, that are so much vaster and fairer! How deceptive is the human eye!—nearly as deceptive as the human reason. Tell me—why did you not visit the Moon, or the Sun, in your recent wanderings?"

This question caused me some surprise. It was certainly very strange that I had not thought of doing so. Yet, on pondering the matter in my mind, I remembered that during my aerial journey suns and moons had been no more to me than flowers strewn on a meadow. I now regretted that I had not sought to know something of those two fair luminaries which light and warm our earth.

Heliobas, after watching my face intently, resumed:

"You cannot guess the reason of your omission? I will tell you. There is nothing to see in either Sun or Moon. They were both inhabited worlds once; but the dwellers in the Sun have ages ago lived their lives and passed to the Central Sphere. The Sun is nothing now but a burning world, burning rapidly, and surely, away: or rather, IT IS BEING ABSORBED BACK INTO THE ELECTRIC CIRCLE FROM WHICH IT ORIGINALLY SPRANG, TO BE THROWN OUT AGAIN IN SOME NEW AND GRANDER FORM. And so with all worlds, suns and systems, for ever and ever. Hundreds of thousands of those brief time-breathings called years may pass before this consummation of the Sun; but its destruction is going on now, or rather its absorption—and we on our cold small star warm ourselves, and are glad, in the light of an empty world on fire!"

I listened with awe and interest.

"And the Moon?" I asked eagerly.

"The Moon does not exist. What we see is the reflection or the electrograph of what she once was. Atmospherical electricity has imprinted this picture of a long-ago living world upon the heavens, just as Raphael drew his cartoons for the men of to-day to see."

"But," I exclaimed in surprise, "how about the Moon's influence on the tides? and what of eclipses?"

"Not the Moon, but the electric photograph of a once living but now absorbed world, has certainly an influence on the tides. The sea is impregnated with electricity. Just as the Sun will absorb colours, so the electricity in the sea is repelled or attracted by the electric picture of the Moon in Heaven. Because, as a painting is full of colour, so is that faithful sketch of a vanished sphere, drawn with a pencil of pure light, full of immense electricity; and to carry the simile further, just as a painting may be said to be formed of various dark and light tints, so the electric portrait of the Moon contains various degrees of electric force—which, coming in contact with the electricity of the Earth's atmosphere, produces different effects on us and on the natural scenes amid which we dwell. As for eclipses—if you slowly pass a round screen between yourself and a blazing fire, you will only see the edges of the fire. In the same way the electrograph of the Moon passes at stated intervals between the Earth and the burning world of the Sun."

"Yet surely," I said, "the telescope has enabled us to see the Moon as a solid globe—we have discerned mountains and valleys on its surface; and then it revolves round us regularly—how do you account for these facts?"

"The telescope," returned Heliobas, "is merely an aid to the human eye; and, as I told you before, nothing is so easily deceived as our sense of vision, even when assisted by mechanical appliances. The telescope, like the stereoscope, simply enables us to see the portrait of the Moon more clearly; but all the same, the Moon, as a world, does not exist. Her likeness, taken by electricity, may last some thousands of years, and as long as it lasts it must revolve around us, because everything in the universe moves, and moves in a circle. Besides which, this portrait of the moon being composed of pure electricity, is attracted and forced to follow the Earth by the compelling influence of the Earth's own electric power. Therefore, till the picture fades, it must attend the Earth like the haunting spectre of a dead joy. You can understand now why we never see what we imagine to be the OTHER SIDE of the Moon. It simply has No other side, except space. Space is the canvas—the Moon is a sketch. How interested we are when a discovery is made of some rare old painting, of which the subject is a perfectly beautiful woman! It bears no name—perhaps no date—but the face that smiles at us is exquisite—the lips yet pout for kisses—the eyes brim over, with love! And we admire it tenderly and reverently—we mark it 'Portrait of a lady,' and give it an honoured place among our art collections. With how much more reverence and tenderness ought we to look up at the 'Portrait of a Fair Lost Sphere,' circling yonder in that dense ever-moving gallery of wonders where the hurrying throng of spectators are living and dying worlds!"

I had followed the speaker's words with fascinated attention, but now I said:

"Dying, Heliobas? There is no death."

"True!" he answered, with hesitating slowness. "But there is what we call death—transition—and it is always a parting."

"But not for long!" I exclaimed, with all the gladness and eagerness of my lately instructed soul. "As worlds are absorbed into the Electric Circle and again thrown out in new and more glorious forms, so are we absorbed and changed into shapes of perfect beauty, having eyes that are strong and pure enough to look God in the face. The body perishes—but what have WE to do with the body—our prison and place of experience, except to rejoice when we shake off its weight for ever!"

Heliobas smiled gravely.

"You have learned your high lesson well," he said. "You speak with the assurance and delight of a spirit satisfied. But when I talk of DEATH, I mean by that word the parting asunder of two souls who love each other; and though such separation may be brief, still it is always a separation. For instance, suppose—" he hesitated: "suppose Zara were to die?"

"Well, you would soon meet her again," I answered. "For though you might live many years after her, still you would know in yourself that those years were but minutes in the realms of space—"

"Minutes that decide our destinies," he interrupted with solemnity. "And there is always this possibility to contemplate—suppose Zara were to leave me now, how can I be sure that I shall be strong enough to live out my remainder of life purely enough to deserve to meet her again? And if not then Zara's death would mean utter and almost hopeless separation for ever—though perhaps I might begin over again in some other form, and so reach the goal."

He spoke so musingly and seriously that I was surprised, for I had thought him impervious to such a folly as the fear of death.

"You are melancholy, Heliobas," I said. "In the first place, Zara is not going to leave you yet; and secondly, if she did, you know your strongest efforts would be brought to bear on your career, in order that no shadow of obstinacy or error might obstruct your path. Why, the very essence of our belief is in the strength of Will-power. What we WILL to do, especially if it be any act of spiritual progress, we can always accomplish."

Heliobas took my hand and pressed it warmly.

"You are so lately come from the high regions," he said, "that it warms and invigorates me to hear your encouraging words. Pray do not

MARIE CORELLI

think me capable of yielding long to the weakness of foreboding. I am, in spite of my advancement in electric science, nothing but a man, and am apt to be hampered oftentimes by my mortal trappings. We have prolonged our conversation further than I intended. I assure you it is better for you to try to sleep, even though, as I know, you feel so wide awake. Let me give you a soothing draught; it will have the effect of composing your physical nerves into steady working order."

He poured something from a small phial into a glass, and handed it to me. I drank it at once, obediently, and with a smile.

"Good-night, my Master!" I then said. "You need have no fear of your own successful upward progress. For if there were the slightest chance of your falling into fatal error, all those human souls you have benefited would labour and pray for your rescue; and I know now that prayers reach Heaven, so long as they are unselfish. I, though I am one of the least of your disciples, out of the deep gratitude of my heart towards you, will therefore pray unceasingly for you, both here and hereafter."

He bent his head.

"I thank you!" he said simply. "More deeds are wrought by prayer than this world dreams of! That is a true saying. God bless you, my child. Good-night!"

And he opened the door of his study for me to pass out. As I did so, he laid his hand lightly on my head in a sort of unspoken benediction— then he closed his door, and I found myself alone in the great hall. A suspended lamp was burning brightly, and the fountain was gurgling melodiously to itself in a subdued manner, as if it were learning a new song for the morning. I sped across the mosaic pavement with a light eager step, and hurried up the stairs, intent on finding Zara to tell her how happy I felt, and how satisfied I was with my wonderful experience. I reached the door of her bedroom—it was ajar. I softly pushed it farther open, and looked in. A small but exquisitely modelled statue of an "Eros" ornamented one corner. His uplifted torch served as a light which glimmered faintly through a rose-coloured glass, and shed a tender lustre over the room; but especially upon the bed, ornamented with rich Oriental needlework, where Zara lay fast asleep. How beautiful she looked! Almost as lovely as any one of the radiant spirits I had met in my aerial journey! Her rich dark hair was scattered loosely on the white pillows; her long silky lashes curled softly on the delicately tinted cheeks; her lips, tenderly red, like the colour on budding apple-blossoms in early spring, were slightly parted, showing the glimmer of the small white teeth within; her night-dress was slightly undone, and half displayed and half disguised her neck and daintily rounded bosom, on which the electric jewel she always wore glittered brilliantly as it rose and sank with her regular and quiet breathing. One fair hand lay outside the coverlet, and the reflection from the lamp of the "Eros" flickered on a ring which adorned it, making its central diamond flash like a wandering star.

I looked long and tenderly on this perfect ideal of a "Sleeping Beauty," and then thought I would draw closer and see if I could kiss her without awaking her. I advanced a few steps into the room—when suddenly I was stopped. Within about a yard's distance from the bed a SOMETHING opposed my approach! I could not move a foot forward—I tried vigorously, but in vain! I could step backward, and that was all. Between me and Zara there seemed to be an invisible barrier, strong, and absolutely impregnable. There was nothing to be seen—nothing but the softly-shaded room—the ever-smiling "Eros," and the exquisite reposeful figure of my sleeping friend. Two steps, and I could have touched her; but those two steps I was forcibly prevented from making—as forcibly as though a deep ocean had rolled between her and me. I did not stop long to consider this strange occurrence—I felt sure it had something to do with her spiritual life and sympathy, therefore it neither alarmed nor perplexed me. Kissing my hand tenderly towards my darling, who lay so close to me, and who was yet so jealously and invisibly guarded during her slumbers, I softly and reverently withdrew. On reaching my own apartment, I was more than half inclined to sit up reading and studying the parchments Heliobas had given me; but on second thoughts I resolved to lock up these precious manuscripts and go to bed. I did so, and before preparing to sleep I remembered to kneel down and offer up praise and honour, with a loving and believing heart, to that Supreme Glory, of which I had been marvellously permitted to enjoy a brief but transcendent glimpse. And as I knelt, absorbed and happy, I heard, like a soft echo falling through the silence of my room, a sound like distant music, through which these words floated towards me: "A new commandment give I unto you, that you love one another, even as I have loved you!"

XIII

SOCIABLE CONVERSE

The next morning Zara came herself to awaken me, looking as fresh and lovely as a summer morning. She embraced me very tenderly, and said:

"I have been talking for more than an hour with Casimir. He has told me everything. What wonders you have seen! And are you not happy, dearest? Are you not strong and satisfied?"

"Perfectly!" I replied. "But, O Zara! what a pity that all the world should not know what we know!"

"All have not a desire for knowledge," replied Zara. "Even in your vision of the garden you possessed, there were only a few who still sought you; for those few you would have done anything, but for the others your best efforts were in vain."

"They might not have been always in vain," I said musingly.

"No, they might not," agreed Zara. "That is just the case of the world to-day. While there is life in it, there is also hope. And talking of the world, let me remind you that you are back in it now, and must therefore be hampered with tiresome trivialities. Two of these are as follows; First, here is a letter for you, which has just come; secondly, breakfast will be ready in twenty minutes!"

I looked at her smiling face attentively. She was the very embodiment of vigorous physical health and beauty; it seemed like a dream to remember her in the past night, guarded by that invincible barrier, the work of no mortal hand. I uttered nothing, however, of these thoughts, and responding to her evident gaiety of heart, I smiled also.

"I will be down punctually at the expiration of the twenty minutes," I said. "I assure you, Zara, I am quite sensible of the claims of earthly existence upon me. For instance, I am very hungry, and I shall enjoy breakfast immensely if you will make the coffee."

Zara, who among her other accomplishments had the secret of making coffee to perfection, promised laughingly to make it extra well, and flitted from the room, singing softly as she went a fragment of the Neapolitan Stornello:

> *"Fior di mortelle*
> *Queste manine tue son tanto belle!*
> *Fior di limone*
> *Ti voglio far morire di passione*
> *Salta! lari—lira."*

The letter Zara had brought me was from Mrs. Everard, announcing that she would arrive in Paris that very day, Sunday.

> "By the time you get this note," so ran her words, "we shall have landed at the Grand Hotel. Come and see us at once, if you can. The Colonel is anxious to judge for himself how you are looking. If you are really recovered sufficiently to leave your medical pension, we shall be delighted to have you with us again. I, in particular, shall be glad, for it is real lonesome when the Colonel is out, and I do hate to go shopping by myself, So take pity upon your affectionate
>
> AMY

Seated at breakfast, I discussed this letter with Heliobas and Zara, and decided that I would call at the Grand Hotel that morning.

"I wish you would come with me, Zara," I said wistfully.

To my surprise, she answered:

"Certainly I will, if you like. But we will attend High Mass at Notre Dame first. There will be plenty of time for the call afterwards."

I gladly agreed to this, and Heliobas added with cheerful cordiality:

"Why not ask your friends to dine here to-morrow? Zara's call will be a sufficient opening formality; and you yourself have been long enough with us now to know that any of your friends will be welcome here. We might have a pleasant little party, especially if you add Mr. and Mrs. Challoner and their daughters to the list. And I will ask Ivan."

I glanced at Zara when the Prince's name was uttered, but she made no sign of either offence or indifference.

"You are very hospitable," I said, addressing Heliobas; "but I really see no reason why you should throw open your doors to my friends, unless, indeed, you specially desire to please me."

"Why, of course I do!" he replied heartily; and Zara looked up and smiled.

"Then," I returned, "I will ask them to come. What am I to say about my recovery, which I know is little short of miraculous?"

"Say," replied Heliobas, "that you have been cured by electricity. There is nothing surprising in such a statement nowadays. But say nothing of the HUMAN electric force employed upon you—no one would believe you, and the effort to persuade unpersuadable people is always a waste of time."

An hour after this conversation Zara and I were in the cathedral of Notre Dame. I attended the service with very different feelings to those I had hitherto experienced during the same ceremony. Formerly my mind had been distracted by harassing doubts and perplexing contradictions; now everything had a meaning for me—high, and solemn, and sweet. As the incense rose, I thought of those rays of connecting light I had seen, on which prayers travel exactly as sound travels through the telephone. As the grand organ pealed sonorously through the fragrant air, I remembered the ever youthful and gracious Spirits of Music, one of whom, Aeon, had promised to be my friend. Just to try the strength of my own electric force, I whispered the name and looked up. There, on a wide slanting ray of sunlight that fell directly across the altar was the angelic face I well remembered!—the delicate hands holding the semblance of a harp in air! It was but for an instant I saw it—one brief breathing-space in which its smile mingled with the sunbeams and then it vanished. But I knew I was not forgotten, and the deep satisfaction of my soul poured itself in unspoken praise on the flood of the "Sanctus! Sanctus!" that just then rolled triumphantly through the aisles of Notre Dame. Zara was absorbed in silent prayer throughout the Mass; but at its conclusion, when we came out of the cathedral, she was unusually gay and elate. She conversed vivaciously with me concerning the social merits and accomplishments of the people we were going to visit; while the brisk walk through the frosty air brightened her eyes and cheeks into warmer lustre, so that on our arrival at the Grand Hotel she looked to my fancy even lovelier than usual.

Mrs. Everard did not keep us waiting long in the private salon to which we were shown. She fluttered down, arrayed in a wonderful "art" gown of terra-cotta and pale blue hues cunningly intermixed, and proceeded to hug me with demonstrative fervour. Then she held me a little distance off, and examined me attentively.

"Do you know," she said, "you are simply in lovely condition! I never would have believed it. You are actually as plump and pink as a peach.

And you are the same creature that wailed and trembled, and had palpitations and headaches and stupors! Your doctor must be a perfect magician. I think I must consult him, for I am sure I don't look half as well as you do."

And indeed she did not. I thought she had a tired, dragged appearance, but I would not say so. I knew her well, and I was perfectly aware that though she was fascinating and elegant in every way, her life was too much engrossed in trifles ever to yield her healthy satisfaction.

After responding warmly to her affectionate greeting, I said:

"Amy, you must allow me to introduce the sister of my doctor to you. Madame Zara Casimir—Mrs. Everard."

Zara, who had moved aside a little way out of delicacy, to avoid intruding on our meeting, now turned, and with her own radiant smile and exquisite grace, stretched out her little well-gloved hand.

"I am delighted to know you!" she said, in those sweet penetrating accents of hers which were like music. "Your friend," here indicating me by a slight yet tender gesture, "has also become mine; but I do not think we shall be jealous, shall we?"

Mrs. Everard made some attempt at a suitable reply, but she was so utterly lost in admiration of Zara's beauty, that her habitual self-possession almost deserted her. Zara, however, had the most perfect tact, and with it the ability of making herself at home anywhere, and we were soon all three talking cheerfully and without constraint. When the Colonel made his appearance, which he did very shortly, he too was "taken off his feet," as the saying is, by Zara's loveliness, and the same effect was produced on the Challoners, who soon afterwards joined us in a body. Mrs. Challoner, in particular, seemed incapable of moving her eyes from the contemplation of my darling's sweet face, and I glowed with pride and pleasure as I noted how greatly she was admired. Miss Effie Challoner alone, who was, by a certain class of young men, considered "doocid pretty, with go in her," opposed her stock of physical charms to those of Zara, with a certain air of feminine opposition; but she was only able to keep this barrier up for a little time. Zara's winning power of attraction was too much for her, and she, like all present, fell a willing captive to the enticing gentleness, the intellectual superiority, and the sympathetic influence exercised by the evenly balanced temperament and character of the beautiful woman I loved so well.

After some desultory and pleasant chat, Zara, in the name of her brother and herself, invited Colonel and Mrs. Everard and the Challoner family to dine at the Hotel Mars next day—an invitation which was accepted by all with eagerness. I perceived at once that every one of them was anxious to know more of Zara and her surroundings—a curiosity which I could not very well condemn. Mrs. Everard then wanted me to remain with her for the rest of the afternoon; but an instinctive feeling came upon me, that soon perhaps I should have to part from Heliobas and Zara, and all the wonders and delights of their household, in order to resume my own working life—therefore I determined I would drain my present cup of pleasure to the last drop. So I refused Amy's request, pleading as an excuse that I was still under my doctor's authority, and could not indulge in such an excitement as an afternoon in her society without his permission. Zara bore me out in this assertion, and added for me to Mrs. Everard:

"Indeed, I think it will be better for her to remain perfectly quiet with us for a day or two longer; then she will be thoroughly cured, and free to do as she likes."

"Well!" said Mrs. Challoner; "I must say she doesn't look as if anything were the matter with her. In fact, I never saw two more happy, healthy-looking girls than you both. What secret do you possess to make yourselves look so bright?"

"No secret at all," replied Zara, laughing; "we simply follow the exact laws of health, and they suffice."

Colonel Everard, who had been examining me critically and asking me a few questions, here turned to Zara and said:

"Do you really mean to say, Madame Casimir, that your brother cured this girl by electricity?"

"Purely so!" she answered earnestly.

"Then it's the most wonderful recovery *I* ever saw. Why, at Cannes, she was hollow-eyed, pale, and thin as a willow-wand; now she looks— well, she knows how she is herself—but if she feels as spry as she looks, she's in first-rate training!"

I laughed.

"I Do feel spry, Colonel," I said. "Life seems to me like summer sunshine."

"Brava!" exclaimed Mr. Challoner. He was a staid, rather slow Kentuckian who seldom spoke; and when he did, seemed to find it rather an exertion. "If there's one class of folk I detest more than another, it is those all-possessed people who find life unsuited to their fancies. Nobody asked them to come into it—nobody would miss them if they went out of it. Being in it, it's barely civil to grumble at the Deity who sent them along here. I never do it myself if I can help it."

We laughed, and Mrs. Challoner's eyes twinkled.

"In England, dear, for instance," she said, with a mischievous glance at her spouse—"in England you never grumbled, did you?"

Mr. Challoner looked volumes—his visage reddened, and he clenched his broad fist with ominous vigour.

"Why, by the Lord!" he said, with even more than his usual deliberate utterance, "in England the liveliest flea that ever gave a triumphal jump in air would find his spirits inclined to droop! I tell you, ma'am," he continued, addressing himself to Zara, whose merry laugh rang out like a peal of little golden bells at this last remark—"I tell you that when I walked in the streets of London I used to feel as if I were one of a band of criminals. Every person I met looked at me as if the universe were about to be destroyed next minute, and they had to build another up right away without God to help 'em!"

"Well, I believe I agree with you," said Colonel Everard. "The English take life too seriously. In their craze for business they manage to do away with pleasure altogether. They seem afraid to laugh, and they even approach the semblance of a smile with due caution."

"I'm free to confess," added his wife, "that I'm not easily chilled through. But an English 'at home' acts upon me like a patent refrigerator—I get regularly frozen to the bone!"

"Dear me!" laughed Zara; "you give very bad accounts of Shakespeare's land! It must be very sad!"

"I believe it wasn't always so," pursued Colonel Everard; "there are legends which speak of it as Merrie England. I dare say it might have been merry once, before it was governed by shopkeepers; but now, you must get away from it if you want to enjoy life. At least such is my opinion. But have you never been in England, Madame Casimir? You speak English perfectly."

"Oh, I am a fairly good linguist," replied Zara, "thanks to my brother. But I have never crossed the Channel."

The Misses Challoner looked politely surprised; their father's shrewd face wore an expression of grim contentment.

"Don't cross it, ma'am," he said emphatically, "unless you have a special desire to be miserable. If you want to know how Christians love one another and how to be made limply and uselessly wretched, spend a Sunday in London."

"I think I will not try the experiment, Mr. Challoner," returned Zara gaily. "Life is short, and I prefer to enjoy it."

"Say," interrupted Mrs. Challoner, turning to me at this juncture, "now you are feeling so well, would it be asking you too much to play us a piece of your own improvising?"

I glanced at the grand piano, which occupied a corner of the salon where we sat, and hesitated. But at a slight nod from Zara, I rose, drew off my gloves, and seated myself at the instrument. Passing my hands lightly over the keys, I wandered through a few running passages; and as I did so, murmured a brief petition to my aerial friend Aeon. Scarcely had I done this, when a flood of music seemed to rush to my brain and thence to my fingers, and I played, hardly knowing what I played, but merely absorbed in trying to give utterance to the sounds which were falling softly upon my inner sense of hearing like drops of summer rain on a thirsty soil. I was just aware that I was threading the labyrinth of a minor key, and that the result was a network of delicate and tender melody reminding me of Heinrich Heine's words:

"Lady, did you not hear the nightingale sing? A beautiful silken voice—a web of happy notes—and my soul was taken in its meshes, and strangled and tortured thereby."

A few minutes, and the inner voice that conversed with me so sweetly, died away into silence, and at the same time my fingers found their way to the closing chord. As one awaking from a dream, I looked up. The little group of friendly listeners were rapt in the deepest attention; and when I ceased, a murmur of admiration broke from them all, while Zara's eyes glistened with sympathetic tears.

"How can you do it?" asked Mrs. Challoner in good-natured amazement. "It seems to me impossible to compose like that while seated at the piano, and without taking previous thought!"

"It is not My doing," I began; "it seems to come to me from—"

But I was checked by a look from Zara, that gently warned me not to hastily betray the secret of my spiritual communion with the unseen sources of harmony. So I smiled and said no more. Inwardly I was full of a great rejoicing, for I knew that however well I had played in past days, it was nothing compared to the vigour and ease which were now given to me—a sort of unlocking of the storehouse of music, with freedom to take my choice of all its vast treasures.

"Well, it's what WE call inspiration," said Mr. Challoner, giving my hand a friendly grasp; "and wherever it comes from, it must be a great happiness to yourself as well as to others."

"It is," I answered earnestly. "I believe few are so perfectly happy in music as I am."

Mrs. Everard looked thoughtful.

"No amount of practice could make ME play like that," she said; "yet I have had two or three masters who were supposed to be first-rate. One of them was a German, who used to clutch his hair like a walking tragedian whenever I played a wrong note. I believe he got up his reputation entirely by that clutch, for he often played wrong notes himself without minding it. But just because he worked himself into a sort of frenzy when others went wrong, everybody praised him, and said he had such an ear and was so sensitive that he must be a great musician. He worried me nearly to death over Bach's 'Well-tempered Klavier'— all to no purpose, for I can't play a note of it now, and shouldn't care to if I could. I consider Bach a dreadful old bore, though I know it is heresy to say so. Even Beethoven is occasionally prosy, only no one will be courageous enough to admit it. People would rather go to sleep over classical music than confess they don't like it."

"Schubert would have been a grander master than Beethoven, if he had only lived long enough," said Zara; "but I dare say very few will agree with me in such an assertion. Unfortunately most of my opinions differ from those of everyone else."

"You should say FORTUNATELY, madame," said Colonel Everard, bowing gallantly; "as the circumstance has the happy result of making you perfectly original as well as perfectly charming."

Zara received this compliment with her usual sweet equanimity, and we rose to take our leave. As we were passing out, Amy Everard drew me back and crammed into the pocket of my cloak a newspaper.

"Read it when you are alone," she whispered; "and you will see what Raffaello Cellini has done with the sketch he made of you."

We parted from these pleasant Americans with cordial expressions of goodwill, Zara reminding them of their engagement to visit her at her own home next day, and fixing the dinner-hour for half-past seven.

On our return to the Hotel Mars, we found Heliobas in the drawing-room, deep in converse with a Catholic priest—a fine-looking man of venerable and noble features. Zara addressed him as "Father Paul," and bent humbly before him to receive his blessing, which he gave her with almost parental tenderness. He seemed, from his familiar manner with them, to be a very old friend of the family.

On my being introduced to him, he greeted me with gentle courtesy, and gave me also his simple unaffected benediction. We all partook of a light luncheon to-gether, after which repast Heliobas and Father Paul withdrew together. Zara looked after their retreating figures with a sort of meditative pathos in her large eyes; and then she told me she had something to finish in her studio—would I excuse her for about an hour? I readily consented, for I myself was desirous of passing a little time in solitude, in order to read the manuscripts Heliobas had given me. "For," thought I, "if there is anything in them not quite clear to me, he will explain it, and I had better take advantage of his instruction while I can."

As Zara and I went upstairs together, we were followed by Leo—a most unusual circumstance, as that faithful animal was generally in attendance on his master. Now, however, he seemed to have something oppressive on his mind, for he kept close to Zara, and his big brown eyes, whenever he raised them to her face, were full of intense melancholy. His tail drooped in a forlorn way, and all the vivacity of his nature seemed to have gone out of him.

"Leo does not seem well," I said, patting the dog's beautiful silky coat, an attention to which he responded by a heavy sigh and a wistful gaze approaching to tears. Zara looked at him.

"Poor Leo!" she murmured caressingly. "Perhaps he feels lonely. Do you want to come with your mistress to-day, old boy? So you shall. Come along—cheer up, Leo!"

And, nodding to me, she passed into her studio, the dog following her. I turned into my own apartment, and then bethought myself of the newspaper Mrs. Everard had thrust into my pocket. It was a Roman journal, and the passage marked for my perusal ran as follows:

"The picture of the Improvisatrice, painted by our countryman Signor Raffaello Cellini, has been purchased by Prince N—— for the sum of forty thousand francs. The Prince generously permits it to remain on view for a few days longer, so that those who have not yet enjoyed its attraction, have still time to behold one of the most wonderful pictures of the age. The colouring yet remains a marvel to both students and connoisseurs, and the life-like appearance of the girl's figure, robed in its clinging white draperies ornamented with lilies of the valley, is so strong, that one imagines she will step out of the canvas and confront the bystanders. Signor Cellini must now be undoubtedly acknowledged as one of the greatest geniuses of modern times."

I could see no reason, as I perused this, to be sure that *I* had served as the model for this successful work of art, unless the white dress and the lilies of the valley, which I had certainly worn at Cannes, were sufficient authority for forming such a conclusion. Still I felt quite a curiosity about the picture—the more so as I could foresee no possible chance of my ever beholding it. I certainly should not go to Rome on purpose, and in a few days it would be in the possession of Prince N——, a personage whom in all probability I should never know. I put the newspaper carefully by, and then turned my mind to the consideration of quite another subject—namely, the contents of my parchment documents. The first one I opened was that containing the private instructions of Heliobas to myself for the preservation of my own health, and the cultivation of the electric force within me. These were so exceedingly simple, and yet so wonderful in their simplicity, that I was surprised. They were based upon the plainest and most reasonable common-sense arguments—easy enough for a child to understand. Having promised never to make them public, it is impossible for me to give the slightest hint of their purport; but I may say at once, without trespassing the bounds of my pledged word, that if these few concise instructions were known and practised by everyone, doctors would be entirely thrown out of employment, and chemists' shops would no longer cumber the streets. Illness would be very difficult of attainment—though in the event of its occurring each individual would know how to treat him or herself—and life could be prolonged easily and comfortably to more than a hundred years, barring, of course, accidents by sea, rail and road, or by deeds of violence. But it will take many generations before the world is UNIVERSALLY self-restrained enough to follow such plain maxims as those laid down for me in the writing of my benefactor, Heliobas—even if it be ever self-restrained at all, which, judging from the present state of society, is much to be doubted. Therefore, no more of the subject, on which, indeed, I am forbidden to speak.

The other document, called "The Electric Principle of Christianity," I found so curious and original, suggesting so many new theories concerning that religion which has civilized a great portion of humanity, that, as I am not restrained by any promise on this point, I have resolved to give it here in full. My readers must not be rash enough to jump to the conclusion that I set it forward as an explanation or confession of my own faith; my creed has nothing to do with anyone save myself. I simply copy the manuscript I possess, as the theory of a deeply read and widely intelligent man, such as Heliobas undoubtedly WAS and IS; a man, too, in whose veins runs the blood of the Chaldean kings—earnest and thoughtful Orientals, who were far wiser in their generation perhaps than we, with all our boasted progress, are in ours. The coincidences which have to do with electrical science will, I believe, be generally admitted to be curious if not convincing. To me, of course, they are only fresh proofs of WHAT *I* KNOW, because *I* HAVE SEEN THE GREAT ELECTRIC CIRCLE, and know its power (guided as it is by the Central Intelligence within) to be capable of anything, from the sending down of a minute spark of instinct into the heart of a flower, to the perpetual manufacture and re-absorption of solar systems by the million million. And it is a circle that ever widens without end. What more glorious manifestation can there be of the Creator's splendour and wisdom! But as to how this world of ours span round in its own light littleness farther and farther from the Radiant Ring, till its very Sun began to be re-absorbed, and till its Moon disappeared and became a mere picture—till it became of itself like a small blot on the fair scroll of the Universe, while its inhabitants grew to resent all heavenly attraction; and how it was yet thought worth God's patience and tender consideration, just for the sake of a few human souls upon it who still remembered and loved Him, to give it one more chance before it should be drawn back into the Central Circle like a spark within a fire—all this is sufficiently set forth in the words of Heliobas, quoted in the next chapter.

XIV

THE ELECTRIC CREED

The "Electric Principle of Christianity" opened as follows:

"From all Eternity God, or the SUPREME SPIRIT OF LIGHT, existed, and to all Eternity He will continue to exist. This is plainly stated in the New Testament thus: 'God is a SPIRIT, and they that worship Him must worship Him IN SPIRIT and in truth.'

"He is a Shape of pure Electric Radiance. Those who may be inclined to doubt this may search the Scriptures on which they pin their faith, and they will find that all the visions and appearances of the Deity there chronicled were electric in character.

"As a poet forms poems, or a musician melodies, so God formed by a Thought the Vast Central Sphere in which He dwells, and peopled it with the pure creations of His glorious fancy. And why? Because, being pure Light, He is also pure Love; the power or capacity of Love implies the necessity of Loving; the necessity of loving points to the existence of things to be loved—hence the secret of creation. From the ever-working Intelligence of this Divine Love proceeded the Electric Circle of the Universe, from whence are born all worlds.

"This truth vaguely dawned upon the ancient poets of Scripture when they wrote: 'Darkness was upon the face of the deep. And the Spirit of God moved upon the face of the waters. And God said, Let there be light. And there was light.'

"These words apply SOLELY to the creation or production of OUR OWN EARTH, and in them we read nothing but a simple manifestation of electricity, consisting in a HEATING PASSAGE OF RAYS from the Central Circle to the planet newly propelled forth from it, which caused that planet to produce and multiply the wonders of the animal, vegetable, and mineral kingdoms which we call Nature.

"Let us now turn again to the poet-prophets of Scripture: 'And God said, Let us make man in our image.' The word 'OUR' here implies an instinctive idea that God was never alone. This idea is correct. Love cannot exist in a chaos; and God by the sheer necessity of His Being has for ever been surrounded by radiant and immortal Spirits emanating from His own creative glory—beings in whom all beauty and all purity are found. In the IMAGES, therefore (only the IMAGES), of these Children of Light and of Himself, He made Man—that is, He caused the Earth to be inhabited and DOMINATED by beings composed of Earth's component parts, animal, vegetable, and mineral, giving them their superiority by placing within them His 'LIKENESS' in the form of an ELECTRIC FLAME or GERM of spiritual existence combined with its companion working-force of WILL-POWER.

"Like all flames, this electric spark can either be fanned into a fire or it can be allowed to escape in air—IT CAN NEVER BE DESTROYED. It can be fostered and educated till it becomes a living Spiritual Form of absolute beauty—an immortal creature of thought, memory, emotion, and working intelligence. If, on the contrary, he is neglected or forgotten, and its companion Will is drawn by the weight of Earth to work for earthly aims alone, then it escapes and seeks other chances of development in OTHER FORMS on OTHER PLANETS, while the body it leaves, SUPPORTED ONLY BY PHYSICAL SUSTENANCE DRAWN FROM THE EARTH ON WHICH IT DWELLS, becomes a mere lump of clay ANIMATED BY MERE ANIMAL LIFE SOLELY, full of inward ignorance and corruption and outward incapacity. Of such material are the majority of men composed BY THEIR OWN FREE-WILL AND CHOICE, because they habitually deaden the voice of conscience and refuse to believe in the existence of a spiritual element within and around them.

"To resume: the Earth is one of the smallest of planets; and not only this, but, from its position in the Universe, receives a less amount of direct influence from the Electric Circle than other worlds more happily situated. Were men wise enough to accept this fact, they would foster to the utmost the germs of electric sympathy within themselves, in order to form a direct communication, or system of attraction, between this planet and the ever-widening Ring, so that some spiritual benefit might accrue to them thereby. But as the ages roll on, their chances of doing this diminish. The time is swiftly approaching when the invincible Law of Absorption shall extinguish Earth as easily as we blow out the flame of a candle. True, it may be again reproduced, and again thrown out on space; but then it will be in a new and grander form, and will doubtless have more godlike inhabitants.

"In the meantime—during those brief cycles of centuries which are as a breath in the workings of the Infinite, and which must yet elapse before this world, as we know it, comes to an end—God has taken pity on the few, very few souls dwelling here, pent up in mortal clay, who have blindly tried to reach Him, like plants straining up to the light, and has established a broad stream of sympathetic electric communication with Himself, which all who care to do so may avail themselves of.

"Here it may be asked: Why should God take pity? Because that Supreme Shape of Light finds a portion of Himself in all pure souls that love Him, and HE CANNOT DESPISE HIMSELF. Also because He is capable of all the highest emotions known to man, in a far larger and grander degree, besides possessing other sentiments and desires unimaginable to the human mind. It is enough to say that all the attributes that accompany perfect goodness He enjoys; therefore He can feel compassion, tenderness, forgiveness, patience—all or any of the emotions that produce pure, unselfish pleasure.

"Granting Him, therefore, these attributes (and it is both blasphemous and unreasonable to DENY HIM THOSE VIRTUES WHICH DISTINGUISH THE BEST OF MEN), it is easily understood how He, the All-Fair Beneficent Ruler of the Central Sphere, perceiving the long distance to which the Earth was propelled, like a ball flung too far out, from the glory of His Electric Ring, saw also that the creatures He had made in His image were in danger of crushing that image completely out, and with it all remembrance of Him, in the fatal attention they gave to their merely earthly surroundings, lacking, as they did, and not possessing sufficient energy to seek, electric attraction. In brief, this Earth and God's World were like America and Europe before the Atlantic Cable was laid. Now the messages of goodwill flash under the waves, heedless of the storms. So also God's Cable is laid between us and His Heaven in the person of Christ.

"For ages (always remembering that our ages are with God a moment) the idea of WORSHIP was in the mind of man. With this idea came also the sentiment of PROPITIATION. The untamed savage has from time immemorial instinctively felt the necessity of looking up to a Being greater than Himself, and also of seeking a reconciliation with that Being for some fault or loss in himself which he is aware of, yet cannot explain. This double instinct—worship and propitiation—is the key-note of all the creeds of the world, and may be called God's first thought of the cable to be hereafter laid—a lightning-thought which He instilled into the human race to prepare it, as one might test a telegraph-wire from house to house, before stretching it across a continent.

"All religions, as known to us, are mere types of Christianity. It is a notable fact that some of the oldest and most learned races in the world, such as the Armenians and Chaldeans, were the first to be convinced of the truth of Christ's visitation. Buddhism, of which there are so many million followers, is itself a type of Christ's teaching; only it lacks the supernatural element. Buddha died a hermit at the age of eighty, as any wise and ascetic man might do to-day. The death and resurrection of Christ were widely different. Anyone can be a Buddha again; anyone can Not be a Christ. That there are stated to be more followers of Buddhism than of Christianity is no proof of any efficacy in the former or lack of power in the latter. Buddhists help to swell that very large class of persons who prefer a flattering picture to a plain original; or who, sheep-like by nature, finding themselves all together in one meadow, are too lazy, as well as too indifferent, to seek pastures fresher and fairer.

"Through the divine influence of an Electric Thought, then, the world unconsciously grew to expect SOMETHING—they knew not what. The old creeds of the world, like sunflowers, turned towards that unknown Sun; the poets, prophets, seers, all spoke of some approaching consolation and glory; and to this day the fated Jews expect it, unwilling to receive as their Messiah the Divine Martyr they slew, though their own Scriptures testify to His identity.

"Christ came, born of a Virgin; that is, a radiant angel from God's Sphere was in the first place sent down to Earth to wear the form of Mary of Bethlehem, in Judea. Within that vessel of absolute purity God placed an Emanation of His own radiance—no germ or small flame such as is given to us in our bodies to cultivate and foster, but a complete immortal Spirit, a portion of God Himself, wise, sinless, and strong. This Spirit, pent up in clay, was born as a helpless babe, grew up as man—as man taught, comforted, was slain and buried; but as pure Spirit rose again and returned in peace to Heaven, His mission done.

"It was necessary, in order to establish what has been called an electric communication between God's Sphere and this Earth, that an actual immortal, untainted Spirit in the person of Christ should walk this world, sharing with men sufferings, difficulties, danger, and death. Why? In order that we might first completely confide in and trust Him, afterwards realizing His spiritual strength and glory by His resurrection. And here may be noted the main difference between the Electric Theory of Christianity and other theories. CHRIST DID NOT DIE BECAUSE GOD NEEDED A SACRIFICE. The idea of sacrifice is a relic of heathen barbarism; God is too infinitely loving to desire the sacrifice of the smallest flower. He is too patient to be ever wrathful; and barbaric ignorance confronts us again in the notion that He should need to be appeased. And the fancy that He should desire Himself or part of Himself to become a sacrifice to Himself has arisen out of the absurd and conflicting opinions of erring humanity, wherein right and wrong are so jumbled together that it is difficult to distinguish one from the other. Christ's death was not a sacrifice; it was simply a means of confidence and communion with the Creator. A sinless Spirit suffered to show us how to suffer; lived on earth to show us how to live; prayed to show us how to pray; died to show us how to die; rose again to impress strongly upon us that there was in truth a life beyond this one, for which He strove to prepare our souls. Finally, by His re-ascension into Heaven He established that much-needed electric communication between us and the Central Sphere.

"It can be proved from the statements of the New Testament that in Christ was an Embodied Electric Spirit. From first to last His career was attended by ELECTRIC PHENOMENA, of which eight examples are here quoted; and earnest students of the matter can find many others if they choose to examine for themselves.

"1. The appearance of the Star and the Vision of Angels on the night of His birth. The Chaldeans saw His 'star in the east,' and they came to worship Him. The Chaldeans were always a learned people, and electricity was an advanced science with them. They at once recognized the star to be no new planet, but simply a star-shaped flame flitting through space. They knew what this meant. Observe, too, that they had no doubts upon the point; they came 'to worship him,' and provided themselves with gifts to offer to this radiant Guest, the offspring of pure Light. The vision of the angels appearing to the shepherds was simply a joyous band of the Singing Children of the Electric Ring, who out of pure interest and pleasure floated in sight of Earth, drawn thither partly by the already strong attractive influence of the Radiance that was imprisoned there in the form of the Babe of Bethlehem.

"2. When Christ was baptized by John the Baptist, 'THE HEAVENS OPENED.'

"3. The sympathetic influence of Christ was so powerful that when He selected His disciples, He had but to speak to them, and at the sound of His voice, though they were engaged in other business, 'THEY LEFT ALL AND FOLLOWED HIM."

"4. Christ's body was charged with electricity. Thus He was easily able to heal sick and diseased persons by a touch or a look. The woman who caught at His garment in the crowd was cured of her long-standing ailment; and we see that Christ was aware of His own electric force by the words He used on that occasion: 'WHO TOUCHED ME? FOR I FEEL THAT SOME VIRTUE IS GONE OUT OF ME'—which is the exact feeling that a physical electrician experiences at this day after employing his powers on a subject. The raising of Jairus's daughter, of the widow's son at Nain, and of Lazarus, were all accomplished by the same means.

"5. The walking on the sea was a purely electric effort, AND CAN BE ACCOMPLISHED NOW BY ANYONE who has cultivated sufficient inner force. The sea being full of electric particles will support anybody sufficiently and similarly charged—the two currents combining to procure the necessary equilibrium. Peter, who was able to walk a little way, lost his power directly his will became vanquished by fear—because the sentiment of fear disperses electricity, and being purely HUMAN emotion, does away with spiritual strength for the time.

"6. The Death of Christ was attended by electric manifestations— by the darkness over the land during the Crucifixion; the tearing of the temple veil in twain; and the earthquake which finally ensued.

"7. The Resurrection was a most powerful display of electric force. It will be remembered that the angel who was found sitting at the entrance of the empty sepulchre 'had a countenance like LIGHTNING,' i.e., like electric flame. It must also be called to mind how the risen Christ addressed Mary Magdalene: 'TOUCH ME NOT, for I am but newly risen!' Why should she not have touched Him? Simply because His strength then was the strength of concentrated in-rushing currents of electricity; and to touch him at that moment would have been for Magdalene instant death by lightning. This effect of embodied electric force has been shadowed forth in the Greek legends of Apollo, whose glory consumed at a breath the mortal who dared to look upon him.

"8. The descent of the Holy Ghost, by which term is meant an ever-flowing current of the inspired working Intelligence of the Creator, was purely electric in character: 'Suddenly there came a sound from Heaven as of a rushing mighty wind, and it filled all the house where they were sitting. And there appeared unto them CLOVEN TONGUES LIKE AS OF FIRE, and sat upon each of them.' It may here be noted that the natural electric flame is DUAL or 'cloven' in shape.

"Let us now take the Creed as accepted to-day by the Christian Church, and see how thoroughly it harmonizes with the discoveries of spiritual electricity. 'I believe in one God the Father Almighty, Maker of Heaven and Earth, and of all things VISIBLE AND INVISIBLE.' This is a brief and simple description of the Creator as He exists—a Supreme Centre of Light, out of whom MUST spring all life, all love, all wisdom.

"'And in one Lord Jesus Christ, the only begotten Son of God, born of the Father before all ages.' This means that the only absolute Emanation of His own PERSONAL Radiance that ever wore such mean garb as our clay was found in Christ—who, as part of God, certainly existed 'BEFORE ALL AGES.' For as the Creed itself says, He was 'God of God, LIGHT OF LIGHT. Then we go on through the circumstances of Christ's birth, life, death, and resurrection, and our profession of faith brings us to 'I believe in the Holy Ghost, the Lord and Giver of Life, who proceedeth from the Father and the Son,' etc. This, as already stated, means that we believe that since Christ ascended into Heaven, our electric communication with the Creator has been established, and an ever-flowing current of divine inspiration is turned beneficially in the direction of our Earth, 'proceeding from the Father and the Son.' We admit in the Creed that this inspiration manifested itself before Christ came and 'SPAKE BY THE PROPHETS;' but, as before stated, this only happened at rare and difficult intervals, while now Christ Himself speaks through those who most strongly adhere to His teachings.

"It may here be mentioned that few seem to grasp the fact of the SPECIAL MESSAGE TO WOMEN intended to be conveyed in the person of the Virgin Mary. She was actually one of the radiant Spirits of the Central Sphere, imprisoned by God's will in woman's form. After the birth of Christ, she was still kept on earth, to follow His career to the end. There was a secret understanding between Himself and her. As for instance, when she found Him among the doctors of the law, she for one moment suffered her humanity to get the better of her in anxious inquiries; and His reply, 'Why sought ye Me? Wist ye not that I must be about My Father's business?' was a sort of reminder to her, which she at once accepted. Again, at the marriage feast in Cana of Galilee, when Christ turned the water into wine, He said to His mother, 'WOMAN, what have I to do with thee?' which meant simply: What have I to do with thee as WOMAN merely?—which was another reminder to her of her spiritual origin, causing her at once to address the servants who stood by as follows: 'Whatsoever He saith unto you, do it.' And why, it may be asked, if Mary was really an imprisoned immortal Spirit, sinless and joyous, should she be forced to suffer all the weaknesses, sorrows, and anxieties of any ordinary woman and mother? SIMPLY AS AN EXAMPLE TO WOMEN who are the mothers of the human race; and who, being thus laid under a heavy responsibility, need sympathetic guidance. Mary's life teaches women that the virtues they need are—obedience, purity, meekness, patience, long-suffering, modesty, self-denial, and endurance. She loved to hold a secondary position; she placed herself in willing subjection to Joseph—a man of austere and simple life, advanced in years, and weighted with the cares of a family by a previous marriage—who wedded her by AN INFLUENCE WHICH COMPELLED HIM to become her protector in the eyes of the world. Out of these facts, simple as they are, can be drawn the secret of happiness for women—a secret and a lesson that, if learned by heart, would bring them and those they love out of storm and bewilderment into peace and safety.

"FOR THOSE WHO HAVE ONCE BECOME AWARE OF THE EXISTENCE OF THE CENTRAL SPHERE AND OF THE ELECTRIC RING SURROUNDING IT, AND WHO ARE ABLE TO REALISE TO THE FULL THE GIGANTIC AS WELL AS MINUTE WORK PERFORMED BY THE ELECTRIC WAVES AROUND US AND WITHIN US, there can no longer be any doubt as to all the facts of Christianity, as none of them, VIEWED BY THE ELECTRIC THEORY, are otherwise than in accordance with the Creator's love and sympathy with even the smallest portion of His creation.

"Why then, if Christianity be a Divine Truth, are not all people Christians? As well ask, if music and poetry are good things, why all men are not poets and musicians. Art seeks art; in like manner God seeks God—that is, He seeks portions of His own essence among His creatures. Christ Himself said, 'Many are called, but few are chosen;' and it stands to reason that very few souls will succeed in becoming pure enough to enter the Central Sphere without hindrance. Many, on leaving Earth, will be detained in the Purgatory of Air, where thousands of spirits work for ages, watching over others, helping and warning others, and in this unselfish labour succeed in raising themselves, little by little, higher and ever higher, till they at last reach the longed-for goal. It must also be remembered that not only from Earth, but from All Worlds, released souls seek to attain final happiness in the Central Sphere where God is; so that, however great the number of those that are permitted to proceed thither from this little planet, they can only form, as it were, one drop in a mighty ocean.

"It has been asked whether the Electric Theory of Christianity includes the doctrine of Hell, or a place of perpetual punishment. Eternal Punishment is merely a form of speech for what is really Eternal Retrogression. For as there is a Forward, so there must be a Backward. The electric germ of the Soul—delicate, fiery, and imperishable as it is—can be forced by its companion Will to take refuge in a lower form of material existence, dependent on the body it first inhabits. For instance, a man who is obstinate in pursuing Active Evil can so retrograde the progress of any spiritual life within him, that it shall lack the power to escape, as it might do, from merely lymphatic and listless temperaments, to seek some other chance of development, but shall sink into the form of quadrupeds, birds, and other creatures dominated by purely physical needs. But there is one thing it can never escape from— Memory. And in that faculty is constituted Hell. So that if a man, by choice, forces his soul Downward to inhabit hereafter the bodies of dogs, horses, and other like animals, he should know that he does so at the cost of everything except Remembrance. Eternal Retrogression means that the hopelessly tainted electric germ recoils further and further from the Pure Centre whence it sprang, Always Bearing Within Itself the knowledge of What It Was Once and What It Might Have Been. There is a pathetic meaning in the eyes of a dog or a seal; in the melancholy, patient gaze of the oxen toiling at the plough; there is an unuttered warning in the silent faces of flowers; there is more tenderness of regret in the voice of the nightingale than love; and in the wild upward soaring of the lark, with its throat full of passionate, shouting prayer, there is shadowed forth the yearning hope that dies away in despair as the bird sinks to earth again, his instincts not half satisfied. There is no greater torture than to be compelled to remember, in suffering, joys and glorious opportunities gone for ever.

"Regarding the Electric Theory of Religion, it is curious to observe how the truth of it has again and again been dimly shadowed forth in the prophecies of Art, Science, and Poesy. The old painters who depicted a halo of light round the head of their Virgins and Saints did so out of a correct impulse which they did not hesitate to obey.* The astronomers who, after years of profound study, have been enabled to measure the flames of the burning sun, and to find out that these are from two to four thousand miles high, are nearly arrived at the conclusion that it is a world in a state of conflagration, in which they will be perfectly right. Those who hold that this Earth of ours was once self-luminous are also right; for it was indeed so when first projected from the Electric Ring. The compilers or inventors of the 'Arabian Nights' also hit upon a truth when they described human beings as forced through evil influences to take the forms of lower animals—a truth just explained in the Law of Retrogression. All art, all prophecy, all poesy, should therefore be accepted eagerly and studied earnestly, for in them we find ELECTRIC INSPIRATION out of which we are able to draw lessons for our guidance hereafter. The great point that scientists and artists have hitherto failed to discover, is the existence of the Central Sphere and its Surrounding Electric Circle. Once realize these two great facts, and all the wonders and mysteries of the Universe are perfectly easy of comprehension.

"In conclusion, I offer no opinion as to which is Christ's Church, or the Fountain-head of spirituality in the world. In all Churches errors have intruded through unworthy and hypocritical members. In a crowded congregation of worshippers there may perhaps be only one or two who are free from self-interest and personal vanity. In Sectarianism, for instance, there is no shred of Christianity. Lovers of God and followers of Christ must, in the first place, have perfect Unity; and the bond uniting them must be an electric one of love and faith. No true Christian should be able to hate, despise, or envy the other. Were I called upon to select among the churches, I should choose that which has most electricity working within it, and which is able to believe in a positive electrical communication between Christ and herself taking place daily on her altars—a Church which holds, as it were, the other end of the

---

* An impulse which led them vaguely to foresee, though, not to explain, the electric principle of spiritual life.

telegraphic ray between Earth and the Central Sphere, and which is, therefore, able to exist among the storms of modern opinions, affording refuge and consolation to the few determined travellers who are bound onward and upward. I shall not name the Church I mean, because it is the duty of everyone to examine and find it out for himself or herself. And even though this Church instinctively works in the right direction, it is full of errors introduced by ignorant and unworthy members— errors which must be carefully examined and cast aside by degrees. But, as I said before, it is the only Church which has Principles of Electricity within it, and is therefore destined to live, because electricity is life.

"Now I beseech the reader of this manuscript to which I, Heliobas, append my hand and seal, to remember and realize earnestly the following invincible facts: first that God and His Christ Exist; secondly, that while the little paltry affairs of our temporal state are being built up as crazily as a child's house of cards, the huge Central Sphere revolves, and the Electric Ring, strong and indestructible, is ever at its work of production and re-absorption; thirdly, that every thought and word of Every Habitant On Every Planet is reflected in lightning language before the Creator's eyes as easily as we receive telegrams; fourthly, that this world is The Only Spot In The Universe where His existence is actually questioned and doubted. And the general spread of modern positivism, materialism and atheism is one of the most terrific and meaning signs of the times. The work of separating the wheat from the chaff is beginning. Those who love and believe in God and Spiritual Beauty are about to be placed on one side; the millions who worship Self are drawing together in vast opposing ranks on the other; and the moment approaches which is prophesied to be 'as the lightning that lighteneth out of the one part under heaven, and shineth even to the other part.' In other words, the fiery whirlpool of the Ring is nearly ready to absorb our planet in its vortex; and out of all who dwell upon its surface, how many shall reach the glorious Central World of God? Of two men working in the same field, shall it not be as Christ foretold—'the one shall be taken, and the other left'?

"Friend, or Pupil, Reader! Whoever thou art, take heed and foster thine own soul! For know that nothing can hinder the Immortal Germ within us from taking the form imposed upon it by our Wills. Through Love and Faith, it can become an Angel, and perform wonders even while in its habitation of clay; through indifference and apathy, it can desert us altogether and for ever; through mockery and blasphemous

MARIE CORELLI

disbelief, it can sink into even a lower form than that of snake or toad. In our own unfettered hand lies our eternal destiny. Wonderful and terrible responsibility! Who shall dare to say we have no need of prayer?"

This document was signed "Casimir Heliobas," and bore a seal on which the impression seemed to consist of two Arabic or Sanskrit words, which I could not understand. I put it carefully away with its companion Ms. under lock and key, and while I was yet pausing earnestly on its contents, Zara came into my room. She had finished her task in the studio, she said, and she now proposed a drive in the Bois as an agreeable way of passing the rest of the afternoon.

"I want to be as long as possible in your company," she added, with a caressing sweetness in her manner; "for now your friends have come to Paris, I expect you will soon be leaving us, so I must have as much of you as I can."

My heart sank at the thought of parting from her, and I looked wistfully at her lovely face. Leo had followed her in from the studio, and seemed still very melancholy.

"We shall always be good friends, Zara dearest," I said, "shall we not? Close, fond friends, like sisters?"

"Sisters are not always fond of each other," remarked Zara, half gaily. "And you know 'there is a friend that sticketh closer than a brother'!"

"And what friend is that in YOUR case?" I asked, half jestingly, half curiously.

"Death!" she replied with a strange smile, in which there was both pathos and triumph.

I started at her unexpected reply, and a kind of foreboding chilled my blood. I endeavoured, however, to speak cheerfully as I said:

"Why, of course, death sticks more closely to us than any friend or relative. But you look fitter to receive the embraces of life than of death, Zara."

"They are both one and the same thing," she answered; "or rather, the one leads to the other. But do not let us begin to philosophize. Put on your things and come. The carriage is waiting."

I readily obeyed her, and we enjoyed an exhilarating drive together. The rest of the day passed with us all very pleasantly and our conversation had principally to do with the progress of art and literature in many lands, and maintained itself equally on the level of mundane affairs. Among other things, we spoke of the Spanish violinist Sarasate, and I amused Heliobas by quoting to him some of the criticisms of the

London daily papers on this great artist, such as, "He plays pieces which, though adapted to show his wonderful skill, are the veriest clap-trap;" "He lacks breadth and colour;" "A true type of the artist virtuoso," etc., etc.

"Half these people do not know in the least what they mean by 'breadth and colour' or 'virtuosity,'" said Heliobas, with a smile. "They think emotion, passion, all true sentiment combined with extraordinary TECHNIQUE, must be 'clap-trap.' Now the Continent of Europe acknowledges Pablo de Sarasate as the first violinist living, and London would not be London unless it could thrust an obtuse opposing opinion in the face of the Continent. England is the last country in the world to accept anything new. Its people are tired and blase; like highly trained circus-horses, they want to trot or gallop always in the old grooves. It will always be so. Sarasate is like a brilliant meteor streaming across their narrow bit of the heaven of music; they stare, gape, and think it is an unnatural phenomenon—a 'virtuosity' in the way of meteors, which they are afraid to accept lest it set them on fire. What would you? The meteor shines and burns; it is always a meteor!"

So, talking lightly, and gliding from subject to subject, the hours wore away, and we at last separated for the night.

I shall always be glad to remember how tenderly Zara kissed me and wished me good repose; and I recall now, with mingled pain, wonder, and gratitude, how perfectly calm and contented I felt as, after my prayers, I sank to sleep, unwarned, and therefore happily unconscious, of what awaited me on the morrow.

XV

DEATH BY LIGHTNING

The morning of the next day dawned rather gloomily. A yellowish fog obscured the air, and there was a closeness and sultriness in the atmosphere that was strange for that wintry season. I had slept well, and rose with the general sense of ease and refreshment that I always experienced since I had been under the treatment of Heliobas. Those whose unhappy physical condition causes them to awake from uneasy slumber feeling almost more fatigued than when they retired to rest, can scarcely have any idea of the happiness it engenders to open untired, glad eyes with the morning light; to feel the very air a nourishment; to stand with lithe, rested limbs in the bath of cool, pure water, finding that limpid element obediently adding its quota to the vigour of perfect health; to tingle from head to foot with the warm current of life running briskly through the veins, making the heart merry, the brain clear, and all the powers of body and mind in active working condition. This is indeed most absolute enjoyment. Add to it the knowledge of the existence of one's own inner Immortal Spirit—the beautiful germ of Light in the fostering of which no labour is ever taken in vain—the living, wondrous thing that is destined to watch an eternity of worlds bloom and fade to bloom again, like flowers, while itself, superior to them all, shall become ever more strong and radiant—with these surroundings and prospects, who shall say life is not worth living?

Dear Life! sweet Moment! gracious Opportunity! brief Journey so well worth the taking! gentle Exile so well worth enduring!—thy bitterest sorrows are but blessings in disguise; thy sharpest pains are brought upon us by ourselves, and even then are turned to warnings for our guidance; while above us, through us, and around us radiates the Supreme Love, unalterably tender!

These thoughts, and others like them, all more or less conducive to cheerfulness, occupied me till I had finished dressing. Melancholy was now no part of my nature, otherwise I might have been depressed by the appearance of the weather and the murkiness of the air. But since I learned the simple secrets of physical electricity, atmospheric influences have had no effect upon the equable poise of my temperament—a fact for which I cannot be too grateful, seeing how many of my fellow-creatures permit themselves to be affected by changes in the wind, intense heat, intense cold, or other things of the like character.

I went down to breakfast, singing softly on my way, and I found Zara already seated at the head of her table, while Heliobas was occupied in reading and sorting a pile of letters that lay beside his plate. Both greeted me with their usual warmth and heartiness.

During the repast, however, the brother and sister were strangely silent, and once or twice I fancied that Zara's eyes filled with tears, though she smiled again so quickly and radiantly that I felt I was mistaken.

A piece of behaviour on the part of Leo, too, filled me with dismay. He had been lying quietly at his master's feet for some time, when he suddenly arose, sat upright, and lifting his nose in air, uttered a most prolonged and desolate howl. Anything more thoroughly heartbroken and despairing than that cry I have never heard. After he had concluded it, the poor animal seemed ashamed of what he had done, and creeping meekly along, with drooping head and tail, he kissed his master's hand, then mine, and lastly Zara's. Finally, he went into a distant corner and lay down again, as if his feelings were altogether too much for him.

"Is he ill?" I asked pityingly.

"I think not," replied Heliobas. "The weather is peculiar to-day—close, and almost thunderous; dogs are very susceptible to such changes."

At that moment the page entered bearing a silver salver, on which lay a letter, which he handed to his master and immediately retired.

Heliobas opened and read it.

"Ivan regrets he cannot dine with us to-day," he said, glancing at his sister; "he is otherwise engaged. He says, however, that he hopes to have the pleasure of looking in during the latter part of the evening."

Zara inclined her head gently, and made no other reply.

A few seconds afterwards we rose from table, and Zara, linking her arm through mine, said:

"I want to have a talk with you while we can be alone. Come to my room."

We went upstairs together, followed by the wise yet doleful Leo, who seemed determined not to let his mistress out of his sight. When we arrived at our destination, Zara pushed me gently into an easy-chair, and seated herself in another one opposite.

MARIE CORELLI

"I am going to ask a favour of you," she began; "because I know you will do anything to please me or Casimir. Is it not so?"

I assured her she might rely upon my observing; with the truest fidelity any request of hers, small or great.

She thanked me and resumed:

"You know I have been working secretly in my studio for some time past. I have been occupied in the execution of two designs—one is finished, and is intended as a gift to Casimir. The other"—she hesitated—"is incomplete. It is the colossal figure which was veiled when you first came in to see my little statue of 'Evening'. I made an attempt beyond my powers—in short, I cannot carry out the idea to my satisfaction. Now, dear, pay great attention to what I say. I have reason to believe that I shall be compelled to take a sudden journey—promise me that when I am gone you will see that unfinished statue completely destroyed—utterly demolished."

I could not answer her for a minute or two, I was so surprised by her words.

"Going on a journey, Zara?" I said. "Well, if you are, I suppose you will soon return home again; and why should your statue be destroyed in the meantime? You may yet be able to bring it to final perfection."

Zara shook her head and smiled half sadly.

"I told you it was a favour I had to ask of you," she said; "and now you are unwilling to grant it."

"I am not unwilling—believe me, dearest, I would do anything to please you," I assured her; "but it seems so strange to me that you should wish the result of your labour destroyed, simply because you are going on a journey."

"Strange as it seems, I desire it most earnestly," said Zara; "otherwise—but if you will not see it done for me, I must preside at the work of demolition myself, though I frankly confess it would be most painful to me."

I interrupted her.

"Say no more, Zara!" I exclaimed; "I will do as you wish. When you are gone, you say—"

"When I am gone," repeated Zara firmly, "and before you yourself leave this house, you will see that particular statue destroyed. You will thus do me a very great service."

"Well," I said, "and when are you coming back again? Before I leave Paris?"

"I hope so—I think so," she replied evasively; "at any rate, we shall meet again soon."

"Where are you going?" I asked.

She smiled. Such a lovely, glad, and triumphant smile!

"You will know my destination before to-night has passed away," she answered. "In the meanwhile I have your promise?"

"Most certainly."

She kissed me, and as she did so, a lurid flash caught my eyes and almost dazzled them. It was a gleam of fiery lustre from the electric jewel she wore.

The day went on its usual course, and the weather seemed to grow murkier every hour. The air was almost sultry, and when during the afternoon I went into the conservatory to gather some of the glorious Marechal Niel roses that grew there in such perfection, the intense heat of the place was nearly insupportable. I saw nothing of Heliobas all day, and, after the morning, very little of Zara. She disappeared soon after luncheon, and I could not find her in her rooms nor in her studio, though I knocked at the door several times. Leo, too, was missing. After being alone for an hour or more, I thought I would pay a visit to the chapel. But on attempting to carry out this intention I found its doors locked—an unusual circumstance which rather surprised me. Fancying that I heard the sound of voices within, I paused to listen. But all was profoundly silent. Strolling into the hall, I took up at random from a side-table a little volume of poems, unknown to me, called "Pygmalion in Cyprus;" and seating myself in one of the luxurious Oriental easy-chairs near the silvery sparkling fountain, I began to read. I opened the book I held at "A Ballad of Kisses," which ran as follows:

> "There are three kisses that I call to mind,
> And I will sing their secrets as I go,—
> The first, a kiss too courteous to be kind,
> Was such a kiss as monks and maidens know,
> As sharp as frost, as blameless as the snow.

> "The second kiss, ah God! I feel it yet,—
> And evermore my soul will loathe the same,—
> The toys and joys of fate I may forget,
> But not the touch of that divided shame;
> It clove my lips—it burnt me like a flame.

> *"The third, the final kiss, is one I use*
> *Morning and noon and night, and not amiss.*
> *Sorrow be mine if such I do refuse!*
> *And when I die, be Love enrapt in bliss*
> *Re-sanctified in heaven by such a kiss!"*

This little gem, which I read and re-read with pleasure, was only one of many in the same collection, The author was assuredly a man of genius. I studied his word-melodies with intense interest, and noted with some surprise how original and beautiful were many of his fancies and similes. I say I noted them with surprise, because he was evidently a modern Englishman, and yet unlike any other of his writing species. His name was not Alfred Tennyson, nor Edwin Arnold, nor Matthew Arnold, nor Austin Dobson, nor Martin Tupper. He was neither plagiarist nor translator—he was actually an original man. I do not give his name here, as I consider it the duty of his own country to find him out and acknowledge him, which, as it is so proud of its literary standing, of course it will do in due season. On this, my first introduction to his poems, I became speedily absorbed in them, and was repeating to myself softly a verse which I remember now:

> *"Hers was sweetest of sweet faces,*
> *Hers the tenderest eyes of all;*
> *In her hair she had the traces*
> *Of a heavenly coronal,*
> *Bringing sunshine to sad places*
> *Where the sunlight could not fall."*

Then I was startled by the sound of a clock striking six. I bethought myself of the people who were coming to dinner, and decided to go to my room and dress. Replacing the "Pygmalion" book on the table whence I had taken it, I made my way upstairs, thinking as I went of Zara and her strange request, and wondering what journey she was going upon.

I could not come to any satisfactory conclusion on this point, besides, I had a curious disinclination to think about it very earnestly, though the subject kept recurring to my mind. Yet always some inward monitor seemed to assure me, as plainly as though the words were spoken in my ear:

"It is useless for you to consider the reason of this, or the meaning of that. Take things as they come in due order: one circumstance explains the other, and everything is always for the best."

I prepared my Indian crepe dress for the evening, the same I had worn for Madame Didier's party at Cannes; only, instead of having lilies of the valley to ornament it with, I arranged some clusters of the Marechal Niel roses I had gathered from the conservatory—lovely blossoms, with their dewy pale-gold centres forming perfect cups of delicious fragrance. These, relieved by a few delicate sprays of the maiden-hair fern, formed a becoming finish to my simple costume. As I arrayed myself, and looked at my own reflection in the long mirror, I smiled out of sheer gratitude. For health, joyous and vigorous, sparkled in my eyes, glowed on my cheeks, tinted my lips, and rounded my figure. The face that looked back at me from the glass was a perfectly happy one, ready to dimple into glad mirth or bright laughter. No shadow of pain or care remained upon it to remind me of past suffering, and I murmured half aloud: "Thank God!"

"Amen!" said a soft voice, and, turning round, I saw Zara.

But how shall I describe her? No words can adequately paint the glorious beauty in which, that night, she seemed to move as in an atmosphere of her own creating. She wore a clinging robe of the richest, softest white satin, caught in at the waist by a zone of pearls—pearls which, from their size and purity, must have been priceless. Her beautiful neck and arms were bare, and twelve rows of pearls were clasped round her slender throat, supporting in their centre the electric stone, which shone with a soft, subdued radiance, like the light of the young moon. Her rich, dark hair was arranged in its usual fashion—that is, hanging down in one thick plait, which on this occasion was braided in and out with small pearls. On her bosom she wore a magnificent cluster of natural orange-blossoms; and of these, while I gazed admiringly at her, I first spoke:

"You look like a bride, Zara! You have all the outward signs of one—white satin, pearls, and orange-blossoms!"

She smiled.

"They are the first cluster that has come out in our conservatory," she said; "and I could not resist them. As to the pearls, they belonged to my mother, and are my favourite ornaments; and white satin is now no longer exclusively for brides. How soft and pretty that Indian crepe is! Your toilette is charming, and suits you to perfection. Are you quite ready?"

"Quite," I answered.

She hesitated and sighed. Then she raised her lovely eyes with a sort of wistful tenderness.

"Before we go down I should like you to kiss me once," she said.

I embraced her fondly, and our lips met with a lingering sisterly caress.

"You will never forget me, will you?" she asked almost anxiously; "never cease to think of me kindly?"

"How fanciful you are to-night, Zara dear!" I said. "As if I COULD forget you! I shall always think of you as the loveliest and sweetest woman in the world."

"And when I am out of the world—what then?" she pursued.

Remembering her spiritual sympathies, I answered at once:

"Even then I shall know you to be one of the fairest of the angels. So you see, Zara darling, I shall always love you."

"I think you will," she said meditatively; "you are one of us. But come! I hear voices downstairs. I think our expected guests have arrived, and we must be in the drawing-room to receive them. Good-bye, little friend!" And she again kissed me.

"Good-bye!" I repeated in astonishment; "why 'good-bye'?"

"Because it is my fancy to say the word," she replied with quiet firmness. "Again, dear little friend, good-bye!"

I felt bewildered, but she would not give me time to utter another syllable. She took my hand and hurried me with her downstairs, and in another moment we were both in the drawing-room, receiving and saying polite nothings to the Everards and Challoners, who had all arrived together, resplendent in evening costume. Amy Everard, I thought, looked a little tired and fagged, though she rejoiced in a superb "arrangement" by Worth of ruby velvet and salmon-pink. But, though a perfect dress is consoling to most women, there are times when even that fails of its effect; and then Worth ceases to loom before the feminine eye as a sort of demi-god, but dwindles insignificantly to the level of a mere tailor, whose prices are ruinous. And this, I think, was the state of mind in which Mrs. Everard found herself that evening; or else she was a trifle jealous of Zara's harmonious grace and loveliness. Be this as it may, she was irritable, and whisperingly found fault with, me for being in such good health.

"You will have too much colour if you don't take care," she said almost pettishly, "and nothing is so unfashionable."

"I know!" I replied with due meekness. "It is very bad style to be quite well—it is almost improper."

She looked at me, and a glimmering smile lighted her features. But she would not permit herself to become good-humoured, and she furled and unfurled her fan of pink ostrich feathers with some impatience.

"Where did that child get all those pearls from?" she next inquired, with a gesture of her head towards Zara.

"They belonged to her mother," I answered, smiling as I heard Zara called a CHILD, knowing, as I did, her real age.

"She is actually wearing a small fortune on her person," went on Amy; "I wonder her brother allows her. Girls never understand the value of things of that sort. They should be kept for her till she is old enough to appreciate them."

I made no reply; I was absorbed in watching Heliobas, who at that moment entered the room accompanied by Father Paul. He greeted his guests with warmth and unaffected heartiness, and all present were, I could see, at once fascinated by the dignity of his presence and the charm of his manner. To an uninstructed eye there was nothing unusual about him; but to me there was a change in his expression which, as it were, warned and startled me. A deep shadow of anxiety in his eyes made them look more sombre and less keen; his smile was not so sweet as it was stern, and there was an undefinable SOMETHING in his very bearing that suggested—what? Defiance? Yes, defiance; and it was this which, when I had realized it, curiously alarmed me. For what had he, Heliobas, to do with even the thought of defiance? Did not all his power come from the knowledge of the necessity of obedience to the spiritual powers within and without? Quick as light the words spoken to me by Aztul regarding him came back to my remembrance: "Even as he is my Beloved, so let him not fail to hear my voice." What if he SHOULD fail? A kind of instinct came upon me that some immediate danger of this threatened him, and I braced myself up to a firm determination, that, if this was so, I, out of my deep gratitude to him, would do my utmost best to warn him in time. While these thoughts possessed me, the hum of gay conversation went on, and Zara's bright laughter ever and again broke like music on the air. Father Paul, too, proved himself to be of quite a festive and jovial disposition, for he made himself agreeable to Mrs. Challoner and her daughters, and entertained them with the ease and bonhomie of an accomplished courtier and man of the world.

Dinner was announced in the usual way—that is, with the sound of music played by the electric instrument devoted to that purpose, a performance which elicited much admiration from all the guests. Heliobas led the way into the dining-room with Mrs. Everard; Colonel Everard followed, with Zara on one arm and the eldest Miss Challoner on the other; Mr. Challoner and myself came next; and Father Paul, with Mrs. Challoner and her other daughter Effie, brought up the rear. There was a universal murmur of surprise and delight as the dinner-table came in view; and its arrangement was indeed a triumph of art. In the centre was placed a large round of crystal in imitation of a lake, and on this apparently floated a beautiful gondola steered by the figure of a gondolier, both exquisitely wrought in fine Venetian glass. The gondolier was piled high with a cargo of roses; but the wonder of it all was, that the whole design was lit up by electricity. Electric sparkles, like drops of dew, shone on the leaves of the flowers; the gondola was lit from end to end with electric stars, which were reflected with prismatic brilliancy in the crystal below; the gondolier's long pole glittered with what appeared to be drops of water tinged by the moonlight, but which was really an electric wire, and in his cap flashed an electric diamond. The whole ornament scintillated and glowed like a marvellous piece of curiously contrived jewel-work. And this was not all. Beside every guest at table a slender vase, shaped like a long-stemmed Nile lily, held roses and ferns, in which were hidden tiny electric stars, causing the blossoms to shine with a transparent and almost fairy-like lustre.

Four graceful youths, clad in the Armenian costume, stood waiting silently round the table till all present were seated, and then they commenced the business of serving the viands, with swift and noiseless dexterity. As soon as the soup was handed round, tongues were loosened, and the Challoners, who had been gazing at everything in almost open-mouthed astonishment, began to relieve their feelings by warm expressions of unqualified admiration, in which Colonel and Mrs. Everard were not slow to join.

"I do say, and I will say, this beats all I've ever seen," said good Mrs. Challoner, as she bent to examine the glittering vase of flowers near her plate.

"And this is real electric light? And is it perfectly harmless?"

Heliobas smilingly assured her of the safety of his table decorations. "Electricity," he said, "though the most powerful of masters, is the most docile of slaves. It is capable of the smallest as well as of the greatest uses. It can give with equal certainty life or death; in fact, it is the key-note of creation."

"Is that your theory, sir?" asked Colonel Everard.

"It is not only my theory," answered Heliobas, "it is a truth, indisputable and unalterable, to those who have studied the mysteries of electric science."

"And do you base all your medical treatment on this principle?" pursued the Colonel.

"Certainly. Your young friend here, who came to me from Cannes, looking as if she had but a few months to live, can bear witness to the efficacy of my method."

Every eye was now turned upon me, and I looked up and laughed.

"Do you remember, Amy," I said, addressing Mrs. Everard, "how you told me I looked like a sick nun at Cannes? What do I look like now?"

"You look as if you had never been ill in your life," she replied.

"I was going to say," remarked Mr. Challoner in his deliberate manner, "that you remind me very much of a small painting of Diana that I saw in the Louvre the other day. You have the same sort of elasticity in your movements, and the same bright healthy eyes."

I bowed, still smiling. "I did not know you were such a flatterer, Mr. Challoner! Diana thanks you!"

The conversation now became general, and turned, among other subjects, upon the growing reputation of Raffaello Cellini.

"What surprises me in that young man," said Colonel Everard, "is his colouring. It is simply marvellous. He was amiable enough to present me with a little landscape scene; and the effect of light upon it is so powerfully done that you would swear the sun was actually shining through it."

The fine sensitive mouth of Heliobas curved in a somewhat sarcastic smile.

"Mere trickery, my dear sir—a piece of clap-trap," he said lightly. "That is what would be said of such pictures—in England at least. And it WILL be said by many oracular, long-established newspapers, while Cellini lives. As soon as he is dead—ah! c'est autre chose!—he will then most probably be acknowledged the greatest master of the age. There may even be a Cellini 'School of Colouring,' where a select company of daubers will profess to know the secret that has died with him. It is the way of the world!"

Mr. Challoner's rugged face showed signs of satisfaction, and his shrewd eyes twinkled.

"Right you are, sir!" he said, holding up his glass of wine. "I drink to you! Sir, I agree with you! I calculate there's a good many worlds flying round in space, but a more ridiculous, feeble-minded, contrary sort of world than this one, I defy any archangel to find!"

Heliobas laughed, nodded, and after a slight pause resumed:

"It is astonishing to me that people do not see to what an infinite number of uses they could put the little re-discovery they have made of LUMINOUS PAINT. In that simple thing there is a secret, which as yet they do not guess—a wonderful, beautiful, scientific secret, which may perhaps take them a few hundred years to find out. In the meantime they have got hold of one end of the thread; they can make luminous paint, and with it they can paint light-houses, and, what is far more important—ships. Vessels in mid-ocean will have no more need of fog-signals and different-coloured lamps; their own coat of paint will be sufficient to light them safely on their way. Even rooms can be so painted as to be perfectly luminous at night. A friend of mine, residing in Italy, has a luminous ballroom, where the ceiling is decorated with a moon and stars in electric light. The effect is exceedingly lovely; and though people think a great deal of money must have been laid out upon it, it is perhaps the only great ballroom in Italy that has been really cheaply fitted up. But, as I said before, there is another secret behind the invention or discovery of luminous paint—a secret which, when once unveiled, will revolutionize all the schools of art in the world."

"Do you know this secret?" asked Mrs. Challoner.

"Yes, madame—perfectly."

"Then why don't you disclose it for the benefit of everybody?" demanded Erne Challoner.

"Because, my dear young lady, no one would believe me if I did. The time is not yet ripe for it. The world must wait till its people are better educated."

"Better educated!" exclaimed Mrs. Everard. "Why, there is nothing talked of nowadays but education and progress! The very children are wiser than their parents!"

"The children!" returned Heliobas, half inquiringly, half indignantly. "At the rate things are going, there will soon be no children left; they will all be tired little old men and women before they are in their teens. The very babes will be born old. Many of them are being brought up without any faith in God or religion; the result will be an increase of vice and crime. The purblind philosophers, miscalled wise men, who teach the children by the light of poor human reason only, and do away with faith in spiritual things, are bringing down upon the generations to come an unlooked-for and most terrific curse. Childhood, the happy, innocent, sweet, unthinking, almost angelic age, at which Nature would have us believe in fairies and all the delicate aerial fancies of poets, who are, after all, the only true sages—childhood, I say, is being gradually stamped out under the cruel iron heel of the Period—a period not of wisdom, health, or beauty, but one of drunken delirium, in which the world rushes feverishly along, its eyes fixed on one hard, glittering, stony-featured idol—Gold. Education! Is it education to teach the young that their chances of happiness depend on being richer than their neighbours? Yet that is what it all tends to. Get on!—be successful! Trample on others, but push forward yourself! Money, money!—let its chink be your music; let its yellow shine be fairer than the eyes of love or friendship! Let its piles accumulate and ever accumulate! There are beggars in the streets, but they are impostors! There is poverty in many places, but why seek to relieve it? Why lessen the sparkling heaps of gold by so much as a coin? Accumulate and ever accumulate! Live so, and then—die! And then—who knows what then?"

His voice had been full of ringing eloquence as he spoke, but at these last words it sank into a low, thrilling tone of solemnity and earnestness. We all looked at him, fascinated by his manner, and were silent.

Mr. Challoner was the first to break the impressive pause.

"I'm not a speaker, sir," he observed slowly, "but I've got a good deal of feeling somewheres; and you'll allow me to say that I feel your words—I think they're right true. I've often wanted to say what you've said, but haven't seen my way clear to it. Anyhow, I've had a very general impression about me that what we call Society has of late years been going, per express service, direct to the devil—if the ladies will excuse me for plain speaking. And as the journey is being taken by choice and free-will, I suppose there's no hindrance or stoppage possible. Besides, it's a downward line, and curiously free from obstructions."

"Bravo, John!" exclaimed Mrs. Challoner. "You are actually corning out! I never heard you indulge in similes before."

"Well, my dear," returned her husband, somewhat gratified, "better late than never. A simile is a good thing if it isn't overcrowded. For instance, Mr. Swinburne's similes are laid on too thick sometimes.

MARIE CORELLI

There is a verse of his, which, with all my admiration for him, I never could quite fathom. It is where he earnestly desires to be as 'Any leaf of any tree;' or, failing that, he wouldn't mind becoming 'As bones under the deep, sharp sea.' I tried hard to see the point of that, but couldn't fix it."

We all laughed. Zara, I thought, was especially merry, and looked her loveliest. She made an excellent hostess, and exerted herself to the utmost to charm—an effort in which she easily succeeded.

The shadow on the face of her brother had not disappeared, and once or twice I noticed that Father Paul looked at him with a certain kindly anxiety.

The dinner approached its end. The dessert, with its luxurious dishes of rare fruit, such as peaches, plantains, hothouse grapes, and even strawberries, was served, and with it a delicious, sparkling, topaz-tinted wine of Eastern origin called Krula, which was poured out to us in Venetian glass goblets, wherein lay diamond-like lumps of ice. The air was so exceedingly oppressive that evening that we found this beverage most refreshing. When Zara's goblet was filled, she held it up smiling, and said:

"I have a toast to propose."

"Hear, hear!" murmured the gentlemen, Heliobas excepted.

"To our next merry meeting!" and as she said this she kissed the rim of the cup, and made a sign as though wafting it towards her brother.

He started as if from a reverie, seized his glass, and drained off its contents to the last drop.

Everyone responded with heartiness to Zara's toast and then Colonel Everard proposed the health of the fair hostess, which was drunk with enthusiasm.

After this Zara gave the signal, and all the ladies rose to adjourn to the drawing-room. As I passed Heliobas on my way out, he looked so sombre and almost threatening of aspect, that I ventured to whisper:

"Remember Azul!"

"She has forgotten ME!" he muttered.

"Never—never!" I said earnestly. "Oh, Heliobas! what is wrong with you?"

He made no answer, and there was no opportunity to say more, as I had to follow Zara. But I felt very anxious, though I scarcely knew why, and I lingered at the door and glanced back at him. As I did so, a low, rumbling sound, like chariot-wheels rolling afar off, broke suddenly on our ears.

"Thunder," remarked Mr. Challoner quietly. "I thought we should have it. It has been unnaturally warm all day. A good storm will clear the air."

In my brief backward look at Heliobas, I noted that when that far-distant thunder sounded, he grew very pale. Why? He was certainly not one to have any dread of a storm—he was absolutely destitute of fear. I went into the drawing-room with a hesitating step—my instincts were all awake and beginning to warn me, and I murmured softly a prayer to that strong, invisible majestic spirit which I knew must be near me—my guardian Angel. I was answered instantly—my foreboding grew into a positive certainty that some danger menaced Heliobas, and that if I desired to be his friend, I must be prepared for an emergency. Receiving this, as all such impressions should be received, as a direct message sent me for my guidance, I grew calmer, and braced up my energies to oppose SOMETHING, though I knew not what.

Zara was showing her lady-visitors a large album of Italian photographs, and explaining them as she turned the leaves. As I entered the room, she said eagerly to me:

"Play to us, dear! Something soft and plaintive. We all delight in your music, you know."

"Did you hear the thunder just now?" I asked irrelevantly.

"It WAS thunder? I thought so!" said Mrs. Everard. "Oh, I do hope there is not going to be a storm! I am so afraid of a storm!"

"You are nervous?" questioned Zara kindly, as she engaged her attention with some very fine specimens among the photographs, consisting of views from Venice.

"Well, I suppose I am," returned Amy, half laughing. "Yet I am plucky about most things, too. Still I don't like to hear the elements quarrelling together—they are too much in earnest about it—and no person can pacify them."

Zara smiled, and gently repeated her request to me for some music—a request in which Mrs. Challoner and her daughters eagerly joined. As I went to the piano I thought of Edgar Allan Poe's exquisite poem:

> "In Heaven a spirit doth dwell,
> Whose heart-strings are a lute;
> None sing so wildly well
> As the angel Israfel,

MARIE CORELLI

> And the giddy stars, so legends tell,
> Ceasing their hymns, attend the spell
> Of his voice—all mute."

As I poised my fingers above the keys of the instrument, another long, low, ominous roll of thunder swept up from the distance and made the room tremble.

"Play—play, for goodness' sake!" exclaimed Mrs. Everard; "and then we shall not be obliged to fix our attention on the approaching storm!"

I played a few soft opening arpeggio passages, while Zara seated herself in an easy-chair near the window, and the other ladies arranged themselves on sofas and ottomans to their satisfaction. The room was exceedingly close: and the scent of the flowers that were placed about in profusion was almost too sweet and overpowering.

> "And they say (the starry choir
> And the other listening things)
> That Israfeli's fire
> Is owing to that lyre,
> By which lie sits and sings,—
> The trembling living wire
> Of those unusual strings."

How these verses haunted me! With them floating in my mind, I played—losing myself in mazes of melody, and travelling harmoniously in and out of the different keys with that sense of perfect joy known only to those who can improvise with ease, and catch the unwritten music of nature, which always appeals most strongly to emotions that are unspoilt by contact with the world, and which are quick to respond to what is purely instinctive art. I soon became thoroughly absorbed, and forgot that there were any persons present. In fancy I imagined myself again in view of the glory of the Electric Ring—again I seemed to behold the opaline radiance of the Central Sphere:

> "Where Love's a grown-up God,
> Where the Houri glances are
> Imbued with all the beauty
> Which we worship in a star."

By-and-by I found my fingers at the work of tenderly unravelling a little skein of major melody, as soft and childlike as the innocent babble of a small brooklet flowing under ferns. I followed this airy suggestion obediently, till it led me of itself to its fitting end, when I ceased playing. I was greeted by a little burst of applause, and looking up, saw that all the gentlemen had come in from the dining-room, and were standing near me. The stately figure of Heliobas was the most prominent in the group; he stood erect, one hand resting lightly on the framework of the piano, and his eyes met mine fixedly.

"You were inspired," he said with a grave smile, addressing me; "you did not observe our entrance."

I was about to reply, when a loud, appalling crash of thunder rattled above us, as if some huge building had suddenly fallen into ruins. It startled us all into silence for a moment, and we looked into each other's faces with a certain degree of awe.

"That was a good one," remarked Mr. Challoner. "There was nothing undecided about that clap. Its mind was made up."

Zara suddenly rose from her seat, and drew aside the window-curtains.

"I wonder if it is raining," she said.

Amy Everard uttered a little shriek of dismay.

"Oh, don't open the blinds!" she exclaimed. "It is really dangerous!"

Heliobas glanced at her with a little sarcastic smile.

"Take a seat on the other side of the room, if you are alarmed, madame," he said quietly, placing a chair in the position he suggested, which Amy accepted eagerly.

She would, I believe, have gladly taken refuge in the coal-cellar had he offered it. Zara, in the meantime, who had not heard Mrs. Everard's exclamation of fear, had drawn up one of the blinds, and stood silently looking out upon the night. Instinctively we all joined her, with the exception of Amy, and looked out also. The skies were very dark; a faint moaning wind stirred the tops of the leafless trees; but there was no rain. A dry volcanic heat pervaded the atmosphere—in fact we all felt the air so stifling, that Heliobas threw open the window altogether, saying, as he did so:

"In a thunderstorm, it is safer to have the windows open than shut; besides, one cannot suffocate."

A brilliant glare of light flashed suddenly upon our vision. The heavens seemed torn open from end to end, and a broad lake of pale

MARIE CORELLI

blue fire lay quivering in the heart of the mountainous black clouds—for a second only. An on-rushing, ever-increasing, rattling roar of thunder ensued, that seemed to shake the very earth, and all was again darkness.

"This is magnificent!" cries Mrs. Challoner, who, with her family, had travelled a great deal, and was quite accustomed to hurricanes and other inconveniences caused by the unaccommodating behaviour of the elements. "I don't think I ever saw anything like it, John dear, even that storm we saw at Chamounix was not any better than this."

"Well," returned her husband meditatively, "you see we had the snow mountains there, and the effect was pretty lively. Then there were the echoes—those cavernous echoes were grand! What was that passage in Job, Effie, that I used to say they reminded me of?"

"'The pillars of heaven tremble, and are astonished at His reproof. . . The thunder of His power, who can understand?'" replied Effie Challoner reverently.

"That's it!" he replied. "I opine that Job was pretty correct in his ideas—don't you, reverend sir?" turning to Father Paul.

The priest nodded, and held up his finger warningly.

"That lady—Mrs. Everard—is going to sing or play, I think," he observed. "Shall we not keep silence?"

I looked towards Amy in some surprise. I knew she sang very prettily, but I had thought she was rendered too nervous by the storm to do aught but sit quiet in her chair. However, there she was at the piano, and in another moment her fresh, sweet mezzo-soprano rang softly through the room in Tosti's plaintive song, "Good-bye!" We listened, but none of us moved from the open window where we still inhaled what air there was, and watched the lowering sky.

> *"Hush! a voice from the far-away,*
> *'Listen and learn,' it seems to say;*
> *'All the to-morrows shall be as to-day,'"*

sang Amy with pathetic sweetness. Zara suddenly moved, as if oppressed, from her position among us as we stood clustered together, and stepped out through the French window into the outside balcony, her head uncovered to the night.

"You will catch cold!" Mrs. Challoner and I both called to her simultaneously. She shook her head, smiling back at us; and folding her arms lightly on the stone balustrade, leaned there and looked up at the clouds.

> *"The link must break, and the lamp must die;*
> *Good-bye to Hope! Good-bye—good-bye!"*

Amy's voice was a peculiarly thrilling one, and on this occasion sounded with more than its usual tenderness. What with her singing and the invisible presence of the storm, an utter silence possessed us—not one of us cared to move.

Heliobas once stepped to his sister's side in the open balcony, and said something, as I thought, to warn her against taking cold; but it was a very brief whisper, and he almost immediately returned to his place amongst us. Zara looked very lovely out there; the light coming from the interior of the room glistened softly on the sheen of her satin dress and its ornaments of pearls; and the electric stone on her bosom shone faintly, like a star on a rainy evening. Her beautiful face, turned upwards to the angry sky, was half in light and half in shade; a smile parted her lips, and her eyes were bright with a look of interest and expectancy. Another sudden glare, and the clouds were again broken asunder; but this time in a jagged and hasty manner, as though a naked sword had been thrust through them and immediately withdrawn.

"That was a nasty flash," said Colonel Everard, with an observant glance at the lovely Juliet-like figure on the balcony. "Mademoiselle, had you not better come in?"

"When it begins to rain I will come in," she said, without changing her posture. "I hear the singing so well out here. Besides, I love the storm."

A tumultuous crash of thunder, tremendous for its uproar and the length of time it was prolonged, made us look at each other again with anxious faces.

> *"What are we waiting for? Oh, my heart!*
> *Kiss me straight on the brows and part!*
> *Again! again, my heart, my heart!*
> *What are we waiting for, you and I?*
> *A pleading look—a stifled cry!*
> *Good-bye for ever—"*

MARIE CORELLI

Horror! what was that? A lithe swift serpent of fire twisting venomously through the dark heavens! Zara raised her arms, looked up, smiled, and fell—senseless! With such appalling suddenness that we had scarcely recovered from the blinding terror of that forked lightning-flash, when we saw her lying prone before us on the balcony where one instant before she had stood erect and smiling! With exclamations of alarm and distress we lifted and bore her within the room and laid her tenderly down upon the nearest sofa. At that moment a deafening, terrific thunder-clap—one only—as if a huge bombshell had burst in the air, shook the ground under our feet; and then with a swish and swirl of long pent-up and suddenly-released wrath, down came the rain.

Amy's voice died away in a last "Good-bye!" and she rushed from the piano, with pale face and trembling lips, gasping out:

"What has happened? What is the matter?"

"She has been stunned by a lightning-flash," I said, trying to speak calmly, while I loosened Zara's dress and sprinkled her forehead with eau-de-Cologne from a scent-bottle Mrs. Challoner had handed to me. "She will recover in a few minutes."

But my limbs trembled under me, and tears, in spite of myself, forced their way into my eyes.

Heliobas meanwhile—his countenance white and set as a marble mask—shut the window fiercely, pulled down the blind, and drew the heavy silken curtains close. He then approached his sister's senseless form, and, taking her wrist tenderly, felt for her pulse. We looked on in the deepest anxiety. The Challoner girls shivered with terror, and began to cry. Mrs. Everard, with more self-possession, dipped a handkerchief in cold water and laid it on Zara's temples; but no faint sigh parted the set yet smiling lips—no sign of life was visible. All this while the rain swept down in gusty torrents and rattled furiously against the window-panes; while the wind, no longer a moan, had risen into a shriek, as of baffled yet vindictive anger. At last Heliobas spoke.

"I should be glad of other medical skill than my own," he said, in low and stifled accents. "This may be a long fainting-fit."

Mr. Challoner at once proffered his services.

"I'll go for you anywhere you like," he said cheerily; "and I think my wife and daughters had better come with me. Our carriage is sure to be in waiting. It will be necessary for the lady to have perfect quiet when she recovers, and visitors are best away. You need not be alarmed, I am sure. By her colour it is evident she is only in a swoon. What doctor shall I send?"

Heliobas named one Dr. Morini, 10, Avenue de l'Alma.

"Right! He shall be here straight. Come, wife—come, girls! Mrs. Everard, we'll send back our carriage for you and the Colonel. Good-night! We'll call to-morrow and inquire after mademoiselle."

Heliobas gratefully pressed his hand as he withdrew, and his wife and daughters, with whispered farewells, followed him. We who were left behind all remained near Zara, doing everything we could think of to restore animation to that senseless form.

Some of the servants, too, hearing what had happened, gathered in a little cluster at the drawing-room door, looking with pale and alarmed faces at the death-like figure of their beautiful mistress. Half an hour or more must have passed in this manner; within the room there was a dreadful silence—but outside the rain poured down in torrents, and the savage wind howled and tore at the windows like a besieging army. Suddenly Amy Everard, who had been quietly and skilfully assisting me in rubbing Zara's hands and bathing her forehead, grew faint, staggered, and would have fallen had not her husband caught her on his arm.

"I am frightened," she gasped. "I cannot bear it—she looks so still, and she is growing—rigid, like a corpse! Oh, if she should be dead!" And she hid her face on her husband's breast.

At that moment we heard the grating of wheels on the gravel outside; it was the Challoners' carriage returned. The coachman, after depositing his master and family at the Grand Hotel, had driven rapidly back in the teeth of the stinging sleet and rain to bring the message that Dr. Morini would be with us as soon as possible.

"Then," whispered Colonel Everard gently to me, "I'll take Amy home. She is thoroughly upset, and it's no use having her going off into hysterics. I'll call with Challoner to-morrow;" and with a kindly parting nod of encouragement to us all, he slipped softly out of the room, half leading, half carrying his trembling wife; and in a couple of minutes we heard the carriage again drive away.

Left alone at last with Heliobas and Father Paul, I, kneeling at the side of my darling Zara, looked into their faces for comfort, but found none. The dry-eyed despair on the countenance of Heliobas pierced me to the heart; the pitying, solemn expression of the venerable priest touched me as with icy cold. The lovely, marble-like whiteness and stillness of the figure before me filled me with a vague terror. Making a strong effort to control my voice, I called, in a low, clear tone:

"Zara! Zara!"

No sign—not the faintest flicker of an eyelash! Only the sound of the falling rain and the moaning wind—the thunder had long ago ceased. Suddenly a something attracted my gaze, which first surprised and then horrified me. The jewel—the electric stone on Zara's bosom no longer shone! It was like a piece of dull unpolished pebble. Grasping at the meaning of this, with overwhelming instinctive rapidity, I sprang up and caught the arm of Heliobas.

"You—you!" I whispered hurriedly. "You can restore her! Do as you did with Prince Ivan; you can—you must! That stone she wears—the light has gone out of it. If that means—and I am sure it does—that life has for a little while gone out of Her, You can bring it back. Quick—Quick! You have the power!"

He looked at me with burning grief-haunted eyes; and a sigh that was almost a groan escaped his lips.

"I have No power," he said. "Not over her. I told you she was dominated by a higher force than mine. What can I do? Nothing—worse than nothing—I am utterly helpless."

I stared at him in a kind of desperate horror.

"Do you mean to tell me," I said slowly, "that she is dead—really dead?"

He was about to answer, when one of the watching servants announced in a low tone: "Dr. Morini."

The new-comer was a wiry, keen-eyed little Italian; his movements were quick, decisive, and all to the point of action. The first thing he did was to scatter the little group of servants right and left, and send them about their business. The next, to close the doors of the room against all intrusion. He then came straight up to Heliobas, and pressing his hand in a friendly manner, said briefly:

"How and when did this happen?"

Heliobas told him in as few words as possible. Dr. Morini then bent over Zara's lifeless form, and examined her features attentively. He laid his ear against her heart and listened. Finally, he caught sight of the round, lustreless pebble hanging at her neck suspended by its strings of pearls. Very gently he moved this aside; looked, and beckoned us to come and look also. Exactly on the spot where the electric stone had rested, a small circular mark, like a black bruise, tainted the fair soft skin—a mark no larger than a small finger-ring.

"Death by electricity," said Dr. Morini quietly. "Must have been instantaneous. The lightning-flash, or downward electric current, lodged itself here, where this mark is, and passed directly through the heart. Perfectly painless, but of course fatal. She has been dead some time."

And, replacing the stone ornament in its former position, he stepped back with a suggestive glance at Father Paul. I listened and saw—but I was in a state of stupefaction. Dead? My beautiful, gay, strong Zara DEAD? Impossible! I knelt beside her; I called her again and again by every endearing and tender name I could think of; I kissed her sweet lips. Oh, they were cold as ice, and chilled my blood! As one in a dream, I saw Heliobas advance; he kissed her forehead and mouth; he reverently unclasped the pearls from about her throat, and with them took off the electric stone. Then Father Paul stepped slowly forward, and in place of that once brilliant gem, now so dim and destitute of fire, he laid a crucifix upon the fair and gentle breast, motionless for ever.

At sight of this sacred symbol, some tense cord seemed to snap in my brain, and I cried out wildly:

"Oh, no, no! Not that! That is for the dead; Zara is not dead! It is all a mistake—a mistake! She will be quite well presently; and she will smile and tell you how foolish you were to think her dead! Dead? She cannot be dead; it is impossible—quite impossible!" And I broke into a passion of sobs and tears.

Very gently and kindly Dr. Morini drew me away, and by dint of friendly persuasion, in which there was also a good deal of firm determination, led me into the hall, where he made me swallow a glass of wine. As I could not control my sobs, he spoke with some sternness:

"Mademoiselle, you can do no good by giving way in this manner. Death is a very beautiful and solemn thing, and it is irreverent to show unseemly passion in such a great Presence. You loved your friend—let it be a comfort to you that she died painlessly. Control yourself, in order to assist in rendering her the last few gentle services necessary; and try to console the desolate brother, who looks in real need of encouragement."

These last words roused me. I forced back my tears, and dried my eyes.

"I will, Dr. Morini," I said, in a trembling voice. "I am ashamed to be so weak. I know what I ought to do, and I will do it. You may trust me."

He looked at me approvingly.

MARIE CORELLI

"That is well," he said briefly. "And now, as I am of no use here, I will say good-night. Remember, excessive grief is mere selfishness; resignation is heroism."

He was gone. I nerved myself to the task I had before me, and within an hour the fair casket of what had been Zara lay on an open bier in the little chapel, lights burning round it, and flowers strewn above it in mournful profusion.

We left her body arrayed in its white satin garb; the cluster of orange-blossoms she had gathered still bloomed upon the cold breast, where the crucifix lay; but in the tresses of the long dark hair I wove a wreath of lilies instead of the pearls we had undone.

And now I knelt beside the bier absorbed in thought. Some of the weeping servants had assembled, and knelt about in little groups. The tall candles on the altar were lit, and Father Paul, clad in mourning priestly vestments, prayed there in silence. The storm of rain and wind still raged without, and the windows of the chapel shook and rattled with the violence of the tempest.

A distant clock struck One! with a deep clang that echoed throughout the house. I shuddered. So short a time had elapsed since Zara had been alive and well; now, I could not bear to think that she was gone from me for ever. For ever, did I say? No, not for ever—not so long as love exists—love that shall bring us together again in that far-off Sphere where—

Hush! what was that? The sound of the organ? I looked around me in startled wonderment. There was no one seated at the instrument; it was shut close. The lights on the altar and round the bier burnt steadily; the motionless figure of the priest before the tabernacle; the praying servants of the household—all was unchanged. But certainly a flood of music rolled grandly on the ear—music that drowned for a moment the howling noise of the battering wind. I rose softly, and touched one of the kneeling domestics on the shoulder.

"Did you hear the organ?" I said.

The woman looked up at me with tearful, alarmed eyes.

"No, mademoiselle."

I paused, listening. The music grew louder and louder, and surged round me in waves of melody. Evidently no one in the chapel heard it but myself. I looked about for Heliobas, but he had not entered. He was most probably in his study, whither he had retired to grieve in secret when we had borne Zara's body to its present couch of dreamless sleep.

These sounds were meant for me alone, then? I waited, and the music gradually died away; and as I resumed my kneeling position by the bier all was again silence, save for the unabated raging of the storm.

A strange calmness now fell on my spirits. Some invisible hand seemed to hold me still and tearless. Zara was dead. I realized it now. I began to consider that she must have known her fate beforehand. This was what she had meant when she said she was going on a journey. The more I thought of this the quieter I became, and I hid my face in my hands and prayed earnestly.

A touch roused me—an imperative, burning touch. An airy brightness, like a light cloud with sunshine falling through it, hovered above Zara's bier! I gazed breathlessly; I could not move my lips to utter a sound. A face looked at me—a face angelically beautiful! It smiled. I stretched out my hands; I struggled for speech, and managed to whisper:

"Zara, Zara! you have come back!"

Her voice, so sweetly familiar, answered me: "To life? Ah, never, never again! I am too happy to return. But save him—save my brother! Go to him; he is in danger; to you is given the rescue. Save him; and for me rejoice, and grieve no more!"

The face vanished, the brightness faded, and I sprang up from my knees in haste. For one instant I looked at the beautiful dead body of the friend I loved, with its set mouth and placid features, and then I smiled. This was not Zara—SHE was alive and happy; this fair clay was but clay doomed to perish, but SHE was imperishable.

"Save him—save my brother!" These words rang in my ears. I hesitated no longer—I determined to seek Heliobas at once. Swiftly and noiselessly I slipped out of the chapel. As the door swung behind me I heard a sound that first made me stop in sudden alarm, and then hurry on with increased eagerness. There was no mistaking it—it was the clash of steel!

XVI

A Struggle For the Mastery

I rushed to the study-door, tore aside the velvet hangings, and faced Heliobas and Prince Ivan Petroffsky. They held drawn weapons, which they lowered at my sudden entrance, and paused irresolutely.

"What are you doing?" I cried, addressing myself to Heliobas. "With the dead body of your sister in the house you can fight! You, too!" and I looked reproachfully at Prince Ivan; "you also can desecrate the sanctity of death, and yet—you LOVED her!"

The Prince spoke not, but clenched his sword-hilt with a fiercer grasp, and glared wildly on his opponent. His eyes had a look of madness in them—his dress was much disordered—his hair wet with drops of rain—his face ghastly white, and his whole demeanour was that of a man distraught with grief and passion. But he uttered no word. Heliobas spoke; he was coldly calm, and balanced his sword lightly on his open hand as if it were a toy.

"This GENTLEMAN," he said, with deliberate emphasis, "happened, on his way thither, to meet Dr. Morini, who informed him of the fatal catastrophe which has caused my sister's death. Instead of respecting the sacredness of my solitude under the circumstances, he thrust himself rudely into my presence, and, before I could address him, struck me violently in the face, and accused me of being my sister's murderer. Such conduct can only meet with one reply. I gave him his choice of weapons: he chose swords. Our combat has just begun—we are anxious to resume it; therefore if you, mademoiselle, will have the goodness to retire—"

I interrupted him.

"I shall certainly not retire," I said firmly. "This behaviour on both your parts is positive madness. Prince Ivan, please to listen to me. The circumstances of Zara's death were plainly witnessed by me and others— her brother is as innocent of having caused it as I am."

And I recounted to him quietly all that had happened during that fatal and eventful evening. He listened moodily, tracing out the pattern of the carpet with the point of his sword. When I had finished he looked up, and a bitter smile crossed his features.

"I wonder, mademoiselle," he said, "that your residence in this accursed house has not taught you better. I quite believe all you say, that Zara, unfortunate girl that she was, received her death by a lightning-flash. But answer me this: Who made her capable of attracting atmospheric electricity? Who charged her beautiful delicate body with a vile compound of electrical fluid, so that she was as a living magnet, bound to draw towards herself electricity in all its forms? Who tampered with her fine brain and made her imagine herself allied to a spirit of air? Who but HE—HE!—yonder unscrupulous wretch!—he who in pursuit of his miserable science, practised his most dangerous experiments on his sister, regardless of her health, her happiness, her life! I say he is her murderer—her remorseless murderer, and a thrice-damned villain!"

And he sprang forward to renew the combat. I stepped quietly, unflinchingly between him and Heliobas.

"Stop!" I exclaimed; "this cannot go on. Zara herself forbids it!"

The Prince paused, and looked at me in a sort of stupefaction.

"Zara forbids it!" he muttered. "What do you mean?"

"I mean," I went on, "that I have seen Zara since her death; I have spoken to her. She herself sent me here."

Prince Ivan stared, and then burst into a fit of wild laughter.

"Little fool!" he cried to me; "he has maddened you too, then! You are also a victim! Miserable girl! out of my path! Revenge—revenge! while I am yet sane!"

Then pushing me roughly aside, he cast away his sword, and shouted to Heliobas:

"Hand to hand, villain! No more of these toy-weapons! Hand to hand!"

Heliobas instantly threw down his sword also, and rushing forward simultaneously, they closed together in savage conflict. Heliobas was the taller and more powerful of the two, but Prince Ivan seemed imbued with the spirit of a hundred devils, and sprang at his opponent's throat with the silent breathless ferocity of a tiger. At first Heliobas appeared to be simply on the defensive, and his agile, skilful movements were all used to parry and ward off the other's grappling eagerness. But as I watched the struggle, myself speechless and powerless, I saw his face change. Instead of its calm and almost indifferent expression, there came a look which was completely foreign to it—a look of savage determination bordering on positive cruelty. In a moment I saw what was taking place in his mind. The animal passions of the mere MAN were aroused—the spiritual force was utterly forgotten. The excitement of the contest was beginning to tell, and the desire of victory was dominant in the breast of him whose ideas were generally—and should have been now—those of patient endurance and large generosity. The fight grew closer, hotter, and more terrible. Suddenly the Prince swerved aside and fell, and within a second Heliobas held him down, pressing one knee firmly against his chest. From my point of observation I noted with alarm that little by little Ivan ceased his violent efforts to rise, and that he kept his eyes fixed on the overshadowing face of his foe with an unnatural and curious pertinacity. I stepped forward. Heliobas pressed his whole weight heavily down on the young man's prostrate body, while with both hands he held him by the shoulders, and gazed with terrific meaning into his fast-paling countenance. Ivan's lips turned blue; his eyes appeared to start from their sockets; his throat rattled. The spell that held me silent was broken; a flash of light, a flood of memory swept over my intelligence. I knew that Heliobas was exciting the whole battery of his inner electric force, and that thus employed for the purposes of vengeance, it must infallibly cause death. I found my speech at last.

"Heliobas!" I cried "Remember, remember Azul! When Death lies like a gift in your hand, withhold it. Withhold it, Heliobas; and give Life instead!"

He started at the sound of my voice, and looked up. A strong shudder shook his frame. Very slowly, very reluctantly, he relaxed his position; he rose from his kneeling posture on the Prince's breast—he left him and stood upright. Ivan at the same moment heaved a deep sigh, and closed his eyes, apparently insensible.

Gradually one by one the hard lines faded out of the face of Heliobas, and his old expression of soft and grave beneficence came back to it as graciously as sunlight after rain. He turned to me, and bent his head in a sort of reverential salutation.

"I thank and bless you," he said; "you reminded me in time! Another moment and it would have been too late. You have saved me."

"Give him his life," I said, pointing to Ivan.

"He has it," returned Heliobas; "I have not taken it from him, thank God! He provoked me; I regret it. I should have been more patient with him. He will revive immediately. I leave him to your care. In dealing with him, I ought to have remembered that human passion like his, unguided by spiritual knowledge, was to be met with pity and forbearance. As it is, however, he is safe. For me, I will go and pray for Zara's pardon, and that of my wronged Azul."

As he uttered the last words, he started, looked up, and smiled.

"My beautiful one! Thou HAST pardoned me? Thou wilt love me still? Thou art with me, Azul, my beloved? I have not lost thee, oh my best and dearest! Wilt thou lead me? Whither? Nay—no matter whither—I come!"

And as one walking in sleep, he went out of the room, and I heard his footsteps echoing in the distance on the way to the chapel.

Left alone with the Prince, I snatched a glass of cold water from the table, and sprinkled some of it on his forehead and hands. This was quite sufficient to revive him; and he drew a long breath, opened his eyes, and stared wildly about him. Seeing no one but me he grew bewildered, and asked:

"What has happened?"

Then catching sight of the drawn swords lying still on the ground where they had been thrown, he sprang to his feet, and cried:

"Where is the coward and murderer?"

I made him sit down and hear with patience what I had to say. I reminded him that Zara's health and happiness had always been perfect, and that her brother would rather have slain himself than her. I told him plainly that Zara had expected her death, and had prepared for it—had even bade me good-bye, although then I had not understood the meaning of her words. I recalled to his mind the day when Zara had used her power to repulse him.

"Disbelieve as you will in electric spiritual force," I said. "Your message to her then through me was—TELL HER I HAVE SEEN HER LOVER."

At these words a sombre shadow flitted over the Prince's face.

"I tell you," he said slowly, "that I believe I was on that occasion the victim of an hallucination. But I will explain to you what I saw. A superb figure, like, and yet unlike, a man, but of a much larger and grander form, appeared to me, as I thought, and spoke. 'Zara is mine,' it said—'mine by choice; mine by freewill; mine till death; mine after death; mine through eternity. With her thou hast naught in common; thy way lies elsewhere. Follow the path allotted to thee, and presume no more upon an angel's patience.' Then this Strange majestic-looking creature, whose face, as I remember it, was extraordinarily beautiful,

MARIE CORELLI

and whose eyes were like self-luminous stars, vanished. But, after all, what of it? The whole thing was a dream."

"I am not so sure of that," I said quietly, "But, Prince Ivan, now that you are calmer and more capable of resignation, will you tell me why you loved Zara?"

"Why!" he broke out impetuously. "Why, because it was impossible to help loving her."

"That is no answer," I replied. "Think! You can reason well if you like—I have heard you hold your own in an argument. What made you love Zara?"

He looked at me in a sort of impatient surprise, but seeing I was very much in earnest, he pondered a minute or so before replying.

"She was the loveliest woman I have ever seen!" he said at last, and in his voice there was a sound of yearning and regret.

"Is THAT all?" I queried, with a gesture of contempt. "Because her body was beautiful—because she had sweet kissing lips and a soft skin; because her hand was like a white flower, and her dark hair clustering over her brow reminded one of a misty evening cloud hiding moonlight; because the glance of her glorious eyes made the blood leap through your veins and sting you with passionate desire—are these the reasons of your so-called love? Oh, give it some other and lower name! For the worms shall feed on the fair flesh that won your admiration—their wet and slimy bodies shall trail across the round white arms and tender bosom—unsightly things shall crawl among the tresses of the glossy hair; and nothing, nothing shall remain of what you loved, but dust. Prince Ivan, you shudder; but I too loved Zara—I loved HER, not the perishable casket in which, like a jewel, she was for a time enshrined. I love her still—and for the being I love there is no such thing as death."

The Prince was silent, and seemed touched. I had spoken with real feeling, and tears of emotion stood in my eyes.

"I loved her as a man generally loves," he said, after a little pause. "Nay—more than most men love most women!"

"Most men are too often selfish in both their loves and hatreds," I returned. "Tell me if there was anything in Zara's mind and intelligence to attract you? Did you sympathize in her pursuits; did you admire her tastes; had you any ideas in common with her?"

"No, I confess I had not," he answered readily. "I considered her to be entirely a victim to her brother's scientific experiments. I thought, by making her my wife, to release her from such tyranny and give her rescue and refuge. To this end I found out all I could from—Him"—he approached the name of Heliobas with reluctance—"and I made up my mind that her delicate imagination had been morbidly excited; but that marriage and a life like that led by other women would bring her to a more healthy state of mind."

I smiled with a little scorn.

"Your presumption was almost greater than your folly, Prince," I said, "that with such ideas as these in your mind you could dream of winning Zara for a wife. Do you think she could have led a life like that of other women? A frivolous round of gaiety, a few fine dresses and jewels, small-talk, society scandal, stale compliments—you think such things would have suited Her? And would she have contented herself with a love like yours? Come! Come and see how well she has escaped you!"

And I beckoned him towards the door. He hesitated.

"Where would you take me?" he asked.

"To the chapel. Zara's body lies there."

He shuddered.

"No, no—not there! I cannot bear to look upon her perished loveliness—to see that face, once so animated, white and rigid—death in such a form is too horrible!"

And he covered his eyes with his hand—I saw tears slowly drop through his fingers. I gazed at him, half in wonder, half in pity.

"And yet you are a brave man!" I said.

These words roused him. He met my gaze with such a haggard look of woe that my heart ached for him. What comfort had he now? What joy could he ever expect? All his happiness was centred in the fact of Being Alive—alive to the pleasures of living, and to the joys the world could offer to a man who was strong, handsome, rich, and accomplished—how could he look upon death as otherwise than a loathsome thing—a thing not to be thought of in the heyday of youthful blood and jollity—a doleful spectre, in whose bony hands the roses of love must fall and wither! With a sense of deep commiseration in me, I spoke again with great gentleness.

"You need not look upon Zara's corpse unless you wish it, Prince," I said. "To you, the mysteries of the Hereafter have not been unlocked, because there is something in your nature that cannot and will not believe in God. Therefore to you, death must be repellent. I know you are one of those for whom the present alone exists—you easily forget the past, and take no trouble for the future. Paris is your heaven, or

St. Petersburg, or Vienna, as the fancy takes you; and the modern atheistical doctrines of French demoralization are in your blood. Nothing but a heaven-sent miracle could make you other than you are, and miracles do not exist for the materialist. But let me say two words more before you go from this house. Seek no more to avenge yourself for your love-disappointment on Heliobas—for you have really nothing to avenge. By your own confession you only cared for Zara's body—that body was always perishable, and it has perished by a sudden but natural catastrophe. With her soul, you declare you had nothing in common—that was herself—and she is alive to us who love her as she sought to be loved. Heliobas is innocent of having slain her body; he but helped to cultivate and foster that beautiful Spirit which he knew to be HER—for that he is to be honored and commended. Promise me, therefore, Prince Ivan, that you will never approach him again except in friendship—indeed, you owe him an apology for your unjust accusation, as also your gratitude for his sparing your life in the recent struggle."

The Prince kept his eyes steadily fixed upon me all the time I was speaking, and as I finished, he sighed and moved restlessly.

"Your words are compelling, mademoiselle," he said; "and you have a strange attraction for me. I know I am not wrong in thinking that you are a disciple of Heliobas, whose science I admit, though I doubt his theories. I promise you willingly what you ask—nay, I will even offer him my hand if he will accept it."

Overjoyed at my success, I answered: "He is in the chapel, but I will fetch him here."

Over the Prince's face a shadow of doubt, mingled with dread, passed swiftly, and he seemed to be forming a resolve in his own mind which was more or less distasteful to him. Whatever the feeling was he conquered it by a strong effort, and said with firmness:

"No; I will go to him myself. And I will look again upon—upon the face I loved. It is but one pang the more, and why should I not endure it?"

Seeing him thus inclined, I made no effort to dissuade him, and without another word I led the way to the chapel. I entered it reverently, he following me closely, with slow hushed footsteps. All was the same as I had left it, save that the servants of the household had gone to take some needful rest before the morning light called them to their daily routine of labour. Father Paul, too, had retired, and Heliobas alone knelt beside all that remained of Zara, his figure as motionless as though carved in bronze, his face hidden in his hands. As we approached, he neither stirred nor looked up, therefore I softly led the Prince to the opposite side of the bier, that he might look quietly on the perished loveliness that lay there at rest for ever. Ivan trembled, yet steadfastly gazed at the beautiful reposeful form, at the calm features on which the smile with which death had been received, still lingered—at the folded hands, the fading orange-blossoms—at the crucifix that lay on the cold breast like the final seal on the letter of life. Impulsively he stooped forward, and with a tender awe pressed his lips on the pale forehead, but instantly started back with the smothered, exclamation:

"O God! how cold!"

At the sound of his voice Heliobas rose up erect, and the two men faced each other, Zara's dead body lying like a barrier betwixt them.

A pause followed—a pause in which I heard my own heart beating loudly, so great was my anxiety. Heliobas suffered a few moments to elapse, then stretched his hand across his sister's bier.

"In HER name, let there be peace between us, Ivan," he said in accents that were both gentle and solemn.

The Prince, touched to the quick, responded to these kindly words with eager promptness, and they clasped hands over the quiet and lovely form that lay there—a silent, binding witness of their reconciliation.

"I have to ask your pardon, Casimir," then whispered Ivan. "I have also to thank you for my life."

"Thank the friend who stands beside you," returned Heliobas, in the same low tone, with a slight gesture towards me. "She reminded me of a duty in time. As for pardon, I know of no cause of offence on your part save what was perfectly excusable. Say no more; wisdom comes with years, and you are yet young."

A long silence followed. We all remained looking wistfully down upon the body of our lost darling, in thought too deep for words or weeping. I then noticed that another humble mourner shared our watch—a mourner whose very existence I had nearly forgotten. It was the faithful Leo. He lay couchant on the stone floor at the foot of the bier, almost as silent as a dog of marble; the only sign of animation he gave being a deep sigh which broke from his honest heart now and then. I went to him and softly patted his shaggy coat. He looked up at me with big brown eyes full of tears, licked my hand meekly, and again laid his head down upon his two fore-paws with a resignation that was most pathetic.

MARIE CORELLI

The dawn began to peer faintly through the chapel windows—the dawn of a misty, chilly morning. The storm of the past night had left a sting in the air, and the rain still fell, though gently. The wind had almost entirely sunk into silence. I re-arranged the flowers that were strewn on Zara's corpse, taking away all those that had slightly faded. The orange-blossom was almost dead, but I left that where it was— where the living Zara had herself placed it. As I performed this slight service, I thought, half mournfully, half gladly—

> *"Yes, Heaven is thine, but this*
> *Is a world of sweets and sours—*
> *Our flowers are merely FLOWERS;*
> *And the shadow of thy perfect bliss*
> *Is the sunshine of ours."*

Prince Ivan at last roused himself as from a deep and melancholy reverie, and, addressing himself to Heliobas, said softly:

"I will intrude no longer on your privacy, Casimir. Farewell! I shall leave Paris to-night."

For all answer Heliobas beckoned him and me also out of the chapel. As soon as its doors closed behind us, and we stood in the centre hall, he spoke with affectionate and grave earnestness:

"Ivan, something tells me that you and I shall not meet again for many years, if ever. Therefore, when you say 'farewell,' the word falls upon my ears with double meaning. We are friends—our friendship is sanctified by the dead presence of one whom we both loved, in different ways; therefore you will take in good part what I now say to you. You know, you cannot disguise from yourself that the science I study is fraught with terrible truth and marvellous discoveries; the theories I deduce from it you disbelieve, because you are nearly a materialist. I say NEARLY—not quite. That 'not quite' makes me love you, Ivan: I would save the small bright spark that flickers within you from both escape and extinction. But I cannot—at least, not as yet. Still, in order that you may know that there is a power in me higher than ordinary human reason, before you go from me to-night hear my prophecy of your career. The world waits for you, Ivan—the world, all agape and glittering with a thousand sparkling toys; it waits greedy for your presence, ready to fawn upon you for a smile, willing to cringe to you for a nod of approval. And why? Because wealth is yours—vast, illimitable wealth. Aye—you need not start or look incredulous—you will find it as I say. You, whose fortune up to now has barely reached a poor four thousand per annum—you are at this moment the possessor of millions. Only last night a relative of yours, whose name you scarcely know, expired, leaving all his hoarded treasures to you. Before the close of this present day, on whose threshold we now stand, you will have the news. When you receive it remember me, and acknowledge that at least for once I knew and spoke the truth. Follow the broad road, Ivan, laid out before you—a road wide enough not only for you to walk in, but for the crowd of toadies and flatterers also, who will push on swiftly after you and jostle you on all sides; be strong of heart and merry of countenance! Gather the roses; press the luscious grapes into warm, red wine that, as you quaff it, shall make your blood dance a mad waltz in your veins, and fair women's faces shall seem fairer to you than ever, their embraces more tender, their kisses more tempting! Spin the ball of Society like a toy in the palm of your hand! I see your life stretching before me like a brilliant, thread-like ephemeral ray of light! But in the far distance across it looms a shadow—a shadow that your power alone can never lift. Mark me, Ivan! When the first dread chill of that shadow makes itself felt, come to me—I shall yet be living. Come; for then no wealth can aid you—at that dark hour no boon companions can comfort. Come; and by our friendship so lately sworn—by Zara's pure soul—by God's existence, I will not die till I have changed that darkness over you into light eternal!—Fare you well!"

He caught the Prince's hand, and wrung it hard; then, without further word, look, or gesture, turned and disappeared again within the chapel.

His words had evidently made a deep impression on the young nobleman, who gazed after his retreating figure with a certain awe not unmingled with fear.

I held out my hand in silent farewell. Ivan took it gently, and kissed it with graceful courtesy.

"Casimir told me that your intercession saved my life, mademoiselle," he said. "Accept my poor thanks. If his present prophet-like utterances be true—"

"Why should you doubt him?" I asked, with some impatience. "Can you believe in Nothing?"

The Prince, still holding my hand, looked at me in a sort of grave perplexity.

MARIE CORELLI

"I think you have hit it," he observed quietly. "I doubt everything except the fact of my own existence, and there are times when I am not even sure of that. But if, as I said before, the prophecy of my Chaldean friend, whom I cannot help admiring with all my heart, turns out to be correct, then my life is more valuable to me than ever with such wealth to balance it, and I thank you doubly for having saved it by a word in time."

I withdrew my hand gently from his.

"You think the worth of your life increased by wealth?" I asked.

"Naturally! Money is power."

"And what of the shadow also foretold as inseparable from your fate?"

A faint smile crossed his features.

"Ah, pardon me! That is the only portion of Casimir's fortune-telling that I am inclined to disbelieve thoroughly."

"But," I said, "if you are willing to accept the pleasant part of his prophecy, why not admit the possibility of the unpleasant occurring also?"

He shrugged his shoulders.

"In these enlightened times, mademoiselle, we only believe what is agreeable to us, and what suits our own wishes, tastes, and opinions. Ca va sans dire. We cannot be forced to accept a Deity against our reason. That is a grand result of modern education."

"Is it?" and I looked at him with pity. "Poor human reason! It will reel into madness sometimes for a mere trifle—an overdose of alcohol will sometimes upset it altogether—what a noble omnipotent thing is human reason! But let me not detain you. Good-bye, and—as the greeting of olden times used to run—God save you!"

He bent his head with a light reverence.

"I believe you to be a good, sweet woman," he said, "therefore I am grateful for your blessing. My mother," and here his eyes grew dreamy and wistful—"poor soul! she died long ago—my mother would never let me retire to rest without signing the cross on my brow. Ah well, that is past! I should like, mademoiselle," and his voice sank very low, "to send some flowers for—her—you understand?"

I did understand, and readily promised to lay whatever blossoms he selected tenderly above the sacred remains of that earthly beauty he had loved, as he himself said, "more than most men love most women."

He thanked me earnestly, and seemed relieved and satisfied. Casting a look of farewell around the familiar hall, he wafted a parting kiss towards the chapel—an action which, though light, was full of tenderness and regret. Then, with a low salute, he left me. The street-door opened and closed after him in its usual noiseless manner. He was gone.

The morning had now fairly dawned, and within the Hotel Mars the work of the great mansion went on in its usual routine; but a sombre melancholy was in the atmosphere—a melancholy that not all my best efforts could dissipate. The domestics looked sullen and heavy-eyed; the only ones in their number who preserved their usual equanimity were the Armenian men-servants and the little Greek page. Preparations for Zara's funeral went on apace; they were exceedingly simple, and the ceremony was to be quite private in character. Heliobas issued his orders, and saw to the carrying out of his most minute instructions in his usual calm manner; but his eyes looked heavy, and his fine countenance was rendered even more majestic by the sacred, resigned sorrow that lay upon it like a deep shadow. His page served him with breakfast in his private room: but he left the light meal untasted. One of the women brought me coffee; but the very thought of eating and drinking seemed repulsive, and I could not touch anything. My mind was busy with the consideration of the duty I had to perform—namely, to see the destruction of Zara's colossal statue, as she had requested. After thinking about it for some time, I went to Heliobas and told him what I had it in charge to do. He listened attentively.

"Do it at once," he said decisively. "Take my Armenians; they are discreet, obedient, and they ask no questions—with strong hammers they will soon crush the clay. Stay! I will come with you." Then looking at me scrutinizingly, he added kindly: "You have eaten nothing, my child? You cannot? But your strength will give way—here, take this." And lie held out a small glass of a fluid whose revivifying properties I well knew to be greater than any sustenance provided by an ordinary meal. I swallowed it obediently, and as I returned the empty glass to him he said: "I also have a commission in charge from Zara. You know, I suppose, that she was prepared for her death?"

"I did not know; but I think she must have been," I answered.

"She was. We both were. We remained together in the chapel all day, saying what parting words we had to say to one another. We knew her death, or rather her release, was to occur at some hour that night; but in what way the end was destined to come, we knew not. Till I heard the first peals of thunder, I was in suspense; but after that

MARIE CORELLI

I was no longer uncertain. You were a witness of the whole ensuing scene. No death could have been more painless than hers. But let me not forget the message she gave me for you." Here he took from a secret drawer the electric stone Zara had always worn. "This jewel is yours," he said. "You need not fear to accept it—it contains no harm! it will bring you no ill-fortune. You see how all the sparkling brilliancy has gone out of it? Wear it, and within a few minutes it will be as lustrous as ever. The life throbbing in your veins warms the electricity contained in it; and with the flowing of your blood, its hues change and glow. It has no power to attract; it can simply absorb and shine. Take it as a remembrance of her who loved you and who loves you still."

I was still in my evening dress, and my neck was bare. I slipped the chain, on which hung the stone, round my throat, and watched the strange gem with some curiosity. In a few seconds a pale streak of fiery topaz flashed through it, which deepened and glowed into a warm crimson, like the heart of a red rose; and by the time it had become thoroughly warmed against my flesh, it glittered as brilliantly as ever.

"I will always wear it," I said earnestly. "I believe it will bring me good fortune."

"I believe it will," returned Heliobas simply. "And now let us fulfil Zara's other commands."

On our way across the hall we were stopped by the page, who brought us a message of inquiry after Zara's health from Colonel Everard and his wife, and also from the Challoners. Heliobas hastily wrote a few brief words in pencil, explaining the fatal result of the accident, and returned it to the messenger, giving orders at the same time that all the blinds should be pulled down at the windows of the house, that visitors might understand there was no admittance. We then proceeded to the studio, accompanied by the Armenians carrying heavy hammers. Reverently, and with my mind full of recollections of Zara's living presence, I opened the familiar door. The first thing that greeted us was a most exquisitely wrought statue in white marble of Zara herself, full length, and arrayed in her customary graceful Eastern costume. The head was slightly raised: a look of gladness lighted up the beautiful features; and within the loosely clasped hands was a cluster of roses. Bound the pedestal were carved the words, "Omnia vincit Amor," with Zara's name and the dates of her birth and death. A little slip of paper lay at the foot of the statue, which Heliobas perceived, and taking it he read and passed it to me. The lines were in Zara's handwriting, and ran as follows:

"To my beloved Casimir—my brother, my friend, my guide and teacher, to whom I owe the supreme happiness of my life in this world and the next—let this poor figure of his grateful Zara be a memento of happy days that are gone, only to be renewed with redoubled happiness hereafter."

I handed back the paper silently, with tears in my eyes, and we turned our attention to the colossal figure we had come to destroy. It stood at the extreme end of the studio, and was entirely hidden by white linen drapery. Heliobas advanced, and by a sudden dexterous movement succeeded in drawing off the coverings with a single effort, and then we both fell back and gazed at the clay form disclosed in amazement. What did it represent? A man? a god? an angel? or all three united in one vast figure?

It was an unfinished work. The features of the face were undeclared, save the brow and eyes; and these were large, grand, and full of absolute wisdom and tranquil consciousness of power. I could have gazed on this wonderful piece of Zara's handiwork for hours, but Heliobas called to the Armenian servants, who stood near the door awaiting orders, and commanded them to break it down. For once these well-trained domestics showed signs of surprise, and hesitated. Their master frowned. Snatching a hammer from one of them, he himself attacked the great statue as if it were a personal foe. The Armenians, seeing he was in earnest, returned to their usual habits of passive obedience, and aided him in his labour. Within a few minutes the great and beautiful figure lay in fragments on the floor, and these fragments were soon crushed into indistinguishable atoms. I had promised to witness this work of destruction, and witness it I did, but it was with pain and regret. When all was finished, Heliobas commanded his men to carry the statue of Zara's self down to his own private room, and then to summon all the domestics of the household in a body to the great hall, as he wished to address them. I heard him give this order with some surprise, and he saw it. As the Armenians slowly disappeared, carrying with great care the marble figure of their late mistress, he turned to me, as he locked up the door of the studio, and said quietly:

"These ignorant folk, who serve me for money and food—money that they have eagerly taken, and food that they have greedily devoured—

they think that I am the devil or one of the devil's agents, and I am going to prove their theories entirely to their satisfaction. Come and see!"

I followed him, somewhat mystified. On the way downstairs he said:

"Do you know why Zara wished that statue destroyed?"

"No," I said frankly; "unless for the reason that it was incomplete."

"It always would have been incomplete," returned Heliobas; "even had she lived to work at it for years. It was a daring attempt, and a fruitless one. She was trying to make a clay figure of one who never wore earthly form—the Being who is her Twin-Soul, who dominates her entirely, and who is with her now. As well might she have tried to represent in white marble the prismatic hues of the rainbow!"

We had now reached the hall, and the servants were assembling by twos and threes. They glanced at their master with looks of awe, as he took up a commanding position near the fountain, and faced them with a glance of calm scrutiny and attention. I drew a chair behind one of the marble columns and seated myself, watching everything with interest. Leo appeared from some corner or other, and laid his rough body down close at his master's feet.

In a few minutes all the domestics, some twenty in number, were present, and Heliobas, raising his voice, spoke with a clear deliberate enunciation:

"I have sent for you all this morning, because I am perfectly aware that you have all determined to give me notice."

A stir of astonishment and dismay ensued on the part of the small audience, and I heard one voice near me whisper:

"He Is the devil, or how could he have known it?"

The lips of Heliobas curled in a fine sarcastic smile. He went on:

"I spare you this trouble. Knowing your intentions, I take upon myself to dismiss you at once. Naturally, you cannot risk your characters by remaining in the service of the devil. For my own part, I wonder the devil's money has not burnt your hands, or his food turned to poison in your mouths. My sister, your kind and ever-indulgent mistress, is dead. You know this, and it is your opinion that I summoned up the thunderstorm which caused her death. Be it so. Report it so, if you will, through Paris; your words do not affect me. You have been excellent machines, and for your services many thanks! As soon as my sister's funeral is over, your wages, with an additional present, will be sent to you. You can then leave my house when you please; and, contrary to the usual custom of accepted devils, I am able to say, without perishing in the effort—God speed you all!"

The faces of those he addressed exhibited various emotions while he spoke—fear contending with a good deal of shame. The little Greek page stepped forward timidly.

"The master knows that I will never leave him," he murmured, and his large eyes were moist with tears.

Heliobas laid a gentle hand on the boy's dark curls, but said nothing. One of the four Armenians advanced, and with a graceful rapid gesture of his right hand, touched his head and breast.

"My lord will not surely dismiss Us who desire to devote ourselves to his service? We are willing to follow my lord to the death if need be, for the sake of the love and honour we bear him."

Heliobas looked at him very kindly.

"I am richer in friends than I thought myself to be," he said quietly. "Stay then, by all means, Afra, you and your companions, since you have desired it. And you, my boy," he went on, addressing the tearful page, "think you that I would turn adrift an orphan, whom a dying mother trusted to my care? Nay, child, I am as much your servant as you are mine, so long as your love turns towards me."

For all answer the page kissed his hand in a sort of rapture, and flinging back his clustering hair from his classic brows, surveyed the domestics, who had taken their dismissal in silent acquiescence, with a pretty scorn.

"Go, all of you, scum of Paris!" he cried in his clear treble tones— "you who know neither God nor devil! You will have your money— more than your share—what else seek you? You have served one of the noblest of men; and because he is so great and wise and true, you judge him a fiend! Oh, so like the people of Paris—they who pervert all things till they think good evil and evil good! Look you! you have worked for your wages; but I have worked for HIM—I would starve with him, I would die for him! For to me he is not fiend, but Angel!"

Overcome by his own feelings the boy again kissed his master's hand, and Heliobas gently bade him be silent. He himself looked round on the still motionless group of servants with an air of calm surprise.

"What are you waiting for?" he asked. "Consider yourselves dismissed, and at liberty to go where you please. Any one of you that chooses to apply to me for a character shall not lack the suitable recommendation. There is no more to say."

A lively-looking woman with quick restless black eyes stepped forward.

"I am sure," she said, with a mincing curtsey, "that we are very sorry if we have unintentionally wronged monsieur; but monsieur, who is aware of so many things, must know that many reports are circulated about monsieur that make one to shudder; that madame his sister's death so lamentable has given to all, what one would say, the horrors; and monsieur must consider that poor servants of virtuous reputation—"

"So, Jeanne Claudet!" interrupted Heliobas, in a thrilling low tone. "And what of the child—the little waxen-faced helpless babe left to die on the banks of the Loire? But it did not die, Jeanne—it was rescued; and it shall yet live to loathe its mother!"

The woman uttered a shriek, and fainted.

In the feminine confusion and fuss that ensued, Heliobas, accompanied by his little page and the dog Leo, left the hall and entered his own private room, where for some time I left him undisturbed.

In the early part of the afternoon a note was brought to me. It was from Colonel Everard, entreating me to come as soon as possible to his wife, who was very ill.

"Since she heard of the death of that beautiful young lady, a death so fearfully sudden and unexpected," wrote the Colonel, "she has been quite unlike herself—nervous, hysterical, and thoroughly unstrung. It will be a real kindness to her if you will come as soon as you can—she has such, a strong desire for your company."

I showed this note at once to Heliobas. He read it, and said:

"Of course you must go. Wait till our simple funeral ceremony is over, and then—we part. Not for ever; I shall see you often again. For now I have lost Zara, you are my only female disciple, and I shall not willingly lose sight of you. You will correspond with me?"

"Gladly and gratefully," I replied.

"You shall not lose by it. I can initiate you into many secrets that will be useful to you in your career. As for your friend Mrs. Everard, you will find that your presence will cure her. You have progressed greatly in electric force: the mere touch of your hand will soothe her, as you will find. But never be tempted to try any of the fluids of which you have the recipes on her, or on anybody but yourself, unless you write to me first about it, as Cellini did when he tried an experiment on you. As for your own bodily and spiritual health, you know thoroughly what to do—Keep The Secret; and make a step in advance every day. By-and-by you will have double work."

"How so?" I asked.

"In Zara's case, her soul became dominated by a Spirit whose destiny was fulfilled and perfect, and who never could descend to imprisonment in earthly clay. Now, you will not be dominated—you will be simply Equalized; that is, you will find the exact counterpart of your own soul dwelling also in human form, and you will have to impart your own force to that other soul, which will, in its turn, impart to yours a corresponding electric impetus. There is no union so lovely as such an one—no harmony so exquisite; it is like a perfect chord, complete and indissoluble. There are sevenths and ninths in music, beautiful and effective in their degrees; but perhaps none of them are so absolutely satisfying to the ear as the perfect chord. And this is your lot in life and in love, my child—be grateful for it night and morning on your bended knees before the Giver of all good. And walk warily—your own soul with that other shall need much thought and humble prayer. Aim onward and upward—you know the road—you also know, and you have partly seen, what awaits you at the end."

After this conversation we spoke no more in private together. The rest of the afternoon was entirely occupied with the final preparations for Zara's funeral, which was to take place at Pere-la-Chaise early the next morning. A large and beautiful wreath of white roses, lilies, and maiden-hair arrived from Prince Ivan; and, remembering my promise to him, I went myself to lay it in a conspicuous place on Zara's corpse. That fair body was now laid in its coffin of polished oak, and a delicate veil of filmy lace draped it from head to foot. The placid expression of the features remained unchanged, save for a little extra rigidity of the flesh; the hands, folded over the crucifix, were stiff, and looked as though they were moulded in wax. I placed the wreath in position and paused, looking wistfully at that still and solemn figure. Father Paul, slowly entering from a side-door, came and stood beside me.

"She is happy!" he said; and a cheerful expression irradiated his venerable features.

"Did you also know she would die that night?" I asked softly.

"Her brother sent for me, and told me of her expected dissolution. She herself told me, and made her last confession and communion. Therefore I was prepared."

"But did you not doubt—were you not inclined to think they might be wrong?" I inquired, with some astonishment.

"I knew Heliobas as a child," the priest returned. "I knew his father and mother before him; and I have been always perfectly aware of the immense extent of his knowledge, and the value of his discoveries. If I were inclined to be sceptical on spiritual matters, I should not be of the race I am; for I am also a Chaldean."

I said no more, and Father Paul trimmed the tapers burning round the coffin in devout silence. Again I looked at the fair dead form before me; but somehow I could not feel sad again. All my impulses bade me rejoice. Why should I be unhappy on Zara's account?—more especially when the glories of the Central Sphere were yet fresh in my memory, and when I knew as a positive fact that her happiness was now perfect. I left the chapel with a light step and lighter heart, and went to my own room to pack up my things that all might be in readiness for my departure on the morrow. On my table I found a volume whose quaint binding I at once recognised—"The Letters of a Dead Musician." A card lay beside it, on which was written in pencil:

"Knowing of your wish to possess this book, I herewith offer it for your acceptance. It teaches you a cheerful devotion to Art, and an indifference to the world's opinions—both of which are necessary to you in your career.—HELIOBAS."

Delighted with this gift, I opened the book, and found my name written on the fly-leaf, with the date of the month and year, and the words:

"La musica e il lamento dell' amore o la preghiera a gli Dei." (Music is the lament of love, or a prayer to the Gods.)

I placed this treasure carefully in a corner of my portmanteau, together with the parchment scrolls containing "The Electric Principle of Christianity," and the valuables recipes of Heliobas; and as I did so, I caught sight of myself in the long mirror that directly faced me. I was fascinated, not by my own reflection, but by the glitter of the electric gem I wore. It flashed and glowed like a star, and was really lovely—far more brilliant than the most brilliant cluster of fine diamonds. I may here remark that I have been asked many questions concerning this curious ornament whenever I have worn it in public, and the general impression has been that it is some new arrangement of ornamental electricity. It is, however, nothing of the kind; it is simply a clear pebble, common enough on the shores of tropical countries, which has the property of absorbing a small portion of the electricity in a human body, sufficient to make it shine with prismatic and powerful lustre—a property which has only as yet been discovered by Heliobas, who asserts that the same capability exists in many other apparently lustreless stones which have been untried, and are therefore unknown. The "healing stones," or amulets, still in use in the East, and also in the remote parts of the Highlands (see notes to Archibald Clerk's translation of 'Ossian'), are also electric, but in a different way—they have the property of absorbing DISEASE and destroying it in certain cases; and these, after being worn a suitable length of time, naturally exhaust what virtue they originally possessed, and are no longer of any use. Stone amulets are considered nowadays as a mere superstition of the vulgar and uneducated; but it must be remembered that superstition itself has always had for it a foundation some grain, however small and remote, of fact. I could give a very curious explanation of the formation of ORCHIDS, those strange plants called sometimes "Freaks of Nature," as if Nature ever indulged in a "freak" of any kind! But I have neither time nor space to enter upon the subject now; indeed, if I were once to begin to describe the wonderful, amazing and beautiful vistas of knowledge that the wise Chaldean, who is still my friend and guide, has opened up and continues to extend before my admiring vision, a work of twenty volumes would scarce contain all I should have to say. But I have written this book merely to tell those who peruse it, about Heliobas, and what I myself experienced in his house; beyond this I may not go. For, as, I observed in my introduction, I am perfectly aware that few, if any, of my readers will accept my narrative as more than a mere visionary romance—or that they will admit the mysteries of life, death, eternity, and all the wonders of the Universe to be simply the NATURAL AND SCIENTIFIC OUTCOME OF A RING OF EVERLASTING ELECTRIC HEAT AND LIGHT; but whether they agree to it or no, I can say with Galileo, "E pur si muove!"

XVII

Conclusion

It was a very simple and quiet procession that moved next day from the Hotel Mars to Pere-la-Chaise. Zara's coffin was carried in an open hearse, and was covered with a pall of rich white velvet, on which lay a royal profusion of flowers—Ivan's wreath, and a magnificent cross of lilies sent by tender-hearted Mrs. Challoner, being most conspicuous among them. The only thing a little unusual about it was that the funeral car was drawn by two stately WHITE horses; and Heliobas told me this had been ordered at Zara's special request, as she thought the solemn pacing through the streets of dismal black steeds had a depressing effect on the passers-by.

"And why," she had said, "should anybody be sad, when *I* in reality am so thoroughly happy?"

Prince Ivan Petroffsky had left Paris, but his carriage, drawn by two prancing Russian steeds, followed the hearse at a respectful distance, as also the carriage of Dr. Morini, and some other private persons known to Heliobas. A few people attended it on foot, and these were chiefly from among the very poor, some of whom had benefited by Zara's charity or her brother's medical skill, and had heard of the calamity through rumour, or through the columns of the Figaro, where it was reported with graphic brevity. The weather was still misty, and the fiery sun seemed to shine through tears as Father Paul, with his assistants, read in solemn yet cheerful tones the service for the dead according to the Catholic ritual. One of the chief mourners at the grave was the faithful Leo; who, without obtruding himself in anyone's way, sat at a little distance, and seemed, by the confiding look with which he turned his eyes upon his master, to thoroughly understand that he must henceforth devote his life entirely to him alone. The coffin was lowered, the "Requiem aeternam" spoken—all was over. Those assembled shook hands quietly with Heliobas, saluted each other, and gradually dispersed. I entered a carriage and drove back to the Hotel Mars, leaving Heliobas in the cemetery to give his final instructions for the ornamentation and decoration of his sister's grave.

The little page served me with some luncheon in my own apartment, and by the time all was ready for my departure, Heliobas returned.

I went down to him in his study, and found him sitting pensively in his arm-chair, absorbed in thought. He looked sad and solitary, and my whole heart went out to him in gratitude and sympathy. I knelt beside him as a daughter might have done, and softly kissed his hand.

He started as though awakened suddenly from sleep, and seeing me, his eyes softened, and he smiled gravely.

"Are you come to say 'Good-bye,' my child?" he asked, in a kind tone. "Well, your mission here is ended!"

"Had I any mission at all," I replied, with a grateful look, "save the very selfish one which was comprised in the natural desire to be restored to health?"

Heliobas surveyed me for a few moments in silence.

"Were I to tell you," he said at last, "by what mystical authority and influence you were compelled to come here, by what a marvellously linked chain of circumstances you became known to me long before I saw you; how I was made aware that you were the only woman living to whose companionship I could trust my sister at a time when the society of one of her own sex became absolutely necessary to her; how you were marked out to me as a small point of light by which possibly I might steer my course clear of the darkness which threatened me—I say, were I to tell you all this, you would no longer doubt the urgent need of your presence here. It is, however, enough to tell you that you have fulfilled all that was expected of you, even beyond my best hopes; and in return for your services, the worth of which you cannot realize, whatever guidance I can give you in the future for your physical and spiritual life, is yours. I have done something for you, but not much—I will do more. Only, in communicating with me, I ask you to honour me with your full confidence in all matters pertaining to yourself and your surroundings—then I shall not be liable to errors of judgment in the opinions I form or the advice I give."

"I promise most readily," I replied gladly, for it seemed to me that I was rich in possessing as a friend and counsellor such a man as this student of the loftiest sciences.

"And now one thing more," he resumed, opening a drawer in the table near which he sat. "Here is a pencil for you to write your letters to me with. It will last about ten years, and at the expiration of that time you can have another. Write with it on any paper, and the marks will be like those of an ordinary drawing-pencil; but as fast as they are written they disappear. Trouble not about this circumstance—write all you have to say, and when you have finished your letter your closely covered pages shall seem blank. Therefore, were the eye of a stranger to look at them, nothing could be learned therefrom. But when they reach me, I can make the writing appear and stand out on these apparently unsullied pages as distinctly as though your words had been printed. My letters to you will also, when you receive them, appear blank; but you will only have to press them for about ten minutes in this"—and he handed me what looked like an ordinary blotting-book—"and they will be perfectly legible. Cellini has these little writing implements; he uses them whenever the distances are too great for us to amuse ourselves with the sagacity of Leo—in fact the journeys of that faithful animal have principally been to keep him in training."

"But," I said, as I took the pencil and book from his hand, "why do you not make these convenient writing materials public property? They would be so useful."

"Why should I build up a fortune for some needy stationer?" he asked, with a half-smile. "Besides, they are not new things. They were known to the ancients, and many secret letters, laws, histories, and poems were written with instruments such as these. In an old library, destroyed more than two centuries ago, there was a goodly pile of apparently blank parchment. Had I lived then and known what I know now, I could have made the white pages declare their mystery."

"Has this also to do with electricity?" I asked.

"Certainly—with what is called vegetable electricity. There is not a plant or herb in existence, but has almost a miracle hidden away in its tiny cup or spreading leaves—do you doubt it?"

"Not I!" I answered quickly. "I doubt nothing!"

Heliobas smiled gravely.

"You are right!" he said. "Doubt is the destroyer of beauty—the poison in the sweet cup of existence—the curse which mankind have brought on themselves. Avoid it as you would the plague. Believe in anything or everything miraculous and glorious—the utmost reach of your faith can with difficulty grasp the majestic reality and perfection of everything you can see, desire, or imagine. Mistrust that volatile thing called Human Reason, which is merely a name for whatever opinion we happen to adopt for the time—it is a thing which totters on its throne in a fit of rage or despair—there is nothing infinite about it. Guide yourself by the delicate Spiritual Instinct within you, which tells you that with God all things are possible, save that He cannot destroy

Himself or lessen by one spark the fiery brilliancy of his ever-widening circle of productive Intelligence. But make no attempt to convert the world to your way of thinking—it would be mere waste of time."

"May I never try to instruct anyone in these things?" I asked.

"You can try, if you choose; but you will find most human beings like the herd of swine in the Gospel, possessed by devils that drive them headlong into the sea. You know, for instance, that angels and aerial spirits actually exist; but were you to assert your belief in them, philosophers (so-called) would scout your theories as absurd,—though their idea of a LONELY God, who yet is Love, is the very acme of absurdity. For Love MUST have somewhat to love, and MUST create the beauty and happiness round itself and the things beloved. But why point out these simple things to those who have no desire to see? Be content, child, that YOU have been deemed worthy of instruction—it is a higher fate for you than if you had been made a Queen."

The little page now entered, and told me that the carriage was at the door in waiting. As he disappeared again after delivering this message, Heliobas rose from his chair, and taking my two hands in his, pressed them kindly.

"One word more, little friend, on the subject of your career. I think the time will come when you will feel that music is almost too sacred a thing to be given away for money to a careless and promiscuous public. However this may be, remember that scarce one of the self-styled artists who cater for the crowd deserves to be called MUSICIAN in the highest sense of the word. Most of them seek not music, but money and applause; and therefore the art they profess is degraded by them into a mere trade. But you, when you play in public, must forget that PERSONS with little vanities and lesser opinions exist. Think of what you saw in your journey with Azul; and by a strong effort of your will, you can, if you choose, COMPEL certain harmonies to sound in your ears—fragments of what is common breathing air to the Children of the Ring, some of whom you saw—and you will be able to reproduce them in part, if not in entirety. But if you once admit a thought of Self to enter your brain, those aerial sounds will be silenced instantly. By this means, too, you can judge who are the true disciples of music in this world—those who, like Schubert and Chopin, suffered the heaven-born melodies to descend THROUGH them as though they were mere conductors of sound; or those who, feebly imitating other composers, measure out crotchets and quavers by rule and line, and flood the world with inane and perishable, and therefore useless, productions. And now,—farewell."

"Do you remain in Paris?" I asked.

"For a few days only. I shall go to Egypt, and in travelling accustom myself to the solitude in which I must dwell, now Zara has left me."

"You have Azul," I ventured to remark.

"Ah! but how often do I see her? Only when my soul for an instant is clear from all earthly and gross obstruction; and how seldom I can attain to this result while weighted with my body! But she is near me— that I know—faithful as the star to the mariner's compass!"

He raised his head as he spoke, and his eyes flashed. Never had I seen him look more noble or kingly. The inspired radiance of his face softened down into his usual expression of gentleness and courtesy, and he said, offering me his arm:

"Let me see you to the carriage. You know, it is not an actual parting with us—I intend that we shall meet frequently. For instance, the next time we exchange pleasant greetings will be in Italy."

I suppose I looked surprised; I certainly felt so, for nothing was further from my thoughts than a visit to Italy.

Heliobas smiled, and said in a tone that was almost gay:

"Shall I draw the picture for you? I see a fair city, deep embowered in hills and sheltered by olive-groves. Over it beams a broad sky, deeply blue; many soft bells caress the summer air. Away in the Cascine Woods a gay party of people are seated on the velvety moss; they have mandolins, and they sing for pure gaiety of heart. One of them, a woman with fair hair, arrayed in white, with a red rose at her bosom, is gathering the wild flowers that bloom around her, and weaving them into posies for her companions. A stranger, pacing slowly, book in hand, through the shady avenue, sees her—her eyes meet his. She springs up to greet him; he takes her hand. The woman is yourself; the stranger no other than your poor friend, who now, for a brief space, takes leave of you!"

So rapidly had he drawn up this picture, that the impression made on me was as though a sudden vision had been shown to me in a magic glass. I looked at him earnestly.

"Then our next meeting will be happy?" I said inquiringly.

"Of course. Why not? And the next—and the next after that also!" he answered.

At this reply, so frankly given, I was relieved, and accompanied him readily through the hall towards the street-door. Leo met us here, and intimated, as plainly as a human being could have done, his wish to bid me good-bye. I stooped and kissed his broad head and patted him affectionately, and was rewarded for these attentions by seeing his plume-like tail wave slowly to and fro—a sign of pleasure the poor animal had not betrayed since Zara's departure from the scene of her earthly imprisonment.

At the door the pretty Greek boy handed me a huge basket of the loveliest flowers.

"The last from the conservatory," said Heliobas. "I shall need no more of these luxuries."

As I entered the carriage he placed the flowers beside me, and again took my hand.

"Good-bye, my child!" he said, in earnest and kindly tones. "I have your address, and will write you all my movements. In any trouble, small or great, of your own, send to me for advice without hesitation. I can tell you already that I foresee the time when you will resign altogether the precarious and unsatisfactory life of a mere professional musician. You think no other career would be possible to you? Well, you will see! A few months will decide all. Good-bye again; God bless you!"

The carriage moved off, and Heliobas stood on the steps of his mansion watching it out of sight. To the last I saw his stately figure erect in the light of the winter sunshine—a figure destined from henceforth to occupy a prominent position in my life and memory. The regret I felt at parting from him was greatly mitigated by the assurance he gave me of our future meeting, a promise which has since been fulfilled, and is likely soon to be fulfilled again. That I have such a friend is an advantageous circumstance for me, for through his guidance I am able to judge accurately of many things occurring in the course of the daily life around me—things which, seemingly trivial, are the hints of serious results to come, which, I am thus permitted in part to foresee. There is a drawback, of course, and the one bitter drop in the cup of knowledge is, that the more I progress under the tuition of Heliobas, the less am I deceived by graceful appearances. I perceive with almost cruel suddenness the true characters of all those whom I meet. No smile of lip or eye can delude me into accepting mere surface-matter for real depth, and it is intensely painful for me to be forced to behold hypocrisy in the expression of the apparently devout—sensuality in the face of some radiantly beautiful and popular woman—vice under the mask of virtue—self-interest in the guise of friendship, and spite and malice springing up like a poisonous undergrowth beneath the words of elegant flattery or dainty compliment. I often wish I could throw a rose-coloured mist of illusion over all these things and still more earnestly do I wish I could in a single instance find myself mistaken. But alas! the fatal finger of the electric instinct within me points out unerringly the flaw in every human diamond, and writes "SHAM" across many a cunningly contrived imitation of intelligence and goodness. Still, the grief I feel at this is counterbalanced in part by the joy with which I quickly recognize real virtue, real nobility, real love; and when these attributes flash out upon me from the faces of human beings, my own soul warms, and I know I have seen a vision as of angels. The capability of Heliobas to foretell future events proved itself in his knowledge of the fate of the famous English hero, Gordon, long before that brave soldier met his doom. At the time the English Government sent him out on his last fatal mission, a letter from Heliobas to me contained the following passage:

"I see Gordon has chosen his destiny and the manner of his death. Two ways of dying have been offered him—one that is slow, painful, and inglorious; the other sudden, and therefore sweeter to a man of his temperament. He himself is perfectly aware of the approaching end of his career; he will receive his release at Khartoum. England will lament over him for a little while, and then he will be declared an inspired madman, who rushed recklessly on his own doom; while those who allowed him to be slain will be voted the wisest, the most just and virtuous in the realm."

This prophecy was carried out to the letter, as I fully believe certain things of which I am now informed will also be fulfilled. But though there are persons who pin their faith on "Zadkiel," I doubt if there are any who will believe in such a thing as ELECTRIC DIVINATION. The one is mere vulgar imposture, the other is performed on a purely scientific basis in accordance with certain existing rules and principles; yet I think there can be no question as to which of the two the public en masse is likely to prefer. On the whole, people do not mind being deceived; they hate being instructed, and the trouble of thinking for themselves is almost too much for them. Therefore "Zadkiel" is certain to flourish for many and many a long day, while the lightning instinct of prophecy dormant in every human being remains unused and utterly forgotten except by the rare few.

I HAVE LITTLE MORE TO say. I feel that those among my readers who idly turn over these pages, expecting to find a "NOVEL" in the true acceptation of the term, may be disappointed. My narrative is simply an "experience:" but I have no wish to persuade others of the central truth contained in it—namely, THE EXISTENCE OF POWERFUL ELECTRIC ORGANS IN EVERY HUMAN BEING, WHICH WITH PROPER CULTIVATION ARE CAPABLE OF MARVELLOUS SPIRITUAL FORCE. The time is not yet ripe for this fact to be accepted.

The persons connected with this story may be dismissed in a few words. When I joined my friend Mrs. Everard, she was suffering from nervous hysteria. My presence had the soothing effect Heliobas had assured me of, and in a very few days we started from Paris in company for England. She, with her amiable and accomplished husband, went back to the States a few months since to claim an immense fortune, which they are now enjoying as most Americans enjoy wealth. Amy has diamonds to her heart's content, and toilettes galore from Worth's; but she has no children, and from the tone of her letters to me, I fancy she would part with one at least of her valuable necklaces to have a small pair of chubby arms round her neck, and a soft little head nestling against her bosom.

Raffaello Cellini still lives and works; his paintings are among the marvels of modern Italy for their richness and warmth of colour—colour which, in spite of his envious detractors, is destined to last through ages. He is not very rich, for he is one of those who give away their substance to the poor and the distressed; but where he is known he is universally beloved. None of his pictures have yet been exhibited in England, and he is in no hurry to call upon the London critics for their judgment. He has been asked several times to sell his large picture, "Lords of our Life and Death," but he will not. I have never met him since our intercourse at Cannes, but I hear of him frequently through Heliobas, who has recently forwarded me a proof engraving of the picture "L'IMPROVISATRICE," for which I sat as model. It is a beautiful work of art, but that it is like ME I am not vain enough to admit. I keep it, not as a portrait of myself, but as a souvenir of the man through whose introduction I gained the best friend I have.

News of Prince Ivan Petroffsky reaches me frequently. He is possessor of the immense wealth foretold by Heliobas; the eyes of Society greedily follows his movements; his name figures conspicuously in the "Fashionable Intelligence;" and the magnificence of his recent marriage festivities was for some time the talk of the Continent. He has married the only daughter of a French Duke—a lovely creature, as soulless and heartless as a dressmaker's stuffed model; but she carries his jewels well on her white bosom, and receives his guests with as much dignity as a well-trained major-domo. These qualities suffice to satisfy her husband at present; how long his satisfaction will last is another matter. He has not quite forgotten Zara; for on every recurring Jour des Morts, or Feast of the Dead, he sends a garland or cross of flowers to the simple grave in Pere-la-Chaise. Heliobas watches his career with untiring vigilance; nor can I myself avoid taking a certain interest in the progress of his fate. At the moment I write he is one of the most envied and popular noblemen in all the Royal Courts of Europe; and no one thinks of asking him whether he is happy. He MUST be happy, says the world; he has everything that is needed to make him so. Everything? yes—all except one thing, for which he will long when the shadow of the end draws near.

And now what else remains? A brief farewell to those who have perused this narrative, or a lingering parting word?

In these days of haste and scramble, when there is no time for faith, is there time for sentiment? I think not. And therefore there shall be none between my readers and me, save this—a friendly warning. Belief—belief in God—belief in all things noble, unworldly, lofty, and beautiful, is rapidly being crushed underfoot by—what? By mere lust of gain! Be sure, good people, be very sure that you are RIGHT in denying God for the sake of man—in abjuring the spiritual for the material—before you rush recklessly onward. The end for all of you can be but death; and are you quite positive after all that there is No Hereafter? Is it sense to imagine that the immense machinery of the Universe has been set in motion for nothing? Is it even common reason to consider that the Soul of man, with all its high musings, its dreams of unseen glory, its longings after the Infinite, is a mere useless vapour, or a set of shifting molecules in a perishable brain? The mere fact of the EXISTENCE OF A DESIRE clearly indicates an EQUALLY EXISTING CAPACITY for the GRATIFICATION of that desire; therefore, I ask, would the WISH for a future state of being, which is secretly felt by every one of us, have been permitted to find a place in our natures, IF THERE WERE NO POSSIBLE MEANS OF GRANTING IT? Why all this discontent with the present—why all this universal complaint and despair and world-weariness, if there be No HEREAFTER? For my own part, I have told you frankly

What I Have Seen and What I Know; but I do not ask you to believe me. I only say, If—If you admit to yourselves the possibility of a future and eternal state of existence, would it not be well for you to inquire seriously how you are preparing for it in these wild days? Look at society around you, and ask yourselves: Whither is our "Progress" tending—Forward or Backward—Upward or Downward? Which way? Fight the problem out. Do not glance at it casually, or put it away as an unpleasant thought, or a consideration involving too much trouble—struggle with it bravely till you resolve it, and whatever the answer may be, Abide By It. If it leads you to deny God and the immortal destinies of your own souls, and you find hereafter, when it is too late, that both God and immortality exist, you have only yourselves to blame. We are the arbiters of our own fate, and that fact is the most important one of our lives. Our Will is positively unfettered; it is a rudder put freely into our hands, and with it we can steer Wherever We Choose. God will not Compel our love or obedience. We must ourselves Desire to love and obey—Desire It Above All Things In The World.

As for the Electric Origin of the Universe, a time is coming when scientific men will acknowledge it to be the only theory of Creation worthy of acceptance. All the wonders of Nature are the result of Light And Heat Alone—i.e., are the work of the Electric Ring I have endeavoured to describe, which Must go on producing, absorbing and reproducing worlds, suns and systems for ever and ever. The Ring, in its turn, is merely the outcome of God's own personality—the atmosphere surrounding the World in which He has His existence—a World created by Love and for Love alone. I cannot force this theory on public attention, which is at present claimed by various learned professors, who give ingenious explanations of "atoms" and "molecules;" yet, even regarding these same "atoms," the mild question may be put: Where did the First "atom" come from? Some may answer: "We call the first atom God." Surely it is as well to call Him a Spirit of pure Light as an atom? However, the fact of one person's being convinced of a truth will not, I am aware, go very far to convince others. I have related my "experience" exactly as it happened at the time, and my readers can accept or deny the theories of Heliobas as they please. Neither denial, acceptance, criticism, nor incredulity can affect Me personally, inasmuch as I am not Heliobas, but simply the narrator of an episode connected with him; and as such, my task is finished.

Appendix

(In publishing these selections from letters received concerning the "Romance," I am in honour bound not to disclose the names of my correspondents, and this necessary reticence will no doubt induce the incredulous to declare that they are not genuine epistles, but mere inventions of my own. I am quite prepared for such a possible aspersion, and in reply, I can but say that I hold the originals in my possession, and that some of them have been read by my friend Mr. George Bentley, under whose auspices this book has been successfully launched on the sea of public favour. I may add that my correspondents are all strangers to me personally—not one of them have I ever met. A few have indeed asked me to accord them interviews, but this request I invariably deny, not wishing to set myself forward in any way as an exponent of high doctrine in which I am as yet but a beginner and student.—Author.)

Letter I

Dear Madam,

"You must receive so many letters that I feel it is almost a shame to add to the number, but I cannot resist writing to tell you how very much your book, 'The Romance of Two Worlds,' has helped me. My dear friend Miss F——, who has written to you lately I believe, first read it to me, and I cannot tell you what a want in my life it seemed to fill up. I have been always interested in the so-called Supernatural, feeling very conscious of depths in my own self and in others that are usually ignored. . . I have been reading as many books as I could obtain upon Theosophy, but though thankful for the high thoughts I found in them, I still felt a great want—that of combining this occult knowledge with my own firm belief in the Christian religion. Your book seemed to give me just what I wanted—It Has Deepened And Strengthened My Belief In And Love To God And Has Made The New Testament A New Book To Me. Things which I could not understand before seem clear in the light which your 'Vision' has thrown upon them, and I cannot remain satisfied without expressing to you my sincere gratitude. May your book be read by all who are ready to receive the high truths that it contains! With thanks, I remain, dear Madam,

Yours sincerely,

M. S.

Letter II

Madam,

"I am afraid you will think it very presumptuous of a stranger to address you, but I have lately read your book, 'A Romance of Two Worlds,' and have been much struck with it. It has opened my mind to such new impressions, and seems to be so much what I have been groping for so long, that I thought if you would be kind enough to answer this, I might get a firmer hold on those higher things and be at anchor at last. If you have patience to read so far, you will imagine I must be very much in earnest to intrude myself on you like this, but from the tone of your book I do not believe you would withdraw your hand where you could do good. . . I never thought of or read of the electric force (or spirit) in every human being before, but I do believe in it after reading your book, and You Have Made The Next World A Living Thing To Me, and raised my feelings above the disappointments and trials of this life. . . Your book was put into my hands at a time when I was deeply distressed and in trouble about my future; but you have shown me how small a thing this future of Our life is. . . Would it be asking too much of you to name any books you think might help me in this new vein of thought you have given me? Apologizing for having written, believe me yours sincerely,

B. W. L.

(I answered to the best of my ability the writer of the above, and later on received another letter as follows:)

"Forgive my writing to you again on the subject of your 'Romance,' but I read it so often and think of it so much. I cannot say the wonderful change your book has wrought in my life, and though very likely you are constantly hearing of the good it has done, yet it cannot but be the sweetest thing you can hear—that the seed you have planted is bringing forth so much fruit. . . The Bible is a new book to me since your work came into my hands."

Letter III

(The following terribly pathetic avowal is from a clergyman of the Church of England:)

MADAM,

"Your book, the 'Romance of Two Worlds,' has stopped me on the brink of what is doubtless a crime, and yet I had come to think it the only way out of impending madness. I speak of self-destruction—suicide. And while writing the word, I beg of you to accept my gratitude for the timely rescue of my soul. Once I believed in the goodness of God—but of late years the cry of modern scientific atheism, 'There is No God,' has rung in my ears till my brain has reeled at the desolation and nothingness of the Universe. No good, no hope, no satisfaction in anything—this world only with all its mockery and failure—and afterwards annihilation! Could a God design and create so poor and cruel a jest? So I thought—and the misery of the thought was more than I could bear. I had resolved to make an end. No one knew, no one guessed my intent, till one Sunday afternoon a friend lent me your book. I began to read, and never left it till I had finished the last page—then I knew I was saved. Life smiled again upon me in consoling colours, and I write to tell you that whatever other good your work may do and is no doubt doing, you have saved both the life and reason of one grateful human being. If you will write to me a few lines I shall be still more grateful, for I feel you can help me. I seem to have read Christ's mission wrong—but with patience and prayer it is possible to redeem my error. Once more thanking you, I am,

Yours with more thankfulness than I can write,
L. E. F.

(I lost no time in replying to this letter, and since then have frequently corresponded with the writer, from whose troubled mind the dark cloud has now entirely departed. And I may here venture to remark that the evils of "modern scientific atheism" are far more widely spread and deeply rooted than the majority of persons are aware of, and that many of the apparently inexplicable cases of self-slaughter on which the formal verdict, "Suicide during a state of temporary insanity," is passed, have been caused by long and hopeless brooding on the "nothingness of the Universe"—which, if it were a true theory, would indeed make of Creation a bitter, nay, even a senseless jest. The cruel preachers of such a creed have much to answer for. The murderer who destroys human life for wicked passion and wantonness is less criminal than the proudly learned, yet egotistical, and therefore densely ignorant scientist, who, seeking to crush the soul by his feeble, narrow-minded arguments, and deny its imperishable nature, dares to spread his poisonous and corroding doctrines of despair through the world, draining existence of all its brightness, and striving to erect barriers of distrust between the creature and the Creator. No sin can be greater than this; for it is impossible to estimate the measure of evil that may thus be brought into otherwise innocent and happy lives. The attitude of devotion and faith is natural to Humanity, while nothing can be more UNnatural and disastrous to civilization, morality and law, than deliberate and determined Atheism.—AUTHOR.)

Letter IV

DEAR MADAM,

"I dare say you have had many letters, but I must add mine to the number to thank you for your book, the 'Romance of Two Worlds.' I am deeply interested in the wonderful force we possess, all in a greater or lesser degree—call it influence, electricity, or what you will. I have thought much on Theosophy and Psychical Research—but what struck me in your book was the glorious selflessness inculcated and the perfect Majesty of the Divinity clear throughout—no sweeping away of the Crucified One. I felt a better woman for the reading of it twice: and I know others, too, who are higher and better women for such noble thoughts and teaching. . . People for the most part dream away their lives; one meets so few who really believe in electrical affinity, and I have felt it so often and for so long. Forgive my troubling you with this letter, but I am grateful for your labour of love towards raising men and women.

Sincerely yours,
R. H.

Letter V

"I should like to know if Marie Corelli honestly believes the theory which she enunciates in her book, 'The Romance of Two Worlds;' and also if she has any proof on which to found that same theory?—if so, the authoress will greatly oblige an earnest seeker after Truth if she will give the information sought to

A. S.

(I sent a brief affirmative answer to the above note; the "proof" of the theories set forth in the "Romance" is, as I have already stated, easily to be found in the New Testament. But there are those who do not and will not believe the New Testament, and for them there are no "proofs" of any existing spirituality in earth or heaven. "Having eyes they see not, and hearing they do not understand."—AUTHOR.)

Letter VI

DEAR MADAM,

"I have lately been reading with intense pleasure your 'Romance of Two Worlds,' and I must crave your forbearance towards me when I tell you that it has filled me with envy and wonder. I feel sure that many people must have plied you with questions on the subject already, but I am certain that you are too earnest and too sympathetic to feel bored by what is in no sense idle curiosity, but rather a deep and genuine longing to know the truth. . . To some minds it would prove such a comfort and such, a relief to have their vague longings and beliefs confirmed and made tangible, and, as you know, at the present day so-called Religion, which is often a mere mixture of dogma and superstition, is scarcely sufficient to do this. . . I might say a great deal more and weary your patience, which has already been tried, I fear. But may I venture to hope that you have some words of comfort and assurance out of your own experience to give me? With your expressed belief in the good influence which each may exert over the other, not to speak of a higher and holier incentive in the example of One (in whom you also believe) who bids us for His sake to 'Bear one another's burdens,' you cannot, I think, turn away in impatience from the seeking of a very earnest soul.

Yours sincerely,
B. D.

(I have received about fifty letters written in precisely the same tone as the above—all more or less complaining of the insufficiency of "so-called Religion, which is often a mere mixture of dogma and superstition"— and I ask—What are the preachers of Christ's clear message about that there should be such plaintively eager anxious souls as these, who are evidently ready and willing to live noble lives if helped and encouraged ever so little? Shame on those men who presume to take up the high vocation of the priesthood for the sake of self-love, self-interest, worldly advancement, money or position! These things are not among Christ's teachings. If there are members of the clergy who can neither plant faith, nor consolation, nor proper comprehension of God's infinite Beauty and Goodness in the hearts of their hearers, I say that their continuance in such sacred office is an offence to the Master whom they profess to serve. "It must needs be that offences come, but woe to that man by whom the offence cometh!" To such may be addressed the words, "Hypocrites! for ye shut up the kingdom of heaven against men; ye neither go in yourselves, neither suffer ye them that are entering to go in."—Author.)

Letter VII

Madam,

"I hope you will not think it great presumption my writing to you. My excuse must be that I so much want to believe in he great Spirit that 'makes for righteousness,' and I cannot! Your book puts it all so clearly that if I can only know it to be a true experience of your own, it will go a long way in dispersing the fog that modern writings surround one with. . .

Apologizing for troubling you,
I am faithfully yours,
C.M.E.

Letter VIII

MADAM,

"I trust you will pardon the liberty I take in writing
to you. My excuse must be the very deep interest your
book, 'A Romance of Two Worlds,' has excited in me. I,
of course, understand that the STORY itself is a romance,
but in reading it carefully it seems to me that it is a book
written with a purpose. . . The Electric Creed respecting
Religion seems to explain so much in Scripture which has
always seemed to me impossible to accept blindly without
explanation of any kind; and the theory that Christ came
to die and to suffer for us as an Example and a means of
communication with God, and not as a SACRIFICE, clears
up a point which has always been to me personally a
stumbling-block. I cannot say how grateful I shall be if
you can tell me any means of studying this subject further;
and trusting you will excuse me for troubling you, I am,
Madam,

Yours truly,

H. B.

(Once more I may repeat that the idea of a sacrifice to appease
God's anger is purely JEWISH, and has nothing whatever to do with
Christianity according to Christ. He Himself says, "I am the WAY, the
Truth, and the Life; no man cometh to the Father but BY ME." Surely
these words are plain enough, and point unmistakably to a MEANS
OF COMMUNICATION through Christ between the Creator and this
world. Nowhere does the Divine Master say that God is so furiously
angry that he must have the bleeding body of his own messenger,
Christ, hung up before Him as a human sacrifice, as though He
could only be pacified by the scent of blood! Horrible and profane
idea! and one utterly at variance with the tenderness and goodness of
"Our Father" as pictured by Christ in these gentle words—"Fear not,
little flock; it is your Father's good pleasure to give you the Kingdom."
Whereas that Christ should come to draw us closer to God by the
strong force of His own Divinity, and by His Resurrection prove to us
the reality of the next life, is not at all a strange or ungodlike mission,
and ought to make us understand more surely than ever how infinitely

pitying and forbearing is the All-Loving One, that He should, as it were, with such extreme affection show us a way by which to travel through darkness unto light. To those who cannot see this perfection of goodness depicted in Christ's own words, I would say in the terse Oriental maxim:

> *"Diving, and finding no pearls in the sea,*
> *Blame not the ocean, the fault is in* THEE.*"*
> AUTHOR.)

Letter IX

DEAR MADAM,

"I have lately been reading your remarkable book, 'A Romance of Two Worlds,' and I feel that I must write to you about it. I have never viewed Christianity in the broadly transfigured light you throw upon it, and I have since been studying carefully the four Gospels and comparing them with the theories in your book. The result has been a complete and happy change in my ideas of religion, and I feel now as if I had, like a leper of old, touched the robe of Christ and been healed of a long-standing infirmity. Will you permit me to ask if you have evolved this new and beneficent lustre from the Gospel yourself? or whether some experienced student in mystic matters has been your instructor? I hear from persons who have seen you that you are quite young, and I cannot understand how one of your sex and age seems able so easily to throw light on what to many has been, and is still, impenetrable darkness. I have been a preacher for some years, and I thought the Testament was old and familiar to me; but you have made it a new and marvellous book full of most precious meanings, and I hope I may be able to impart to those whom it is my duty to instruct, something of the great consolation and hope your writing has filled me with.

Believe me,
Gratefully yours,
T.M.

Letter X

MADAM,

"Will you tell me what ground you have for the foundation of the religious theory contained in your book, 'A Romance of Two Worlds'? Is it a part of your own belief? I am MOST anxious to know this, and I am sure you will be kind enough to answer me. Till I read your book I thought myself an Agnostic, but now I am not quite sure of this. I do not believe in the Deity as depicted by the Churches. I CANNOT. Over and over again I have asked myself—If there is a God, why should He be angry? It would surely be easy for Him to destroy this world entirely as one would blow away an offending speck of dust, and it would be much better and BRAVER for Him to do this than to torture His creation. For I call life a torture and certainly a useless and cruel torture if it is to end in annihilation. I know I seem to be blasphemous in these remarks, yet if you only knew what I suffer sometimes! I desire, I LONG to believe. YOU seem so certain of your Creed—a Creed so noble, reasonable and humane—the God you depict so worthy of the adoration of a Universe. I BEG of you to tell me—Do you feel sure of this beneficent all-pervading Love concerning which you write so eloquently? I do not wish to seem an intruder on your most secret thought. I want to believe that YOU believe—and if I felt this, the tenor of my whole life might change. Help me if you can—I stand in real need of help. You may judge I am very deeply in earnest, or I should not have written to you.

Yours faithfully,
A. W. L.

A Note About the Author

Marie Corelli (1855–1924), born Mary Mackay, was a British writer from London, England. Educated at a Parisian convent, she later worked as a pianist before embarking on a literary career. Her first novel, *A Romance of Two Worlds* was published in 1886 and surpassed all expectations. Corelli quickly became one of the most popular fiction writers of her time. Her books featured contrasting themes rooted in religion, science and the supernatural. Some of Corelli's other notable works include *Barabbas: A Dream of the World's Tragedy* (1893) and *The Sorrows of Satan* (1895).

A Note from the Publisher

Spanning many genres, from non-fiction essays to literature classics to children's books and lyric poetry, Mint Edition books showcase the master works of our time in a modern new package. The text is freshly typeset, is clean and easy to read, and features a new note about the author in each volume. Many books also include exclusive new introductory material. Every book boasts a striking new cover, which makes it as appropriate for collecting as it is for gift giving. Mint Edition books are only printed when a reader orders them, so natural resources are not wasted. We're proud that our books are never manufactured in excess and exist only in the exact quantity they need to be read and enjoyed.

Discover more of your favorite classics with Bookfinity™.

- Track your reading with custom book lists.
- Get great book recommendations for your personalized Reader Type.
- Add reviews for your favorite books.
- AND MUCH MORE!

Visit **bookfinity.com** and take the fun Reader Type quiz to get started.

Enjoy our classic and modern companion pairings!

Printed in the USA
CPSIA information can be obtained
at www.ICGtesting.com
LVHW030041070823
754491LV00004B/423

9 781513 277752